fiREBiRDS

fIREBIRDS

aN
anthoLogy
of
oRIGINaL
fantasy
aND
scieNce
fictION

edited by Sharyn November

FIREBIRD

AN IMPRINT OF PENGUIN GROUP (USA) INC.

fIREBIRD—WHERE fantasy takes fLIGHT™

FIREBIRD
Published by Penguin Group
Penguin Group (USA) Inc., 345 Hudson Street, New York, New York 10014, U.S.A.
Penguin Books Ltd, 80 Strand, London WC2R ORL, England
Penguin Books Australia Ltd, 250 Camberwell Road, Camberwell, Victoria 3124, Australia
Penguin Books Canada Ltd, 10 Alcorn Avenue, Toronto, Ontario, Canada M4V 3B2
Penguin Books (N.Z.) Ltd, 182-190 Wairau Road, Auckland 10, New Zealand

First published in the United States of America by Firebird,
an imprint of Penguin Group (USA) Inc., 2003

1   3   5   7   9   10   8   6   4   2

ISBN 0-14-250142-5
Printed in the United States of America

*To the authors included here—thank you
with all my heart.*

contents

Introduction

ere's a confession: I never read introductions until I've finished a book, because I hate it when an editor gives things away. So don't worry—I'm going to let the stories speak for themselves. I want you to read them the way I did when they first came in.

What I *really* want to tell you about isn't *Firebirds*, but Firebird, the imprint.

Firebird started one late night in 1999, when I was walking from my office to the train home. I find that these walks are really some of my best thinking times; when I had a band, that's when I wrote songs in my head. The business of the day drains away and reveals what's important, or unexpected.

I had been working with teenagers in the schools and online since 1996. The more teens I polled (thousands!) and talked to, the more I realized one thing: some of my best and most voracious readers loved fantasy and science fiction. They were going into the adult genre section to find new authors and books, and they couldn't wait to tell me about them. They had really become readers for life—this doesn't happen with everyone, and when it does, it's wonderful. These middle and high school students were going to mature into adults who read fantasy and sf—I knew some of those adults, and they consistently talked about what they'd read at twelve, thirteen, and onward. They bought and re-read those books, too. They were touchstones.

All of these realizations and conversations had been in my head for a while, distilling themselves, and they finally crystallized on that walk. I suddenly thought: *Why can't we have an imprint for this?*

Then, all of the backup information came spilling in. *We do so well with fantasy and sf for younger readers; it's logical that we take this step. What do we already publish that I can use? Who should I talk to?* And, the most important question of all: *What do I need to read?*

The reading's still going on, of course. It always will be.

It took a few years to sort out the details—from the name and logo to the Web site to the cover look to the Editorial Boards to lots of acquisitions—but Firebird finally launched in January 2002.

This anthology is a celebration of Firebird. But it is mainly a celebration of good writing.

The one thing everyone here has in common is their connection to the list, either as part of it or part of its Editorial Board. Each of them does something wholly unique and extraordinary with words (or, in the case of Charles Vess, pictures). Oh, and one more thing: I love their work. When it comes to the *Firebirds* contributors, I am as much of a fangirl as anyone. You can imagine how I felt as the stories began to come in! It was like some sort of extended Hanukkah, and by the end of it I was as lit up as an oversized menorah. I think I am still burning.

Enjoy this book. It's been a pleasure every step of the way.

Sharyn November
June 2003

P.S. You'll notice that a few of the stories here don't look or sound "American." Why? Because their authors aren't. To me, it makes sense to keep things in their "natural" language, including turns of phrase and spelling. Plus it's more fun.

P.P.S. I'd love to hear what you think of *Firebirds*—and, of course, the Firebird imprint. There's a list of books published to date opposite the title page; **www.firebirdbooks.com** has first chapters, a cover gallery, and lots of links. If you have any ideas for books I need to read, authors I should check out and/or work with, lost treasures that deserve republication, or anything else, feel free to e-mail me at **firebird@us.penguingroup.com**—I am a real person, and I do answer!

Delia Sherman

COTILLION

C elia Townsend's mother brought up the subject of debutante balls for the first time in June. It was the day after
graduation, and they were discussing when Celia would
have to be home from Maine at the end of the summer to get
ready for her freshman year at Vassar.

"There's more to do than you think," Mrs. Townsend
warned her. "For one thing, there's your dress. We'll have to
order it and find shoes before you go. It doesn't do to leave
everything to the last minute."

Celia looked blank. "What dress?"

"Your coming-out dress, dear. For the Snow Ball. We need
to talk about an escort, too, but that can wait until you've
been at college a while. It's a pity you don't know any boys."

Celia didn't point out that this wasn't her fault, since her
parents had sent her to an all-girls school so she wouldn't have
any distractions from her schoolwork. But she did roll her
eyes.

"You're not going to be difficult about this, are you,

CeCee?" her mother said anxiously. "I know some of your friends find coming out horribly old-fashioned and irrelevant, but I honestly fail to see what difference it's going to make in Vietnam whether you go to the Snow Ball or not."

Celia shrugged. "I said I'd do it, didn't I?"

It would have been very uncool to admit it, but secretly Celia was looking forward to the Snow Ball Debutante Cotillion. Sure, coming out was old-fashioned. That was the attraction. Celia liked the past—or at least selected bits of it, like long dresses, long hair, castles, anything with lutes in it, or anything implying lutes. She loved Zefferelli's *Romeo and Juliet* and *Tom Jones* and old stories and folk music, the traditional kind: ballads with magic in them and star-crossed lovers. The past was romantic. You could have adventures in it, the clothes were cool, and exciting things happened at balls, like abductions and falling in love. Celia, who had never had a real adventure or been in love, had high hopes for the Snow Ball.

The reality, however, turned out to be about as romantic as a school assembly. She liked her dress, which had organza petals at the hem that rippled when she moved. But her mother wouldn't let her bind up her honey-colored hair with ropes of pearls as she'd wanted to. And there'd been a lot of boring standing around in a drafty hall with thirty other girls and their parents, with her mother poking at her hair and telling her to stand up straight. Then her name had been called, and she'd swept into the ballroom on her father's arm for her Big Moment.

Some Big Moment. The lights had made her squint and she'd wobbled coming up out of her curtsy and her father had stepped on one of the organza petals and ripped it off. Afterwards, she was officially Out. Big deal. Except for the fact that her mother was happy with her for once, she would have preferred to stay In.

Celia extracted a cigarette from her white beaded bag, lit it, and leaned her elbows on the pink tablecloth. Smoking was one of the evil habits she'd taken up in the heady freedom of living away from her mother for the first time in her life. Another was her date, who she'd met at a Yale mixer in the fall. His name was Guy Duvivier, and he was lounging on a gilt bamboo chair with his feet up on the rail of one of the private boxes that ringed the ballroom. He had a long, bony face, heavy-lidded tiger's eyes, and sandy hair pulled back with a rubber band. There was ash on his silk lapel and a slightly foolish expression on his face, inspired by the joint he was palming under the table.

Celia exhaled a disgusted stream of smoke and turned her eyes to the dance floor. Lester Brown and his Band of Renown were playing a foxtrot. The floor was a chiaroscuro swirl of white dresses and black tailcoats, punctuated by the golds and scarlets and royal blues of the mothers' gowns. Celia caught sight of her best friend Helen and her date swaying at the edge of the mass, gazing into each others' eyes and obviously having a wonderful time.

Celia shifted restlessly on the hard, narrow chair. "Let's dance," she said.

"Why?" Guy released a thin haze of sharp-sweet smoke, raised his hand for another toke.

"It's a ball, Guy. You're supposed to dance at a ball."

"It's a mating ritual left over from before the Flood." He leered at her. "We don't need no stinking ritual to mate, eh, C?"

Celia had no intention of mating with Guy at all. When she'd first started to go out with him, she'd thought he was a romantic, but it hadn't taken her long to find out that he just dressed like one. Unfortunately, she'd already asked him to this stupid ball, and he'd accepted. One more crack like that, and she'd break up with him tonight, even if it left her date-less for the rest of the season. There was only so much she was willing to do to make her mother happy.

The number ended to a patter of well-bred applause. Couples milled about the floor, greeting friends, changing partners. The band left time for everyone to settle into the new configurations, then struck up again: a raucous cha-cha-cha. The curtains to the box stirred and someone said, "Carmen Miranda in white gloves. The mind boggles."

Celia didn't recognize the voice. It was vaguely English, a resonant tenor like a clarinet, full of overtones and harmonies. Looking around, she saw a tall figure in a tailcoat holding aside the box's curtain with one hand.

"I thought I was alone," the figure said. "My apologies."

"No, no, come in," said Celia.

"Yeah," said Guy. "Come in. Bring your friends. We can have a party."

The stranger released the curtain and moved forward into the light. Celia's first thought was that he looked as cool and dangerous as Guy would have liked to look. He had long, flat cheeks and a faintly Roman nose, thin lips and a pointed chin.

His skin was very pale and his black hair was pulled back with a black ribbon. There was a pearl dangling from his left ear.

"Guy Duvivier," said Guy, without getting up.

"Enchanted," said the stranger, and bowed. "Valentine Carter." He turned to Celia. "And you are Celia Townsend."

Celia felt herself blushing. "How did you know that?"

"You were formally presented to the whole room not an hour ago." He smiled at her. "I liked your curtsy. It had character."

There was an awkward pause while Celia tried to decide whether he was laughing at her. She didn't think so. His eyes were dark, deeply set, intense as a searchlight, and fixed unwaveringly on hers. It made her feel uncharacteristically shy.

The band slid from the cha-cha into a waltz. Still holding her gaze, Valentine said, "Miss Townsend, may I have the honor?"

"Nice earring," sneered Guy. "Your boyfriend give it to you?"

"You're stoned," said Celia coldly.

"Out of my gourd," Guy agreed. "Only way to fly." He held out a sweaty hand. "Let's make out."

Mortified, Celia glanced at Valentine, who was politely watching the dancers. "I apologize for Guy," she said. "He's not a total jerk, unless he's stoned. I'd love to dance."

Valentine bowed—she'd never before seen a man bow without looking like a dork—and offered her his arm. She laid her fingers on it and swept out of the box, followed by Guy's plaintive, "Oh, man! Celia? Shit!"

The waltz as performed by Valentine Carter was nothing

like the waltz Celia had learned at Miss Corcoran's Dancing School. He skimmed her around the floor like a top, his hand on her shoulder blade guiding her to turn and turn, swooping like a swallow to the syrupy strains of Strauss.

Valentine squeezed her hand. " You are a delicious dancer, Celia Townsend."

Celia looked up warily. His deep eyes caught hers, held them in a long, teasing look. "If I were to kiss you," he said, "would your boyfriend call me out?" His hand moved on her back, drawing her nearer.

Celia was fascinated—and suspicious. Valentine was so much like someone she'd make up, it was hard to believe he was actually for real. Rather breathlessly, she said, "Pistols at dawn? Guy? Not likely. I'd stay out of dark alleys, though."

"Forewarned is forearmed." He swept her into a twirl that made the organza petals on her gown flutter and flare. Laughing, Celia followed his lead. Who cared if he was for real or not? He had brought enchantment to the Snow Ball. And for the moment, at least, he was hers.

Celia stepped out of the bright lobby into the cold night air. Her breath ghosted back to her as she cuddled her coat up to her chin.

Valentine folded her hand in his and drew her down the steps of the Plaza Hotel towards the fountain, heading across town.

"Let's walk," he said. "The fresh air will revive you."

"There is no fresh air in New York," Celia complained, but it was only reflex. She was feeling indecently cheerful, considering that she'd just broken up with Guy—if you could even break up with someone who was nearly too stoned to speak. When Valentine brought her back to the box after the waltz, Guy had let her know that he didn't like her dancing with foreign fags, and she had let him know that she never wanted to see him again. He'd tried to kiss her. Stoned as he was, it was easy to push him away. Valentine had caught him, and a moment later, Guy was in a chair in the corner of the box with his head on the pink linen tablecloth, snoring peacefully.

"Damn," Celia said, disgusted. "Now there's going to be the most incredible scene." Her cigarettes and silver lighter were lying by Guy's hand. She picked up the pack and pulled one out. Valentine took it from her hand and tucked back it into her purse.

"Let's not make a big deal out of this," he said. "Someone might notice that I don't actually have an invitation to this affair. Perhaps one of his friends would be willing to perform a discreet rescue? I'll see you home, if you like."

Celia was momentarily sidetracked from the problem of what to do with Guy. "You crashed the ball? Why?"

Valentine's smile broadened just a little. "To find you," he said.

Everything went smoothly. Helen's date had good-naturedly agreed to convey Guy's snoring body home and Celia danced with Valentine until midnight, then left a note at her parents' table to say she was walking home with a friend and not to worry. Now she was running past the Plaza fountain with her hair blowing back in the wind, hand in hand with the most romantic man she'd ever met in her life.

"That boy," said Valentine. "Do you love him?"

Startled, Celia looked up at him, met an interested gaze, and quickly looked away again. "Guy? No way," she said. "He thinks Herman's Hermits are the pinnacle of musical achievement."

"Does he love you?"

"God, no," said Celia. "He's far too in love with himself. This is a little weird, you know? I mean, we just met. We're supposed to be talking about where we go to school or something."

"Are we? Why?"

The question seemed genuine. "So we can get to know each other better."

"And talking about love does not lead to us knowing each other better?" He smiled down at her. "Never mind. We'll talk about something else. Not school—I don't go to school."

"You don't go to school?" Celia had never met anybody of her generation who wasn't in school. "Are you a drop-out?"

"I am a lutenist," he said. "I play with the consort called the Booke of Ayres. A consort is. . . ."

"A kind of Renaissance band," Celia interrupted him. "I'm not a complete ignoramus. The Booke of Ayres—that sounds Renaissance too."

"It is. Have you heard of John Dowland?"

"Of course I have. He was the greatest composer of madrigals and lute music in Elizabeth's court."

"Close enough." Valentine sounded impressed. "You're full of surprises, Celia."

She laughed. "It's just about my favorite music in the whole world. I don't know all that much about it, really—there's not a lot of records or anything. But I'm in the Madrigal group at school, and I know tons of ballads."

"What do you know?"

Celia's mind went blank. "Um. Let's see. Stuff from Joan Baez, mostly, and Steeleye Span. They're an English group. Do you know them?"

"No," he said. "Sing me something."

"What, here, in the middle of Park Avenue? I can't. What if someone hears?"

He had his arm around her shoulders, so when he turned to look up and down the street, he turned her too. Apart from the colored lights on the Christmas trees, the giant cross of lighted windows on Grand Central Station, and the headlights of a few late taxis, it was dark, and as quiet as Park Avenue ever gets. "There's no one to hear you. And if there were, what's the harm? Who would not want to hear a girl singing on a winter's night, high and pure through the cold air?"

It was an appealing image. Celia said shyly, "I don't know what to sing."

He thought a moment. "Sing 'Greensleeves.' Everyone knows 'Greensleeves.'"

She began very softly, almost under her breath. But once she got through the first verse without some doorman leaping out to tell her she was disturbing the peace, she got into it, and sang more confidently. Her voice did sound nice, purling away into the night. On the third verse, Valentine joined her, winding a supple tenor up and down through the melody. Singing with him was even more fun than dancing with him.

"Greensleeves" was followed, after some discussion, by "The Silver Swan," with Valentine taking the alto part, and "Tam Lin." Valentine bet she didn't know all the verses. Celia bet she did, and launched recklessly into the Steeleye Span version. There are twenty verses to "Tam Lin," and Celia remembered them all. But Valentine won anyway, because he knew a different version, with forty verses. By the time he'd finished singing it, they were on 83rd Street, a block away from Celia's apartment.

Valentine stopped walking. "I don't want to leave you. But even the longest night of the year must end. And this is not the longest night: not yet."

Celia, who had been floating up the blocks from 59th Street on a cloud of music, came to earth with a painful thump. The night hadn't seemed very long to her, and she didn't want it to end. But she couldn't think of anything to say except, "When will I see you again?" which was supposed to be what he said next.

"I am playing tomorrow night," he said. "In the East Village. It's a rehearsal, not a performance, and the music is mostly instrumental. You could come if you wanted."

It wasn't exactly getting down on one knee, and Celia found herself thinking of all the reasons she shouldn't say yes. She didn't want to look too eager, and when it came down to it, Valentine frightened her a little. He was so very good looking.

He folded her hands in his and kissed them. "Please say you will come."

His dark eyes glittered, holding her gaze until the blood fizzed in her ears. If she said "No," she suspected that he would not ask twice. And she did want to see him again. So, "Okay," she said. "I guess so."

Surprisingly, he laughed. Not so surprisingly, he bent his head and put his lips to hers. His kiss was soft and teasing, very unlike Guy's businesslike probing. When he released her, she was trembling.

"Eight o'clock," he said. "I'll wait for you on this corner. Good night."

The next morning was depressingly ordinary. Celia rose late, but not late enough to escape her mother's inquisition about the strange young man she'd been seen dancing with.

"Valentine? What kind of a name is Valentine? Who's his father?"

"Mr. Carter, I guess, unless his mother's remarried."

Mrs. Townsend shut her eyes briefly, as if praying for patience. "Did you meet his parents, then?"

"I'm not planning to marry him, Mother, just date him."

"How old is he?"

"I don't know," answered Celia truthfully. "Does it matter? He's a perfect gentleman and he's taking me to a concert tonight. A lute concert, not a rock concert."

"The kind of concert is not the point, CeCee."

"The point"—Celia was beginning to lose her temper— "the *point* is that I'm almost twenty and you're still treating me like a baby. If I'd met him at college, I would have gone out with him and you wouldn't even know."

Her mother ignored this as irrelevant. "Where is this lute concert, dear? Lincoln Center? Carnegie Hall?"

"It's in the Village."

"No. Absolutely not. You can't go down to the Village, not at night, not with some strange young man your father and I have never met. The subject is closed."

Celia knew that tone of voice. It meant her mother had made up her mind, and nothing short of an act of Congress would make her change it. When she was in high school, Celia had wasted many hours and tears trying to break down that tone. But she was in college now, and she'd sung "Greensleeves" in the middle of Park Avenue. She knew the taste of romance, and she wasn't about to let her mother take it away because it might not be good for her.

In a tone precisely matching her mother's, she said, "How strange could he be? I met him at the Snow Ball Debutante Cotillion. Look. I'm sorry you don't like it, but I'm going out with him anyway."

What do you wear to a rehearsal of Elizabethan music in the Village? Knowing nothing about actual musicians, and not much about the Village except that it was full of hippies, Celia couldn't decide. Not nice-girl dress-up clothes, that was for sure. In the end, she settled for a short green and purple paisley print dress with a high waist and wide sleeves. She wore fishnet stockings and high, lace-up boots with it, and her honey-brown hair brushed loose down her back. She was trying for a kind of mod-medieval effect, and when she looked in the mirror, she thought she'd succeeded.

At the apartment door, Celia's mother approached her with a twenty dollar bill and instructions to take a taxi home.

"This doesn't mean I approve of your decision, Celia. I just want to be sure you can leave the minute you feel you're in over your head. I wish I had more faith in your judgment, but I suppose I should be grateful you're not lying to me about where you're going. I just hope this young man is worth it."

So did Celia. All day, while her mother had tried every trick in her repertoire to make Celia change her mind, she'd been dreaming about Valentine—his fine musician's hands, his dark poet's eyes, his earring, replaying his kiss like a favorite record until she'd worn out the grooves. Now, about to meet the reality at the corner of 83rd Street, she wondered whether she'd still like him, whether he'd still like her.

He was waiting where he'd said, dressed in black jeans, boots, and a black leather jacket, with a gold ring in his ear. He looked impossibly handsome and dangerous, a pirate king or a highwayman. "Celia," he said, lifted her hand, turned it palm-up, and kissed her wrist, just above the edge of her glove. Celia felt herself going scarlet.

"Very nice," he said. "Fair Janet, circa 1969, with her skirt more than a little above the knee." He picked up a large-bellied guitar case from the sidewalk at his feet. "Shall we take the subway?"

When they emerged from the subway at Astor Place, it became very clear to Celia that going to the Village to see *The Fantasticks* with her parents was nothing at all like walking down St. Mark's Place with someone who belonged there. The street was full of men with beards and dirty hair straggling over their shoulders and girls wearing Indian blankets and beaded headbands across their foreheads. The stores were full of fringed leather vests and bongs and rolling papers laid out in colorful rows. Street stands sold strings of love beads and huge, dangly earrings and pewter peace signs hung on leather thongs. Celia clung to Valentine's hand like a child, staring at the shifting, colorful scene, sniffing the sweet ghosts of incense and pot. Anything could happen here. Anything at all.

A couple of blocks east, Valentine opened a cast-iron gate, mounted the steps of a brownstone, pushed a paint-caked button. A buzzer screeched and he opened the door on a long hall at the end of which was a worn wooden stair. Celia sucked in a deep breath tinted with pot and cabbage and wondered if her floaty, slightly panicked feeling might be a contact high.

The apartment was on the third floor. As Celia and Valentine climbed the last steps a door opened, releasing a stream of warm, golden light like honey. An enormous guy with a beard and a furry vest took her coat and hung it up in the branches of a tree growing up inside the door. Curious, Celia touched its trunk. It was cold and hard—metal of some kind. There was another tree by the stove—the front door opened into the kitchen—with pots and pans hanging from its grace-ful branches, and a third shaded the bathtub (the *bathtub*?) occupying an alcove by the sink. Groovy.

The bearlike man herded Valentine through a curtained door, leaving Celia to follow if she felt like it. He hadn't even asked her name. Celia squelched a sudden desire to use her mother's twenty: If she knew exactly what the rules were and what was going to happen next, it wouldn't be an adventure, right? If she ran away now, it would mean she was just the snotty little Upper East Side deb her mother wanted her to be. So she'd hang loose and keep her cool. She could always run away later.

The room behind the curtain was as strange and beautiful as something from a fairy tale. There were no sofas, but only large, soft cushions covered with richly printed fabrics, blue and green and rust and yellow, like a blooming meadow. The walls were covered with more of the silver metal trees, hung with musical instruments—lutes, violins, a small harp carved with leaves—and little lanterns with candles in them. Clustered at the far end were five low stools, three of them occupied by a girl and two men. Valentine was standing in front of them, holding his instrument case across his chest like a shield.

"We missed you last night," said the girl accusingly. She was easily as strange as the room: a pale, angular face, black eyes, eyebrows like accent marks, arms as long and skinny as branches, fingers like white twigs. Her hair was dark, too, but it glimmered in the candlelight. Feeling as if she'd come in halfway through a play, Celia edged through the door and let the curtain fall.

Valentine shrugged. "There was no rehearsal called—I thought I'd take a night off."

"Nobody has a night off at Midwinter," said one of the men. He was fat, or maybe it was only that he looked fat sitting next to the skinny girl. He had a clever, craggy face and bright little eyes that twinkled out through his wildly curly hair like an animal peering through leaves.

The remaining man was relatively normal-looking, except

for a glassy blue glare that made Celia think of basilisks. The air shimmered with tension and unspoken words.

"I'm here now." Valentine put down his case, unclasped it, lifted out a round-bellied lute, and took his place on a vacant stool. The twiggy girl picked up a lute with a neck nearly as long as she was tall and propped it in her lap, Blue Eyes tucked a violin into the hollow of his shoulder, Curly straddled something that looked like a miniature cello, Big Bear screwed a recorder together. They all started tuning, their heads bent over their instruments as if in worship. The tension eased a notch or two. Celia wondered if anyone even knew she was there.

"And *one*," said Twiggy.

As they plunged into the first piece, Celia forgot about leaving. She dove into the music and let it carry her with it as its notes tumbled over one another in a barely ordered chaos, like water over a dam. When the piece was over, Celia found herself breathing as though she'd been swimming in cold water. She was so happy she could hardly bear it.

The musicians exchanged satisfied looks.

"Far out," said Twiggy. She stretched her arms, long and thin as spider's legs. "That was good. Didn't you think so?"

By the time Celia realized that she was being addressed, Twiggy had turned to Valentine. "Nice of you to bring an audience for us. It would have been better if you'd told us first, but now she's here, you'd better ask her to sit down and offer her a beer or something. Otherwise, she might think you're an insensitive jerk."

Valentine put his chin up and tightened his mouth.

"Apologies all around," he said stiffly. "Pull up a cushion, C. Make yourself comfortable."

"What about some wine?" Twiggy suggested. "We've got some rotgut in the fridge. Or some cheese, maybe? I don't want to be inhospitable."

Celia was about to say that wine sounded good when Valentine broke in. "Later, okay? I mean, this is a rehearsal, isn't it? So let's rehearse."

He sounded so angry—at Twiggy? At Celia?—that Celia wished that she'd listened to her mother. Except for the music, the evening was a total disaster. Walking out was definitely an option. But the music rang in the silence it had left behind. She couldn't possibly leave until she'd heard more. And she was damned if she was going to let them know they'd spooked her. As gracefully as she could, she sank into the nearest pile of cushions.

"Don't mind me," she said in her best Miss Debutante 1969 voice. "I can wait until you've done. I wanted to ask, though—what's that instrument you're playing?"

The woman ran her twiggy fingers up the long, slender neck. "It's an arch-lute," she said, in the patient tone of someone explaining the obvious. "Anything else you want to ask?"

Okay, Celia thought, be like that. I can be like that too. "Yes, as a matter of fact," she said, and pointed to Curly's miniature cello. "What's that?"

"A viol da gamba," Twiggy said. "Possibly the only one in New York."

"Cool." For Valentine's benefit, Celia arranged a look of bright interest on her face. But Valentine was retuning his lute. Lutes, Celia soon learned, take a lot of tuning.

The next set of tunes sounded like dance music, and included an instrumental setting of a song Celia had sung in Madrigals. She sang the lyrics under her breath until the melody lost itself in a series of increasingly complex variations and sent her into an enchanted place. It was as if the music drew her soul into her ears, pouring into it those glorious phrases, those trilling runs and intricate harmonies, each more marvelous than the last. Even the inevitable retuning couldn't break the spell. Celia just ran the last tune through her head until the next one came along and displaced it.

Eventually, Twiggy said, "I think it's time for something a little more challenging. What about that new thing? The Midwinter Pavane?"

Excited murmurs from Curly and Blue Eyes, silence from Big Bear. Valentine frowned, caught Twiggy's eye, shrugged, and retuned.

The Midwinter Pavane was dark and stately and full of repeating phrases tossed from strings to recorder and back again, turning on themselves like coiling snakes. After a few phrases, the recorder dropped out and the stringed instruments played on alone in a plangent scurry of notes and chords. Celia closed her eyes blissfully. Behind her lids, shadows spun and leaped like dancers dressed in burgundy and gold and chestnut, then twirled vertiginously down towards a single, silent, lightless point.

Celia gasped and jerked upright, hoping no one had noticed her falling asleep. She needn't have worried. The consort were all watching Valentine, who was playing a solo. He sat with one ankle cocked up on the opposite knee, the lute held in his open lap. The fingers of his left hand pranced along the frets, backing and bowing to his right hand, which skipped lightly across the strings. Watching him, all Celia wanted in the world was to come closer so that she could study the subtle play of the music over his face, like light over water. Blindly, she struggled out of her nest of cushions and knocked into a thing like an extra-large violin.

It made a small wooden complaint as it fell over, followed by an ominous twang. The music faltered to a halt.

"Shit!" Blue Eyes leapt from his stool. "Clumsy girl," he snarled. "Can't you watch where you put your feet? This is a delicate instrument, a rare instrument—you have no idea how rare. If you've broken it, I'll. . . ." He cradled the violin as if it were a cat Celia had just run over.

Tears of mortification pricked the back of Celia's nose. "Don't worry," she said. "If it's broken, I'll pay for it." The musicians stared at her, eyes blank. "I'll write down my address so you can send me the bill," Celia finished up awkwardly. "I guess I'll be going now. I'm really sorry. The music was wonderful."

She managed to keep back her tears until she was in the little kitchen, looking for her coat. It was pitch black, and she couldn't find the light switch among the tree branches, or her coat, or the door. She swore tearfully and felt around the walls again. The sharp edges of the metal leaves nicked her fingers painfully. From the next room came the sound of voices, murmuring urgently.

The lights came up. Valentine was standing by the stove. "Don't go," he said.

Celia fished a handkerchief out of her purse and blew her nose with defiant force. "So now you want me to stay? Why should I? You left me standing in the middle of the floor like an idiot. You didn't introduce me to anybody or explain anything to me. You didn't even ask me if I wanted a glass of water."

"I'm sorry," he said, sounding as if he really was.

Celia was not mollified. "So you're sorry. And I tell you it's okay. Then what?"

He took her hand. His eyes were bright on hers and she felt the phantom pressure of last night's kiss against her lips. She lowered her eyes to his loose white shirt and stared at it blindly.

"Stay," he said softly. "We're taking a break. I need to talk to you. Alone."

He reached behind her and swept open a curtain Celia hadn't noticed before. Behind it was a polished wooden door, and behind that was another room. Celia tried to pretend she was calm while Valentine found a match and lit a candle. The small flame illuminated a wide platform bed with—surprise!—metal trees at the four corners of it, and a moss-green bedspread. Celia swallowed. *This is it*, she thought. *See Celia jump off the Empire State Building into a bucket of water.* Her heart went into a brisk drum-roll.

Valentine sat down on the bed and focused his gaze on her. "I'm in trouble," he said.

It wasn't anything like what she'd expected him to say. She

took a deep breath and tried to pull herself together. "What kind of trouble?"

"You won't believe me. Or maybe you will. I don't know. I thought you were the right one, but what do I know about you, after all?" He raked his hands through his hair and stared at her. "How do I know I can trust you?"

"*You're* worried about trusting *me*?"

His voice was rough with desperation. "I have to trust someone. I need your help. You're my only chance, and you hardly know me. It's probably a stupid idea, but I'm out of time and I'm out of options."

Things were moving a little fast, although not in the direction she'd feared. Or maybe this was his idea of a seduction. If so, she didn't think much of his technique. On the other hand, he was so obviously bummed out, she couldn't help feeling sorry for him. She needed time to think. She dredged around in her purse for her cigarettes and her lighter, pulled one out, and lit up.

Valentine jerked upright, wild-eyed as a frightened dog. "You can't smoke that here," he said. "They hate cigarettes."

"*Who* hates cigarettes? What's the story here? Hey!" He had leaned towards her, snatched the cigarette from her fingers and stubbed it out on the sole of his boot.

"That's the catch," he said. "I can't tell you the story—not all of it. There's a spell. . . ." His mouth worked, his long hand waved the unlit cigarette helplessly. "Anyway, I can't."

The room was just big enough for the bed. No chair, no desk, no chest to sit on. Too curious to be self-conscious, Celia perched on the bed. "A spell? You're putting me on."

Valentine started to shred the cigarette. "Tonight," he said carefully, "is the longest night of the year. There's a dance. At the end of the dance, there's a ceremony"—his mouth worked—"of . . . payment. This year, I play the starring role." He looked up from the mess of filter and tobacco on the polished floor, to her face, searching for understanding.

"That doesn't give me a lot to go on," Celia said.

Running his hands through his hair, he'd pulled it loose. Dark, curly strands hung over his eyes. "Last night, we sang together. Do you remember?"

"'The Silver Swan,'" she said. "'Tam Lin.'"

He stared at her unblinking.

"Tam Lin," she said slowly, "is an earthly knight living in the fairie court. Every seventh year, the fairies have to give a soul to the Devil as tribute—that's the tithe to Hell. Now, it's Tam Lin's turn. On Halloween night, Fair Janet rescues him by holding him in her arms while he turns into freaky stuff like bears and burning brands." She stopped; he nodded encouragement. She said, "Are you trying to tell me you're like Tam Lin? Are you the tithe to. . . ."

"Shut up. Just shut up."

His voice was ragged with pain. Celia wanted to put her arms around him: possibly to comfort him, possibly to comfort herself. She wasn't sure whether the turmoil in her stomach was fear or excitement. She wanted to believe him; she did believe him, but a couple of things bothered her.

"It's not Halloween," she said.

"Midwinter Night is the longest night of the year."

"Janet got instructions."

"So she did."

"Which is why you can't tell me what to do."

For the first time, he smiled at her. "I knew you were bright," he said.

It was excitement. Definitely excitement. This was, no kidding, the best thing that had ever happened to her. "Do I get hints?"

He turned serious again. "Trust your ears, not your eyes."

"That's it?"

He nodded silently. His face was very still. Celia edged closer and put her hand on his. "I'll do my best," she said.

"I know you will, Celia."

In his mouth, her name was an invocation, a declaration, a caress. She'd never heard anyone speak her name like that before. She made the only response she could think of. She kissed him.

It went further than that, of course. Quite a bit further, in fact, but not as far as Janet had gone with Tam Lin. Part of Celia really wanted to go all the way, more than she'd ever wanted anything, and the hell with the consequences. Another part, however, spoke to her in her mother's voice, more sorrowful than angry, of pregnancy and disease and lost self-respect. She tried to ignore it, but it took enough of the enthusiasm out of her kissing that Valentine noticed and drew his mouth away from hers.

Celia felt relieved, frustrated, humiliated, and several other emotions she couldn't put a name to. "Sorry," she muttered.

"No," he said unexpectedly. "It would not be right, not

tonight." He sighed and sat up against the pillows. "Your kisses are very sweet, Celia. And so are you."

Celia smiled at him. She wanted to say something suitably wise and flirtatious, but the bed was incredibly soft and cozy and her eyes heavy.

"One more thing," his voice said, warm and low in her ear. "Things are not as they seem."

"Not as they seem," she murmured. "Got it." And then she was asleep.

Celia woke shivering with cold. The candle had either burned or been blown out. The bed beside her was empty. Her feet were freezing.

She couldn't find the matches or the candle or her boots. She was a little fuzzy on where she was and what she had to do, but she remembered that it had something to do with Valentine, and it was important, so she hauled herself out of the bed and groped through the darkness, looking for a door.

She didn't find a door, but eventually she found herself in a long, paneled corridor, with a rumor of torchlight and lute-song at the far end. Celia padded forward. Golden light and heat swelled towards her and a rhythmical pounding below the music's cheerful havoc.

Six steps short of the corridor's end, Celia stopped dead. It was all coming back to her: the rehearsal, the music, the sweetness of kissing Valentine, the pain of stopping. And she remembered that he'd asked her to reclaim him to the human world just as Janet had reclaimed Tam Lin.

But it wasn't just the same, was it? This wasn't like the ballad, not at all. Celia hadn't plucked a forbidden rose as Janet had, or gone looking for a thrill in a forbidden castle. Valentine had come to the ball looking for her. And he hadn't claimed her virginity as Tam Lin had Janet's—he'd been a perfect gentleman. So how could Celia trust that what had worked for Janet—desperate, pregnant, madly (presumably) in love—would work for Celia? And what would happen to her if it didn't?

That was the question, wasn't it? Why should she risk being turned into a frog or worse for a man she barely knew? Well, Celia answered herself, because she might love him, if she got the chance. And because she'd promised she would, and promises meant something to her. But most of all because she'd regret it the rest of her life if she turned back now. What was the good of dreaming of adventure if you turned your back on the first one that came your way?

Feeling a lot more nervous than she had before her curtsy to Society, Celia Townsend wiped her sweating palms down the purple paisley skirt of her minidress and stepped out of the dark corridor into the soft blaze of torches.

Standing just inside the door, she tried to make sense of the kaleidoscope of colors and shapes unfolding before her. It was a dance, of course, a dance as enchanted as the Snow Ball was dull. Hundreds of brightly dressed figures leapt, bowed, and pranced in perfect time to the music of two lutes, a violin, a viol da gamba, and a recorder. Every gesture was graceful, every step was light and self-assured. And the clothes! Celia had an impression of velvet and chiffon in rich colors—gold and burgundy and deep blue—and long hair piled high or braided with beads and flowers and shells. The men were as showy as the women, with lacy cuffs and beaded vests and ribbons plaited into their beards and hair.

The music was familiar—a dance tune the Booke of Ayres had been rehearsing. Celia took a timid step forward to try and get a look at the band; a dark figure stepped out of the dance, put a fist over its heart, and bowed. Celia looked up at Valentine. He had combed his hair, she noticed, and put on a dark Nehru jacket. "Are we in Elfland?" she asked.

He seemed amused. "We're not in Poughkeepsie," he said, and held out his hand to her, just as he had at the Snow Ball. "Come now, and dance."

Celia hung back. Thinking about him and seeing him were two different things. Just now, she was mostly aware that she was on the verge of a desperate and probably dangerous adventure. She expected him to act at least as if he was aware of what she was going to do for him. Instead, here he was, cool as a Sno-Cone, asking her to dance as if nothing had happened.

"Don't be shy, sweet heart," he said impatiently.

Remembering how desperate he'd been, in the little room with the bed and the trees, how frightened, and then how tender, Celia couldn't help wondering whether he'd been faking her out. Then she noticed that his outstretched hand was trembling. Of course. He was afraid, and he wasn't going to show it, or anything else, in front of his enemies. He knew the rules here; she didn't. If he wanted her to dance, she'd dance.

Celia laid her fingers on his, and allowed herself to be drawn onto the floor.

They'd hardly taken a step before a new partner claimed her, and to her dismay, Celia found herself moving lightly through the complex pattern, changing partners with each measure. Close up, the dancers were even more beautiful than she'd realized, and far stranger. Celia was passed from a boy whose hair clustered like grapes beneath a wreath of leaves to a little dark woman with surprised, golden eyes. As they spun together in the center of a weaving circle, little stars and moons poured from the skirts of her dress to surround them in a coruscating cloud that dispersed when the woman handed her off.

If Celia could have stopped dancing, she would have. Like a girl's in a fairy tale, her feet seemed to have taken on a life of their own, moving her flawlessly through the complex measures of a dance she'd never seen before. Whether she wanted to or not, she had to dance. Even if she was frightened, even if her feet hurt, even if she'd lost sight of Valentine, she had to dance.

Celia's feet skipped her through a winding chain of dancers—left hand, right hand, left hand, right hand—round to Valentine again. She clamped her fingers around his wrist.

"Don't worry," she said. "I've got you now. And I won't let go."

Valentine laughed and changed into a woman with a silver-gilt fall of hair and eyes like golden coins. "You can save him," the woman said happily, "if you can find him."

There were Valentines, suddenly, everywhere Celia looked—bowing, prancing, tossing their partners in the air or spinning them by the waist. Each was dressed differently:

velvet jacket, torn denim, ruffled shirt, jeans, turtleneck. One wore nothing at all but his own tossing curls.

Celia had hardly had time to register the sudden excess of Valentines when a tiny man with a single horn growing from his forehead grabbed her hand and forced her through a complicated set of twirls and turns that left her dizzy and panting. Her feet, still enthusiastically tripping the measure, were bruised and tender. Maybe if she just gave up, she thought, they'd let her stop dancing and go home. Valentine wasn't really her boyfriend, was he? Where did he get off, expecting her to rescue him just because he was cute and needed her to? Serve him right if she just let him go to Hell, like he was supposed to.

A woman made of flowers passed Celia to one of the Valentines, this one with a ruby swinging from his ear. Unlike the first Valentine, this one did not look as if he were enjoying himself. He looked like a whipped dog, and his dark eyes begged Celia to save him. It was impossible to be mad when he looked at her like that, impossible to condemn him just because he'd taken advantage of her. Which he hadn't even done, because she'd kissed him first. She'd come here to rescue him, and she would. If only she could figure out which of him to rescue.

Someone was riffing on the lute, chasing up and down through the scales, leaving a shimmer like gold on the air. "Trust your ears, not your eyes." Okay. Think. All the dancing Valentines looked like Valentine. But they couldn't be. Why not? Because if Valentine was dancing, who was playing the lute?

COTILLION

The movement of the dance hadn't brought Celia to the front of the room, where the musicians were—or if it had, she'd been too busy being passed around like a basketball to notice. Now she focussed her attention towards the music, peering through the shifting mass of dancers, leaving her feet and her partners to look after her place in the pattern. It was the Booke of Ayres, just as she'd thought: Twiggy, Curly, Blue Eyes, and Big Bear. And Valentine. So simple, really, now she'd figured it out. All she had to do was dance her way to the front, jump on Valentine and hold on no matter what happened. Piece of cake.

Choosing her own path through the dance was all but impossible. Since basketballs have very little choice about what part of the court they're in, finally, it was more chance than intention that brought her close to the raised platform where Valentine sat, fingers dancing frantically over the long neck of his lute.

With the desperate sense that it was now or never, Celia tore herself out of her partner's arms and ran for the platform. No one looked at her or tried to stop her. Valentine's dark head was bent over his lute's round body. Its exaggeratedly long neck towered over him, threatening Blue Eyes' bow arm.

Celia veered towards the other lutenist. Twiggy's lute was short-necked. No time to look carefully, no time to work out the possible layers and levels of illusion. Praying she had guessed right, Celia leaped onto the stage and threw her arms around Twiggy, lute and all.

Nothing happened. Celia had time to wonder if she'd

blown it, chosen someone who didn't need saving, and what would happen to her if she had? Would she be stuck dancing here forever? Get turned into a metal tree, or maybe get sent to Hell herself the next time the fairy folk needed a substitute?

Then the air shivered, and Celia was holding a dog, a German Shepherd. Its hackles were up, its teeth were bared, and it was growling.

Celia liked dogs, even big dogs; but she preferred to make friends with them gradually, and at a distance. The German Shepherd was pressed tight against her chest. It twisted back its neck and snapped at her. Sobbing with fear, Celia fought the instinct that would have snatched her hands away from its teeth and held on. Incredibly, the white teeth bit air. Celia buried her face in the dog's fur. Things are not what they seem. This dog was really Valentine, wasn't it? And Valentine wouldn't hurt her. All she had to do was hold on, and everything would come out okay.

But snakes aren't easy to hold on to. There's a lot of them to hold, and it's very muscular. One end keeps slashing at your back, and the other threatens you with a gaping mouth furnished with foot-long fangs. They were dripping venom, too. Celia screamed, but she didn't let go. If the dog hadn't bitten her, the snake wouldn't either. She hoped. How many transformations had Janet endured? Three, in the version she knew. In Valentine's version, the dog had been followed by a snake, a lion, a bear, and a burning brand.

She was almost looking forward to the lion.

There was no lion. What there was instead was a huge rat, with incisors the color of butter, a tail like a whip, scratching pink paws, and a slick coat of coarse fur. It stank like a sewer, and its eyes were red and mad.

Celia closed her eyes again, gritted her teeth, and hung on. Three. Her version, or Valentine's?

For a second, she thought she was done, because there was a man in her arms. But the eyes she encountered when she opened her own were rheumy and red-rimmed, with yellowish whites. The skin around them was gray with ground-in dirt, the hair matted, the cheeks unshaved. The man she embraced smelled worse than the rat, of old sweat and old drink and new vomit. Celia came very near to adding to that smell, and nearer still to opening her arms and getting away from him as fast as she could scramble.

It's just an illusion, she told herself. It's really Valentine. After the first shock, it's not so bad. Only one more to go. Maybe.

Her arms were full of leaves and twigs. And thorns, sharp ones, pricking deep into her wrists, face, and breasts. Pain, Celia found, was harder to resist than fear or disgust. It was all she could do to keep her arms firm around the slippery, prickly mass. She couldn't tighten her grip; it hurt too much.

Something wet trickled down from her temple to the corner of her eye: sweat, maybe, or blood. It stung. Celia blinked furiously and hung on. She didn't even know what she was holding any more, or why. She was just holding, and waiting for it to be over.

A familiar voice said, "Celia."

She had her face against his chest and her arms were pinning his arms to his side. He was naked and shivering. She loosed her hold just enough to get a good look at him. Valentine. He looked as sick as she felt, pale as a dead fish, and his dark curls very nearly as matted as the bum's. His face was wet with tears.

Celia raised her hand to wipe them away. "I don't have a cloak to cover you," she said, her voice shaking.

"I don't mind," he said.

At that point, Twiggy, back in her own shape again, began to swear a blue streak.

It was pretty imaginative, as swearing goes, sexual and scatological and highly insulting to humans in general and musicians in particular. Listening, Celia realized just how sheltered her life had been. She'd never imagined that simple bad language could be so absolutely ugly. But ugly was all it was. There was nothing worse Twiggy could do to them, now, than hurl nasty words at them. She was beaten.

Finally, she ran dry. She shook back her glimmering hair and drew herself upright, like a slender tree. "Very well," she said to Valentine. "You win. I knew you'd find some way out of it. I should have guessed you hadn't lured her here to take your place. Now one of us will have to. We don't get out of the deal, you know, when the designated fall guy gets rescued."

Valentine shrugged. "It's your deal. You honor it."

Twiggy looked as if she was going to start swearing again. Instead she said, "If I'd known what your promises were worth, Valentine Carter, I'd never have taught you to play the lute."

"But you didn't know," Valentine said. "And the promise was forced from me."

"I'd like to cut off your hands," said Twiggy coldly. "But I've got more pressing things to do. Now, get out."

It's hard to make a dignified exit when your feet are killing you and your companion is stark naked. Celia didn't care much about dignity at this point. She was willing to crawl from the room if her swollen feet and aching legs wouldn't carry her. But Valentine picked her up, staggering a little, and walked stolidly through the crowd with her in his arms. They must have looked ridiculous, but nobody was laughing.

It wasn't over at all, Celia realized, not for the dancers. The little one-horned man caught her eye and bowed to her. The little woman with the stars in her dress gave her a sad smile. Tears rose to Celia's eyes.

"I know," Valentine said. "I'm sorry for them, too. But not enough to burn in hell for them."

It seemed like a long walk back to the bedroom. Celia clung to Valentine's neck and tried not to cry. She might be a heroine, but she didn't feel like one. She hurt all over and was tired beyond belief. And when she got home, her mother would kill her.

The bedroom looked different—dirty and bare except for a mattress and a pile of clothes: Valentine's white shirt and black jeans; Celia's boots and fishnet stockings. Valentine lowered Celia onto the mattress with a groan. Their eyes caught and shied away from one another. Celia felt her face heat. She decided against putting on the stockings, and grimly began to work her feet into the boots. Miraculously, they weren't too swollen to fit. In fact, they were fine. The scratches from the thorns were gone, too.

"Celia?" Valentine had dressed and pulled back his hair, but he still looked pretty grotty. Celia suspected she didn't look a whole lot better. And it didn't matter anyway, did it, how they looked? Trust your ears, not your eyes. Yeah.

"What?" It came out sharp and impatient.

Valentine lifted his chin in a familiar gesture. "I just wanted to tell you that I love you. You're smart and you're brave and you're beautiful. You saved me." He took her unresisting hands in his. "I want to marry you."

The end of the fairy tale indeed, as pat and easy as "And they lived happily ever after." Celia felt a huge, warm emotion rise in her, swelling from the pit of her stomach to her throat and head, so that she was sick and dizzy with it. It might have been love and joy and surrender. If it was, Celia wasn't at all sure she liked it. "I hardly know you," she objected.

"I don't understand," Valentine said. "You saved me. You risked you didn't even know what danger to save me. How could you not love me?"

"I did it because it wasn't fair for you to go to Hell when it wasn't even your bargain. And it was an adventure."

"I thought you loved me."

"I might. I just met you. I don't know."

She'd left her hands in his, which might be significant, but was likely to be just inertia. He looked hurt and bewildered and exhausted.

"Look," she said. "I really can't talk about this right now. Do you have someplace to go?"

He shrugged. "This is where I've been staying. Here, and that other place."

"Not a good idea. What if Twiggy has second thoughts?"

"Twiggy?" That astonished a laugh out of him. "You think

of her as *Twiggy*?" He threw his arms around her. "I do love you, Celia. You're—I don't even know what you are. I've never met anyone like you."

She hugged him back, kissed him on his cheek (he needed a shave) and disengaged herself. "Believe me, I've never met anyone like you either. This isn't ballad-land, Valentine. It's New York, December 1969. And it's really late and I've got to go home and face my parents. They didn't want me to come tonight. It's not going to be pretty." She opened her purse, took out all her money, including her mother's twenty, and gave it to him, all but a subway token and a dime for a phone call. "Here," she said. "It might be enough for a room at the Y. I don't really know. Call me around noon, and I'll meet you somewhere. Down here. I think I might like the Village—the human part of it, that is. The same with you. I need to see you both in the light of day."

His chin was up again. "I'm not used to begging."

"Fine." She was at the end of her tether. "So don't call me." She crumpled up the slip of paper on which she'd scribbled her phone number and dropped it on the floor. He picked it up.

"I'm sorry," he said. "I'm not used to being human. It's been a while."

"How long? Never mind, you can tell me tomorrow. I can't take any more wonders."

He kissed her when they parted, a shy, courting kind of kiss. Celia was too tired to care what kind of kiss it was. The crowds were just as thick as they had been earlier, and it was late—very late indeed. Whatever was going to happen at the ball had probably happened by now, and Twiggy, a.k.a. the Fairy Queen, was plucking away on her arch-lute while her subjects danced their sorrow and fear away. And Celia was on her way home to get reamed out by her parents. It didn't seem nearly as scary as it ought to. Maybe it was being tired. Maybe it was knowing that her parents were human, and cared for her. Or perhaps it was knowing that she'd followed her heart and her instincts and had brought Valentine back to the human world. Whatever happened next, she had a good chance, she thought, of living happily ever after.

DELIA SHERMAN was born in Tokyo, Japan, raised in New York City, and now lives in Boston. She is the author of the novels *Through a Brazen Mirror*, *The Porcelain Dove* (winner of the Mythopoeic Award), and *The Freedom Maze*. With fellow fantasist Ellen Kushner, she is co-author of a short story and a novel, both called "The Fall of the Kings." Her many short stories include "Grand Central Park," also set in a magical New York City, which appeared in *The Green Man: Tales from the Mythic Forest* (Viking). With Terri Windling, she co-edited *The Essential Bordertown*. She is a contributing editor for Tor Books and a founding member of the Interstitial Arts Foundation (**www.endicott-studio.com/ia**). She prefers cafés to home for writing, and traveling to staying put.

AUTHOR'S NOTE

Like Celia, I made my bow to society in 1969. It was my mother's idea, and I didn't really enjoy it very much—except for my dress, which had white organdy petals on the skirt. The whole experience seemed very unreal, as if it were taking place in a universe parallel to the one where I went to school and watched the Vietnam War being fought on TV every night. So I thought it might be interesting to take that sense of unreality just one step further, into the magical New York that I always feel around me when I walk in the Village or Central Park or the New York Public Library.

tHE BABY IN tHE NIGHt DEPOSIt BOX

The Elliotville Bank had just added a secure room to their bank vault and filled it with safety deposit boxes. Things rarely changed around Elliotville, and something new always got people's attention, but to be sure that everyone had heard about the service, the bank rented a billboard near the center of town and put a picture up with the slogan, "Your treasure will be safe with us."

The president of the bank, Homer Donnelly, had thought of the slogan himself, and was quite proud of it. More than just the president of the bank, he was the Chief Executive Officer and the Chairman of the Board of Trustees. His family had founded the bank. The old-fashioned iron safe they had started with still sat in the lobby.

The people in the town were not what you would call wealthy, but they were prosperous and hardworking and, Homer thought, certain to have a family heirloom that needed safekeeping. If someone had asked, he would have said they had good moral character in Elliotville, so it was something of a shock to come in early one morning, a week after the billboard had gone up, and find that someone had left a baby in the night deposit box.

The night deposit box was actually a slot in the outside wall of the bank with a slide in it, like the one in a mailbox or the public library's book return. When the bank was closed, customers could put their money and a deposit slip into an envelope, pull down on the handle, put their envelope on the slide, and then let go. Their deposit would drop through the wall and into a bin positioned below. There it would stay, safely inside the bank, to be recorded the next day.

Emptying the bin was the first business of the banking day, and because he arrived before the tellers, Homer frequently did the job himself. That's why he was the one that found the baby. She was there, wrapped in a blanket, sleeping peacefully on the stack of deposits.

Homer could not have been more dumbstruck if the bin had been empty and the night deposits had disappeared. With a shaking hand he opened the folded bit of paper pinned to the baby blanket, afraid that he knew what it would read. He did. In spidery, elegant handwriting it said, "Our treasure, please keep her safe."

Homer moaned and the baby stirred. Silently he backed away. He went to find the security guard who stayed in the building through the night.

"You're fired," he said.

"What?" said the guard.

"Fired," said Homer.

"But . . . "

"But nothing," said Homer. "Fired. Last night while you were reading your magazine, or having your nap, or God only knows what, someone dropped a baby in the night deposit box."

"A what?"

"A BABY," Homer shouted and pointed with his finger, "IN THE NIGHT DEPOSIT BOX!"

"Alive?" asked the guard, blanching.

"OF COURSE!" shouted Homer, and, as if in agreement, a thin cry rose from the bin.

"Oh gosh," said the security guard. "Oh, my gosh." He hurried across the bank and looked into the bin, Homer behind him.

Pepas, the security guard, was older than Homer, the father of three grown children, and the grandfather of five small ones. He flipped the blanket off the baby and looked at it carefully. He lifted the legs and wiggled the arms while the baby howled louder.

"Poor Precious," said Pepas. "Do you have a bump? No, you're not hurt. You look just fine and everything is fine, don't you fuss." Carefully putting his large hand behind the baby's head he picked it up and settled it on his shoulder. "Yes, Precious," he said, "you come to Poppy," and hearing his deep voice and rocking on his shoulder the baby grew quiet. Its eyes opened and it looked over the guard's shoulder at Homer. Homer felt as if the bank vault had dropped from the ceiling and landed on his head.

"Is she all right?" he asked.

"Just fine," said Pepas. "But you can't tell she's a girl. You never know with babies until you look."

"Of course she's a girl. Any idiot can see that she's a girl. Why is she doing that? What's the matter?"

"She's hungry, I think," said the guard.

"I better call the police," said Homer.

"Call my wife first," said the guard.

Homer called the police, but Mrs. Pepas, who lived two doors down from the bank, beat all four of the town's policemen by a quarter of an hour. She banged at the glass doors at the front of the bank and waved a bottle.

Homer went to let her in.

"Where's the baby?" she asked. "Where's the little treasure?"

"She's over here," said Homer.

"She?" asked Mrs. Pepas, over her shoulder as she hurried across the bank. "Did you look?"

Well, it was the first bit of excitement in Elliotville since the truck carrying chicken manure turned over on Main Street. The police showed up at the bank with their lights on and sirens blazing. Mrs. Pepas made the first officer to reach the bank go back outside to turn them off, because they woke the baby, who'd drunk her bottle and fallen asleep. The tellers arrived one by one and all wanted a chance to hold the little girl. She was definitely a girl, about three months old. She had a silver rattle like a tiny barbell with a larger round ball at one end and a smaller ball at the other. She had a teething ring that was also silver, round like a bracelet with intriguing

bumps and ridges to suck on. There was no other sign of iden-
tification with her except the note. Whoever she was, she
seemed unperturbed at having been dropped through a night
deposit box. She smiled indiscriminately at the faces all
around her. Homer wondered if anyone else felt quite as
stunned as he did when he looked into her eyes.

  He had tentatively asserted his right to hold the baby and
was getting careful instruction from a female police officer
when the representative from the Children's Protective Services arrived. She was a tall woman in a crisp business suit
with a short skirt and sharply pointed, heeled shoes. She
plucked the baby out of Homer's arms and after the briefest
discussion with a policeman, carried her through the doors of
the bank. Homer felt like he'd been robbed. Through the glass
doors of the bank he could see the woman fitting the baby
into a plastic seat. There was a flash of lightning and a clap of
thunder. It had been sunny when Homer walked to the bank,
but the day was as dark as night and it began to rain. The CPS
woman had to put the baby seat on the pavement beside the
open door of the getaway car and kneel down in order to drag
the straps over the baby's head. Not that it was a getaway car,
Homer reminded himself. And of course the baby wasn't
being stolen. It just felt that way.

  "Oh," said Mrs. Pepas, "I have her rattle and her teething
ring. I better go give them to that woman."

  Homer, his eyes still on the crying baby, stopped her with
a lifted hand. "I wonder, Mrs. Pepas, if you might just step
into the safety deposit room first?" He hustled the protesting
Mrs. Pepas past the eighteen-inch-thick door into the vault.

"Wait right here," he said and hurried back across the bank and through the front doors.

He snagged the baby out of the car seat with one hand. He forgot whatever it was that the police officer had been telling him about supporting her head. He scooped her up and was pleased to find that she fit right into the crook of his elbow like a football.

"Excuse me," he said to the CPS representative, who was staring up at him in surprise. "We forgot a little something." Feeling just the way he had when he'd scored a winning touchdown in a high school game, Homer swept back through the double doors and into the bank. He hurried across the lobby and into the vault, pulling on the heavy door as he passed. The hinges on the door were huge and the door was carefully balanced. It swung very slowly but steadily with the inertia of its tremendous weight.

Inside the vault, stunned at his own behavior, but still gamely carrying on, Homer handed the baby to Mrs. Pepas. He stepped back out again to face the highly irritated CPS woman.

"Just forgot the rattle," Homer said as the vault door shut behind him with the almost inaudible click of electromagnets. Homer turned. "Oh dear me," he said. "I must have bumped it."

"Mrs. Pepas?" he said, pushing a button next to a small grill set by the door. "Mrs. Pepas, I seem to have shut the vault door by accident. I am terribly sorry. It has a time lock and I will have to override it. It will take a few minutes to get the codes. Will you and the baby be all right? Don't worry about the air, the vault is ventilated. And we put the intercom in just for moments like this." He let go of the button, cutting off Mrs. Pepas's reply.

Homer smiled at the CPS woman. "Terribly sorry. Won't take a minute." And he went off to fetch the instruction booklet for the vault.

Some of the codes were in the booklet, but others, for safety's sake, were elsewhere. Homer had to telephone his aunt to get her part of the code and as it was seven o'clock in the morning she was not pleased. She didn't know the codes off the top of her head. She told Homer she would call him back. Homer had other calls to make, to his mother and his lawyer, and the mayor and his friend who was Elliotville's county judge. It took some time. In between calls, Homer smiled brightly at the CPS woman and the CPS woman fumed, swinging her baby carrier like the Wicked Witch of the West waiting to carry off Toto.

Carrying the instruction manual and pages torn from his memo pad, Homer addressed himself to the vault door. He pushed button after button in careful order, pausing in between to read and reread the instruction manual until finally his lawyer arrived.

"Ah, there we are," said Homer. He rapidly tapped a few more numbers into the keypad and the door clicked obediently.

Mrs. Pepas stepped out with the baby and Homer gently guided her toward his office. "If you will just step this way," he murmured, but they were blocked by the CPS woman, tapping the pointy toe of her high heels.

"If you please, I think we've spent enough time here. I'll take the baby, now."

"No," said Homer, and sidled past her.

"What do you mean, NO?" she asked as she hurried into Homer's office behind the baby and ahead of the lawyer.

"She's going to stay here. We will take good care of her."

"I am afraid that is entirely out of the question, Mr. . . . Mr. . . . ." She had forgotten his name. "The infant will need to be seen at the hospital by a pediatrician and checked for malnutrition as well as disease. She'll need a PKU test and a genetic screening. She'll need to be given vaccinations: DPT, MMR, HIB, Hep A, Hep B. She can't stay here."

Homer smiled at the list of horrors and propelled his reluctant lawyer forward. "This is Harvey Bentwell. He'll explain." Homer patted his lawyer on the shoulder, the sort of pat he hoped would remind Harvey that there weren't many accounts that paid as well as the bank's in a town as small as Elliotville. Then he and Mrs. Pepas and the baby went to look for a changing table.

Harvey Bentwell smiled, but the CPS woman didn't, so Harvey pulled himself together with a sigh and began a long incantation in Latin. The most important words of which turned out to be *in loco parentis*. Harvey explained that legally speaking the baby hadn't been abandoned, she'd been turned over to the care of the bank, so the Children's Protective Services, while a fine and noble organization, really wasn't called on to look after her. The bank would do that. He'd already called upon a pediatrician and a pediatric nurse to make a house call, or a bank call, to examine the baby.

CPS said that this was the most ridiculous thing she'd ever heard of. Harvey smiled. "I want that baby," CPS said. Harvey Bentwell shook his head. "I will have that baby." Harvey shook his head again.

Well, you can imagine the fuss, but Harvey Bentwell wasn't just a small-town lawyer, he was a good small-town lawyer, and in the end there wasn't much the Children's Protective Services could do. They couldn't guarantee the baby a better home than the bank would offer, and they couldn't produce any legal reason why a bank couldn't be guardian for a child. The judge insisted that the baby be brought to the hearings and she screamed right through them.

She had good reason. The weather was terrible. The skies had been clear in the morning the day they dressed the baby to take her to the courthouse, but by the time they got to the car there was thunder and lightning and driving rain. The world seemed full of shadows and reasonless disturbances. A stoplight fell into the street just ahead of them. The light bulbs in the street lamps, turned on in the middle of the day, exploded. Walking from the car to the courthouse, Homer felt there were people invisible behind the screen of the rain. He hurried up the stairs and into the building. Once inside, everyone seemed to want to take the baby away from him. Good-natured people offered to hold the crying infant, saying they could soothe her better, offering their experience with children as credentials. "I had three children, I'm a grandmother, I've got a baby of my own." Homer declined more or less politely. He wouldn't let anyone take the baby. He put her car seat down for a moment by his feet while he took off his coat.

With one arm still in its sleeve he looked down in horror as he saw the car seat sliding away from him. He whirled around and caught the CPS woman, who'd crouched behind him, with one hand under the edge of the seat, pulling it across the floor. With a look of mock sheepishness, she lifted the seat up by the handle. "She's crying, I'll just take her a mo—"

But Homer had the other side of the handle. He snatched the baby back and hurried away with his coat hanging from one sleeve and dragging on the marble floor with a slithering sound.

The baby went on screaming. She was inconsolable until she was carried back through the bank doors where she went right to sleep, just like any tired baby. The CPS woman seemed to take it all very personally and she assured Homer that she would be watching carefully.

Homer said he didn't care, she could watch all she wanted, so long as the baby stayed at the bank.

A crib was set up in the safety deposit box room. One of the tellers made a mobile to hang over it with coins and dollar bills hanging from strings. They took turns carrying her in a pack on their chests while they talked to customers and passed out papers and collected deposits and counted money. On their breaks they fed her her bottled formula and burped her. Homer got over his first shyness around babies and let her sit on his lap while he took care of the business of the bank. The judge had insisted that a birth certificate be created for the baby and Homer had filled it in. He named her Precious Treasure Donnelly, but no one ever called her anything but Penny.

In the evenings Mr. and Mrs. Pepas came to work together and Mrs. Pepas made her husband dinner on a hot plate in the employees' break room. After dinner she fed the baby again and tucked her into her crib in the safety deposit room. Then the vault door was sealed and the intercom was turned on so that Mr. Pepas could hear her if she woke during the night. Homer had a video camera installed in the vault so that they could see her as well, but she slept every night as peacefully as a lamb. In the morning Homer came in, or one of the tellers, to wake her and get her ready for the day. There was probably never a baby so closely supervised as the bank's baby, but she seemed to thrive. She never had a runny nose, never had a fussy day or a toothache. She seemed happy and normal with a smile for one and all.

But she never left the bank. The tellers did try taking her out in a stroller they bought for her, but she screamed so that they quickly brought her back and Homer declared that she wasn't to be taken out of the bank again. At first this wasn't so remarkable. There was plenty of room in the bank and plenty of things to amuse her. The town got used to stepping around a tricycle when they came to cash their checks. She had her own pretend teller window and play money. In the afternoons she sat with Homer while he worked. He taught her the combination to the old-fashioned iron safe in the lobby and she liked to put her rattle and her teething ring, which she still played with, into the safe and spin the dials and then take them back out again. She never left them there. She carried them with her wherever she went, like talismans to remind her of her parents who had left their Penny in the bank for safekeeping.

By the time she was supposed to be going to kindergarten, Penny knew her numbers to a thousand as well as her times tables up to nine, she could add and subtract numbers in her head and was already reading on her own. Of course, there's a law that children of a certain age have to be in school, and that's when the Children's Protective Services stepped back in. The woman in her pointy shoes arrived at the door on the first of September and asked why Penny wasn't at school. Homer had to call Harvey Bentwell and Harvey had to come up with a tutor and a pile of forms all carefully filled out, that would allow Penny to be home-schooled, though obviously it wasn't home-schooling, it was bank-schooling.

CPS must have thought they had a better case, because they dragged the whole thing back into court, saying that no guardian could legally keep a child incarcerated her entire life. Harvey argued that Penny wasn't incarcerated in the bank, she was home and she liked being there. She didn't want to go outside. CPS said no normal child would choose to stay inside. Harvey said she wasn't a normal child, and that much was true. Watching carefully Homer had concluded that yes, most people were a little stunned the first time they looked into her eyes. She seemed happy and she played like any child, and she raced around the lobby on a two-wheeler after the bank had closed and the path was clear, but when you looked into her eyes you seemed to stare into a well of peace, and, well, the only word Homer had for it was security. At least, when she was in the bank. The only time that Homer saw that serenity clouded was during the court hearings about her custody. She didn't scream through them, the way she had as a baby. She was five years old, after all, and had too much self-possession. She sat in a wooden chair with her feet swing-ing down and her hands folded in her lap, an unnaturally quiet and mannered little girl with coffee-colored skin and dark hair tightly curled like a lamb's fur.

The judge had insisted that Penny come to the hearings, but Homer in turn insisted that the judge come to the bank to speak to her at least once before ruling on the case. Homer walked the judge from the door of the bank across the lobby to his office where Penny was waiting. He suggested that Penny stand up and shake hands with the judge and he watched the judge's face carefully as he bent down and looked into her face as he took her hand.

Homer smiled with satisfaction. He quietly closed the office door behind him. He was smiling as he put his arm around the puzzled Harvey's shoulder. "We're all set, Harvey," he said.

The judge emerged twenty minutes later and summoned the concerned parties to his chamber.

"I am considering leaving the child in the sole custody of the bank of Elliotville," he told them. "She seems in every way happy and well cared for."

"Except that she never leaves the bank, Your Honor," said the lawyer for CPS.

"That's true, but I am content that this is in line with the desires of the child and not an imposition."

"Imposition or not, Your Honor, it's unnatural. It's a psy-chosis. She needs treatment."

Homer sat quietly while the argument went back and forth. He wasn't concerned. Penny had had the desired effect.

THE BABY IN THE NIGHT DEPOSIT BOX

The CPS produced a child psychiatrist who said Penny needed medical help, maybe drugs, maybe hospitalization. Harvey Bentwell agreed that it might be an illness, but said that Penny had felt this way since she was a baby and that no court in the world would say that it wasn't the guardian's right to decide on medical treatment for a child. Did the judge have reason to believe that the bank was an inadequate guardian?

"Yes," said the CPS woman, jumping up and interrupting. "The bank is no guardian at all. This child needs a mother and a father. She needs a family to help her deal with her irrational fears of the outside world. Where is her family?"

"We are her family," Homer pointed out gently.

"Are you?" said Ms. CPS. "Show me some instance where you have helped her deal with her fear. As far as I can see, you do nothing but encourage her debility."

"Have you met the child in the bank?"

Ms. CPS had adamantly refused to step into the bank. She hadn't been back inside it since the day Penny was found.

"Then how can you criticize what parenting is available to the child?"

"There is no parenting. Find one example of an adult helping this child overcome her fears."

"Mrs. Pepas helps me." To everyone's amazement, Penny spoke. "When I am afraid she helps me."

"Go on," said the judge gently.

"Sometimes I am afraid that the things that are outside the bank will get in to get me. Sometimes their shadows come in at night. I can see them."

"And?"

"I told Mrs. Pepas. She said that they were just shadows and that shadows all by themselves couldn't hurt anyone. I didn't have to be afraid. I just had to pretend that they were the shadows of bunnies. That any shadow, if you look at it right, could be the shadow of a bunny. She said I should take my rattle, because I always have my rattle with me, and my ring." She held up her arm to show the teething ring that now sat like a bracelet around her wrist. "She said I should point my rattle at the shadows and say 'You're a bunny,' and then I won't be afraid anymore."

"Did it work?" the judge asked, curious.

"Yes."

The judge looked at CPS and raised his eyebrows. The CPS representative was not pleased. Finally she sniffed and said sharply that it would have been more to the point to teach the child to shake her rattle at the things she thought were outside the bank.

She squatted down in front of Penny. "Darling. These are just silly ideas. We want you to see that. There aren't any monsters. There aren't any bad guys. There isn't anything or anyone outside the bank trying to take you away. It's just nonsense, can you understand that?"

Penny looked at her calmly for a moment. "You are outside the bank," she said. "You are trying to take me away."

Ms. CPS flushed to her hairline and stood up quickly.

"Your Honor, the child is sick. She needs help."

"Your help?" the judge asked.

"Our help."

"I disagree." Bang went the gavel and home went Penny to the bank.

THE BABY IN THE NIGHT DEPOSIT BOX

※ ※ ※

CPS tried again and again over the years, but without success and Penny grew up safe in the bank, but in other ways very much like any girl her age. When she was sixteen and had taken the test to secure a high school equivalency, the Children's Protective Services asked again what future she could have if she never left the Elliotville Bank. Penny explained that she had enrolled in a correspondence course in accounting and she intended to become a teller. The CPS woman, now a little gray but no less forceful, nearly choked But Treasure was near the age of her majority. Though CPS cajoled and threatened, there was nothing that the department could do.

To celebrate her new legal independence, Penny pierced her ears, straightened her curly hair, and dyed the tips blonde. She liked the surprise on people's faces. Customers that she had known her entire life were stunned, but once they looked into her eyes, they knew she was still the same Penny. They broke into smiles of relief and admired her hair and her dangling earrings and the odd incongruity of her clothing: a camouflage tank top, a plaid skirt, and over it all a sensible cardigan with pockets to hold her rattle and teething ring, which she still carried with her wherever she went.

She was working the day before her eighteenth birthday, or what the authorities thought her eighteenth birthday might be, when there was an odd disturbance in the doorway. She looked up from the money she was counting, through the glass window that separated her from the lobby. Standing in the bank doorway was an extremely tall woman dressed in a

crisp black skirt and suit coat and carrying a shiny black briefcase. For one moment Penny thought that she was the CPS
woman, but this woman was far more striking. Her hair was
silver blonde and her skin was white like cream. Her eyes,
even from across the bank lobby, were a startling blue. She
stepped into the lobby like a queen followed by her minions
and her minions were even more remarkable and less appealing than herself.

There was a troll, a vampire, a few surly-looking dwarves,
three or four pale greenish individuals with sneering faces,
and quite a few animals with unpleasant horns and teeth all in
a crowd that was partially obscured by the mist coming
through the doorway.

"Is it raining?" asked Penny. It had been sunny earlier that
day.

The queenly figure in black must have heard her voice
through the glass. She stepped toward Penny and lifted her
briefcase onto the countertop. "I would like to withdraw my
niece," she said in a steely voice that hissed on the last sibi-
lant.

Penny swallowed. "Excuse me?" she said.

"My niece," said the woman. "I would like to withdraw my
niece." She looked over her shoulder toward the open doorway to the vault and the safety deposit boxes. "She must be
around here somewhere. I am sure you see the family resemblance. Her father was mortal and I doubt very much she
would take after him."

Penny quickly tilted her head down and pressed a button
that rang an alarm in Homer's office. Homer rushed into the

lobby and slowed to a stop as he saw the crowd there. More slowly he walked behind the counter and came up behind Penny.

"This lady would like to withdraw her niece," Penny said. She and Homer stared at one another.

"Immediately," prodded the woman on the other side of the counter.

"D—d—d—," said Homer.

"Did you make the deposit?" Penny asked.

"No. I did not. My sister and her husband deposited the baby here, but I am now in charge of their affairs. I would like to withdraw her."

The way she said, "in charge of their affairs," made one think it meant no good at all for this unknown mother and father of Penny's.

"And is the original depositor deceased?" Penny asked.

"Deceased?"

"Dead," said Penny.

"No, not yet."

"Well, then, I'm afraid that she will have to make the withdrawal."

"That is impossible."

Penny turned to Homer. "Perhaps a signature on the withdrawal slip would be sufficient?" she asked.

"Uh, huh, yes, I s-suppose so," said Homer.

Penny, very carefully looking down at the paper in front of her, slid a withdrawal slip across the counter. "We'll need to have this filled out and signed," she said in a prim voice.

The elegant creature on the other side of the counter

picked up the piece of paper by one corner and looked at it with disgust. "You want this signed?"

"We can't otherwise release your deposit," Penny explained.

"Very well," said the woman. Dangling the paper in front of her, she carried it out of the bank. She was followed by the vampire, the troll, the green people, and assorted unpleasant others.

Homer sighed. Penny rubbed her hands together. "That's once," she said.

The woman was back the next day, bringing rain and mist behind her. The other customers in the bank scattered, leaving an open path to the tellers. The woman headed for a different window, but Penny managed to slide up the counter and displace the teller there before her aunt finished her trip across the lobby.

"My niece," she said, and slid the deposit slip across the counter. Penny studied the slip a moment, turning her head to one side to read the spidery signature.

"You did say that your sister and her husband made the deposit, didn't you?"

"I did," said the woman.

"I am terribly sorry. If it is a joint deposit, we'll need his signature as well to authorize a withdrawal."

"You didn't mention this yesterday," the woman hissed.

No one was better at dealing with unpleasant customers than Penny. "I'm terribly sorry," she said in an officially earnest voice. "But we do need both signatures."

The woman snatched the paper from the desk and swept

out the door, sucking the mist away in her wake and disappearing before she'd gone more than a few steps down the street. Penny watched them through the glass doors of the bank. "That's twice," she said.

When the woman returned with the deposit slip, signed, Penny was relieved to see, by two people, she clucked sympathetically and said, "They haven't dated it."

"You are joking."

"No, I am afraid it has . . ."

The woman snapped her fingers and Penny flinched as a pen slid across the counter and jumped obediently into the outstretched hand. The woman looked at the little block calendar next to the teller's window and carefully dated the deposit slip.

". . . to be dated by the signatories," Penny finished as the pen dropped back to the counter.

"I am not pleased, young woman."

"I do apologize," Penny said meekly, her eyes cast down, and when the vampires, the trolls, the nixies, monsters and minions were gone with the mist, she smiled a different smile and said to Homer, "That's three."

The next day she told the woman that the deposit slip, because it wasn't filled out in the bank, needed to be notarized by a notary public.

"A what?"

"A notary public."

"Do go on," the woman prompted.

Homer spoke up. He had been standing by Penny every day, holding his ground as best he could, ready to offer her any assistance. "A notary public is an 'individual legally empowered to witness and certify the validity of documents and to take affidavits and depositions.'"

"They have a stamp," Penny explained. "They witness the document being signed and then they stamp it and it is a legal document. Until then"—she slid the deposit slip back to the woman—"until then, it's just a slip of paper." She smiled brightly.

The creature on the far side of the counter inhaled in a hiss and held her breath until Penny thought she might lift off the floor like a gas-filled balloon, or go off with a pop like an over-inflated one. The woman looked around the lobby wall as if for a weapon to use but finding none she turned back with only a glare.

"And where do I find a notary public?" the enchantress asked. "Where? They don't grow on trees where I come from, and while I might be able to arrange that one did, it would take time I don't have to waste."

"Oh," said Penny thoughtfully. "I am a notary public. I could go with you."

She felt Homer's panicked grasp on her wrist, but she turned to reassure him with a look. "Very well, then," said the frightening woman. "Come along, then."

Penny followed her out of the bank. The mist was thinner than it had been before, and rays of sunshine reached through it. Penny, still keeping her eyes cast down, noted that some of the most frightening creatures of the woman's retinue seemed to have shadows shaped like rabbits. She followed the woman into the mist and saw the world around her thin before the mist cleared entirely and she was standing in the middle of a muddy road. On either side were water-soaked fields under low clouds. The fields were deserted and the few trees between them were black and leafless. It was raining and the enchantress was ahead of her, moving down the road. Her short skirt and briefcase were gone. She wore a long black robe with a hood at the back and had a satchel that hung from her shoulder.

"Come," she commanded and Penny followed her. Ahead lay a fairy tale sort of castle that should have glowed in the sunshine with flags flapping in a breeze, but instead it sat gray and sodden and inert in its blighted surroundings.

It was a twenty-minute walk to the castle and in the first five minutes, Penny was soaked to the skin. The mud collected on her boots and they grew heavier and heavier. She noticed that the rain didn't fall on the enchantress, who was still perfectly dry, but the vampires looked miserable, and the trolls were no happier in their bare skin. Only the nixies, being water creatures, were undistressed by the rain. They were, however, unused to the mud. They slipped and slid and occasionally grabbed each other for support. But they weren't pleasant creatures, even to each other, and when one teetered, another was apt to push her over altogether. Once one fell, she dragged at the hems of her passing sisters and pulled them down too, until they were all a sprawling nest of spiteful hissing and scratching. Penny watched with interest as a troll stepped on one of the nixies underfoot and all the others rose up against him. There was a harpy nearby who took the troll's side and buffeted the nixies with her wings, calling them rude names and knocking them back into the mud. The nixies retaliated by grabbing at her feathers and pulling them out in handfuls. The harpy squawked with rage and screamed abuse. The vampires stopped to watch. The various wolflike creatures and the crawling batwinged monsters twisted between the bystanders to get a better look. Penny, who was behind the vampires, had to stop as well. She ran her fingers through her hair and squeezed the rainwater out. As she did so she felt something brush her ankles and she jumped in surprise. A black rabbit with malevolent red eyes was fidgeting past a hop at a time, clearly as eager as the others to see the fight, but just as clearly nervous of the teeth and claws around him.

There was a crack of thunder and simultaneous lightning and all looked guiltily at the enchantress, hastily collected themselves, and hurried on. They passed between rows of broken-down houses, which seemed deserted, huddled behind flat expanses of mud that should have been front gardens. Penny thought she saw a face or two watching from behind the broken windows. When they reached the gates of the castle, the wooden doors were blasted and their hinges broken. The stones of the courtyard beyond were heaved and rumpled as if by a sudden frost. The nixies stumbled again and a troll snarled, but they scurried on as best they could into the main hall where the enchantress stood, smiling in satisfaction before two thrones. On one sat a woman in every way but one identical to the enchantress. She had skin like cream and long hair that fell like a waterfall in moonlight to her shoulders. Her eyes were open and empty as she sat on the throne, covered over in a mass of spiderwebs that bound her to her chair, clinging to her hands and her arms, her eyelids, her lips, the wisping tendrils of her hair. Though she was as still as a statue, Penny could see in a glance that where her sister was all cruelty, this queen was all kindness. Her eyes were as blue, but where her sister's were blue like ice, this queen's were as blue as the sky and as clear. Beside her sat her husband, ensnared the same way, with his eyes open and watching the enchantress. His skin was a warm coffee color and his black hair was as curly as a lamb's new fur coat. Penny was uncomfortably aware of her own hair, with the heavy water wrung out of it, beginning to regain its natural curl.

The hall was silent except for the dripping of rain and the occasional hiss or snarl of the enchantress's minions. When she held up her hand, the hisses and snarls ceased and there was only the sound of the rain.

"Still here?" she asked the motionless figures. "I am so fortunate to have found you at home. Why yes, there is the teensiest favor you can do for me." She smiled. "Oh it's nothing, less than nothing, but I know you're pleased to help out. You see, we need our form filled out again."

She held out her hand and Penny hurried to her side to offer her the blank deposit slip. The enchantress stepped forward and lifted the limp hand of the queen. She drew a quill pen, black and shiny, from the air and fitted it into the unresponsive fingers. "Sign," she commanded and the fingers moved the pen across the slip of paper while the queen's blue eyes remained empty.

"Date," hissed the enchantress and the pen moved again.

The enchantress moved to the king on his throne and lifted his hand. His head turned ever so slightly and his eyes met Penny's.

The enchantress folded his fingers around the pen. "Oh, don't fuss," she said. "We are so close now, so close. Do this one little thing for me and we are nearly done. I will have you and I will have the princess and I will have the crown and the scepter and there will be none to stand against me, Queen of the Realm." She smiled up at him. "One little thing and the princess is mine."

"Sign," she said. "Date," and the pen moved. "It was your idea, wasn't it? To hide her, and the crown and the scepter when you realized I was too strong to be defeated by your paltry virtuous magic, where I wasted eighteen years trying to fetch her out, sending my minions one after another against cold steel and mortal conventions. Did you think I didn't know?" She straightened. "But if I couldn't reach her, neither could you. So she doesn't know the power she has, and I shall see to it that she never will." Pinching the deposit slip between her thumb and long-nailed forefinger she turned to Penny. "Now for our dear friend, the notary public."

Penny stood with her hands tucked into her cardigan pockets and looked back at her. The enchantress stared at Penny, seeing her clearly for the first time in her heavy boots and plaid skirt oddly paired with her sensible cardigan and her black and yellow hair, her earrings, and her clear blue eyes.

Penny pulled her hands free of her pockets. In one hand was her teething ring, in the other, her rattle. She calmly pointed the rattle at the enchantress.

"No—" shrieked the enchantress. "No—"

"You," Penny said firmly, "are a bunny."

Homer came to visit a few weeks later, bringing the rest of
the people from the bank, the tellers, the security guard Mr.
Pepas, and his wife. They arrived in a patch of mist on the
road before the castle. The mud was gone, along with the nixies and the trolls, the vampires and the looming gray clouds.
The fields were greening again and filled with farmers repair-
ing the damages of the war and the Dark Queen's brief rule.
Penny and her family were there on the road and all walked
together to the newly repaired castle. As they passed through
the tiny village below its gates, Homer commented on the
fenced-in boxes set in every garden.

"Hutches," explained the king, smiling at his daughter. "We
have a surplus of rabbits."

MEGAN WHALEN TURNER is the author of the Newbery Honor Book *The Thief* (Puffin) and its sequel, *The Queen of Attolia*, as well as an acclaimed short story collection, *Instead of Three Wishes*. She lives in Menlo Park, California, with her husband, who is a professor, and their children. Her Web site is **home.att.net/~mwturner/**

AUTHOR'S NOTE
Sometimes the idea for a story will unroll itself in my head and all I need to do is follow it from the beginning through the middle to the end. The idea for "The Baby in the Night Deposit Box" dropped from nowhere like a seed and sat for ten years before it finally grew into a story.

Sherwood Smith

Beauty

There ought to be a law that princesses must be pretty.

I mean, what use are mages and their arts if they can't make up a spell to fix nature's mistakes?

Is that the last thing I wrote in this journal?

So much has happened since then, I don't know if I ought to laugh or run howling to the mountains.

But still, I didn't write that so long ago that I don't still feel twinges of what I felt then.

Just consider the three of us. My older brother Alaraec and my younger sister Oria are both gorgeous: tall, gray-eyed, with long, ordered pale locks just like Father's. Not that they care. They could have been born squat as pillows, with noses like spoiled potatoes, and squinty crescent eyes like mine that look like you're laughing even when you're not, and they wouldn't have even noticed, because my brother is too busy learning kingship and my sister's greatest desire is to go learn magic at the Dyranarya Academy, on the plateau in Western Sartor, as soon as she turns fourteen.

That left me, the one who minded very much having a face as round as a full moon and a body shaped like one of the practice lances down in the courtyard.

Hair? No, I didn't get the blond locks, or Mother's wonderful auburn, which I like much better than lemon-colored. My hair—alone of the family—is too dark and dull for blond, but too dull and washed out to be brown.

So did I get any sympathy?

"Stay away from mirrors," my brother said impatiently.

"Can you reach me that book? And where's the inkpot?" my sister said. "And why would you want to be pretty anyway? Boys are disgusting."

Father: "You are all beautiful to me."

Mother? Her eyes teared up as she tried to smile. "Oh, Elestra, you remind me so much of my mother, and I thought she was the most beautiful person in the world."

That made me feel like I deserved a squashed potato nose.

So how about friends? They take dainty, beautiful Tara Savona seriously . . . they even take seriously my curvy, sweet-faced Tlanth cousin, who everyone calls Kitten because everything she does is cute, even sleep. Me? What could good old platter-faced, stick-figured Elestra be but funny?

Last New Year's is a fine example. One snowy morning we were all practicing that new dance from Sartor, and in came Tara, looking more beautiful than ever with her huge sky-colored eyes full of tears and her perfect lips trembling. As usual everyone stopped dancing and rushed to her, murmuring sympathetic questions, to which she cried, as she had so many times ever since we were small, "My mother is so cruel!"

Everyone knows that Tara's mother, the Duchess of Savona, has a temper like a thunderstorm, and Tara and Lady Tamara fight a lot. And doesn't Tara look stunning when she cries!

As always the girls cooed and fussed, petting her, stroking her beautiful golden hair, and the three handsomest boys in the kingdom tripped over one another offering to fetch her a fan, a glass of wine, whatever she liked.

"No . . . no . . . ." she says in a fluttering voice, sinking gracefully onto a pillow. "I'll survive."

Of course whatever was happening is over, and the rest of the gathering is devoted to cheering her up.

A month after that my cousin Kitten comes drooping in, her little hands wringing, her rosebud mouth downturned and says, "We have to go back to Tlanth, and it's sooo boring there. Won't anyone come and visit me?"

Every single boy, and half the girls, scramble up, promising to get permission to ride to the mountains at once.

But what happens not a week later, when I fall off my horse into a snowbank, nearly breaking my neck? I know I didn't look pretty. I stood there shivering, my hair hanging down in a hank that looked like a soggy bird nest, my nose purple with cold.

They all laughed. Laughed! I could just see myself, and I knew if I attempted to cry or wring my hands they'd laugh harder, because I'd look even more laughable, so I said, "Anyone want to dance?"

After which the fellows all walloped me on the back so hard my eyes nearly popped out, saying things like, "That's the spirit, Elestra! Get right up and teach that mare who's the princess!" And the girls laughed and said, "That Princess Elestra! She's so funny, but she's got guts!"

Guts.

Tara and Kitten get glory, and I get left with guts.

So what seemed to me the final blow happened just after I wrote that about laws and pretty princesses. It was a couple of evenings following Midsummer's Eve (ruined by a four-day rainstorm which pleased the farmers, but no one else) and Tara announced one morning that, as the weather made outside sport impossible, she would stage a play. She'd find one during the day and choose the parts that evening.

Evening came, and she said, "We'll do Jaja the Pirate Queen. Lots of action so the boys will come to watch, and lots of good parts for us girls."

"I know that play really well," I exclaimed in delight. "In fact, my tutor made me translate Jaja's speeches into rhyming Sartoran verse, and I still know 'em by heart." For the briefest time I envisioned myself playing the great Jaja, who defeated the evil Brotherhood of Blood pirate fleet—until Tara exchanged looks with all the others and said, sweetly, "But Elestra, this isn't a comedy."

A comedy. How they laughed! It wasn't even mean laughter, so at least I could feel like a victim, which always excuses self-pity (at least to the victim).

No, it was good-natured laughter because of course "good ol' Elestra has guts. She's funny!" You mean *funny looking*, I thought, fighting hard against tears.

So I sat there pretending to grin until Tara had handed out all the parts. And what did I get? "We never have enough boys who want to memorize, and you look quite gallant dressed as a boy, Elestra!"

"Gallant." She meant, and everyone knew she meant, I have no figure, so I can wear the tight waistcoat currently in fashion for the men.

I fled, holding back the tears all right until I almost crashed into Mama, who was just coming out of Oria's rooms with an armload of magic books. She frowned, looking anxiously into my face, and said, "Are you all right, sweeting?"

What could I say? "Rotten mood," I managed.

Mama looked understanding at once. "Go take a ride, or get in some sword practice," she said with rueful sympathy. "I'm afraid you got those moods from me, and nothing ever worked but exercise."

I didn't say that I'd already had a long bout with the sword master that day, and took a long ride, just so I could be calm when Tara picked her players at her evening party. I nodded, tried to smile, and stumbled to the one place no one ever gathered in all of Athanarel Palace outside of court functions: the throne room.

Now, I have to pause and describe the throne room. Someone reading my journal years hence might assume it was a terrible room, but it wasn't. High windows all around let in the light directly during winter and obliquely during summer, the floor was new tile with patterns of vines and blossoms and birds overlaying the very faint peachy tones of a rising sun, as the outer doors opened to the east.

The most important part was the dais, on which there was

no throne, but a great goldenwood tree reaching up three stories, the silver-gilt leaves brushing the dome of glass that my
parents had made when that tree so suddenly took root.

I say "suddenly" because it really wasn't a tree at all, but a
person. To be exact, Lord Flauvic Merindar, who had tried
to kill both my parents in a bid to take over the kingdom. It
wasn't my parents who stopped him, but the mysterious Hill
Folk, who looked to me almost like trees the one time I briefly
glimpsed them, high in the mountains behind Uncle Bran's
castle in Tlanth.

No one knew if Flauvic had lost his humanness when he
became a tree. Mama insisted he could hear, and she admitted to me once that for a year or two after she was crowned
queen, when she was in a snippy mood she used to go in and
lecture the great, beautiful tree on events inside the kingdom—showing that malicious politics and evil mages never
win—but after the horrible war swept across the world just
after Oria was born, she said she no longer had the heart for
lecturing.

And so the tree stood there for years and years, silently
presiding over court petitions and decisions, but otherwise left
in peace.

Until that night.

As soon as I fumbled my way into that dark room to be
alone, a hand clapped over my mouth, pressing hard, and
another snapped round my waist. A very strong one.

A soft voice murmured close to my ear, "I had hoped for
your mother, but you'll do."

Have you ever pricked your finger on a rose thorn? That

shooting pang that lances up your finger was akin to the one that lanced through my entire body. I gasped. Or tried to. The hand over my face tightened so I could scarcely draw breath.

The arm round my middle had taken care to pinion both my arms so all I could do was ineffectually waggle my hands. So I strained my eyes to either side, and discovered that the ghostly pale branches of the Flauvic tree no longer arched overhead.

Lord Flauvic Merindar was a man again.

And I was his prisoner.

"I don't want to have to kill you," he murmured. "Don't fight."

I knew from Mama's stories about that last terrible day that he would mean exactly what he said. I stopped struggling, and he lifted the one hand away from my mouth.

"Come along."

"What?"

He still held my arm in a tight grip. I couldn't see much in the darkness, just the outline of a head and shoulders, and the glint of blue on steel: a knife.

Was he twenty, as he had been when he tried to take the kingdom, or was he closer to forty? Either way, being a tree hadn't weakened him a mite.

"Come along," he repeated. And then he whispered some sort of spell, and the back of my neck prickled. A knife didn't scare me nearly as much as magic did: just before he was made into a tree he had transformed everyone in Athanarel, except for my parents, into stone statues. And one of these

he'd tipped over to break into bits. It had not been transformed back.

The air around me seemed to shimmer now, as if I floated
underwater, looking up at the world through the wavering
surface.

Out we walked, Flauvic's assurance reminding me that he
knew his way around Athanarel, which, after all, probably
hadn't changed much in twenty years. Rain fell softly, silvery
in front of windows, a gray mist elsewhere. My heart thumped
with hope when I spotted sentries standing at their posts in
the alcoves along the roof. Surely they would see us?

No. They stared out, not asleep, and not ensorcelled,
either. One's gaze even swept right past us. I could see his
eyes in the torchlight, but he obviously didn't see me. It was
as if we were invisible—and then I realized what sort of spell
Flauvic had cast, one to make others look away. The rain
helped.

On we walked, past the stable, to the garden, and then
through it, both of us now soaking wet, though the air was not
cold.

Flauvic did not speak and presently I remembered something my sister had said, and I realized he was concentrating
on holding his spell, something I only vaguely understood: a
bit like holding the reins of a wild horse that might throw you
at any moment, only the reins are invisible, and you hold them
with your mind.

Could I break away? How long it would take him to lay
that nasty stone spell on me? When I realized we would be
reaching the border of the garden soon, and the forest

beyond, which was only patrolled at dawn and sunset, I decided the time had come to act.

And just as I was about to reach for that knife, my slipper hooked firmly under a trailing root and down I flopped, full length into the mud. When I tried to get up, there was the knife, pressed against my neck.

"I expect the time has come to negotiate," Flauvic said. His voice was still soft, but I heard a tremor of laughter.

"If you surrender now, I won't be too hard on you," I croaked, hoping for a moment he'd think the ridiculous Princess Elestra so ridiculous he'd leave me behind in disgust.

He snorted a laugh, but then reverted right back to his subject. "This is what I had in mind. You come along without putting me to trouble, and I will contrive the journey in comfort."

"No," I said. "I don't want to go anywhere." It was hard to sound defiant with the side of my face squished into muddy moss.

"I regret the necessity," he returned, "but I require a hostage, just to the border, and you are it."

The border?

"Well? What shall it be? Comfort or duress?" he asked. He added, with polite regret, "I feel obliged to reiterate that you're going either way."

I sighed. A small insect nearly jumped into my mouth. "Pah! Pleh! Foogh!" I spat. "So you're asking my parole. Just to the border. And then you'll let me be?"

"Correct." Now he really was laughing.

I sighed again—with my mouth shut. Well? Obviously no one had seen us go. It was night, and I wouldn't be missed until morning since I never bade my maid to stay up for me. In fact, I might not even be missed then, since I often breakfasted in my room over a book. But. There was the reason why I'd been alone in the first place . . . what if I, somehow, in some way, managed to turn the situation round and capture the Wicked Flauvic? They'd notice me then, and not just for being funny looking!

I nodded once. "I'll do it."

"I have your word, then?"

"Yes!" Figures! Finally someone takes me seriously enough to ask for my word of honor, and it's a villain.

Flauvic put away the knife (I was blinking moss out of my eyes and didn't see where) and reached down to help me up, but I flung away his hand and got to my feet on my own. I tried to mop the worst of the mud from my gown—which had been a delicate shade of rose, and was now the same blotchy brown as my hair—as I began walking.

That was a dreary march, through a dark forest during rain. Despite the care with which I stepped I still managed to trip over unseen tree roots and small stones. From the sound of his breathing (I still couldn't see him, of course) Flauvic had much the same trouble. But we kept on.

It was not long after the midnight bell had tolled once, sending pleasant echoes down the river valley, that I realized he wasn't just walking, he had a destination in mind. I don't know what landmarks he found in that darkness, but he'd stop occasionally, pace around, and then set off in one direction or another.

I struggled after, yawning profusely, and wishing I hadn't

been so stupidly excited about Tara's stupid play that I'd skipped my stupid supper. The play and its problems seemed impossibly remote now, but my growling stomach was right there with me.

Abruptly we stopped.

"It's gone." I don't think he realized he'd spoken.

We stood before a ruin, an old house whose timbers had long ago been burned, leaving only the stone walls and chimney. I recognized it then, for we'd ridden round it often enough when I was small.

"That was used as a guardhouse by the enemy in the war," I said. "My father led a raid. Burned it. No one has been here since." Except children, of course, pretending to be on adventures. Then the question slipped out, "What did you expect to find?"

"Not a ruin," was the answer. He wasn't laughing, either.

We walked on. My heartbeat had quickened because I now knew where we were, except what could I do about it?

Leave a trail, of course.

As we walked I used my off-hand to work one of the white ribbons from the seam down my sleeve, and when it was free, I let the ribbon slip down the side of my skirt onto the ground, end first, so it would point the way we walked. Flauvic appeared not to notice.

Triumph kept me awake, at least, until at last we emerged on the ridge above the estuary opening to the sea. Below lay a small village, one we'd often seen when riding by. Most of the folk were fishers, but some tended sheep on the hills all along the wide, slow waterway.

Our eyes had become so accustomed to the darkness under the leafy canopy that it almost seemed light; I could make out the shapes of houses, and the river, which reflected the dark sky. Sheep on the other side of the river formed little white mounds, like snow.

A break in the clouds filled the valley with faint blue starlight, and Flauvic used it to guide us to a clump of thick willow, under which we sat on long, damp grass. Despite the warmth of summer I felt chilled, and wrapped my silk skirts about me as best I could. Would he sleep?

My eyelids drooped, I slid into dreams . . . which were broken by Flauvic's voice.

"Let's move on."

I was still cold, hungry, and in a very bad mood as I followed Flauvic down a sheep trail to the village. Dawn was not far off; the faintest lifting of darkness made it just possible to see.

Blue light, faint and dreary, was spreading westward when we reached the outskirts of the village. Light glowed in windows, and some people were up and about, feeding animals, getting fishing and cargo boats prepared. Flauvic made his way to an inn, which was a low, L-shaped building next to the bank.

The light was now strong enough for me to make out Flauvic's shape, and as we stepped inside the inn hope made my heart thump: wouldn't we look suspicious, me dressed in a muddy rose silk evening gown, and he in a long fitted tunic and narrow trousers twenty years out of fashion?

"Wait here," he said, leaving me standing beside the stable.

I thought about running, then I thought about how quickly he'd catch up. Fact is, I was too hungry and tired to be heroic right then. Papa had been gone for close to a month, riding patrol along the eastern border where there'd been reports of more Norsundrian warriors turned brigand, so Mama was in charge of the kingdom. If she didn't find my ribbon, and us, then I could effect my stunning capture later, after I'd had something to eat.

So deciding, I sat down on an old wooden stile. The smell of hay was strong on the cool air, the only sounds those of animals stirring.

The sun had topped the hill we'd just descended, sending great slants of golden light, when Flauvic and a maidservant emerged from inside.

I stared at Flauvic in that golden light and got a shock. He stood there in his black velvet, old-fashioned black velvet, which had to be exactly as sodden and muddy as my clothes, but he didn't look it. And you didn't notice his clothes anyhow. What that maid (and I) stared at was a beautiful wide-eyed face, a gentle smile, and long, long golden hair. He wore his hair far longer than anyone did now, but instead of looking silly, or even strange, he was so eye-smitingly beautiful he looked like he'd just stepped out of a portrait.

He bent and kissed the maid's hand, the way aristocrats had in my parents' day, and her face went red and she giggled.

"Thank you, dear lady," he said.

The maid mumbled something, thrust a basket at him, completely ignoring me, and whisked herself back inside.

Flauvic glanced my way once, then headed inside the

stable. I heard his voice, speaking to the stable hands on duty: "Torna sent me to you for two mounts. We need to ride to Mardgar today. We'll arrange to have them sent back."

And not long after we were mounted on two big draft horses, with worn saddle pads strapped on. As we rode away, I glimpsed a trio of maidservants in the windows, their heads turning as Flauvic rode up the pathway.

"That," I said, "was disgusting."

Flauvic smiled.

"You," I said distinctly, "are disgusting."

He just laughed.

We rode toward the south, which would lead to the great port city of Mardgar, but only until we were out of the village, and then Flauvic turned his great, shaggy beast eastward beyond a hill dotted with wild rosebushes and starliss, and then we began to ride north.

North.

My warm inward vision of my mother leading a huge force, finding my ribbon, finding the village, hearing about our trip south, and then surrounding us (to Flauvic's infinite chagrin) vanished like smoke.

As Flauvic and I rode into increasingly wild territory, I realized I was on my own.

By noon we'd finished the food in the basket. Hot, fresh bread, sharp aged cheese, and a fine selection of fresh peaches had been nice while they lasted, but both of us were again hungry; I hadn't eaten the day before, and it had been twenty years for him.

Nightfall brought clouds rolling like gray bowls out of the west. I smelled rain on the wind.

"We'd better stop and find shelter," I suggested finally, when Flauvic kept riding, scanning always ahead, never up.

He looked over at me, frowning slightly.

"I can see it's been a while since you camped out in the woods," I commented.

"I've never camped in the woods."

"No, you were much too finicky for that, weren't you?" I said "Well, I have, and I tell you we're going to have a much worse night than last night from the looks of those clouds. And I'd as soon use the last of the light to find something to eat, since you neglected to provide us with supper."

He glanced around, his eyebrows faintly puckered as if he was bewildered. What did he see? Trees, grass, shrubs, some birds darting hither and yon on unimaginable business?

"I saw some old rows of wild vegetables just back there," I said. "Someone probably had a cottage of some sort around here; there's the remains of an apple orchard, all overgrown. We could have carrots, and apples, and chestnuts as well. Not fancy, but filling," I said.

To my surprise, he slid off his horse. "Show me."

And so I did, after we'd done our best for the horses, and left them cropping soft, sweet summer grass. I taught him how to find carrot tops, and told him about apples (ripe and non-ripe, and what the latter did to your innards if you weren't careful) and how to find the good chestnuts.

While we were gathering the chestnuts we spotted the cottage, or the remains of one: it was just the shell of a stone house, built into the side of a cliff with a stream running just above, making a waterfall not ten steps from the door. The slate roof had been laid well, and so it kept the rain off us when the storm burst, as storms will, after an introductory clap of thunder.

Water roared around us, sending brown streams rushing round both sides of the house to tumble down the path back into the stream. I thought about my mother once being alone with him while a storm burst overhead, and reflected how very strange life could be.

"Why did you say I am disgusting?" he asked.

I turned. Yes, there he was, looking like someone's idea of a dream prince, his beautiful profile dimly outlined against the darker stone of the cottage wall.

He was handsome, all right—I'd never seen anyone half so attractive—but between that and any appreciation I might feel was the matter of his past, and our present.

So I looked away. "If you have to ask, there's no use explaining," I stated.

"Humor me. We're not going anywhere."

"What I think about your behavior with that maid won't put you in any good humor."

"But I didn't do anything except ask for a basket of food, and mounts to borrow."

"Oh, and what was that with the hand kissing?"

"Don't they do it any more?" His tone had changed somehow.

I glanced over, but all I could see was his dim profile, no expression. His voice was soft, and trained for singing, and far too controlled to trust for revealing any true emotion.

"No." I stretched. "They don't. I'm going to sleep," I added, drawing my knees up and crossing my arms on them. I laid my cheek on my arms, facing the other way.

The rain increased unexpectedly, then just as unexpectedly ended, leaving around us the drip and trickle of water from eaves and branches.

He said—abruptly, as if I'd spoken—"They do it in their own heads. The flirting, I mean. They look at me, and bridle, and grin, and it seems there's a romance going on inside their skulls, not mine. They want to possess my face, without any interest in my mind. It's been that way ever since I was little."

"Being pretty must be too big a burden to bear," I drawled, in my nastiest tone.

He didn't speak again until morning.

He was awake first, carrying the saddle gear out to the horses, who seemed much refreshed for their night. An apple each and we were off, riding north, Flauvic looking exactly the same as ever, me feeling itchy and gritty and longing for a bath, and feeling just as itchy and gritty inside. I now hated the sight of my rose silk dress; looking down, I realized one sleeve had a ribbon and one didn't.

Time to try leaving another. But after dark.

As for the inward feeling, I remembered my hateful comment, and how Mama had always told us that sarcasm was a particularly poisonous—and unworthy—weapon. I squared my shoulders and muttered, not very graciously, "I apologize for what I said."

He didn't respond immediately.

Presently he looked over in the pure morning light and said, "Tell me about your parents."

"What is there to tell? My father is the king, my mother the queen, they work hard, they laugh a lot, they have us three as well as the kingdom."

"What," he asked after a time, "can you tell me about my family?"

"You mean you don't know? I thought you could understand things you heard while you were a tree."

"Not in the early days. Voices were too quick, and—" He broke off and shrugged. "I only really began to hear voices in the past few years. This year I began to distinguish who they were."

"Well, that would explain your not hearing my mother, who said she used to go in and talk to you. Lecture you, actually."

He smiled over at the water. "I remember hearing the sound of her voice. I always did like it. Even when she was angry, she always seemed to be on the verge of laughter."

Hearing him talk that way about my mother—who hated him with enthusiasm—made me feel peculiar. "Well, your mother took poison after her plot to take the kingdom failed. Your sister tried to poison my father, and then she went south to some cousins of yours. If my parents ever heard anything more about her, they didn't tell us. And then they had the war taking up their attention."

"The war," he repeated, looking at a line of pale-barked birch trees, their leaves brightening to yellow, along a ridge. "It was silent around me for a long time. Sometimes warriors tramped through, but all I recall are the seasons of silence, and feeling the light change."

"We had to evacuate. They never really stayed here, but

tramped through on their ways to the bigger countries west and north or to the south, though sometimes they chased our people for sport, and of course they forced us to supply them with goods and horses—when they could find them. That was the first year. The second year some tried to stay, to take over, and they chased my father for a long time, especially when they found out he used to guide some really famous people they had on their wanted list—smuggled them through the mountains to some others, who then took them south to Morvende Caves to be hidden."

"Do you remember any of that?"

"I was too small. I just remember how much fun it was up at Tlanth, with Uncle Bran and Aunt Nee and Kitten. My brother worried about Papa, I know. My sister was just a baby."

He didn't answer that. Fine; I didn't want to go into detail anyway.

We rode for a time, picking our way across a low, flat river that rushed over stones, and it was mid-afternoon, and I'd been lost in memories of summers at Tlanth, when Flauvic said, "What happened to my lands? I could never quite make that out."

"Papa holds Merindar," I said. "As far as I know."

Silence. I realized, then, what it all meant: he had come back after twenty years to a family either gone or dead, his land gone, and—

"Someone said," I ventured, "that you'd learned that black magic nastiness at the court of Sles Adran."

He looked quickly over at me, his narrowed eyes

reflecting the light that sparkled along the river beside us.

"You should know that King Bartal was deposed. His allies from Norsunder didn't protect him."

When he said nothing, I recited, like I had to my governess, "The new king took over the kingdom to the west, too. And he rules without any aid of mages. Doesn't trust them, some say."

Silence.

"So, uh, if you were thinking of going that way—Sles Adran lying west and north—"

"I was thinking," he said, "of finding some sort of civilization so that we might achieve a hot meal."

"From someone who will do all the flirting inside her head while you just stand there and smile?"

He looked over at me. "Probably. Why does that bother you?"

I shifted on my horse, who retaliated by tossing her head and snorting. "I think it's awful to behave that way. To use people."

"People who let themselves be used get what they deserve," he retorted.

I was fidgeting with that ribbon as my mind fought against his words. I finally said, "Using people just because you can— oh, if you don't know how reprehensible it is, then there's no use in my saying anything."

"No, there isn't." His gaze shifted down to my hands. "And if you drop that ribbon here, we'll just head east. The direction matters little."

My cheeks burned, but not as hot as my annoyance. I

tossed back my tangled braids and snapped, "How superior you are! I wonder just how long your smug 'Because I can' would last if you met someone prettier than you are, or meaner, or more hateful. Wouldn't the world be a wonderful place, if ruled by those like you!"

"Isn't it? Despite all the moral self-praise, don't those who are smart and strong take over, and rule those who aren't?"

"No," I said, my mind careening wildly. I wished I knew my history as well as my brother did, but unfortunately my reading tended to be the records of princesses like me, and not a lot about the doings of courts.

"Take your father, now. Did he hand off my lands to the poor? No, he took them."

"Held them," I corrected. "'Holds.' That's what he says. There's a steward—whose mother was one of the cooks, by the way—but no one lives in the house, except a few servants my mother hired, because all yours vanished after your mother tried to take the kingdom."

He said derisively, "So it just sits there . . . for what? A deserving recipient to come along, someone perhaps from a suitable humble background? While you all live in peace and plenty, protected by the great kings all around you, after they won the war."

I thought of the seasons when the brigands came down to raid and burn and kill, and my father riding off to scour the hills yet again, sometimes with my mother watching him leave, her face tense with apprehension. A few times over the past years she couldn't bear it and rode with him, and then my brother paced his rooms late at night; like our father, he expresses his feelings not in words or in manner, but in action.

"I wish it were so," I said fervently. And then glared at him. "I wish. And what is so wrong with peace and plenty, as long as there is plenty for everyone?"

He studied me for a time, his lips compressed, and then said, "I was going to point out that those who have never known worry or want are usually the first ones with moral platitudes. But how could you possibly have known either?"

"I've never known want," I said. "There's always a warm fire, and enough to eat, and someone there if I wake in the night. But worry, yes. Did you really think that a war just ends? Like that?" I snapped my fingers, and the mare whickered at me in reproach. "As soon as they knew they were losing, most of Norsunder's forces ran for the hills, taking everything they could get. There are some of them still hiding up that way even now." I pointed north and east, toward the mountains. "Over there is where my father is riding this month, trying to keep the borders safe. I know worry, because we grew up aware that a brigand with a sword wouldn't care if he kills a king or a cook."

Flauvic said derisively, "I take it forming a militia and patrolling for themselves is too warlike for your contented peasantry?"

I took a breath, about to give him a nasty answer, but my own words came back as if to mock me: *Because I can.*

I'd been raised with a brother and sister, and so I knew the difference between sarcasm for the sake of prolonging an

argument and sarcasm that masks a desire—perhaps a need—
to know the truth. He wanted to know the truth.

So I forced myself to tell it. "Oh, there was a wonderful
militia for a few years. I remember going to see a review in
Tlanth, where there still actually is one, when I was little. My
Uncle Bran practices with them every year. In other places,
after years of quiet, people acted like people usually do, my
mother told me: it was always the wrong time, or they didn't
feel well enough for drill, or business claimed them. When my
father goes himself, everyone suddenly starts practicing and
patrolling again."

Flauvic said nothing, just stared straight ahead, where several long-tailed birds streamed just above the treetops, scolding and squawking.

Thinking of my father brought me back to my own situation. What use is a hostage unless there's someone to threat-
en? Was Flauvic really going to stick that knife at my neck if
either of my parents somehow found our trail, and threaten to
kill me unless he was safely seen to the border?

"Your knife," I said, picking long-dried moss off my gown.
"I sure don't remember seeing it sticking out of your tree. But
then your clothes weren't hanging from the branches, either.
Did they stay invisible somewhere, or what?"

"Invisible isn't quite the right word," he said, casting me a
glance that was very hard to interpret, as one of his fingers
made a subtle motion toward the other wrist. Aha: a wrist
sheath. "It's more like they stayed outside of time. As for me,
I seem to have aged as a tree ages, which is far slower than we
do as humans."

"You look twenty to me," I said, thinking about that knife in the wrist sheath, and how I might get it if, at the border, he suddenly turned . . . what? Would he truly try to kill me?

I looked over to see a speculative glance from his light eyes, then he lifted a shoulder. "Age doesn't appear to hold much meaning anymore." Yes, he was alone, and I strongly suspected he was only beginning to understand what it meant.

"Look at those delicious blackberries!" I said, pointing to some shrubs along a very old, mossy stone wall. When in doubt, be ridiculous, that was my usual habit. "I don't know about you, but I'm starving. You have to realize that the old rules concerning the proper abduction of princesses might have included starving them, but I assure you, modern abductions are different."

Flauvic smiled a little as he slid off his horse. We soon sat on the wall, my lap full of blackberries. Who cared about stains? The gown was ruined anyway.

The sun shone, the wind carried the scents of herbs and roses, and the horses lipped at the clover along the roadside.

"So what was it like being a tree?" I asked. "Can you speak with them now?"

He laughed. "If trees speak, it's more than I know."

"Nothing? Nothing at all?"

He tipped back his head, looking at the white lambkin cloud puffs arrayed across the sky. Then he looked at me. "It seems absurd to try to put that experience into words."

"Not at all. It's interesting," I said. "And when I get home, my sister, who studies magic, will ask first thing, 'Did he talk

about what it's like to be a tree?' She won't care about anything else."

"Tell her you hear the Hill Folk singing. Distance doesn't
appear to mean much, though I can't explain how or why. You
feel the rhythm of the seasons, you are sensitive to the turns
of light, north during winter's cold, and then south again,
strong light that sends your roots deep down into the water
running below the ground." He shrugged. "I couldn't hear
words for some time, as I told you. Of late I could. Your friend
Tara was in the throne room often, did you know that? She
sounded to me like an insect, whine, whine, though she was
there to flirt in private."

"She's very beautiful," I muttered. "They all compete to be
with her."

He made an elegant gesture of dismissal. "I couldn't see
her, so I wondered why they came with her. Do you know that
her only subject of interest is herself? Doesn't she ever think
about anything else?"

I thought. "Her admirers consider her just as fascinating as
she does."

"Do they? It seems to me she doesn't keep them long."

"At least she has some—" I began, then I shut my mouth
so fast my teeth clicked. I was not, not, not going to tell the
Evil Flauvic that I'd never had one, was unlikely to ever have
one.

He said, quite abruptly, "Did King Bartal find out I was a
tree?"

"Oh, yes," I said.

He looked over at me. His hands had managed to stay

clean, and his mouth, whereas my fingers were stained with berry juice, and I was sure my mouth was purple.

"Tell me the rest," he said. "It's not like I'll ever see him again, if what you say about him being deposed is true."

"He laughed." The day before I would have said it triumphantly, but now it embarrassed me, and so I busied myself by examining the purple blotches on my gown. It looked quite terrible, of course. I added, "In case you think I'm making it up, you could find your own great-uncle, who was still ambassador before my father recalled him. He told us King Bartal laughed so loud the whole court laughed, and then he said, 'If he's a tree, no doubt he's a pretty one.'"

Flauvic's face showed no expression whatever, but I thought about what it meant: no one, during those twenty years, had tried to disenchant him. Not one of his long-ago allies had even shown up, and it wasn't as if we had any formidable magical protections or traps. He wasn't just alone—his world had passed by, leaving him twenty years distant in memory.

"Let's go," he said.

We began riding again, along old cart paths winding through the great, gnarled trees we encountered more frequently now. When we crossed the good roads he always turned onto pathways, always to the north and west, and though he looked around, sometimes watching the progress of flocks of birds above the treetops, other times studying the hazy purple mountaintops on the horizon, he didn't speak.

I didn't speak either. It was fun to bait the Evil Flauvic

when I was angry with him, but when I wasn't, I found I had to look away, or I was far too aware of the light on his long golden hair, the shape of his shoulders, even the sound of his breathing. What was it like, to inspire desire simply by existing? I'd been watching Tara exert that power for a couple of years now, and I couldn't count how many nights I spent in smoldering envy, but now I wondered: if everywhere you go everyone watches you and wants you, can you truly be yourself?

"What are you thinking?" he asked suddenly, as the light began to slant, weaving long tree-shadows to the right.

"What's it really like to always be the prettiest person in a room? Does it mean you're always acting, as if in a play, because no one stops looking at you?"

"Life is a play, isn't it?"

I sighed. Obviously I wasn't going to get a real answer. "I guess it might be for those who act that way."

"'Act.' How many good people do you really know? I discount those who mouth out platitudes for the edification of the young, and who truly are 'good,' whatever that means."

What a strange subject, and from so strange a person! "Everyone I know is a mixture, some with more good than bad, and it varies on different days," I said, thinking hard, as I watched without any real comprehension some birds flap into the sky from the trees just ahead, scolding and squawking. "My mother told me once she has more than her share of the howling wolf emotions, but she learned that trying to make the good choice—acting good, I guess you might say—made her actually feel good after. Maybe it's that way for a lot of people. You don't think much of Tara—and sometimes neither do I—but I happen to know she's very good to animals, and it's not like they can talk to praise her in company. I think she's good to them because she loves them."

"What if feeling good comes only after you destroy someone you hate?"

"That's not good, that's triumph," I declared. And at the derisive glance he sent me, I felt my face go red, and I stared straight ahead at my mare's hairy ears, which were canted forward. "Well, so I've read. Put it this way, I don't know anyone who would feel good after—"

Birds? Squawking? Mare's ears canted, listening for—

Danger?

I realized something was wrong a heartbeat before three men crashed from the shrubs, running hard. They saw us the same moment we saw them, then two of them veered straight for the horses.

Mine danced back, tossing her head; the man snatched the reins and jerked her violently round with one hand and reached for me with the other. One moment I saw a big hand with short, filthy nails reaching for me, then I rolled off the back of the horse—something my brother and I had practiced years ago, after reading stories about the feats of the western plains riders.

I brought my hands up—and realized the fellow wasn't the least interested in me, only in the horse. He was trying to mount, but my mare had decided she didn't like this new rider, and she was dancing about with all the agility of a hill pony.

I was still slightly dizzy from the roll and drop, but I turned at the sound of harsh voices, to see the other two men arguing over the other horse. One man held her by the reins, the other man swung a sword back and forth as he yelled.

" . . . run . . . coast . . . boat . . ."

I realized they were talking in a form of Sartoran, not the kind they supposedly spoke at the court in Eidervaen, but discernable if I concentrated.

"Right now," the other said.

Where was Flauvic?

He was lying on the other side of a scattering of rocks, with the sword-swinger's boot planted in the middle of his back.

" . . . money," said the one holding his horse, and they both turned and glared at me.

I glanced from Flauvic back at the men. From the look of their haggard faces they were about my father's age, considerably more dirty and disheveled even than I was. I realized then that they were brigands, maybe even former Norsun drians, and that they did not mean us well.

"I want to go *hooome*," I screamed, and knuckled my eyes.

"What did she say?" demanded one.

"Shut her up. We can search them afterward," the other said, in slow, forced words as the mare fought to free herself. His speech was slow enough for me to follow.

I ran around in a circle, stumbled, bent down to the ground to grab a handful of dirt, all the while yelling—hoping that running brigands meant some kind of pursuit. The one with the sword lifted his foot off Flauvic's back and came at me, and that was all Flauvic needed. He was up, the knife out, in the time it took for me to swing my arm and let fly with the dirt straight into the sword-swinger's face.

He howled in rage, chopping in front of him with the sword, but by then I'd whirled, just the way the arms master at home taught me, and used my momentum to kick sideways at his kneecap.

The howls increased, rage turning to pain, as he stumbled. I kept whirling, almost tripped on my skirt, and smacked my heel straight into his gut. He fell, hard.

When I turned both horses were free, the man with the club was down, bleeding at the throat, and the other circled around Flauvic, holding a knife more lethal than the one Flauvic had.

They both glanced my way.

The brigand's look dismissed me. Flauvic's was longer, flickering down to the groaning man on the ground, then up, widening. He stepped sideways, with a slow, deliberate pace. I understood immediately, and while the brigand could still see me, I bent over with my hands covering my face, but I watched between my fingers.

As soon as his shoulder was turned to me, I bent down, picked up a good-sized flat stone. And when Flauvic attacked, causing the other to block and try to stab, I ran up and bashed the stone just under the brigand's ear. He dropped with a thud, his knife clattering on the rubble.

Flauvic and I were both breathing hard as we gathered all the weapons, including the club, and I noticed his hands were shaking as badly as mine were.

"You didn't mention that," he said, tipping his head sideways. He leaned a little to one side, wincing; I hadn't seen his first fight, but it was clear he'd gotten hurt.

"I was hoping you wouldn't have to find out the nasty way," I returned, puffing like a bellows. "My parents made sure we all got trained, from the time we could walk—"

Now we could both hear it: the thud of horse hooves and the crashing of brush.

We both looked up, then at one another.

Pursuit! Someone on my side?

A moment later four horses crashed through a brake of ferns on the other side of the churned-up ground, and plunged to a stop. I looked up, expecting to see the helms and tunics of the border riders, which I did see. But when I glanced at the fourth I stared, gaping, as I recognized my father's silver-streaked hair, and his gray eyes going wide in dismay, and then narrowing.

"Here they are, sire," shouted one of the riders. "All three of them. And—" The man, a very young man, about my brother's age, straightened up, staring at me in my rose-colored evening gown with its decorative mud-splotches and black-berry stains.

"Permit me to introduce you to my daughter, Princess Elestra," Father said, smiling just a little as he dismounted.

The riders all stared at me, then: "Did you do that?" asked another, a gloved hand pointing at the groaner. The other two lay still, one breathing, one not.

"I—ah—" I looked around witlessly, seeing the two horses, still flicking their tails in irritation, the brigands' weapons on the ground, and—

And a glimpse of a pale face beyond the shrubs across the clearing. For a long, strange moment I stared into Flauvic's golden eyes, and then I turned away, and whooshed out a sigh, and said, "Well, yes. Most of it was an accident, though," I began babbling, my voice suddenly going high. Why were my eyes burning and my throat closing? I was safe! "You see, they wanted the horses, and argued, and—"

"Never say too much," my father murmured, and embraced me. I leaned against him, shivering.

Before anyone else could either move or speak, there came the sound of more horse hooves, this time from the cart path. We all looked up (the border riders putting their hands to their weapons, my father standing there with his arms around me, but I heard his breathing go still) and up rode, in neat formation, a patrol of castle guards in their fine blue tunics and chain mail—with my mother at the lead!

"There you are!" she exclaimed, pulling up her horse. Then her triumph changed to amazement. "Danric?"

"Hello, Mel. We've been chasing these three just this side of the river," Father said, and I could hear his smile in his voice as he pointed at the brigands. "I take it you were not on the same mission?"

"Elestra—Flauvic—" Mama said, still on her horse. She put her fists on her hips and glared around. "Where's that sneaking, lying skunk of a Merindar, anyway?"

Father laughed, then said, "I can see that there are a number of questions that must be answered. I suggest we postpone the necessary exchanges until we have reached a place of more comfort. In the meantime . . ." He issued orders in a rapid voice, and the brigands were taken in one direction and the two big plow-mares in another.

Those not assigned to dealing with the brigands fell into formation behind, and Papa pulled me up onto his big war horse. "I'm awfully grubby," I warned, giving in at last to the compelling temptation to look behind me, to see if Flauvic was still there.

He wasn't.

But I could still see that look, that heart-still look, that he had given me, as if he were still before me.

"I'll live," Papa said, still sounding amused.

Mama, of course, couldn't wait. Her favorite mare danced a little, greeting Papa's horse with a snort and an ear-flick as Mama said, "What happened, Elestra? The servants went crazy after they trooped in at dawn to do the throne room floors and found there was no tree—and right after that your maid came in pounding on my door to say you weren't in your room. I figured the worst when one of my search parties found your ribbon, and the girl from the inn down at River-town was brought in with the story about a lady and a golden-haired fellow riding for Mardgar."

"You rode all the way to Mardgar and then north?" I asked, speaking just one of the questions flitting through my mind like fire-singed moths.

"Of course not," she exclaimed, sounding indignant. "This is Flauvic, after all. Oh, I did send a party to Mardgar, just in case, but I figured he took all that care to mention a southern port if he meant to ride north. And I see I was right."

"But—how did you find the right track?"

"Well, I didn't, really. We got hailed by some people in the village just east of here, saying that they'd been robbed this morning by three fellows, and the track was clear for a time—" She stopped, looking at Papa with her brow furrowed. "You were chasing those three?"

"For two days," he said. "They're the last of a gang that has been marauding on both sides of the border since spring. They had been clever enough to elude us until Elestra decided to step in, apparently."

I felt my face heat up.

Mama turned to me. "I gather Flauvic abandoned you as soon as he sniffed the river?" She pointed to the west, and I realized how close to the border we were—and then I realized that we'd been riding parallel to the border probably since morning.

Why?

To answer her I mumbled something inarticulate, and Mama sighed. "And I had been thinking up the choicest insults with which to benefit his pretty ears, and now no one will get to hear them!"

"You shall entertain us with them when we reach the garrison at Kalna," Papa said. "No use in letting them go to waste."

Mama opened her mouth, looked from me to him, closed her mouth, raised her expressive brows, then laughed. "And so you shall. Tell you what. I'll ride ahead and see to it we get a good meal, and not just garrison soup."

How did they do that? All my life they had looked at one another, no words spoken, and somehow they communicated something. I sighed as Mama clucked to her horse and rode on ahead, waving on half her escort as accompaniment.

Papa waited until we'd turned off the cart path onto the wide and well-paved main road.

"I take it you had a reason to let him go," Papa murmured.

Remember that comment about the thorn-pang? I got another one, sharp and cold.

"You saw him?" I managed.

"I may be aging, but I am not quite decrepit enough to miss the sight of long hair the color of gold coins behind a hedge of hemlock. Or the distinct print of shoes made in the manner of my younger days."

"You didn't say anything," I muttered, blushing again.

"I figured you must have your reasons. What happened?"

I told him, as we rode slowly down toward Kalna, whose towers were just visible above the treetops in the east. Papa must have signaled to his border riders, as they maintained a discreet distance behind us.

By the time I was done all the rapid emotions I'd sustained that day drained away, leaving me tired, and hungry, and once again my eyelids burned and my throat as well. Tears? Not me! Not good ol' Elestra, the Princess with Guts!

"I don't know why I did it," I said finally, mopping my stinging eyes with my filthy gown. "It just seemed . . . right."

Papa said nothing for a time, as we clopped steadily toward the city, and Mama, and good food and a bath and something—anything—to wear beside this horrid gown.

Before he spoke he caressed my cheek with his callused thumb, then murmured, "There was a moment in my own career when I was pursuing a fugitive in a river town, and I chose to ride on past. It seemed right at the time. Instinct proved to be a better guide than, ah, the demands of current events."

"Papa." I turned around, and then grimaced. "You're talking about Mama."

He smiled.

"You can't possibly mean I did it out of, well, romance."

"No, not any more than I did. It seemed fair, and right, to give my fugitive a chance at freedom."

I sighed. "But if he goes on and does anything horrid, isn't it my fault?"

Papa waited even longer before he answered. The city walls were in view, down the road past squares of ripening corn and shooting barley when at last he said, "The Merindars were never known for their laughter or inner grace, for their generosity of spirit, for their earnest attempts to see the greater truth in the world, and try to abide by it."

"No," I said, wondering what he was talking about—and then I blushed yet again.

"You mean me."

"He spent a whole day with you, I understand. He could have ridden over the border at dawn."

"But most of the time we just argued."

Papa laughed, and hugged me tight for a moment, just like he had when I was small, and asked to go riding with him. Then he said, "You know, when people first discover beauty, they tend to linger. Even if they don't at first recognize it for what it is."

Beauty. That's what he said.

Is it true, or is it just Papa trying to make me feel better?

I don't know. I'm home, of course, and things are back to normal (they waited on the play—and I'm busy learning my lines as the Gallant Prince) but I keep thinking about what happened.

But I am not languishing at a window, or watching the northern road.

Because I know he'll be back.

SHERWOOD SMITH'S work includes *Crown Duel* and *Court Duel* (published together in Firebird paperback as *Crown Duel*) and three books about the intrepid Wren—*Wren to the Rescue, Wren's Quest,* and *Wren's War.* A fourth book, *Wren Journeymage,* is forthcoming.

Sherwood Smith lives in Southern California. Her Web site is at **www.sff.net/people/sherwood**

AUTHOR'S NOTE
Though this story can stand on its own, it was written for all those readers of my book *Crown Duel* who asked, "What are Meliara's and Shevraeth's children like?" and "What happened to Flauvic?"

Nancy Springer

mariposa

"I 've lost my soul?" Aimee repeated, almost losing her usual perfect control.

The doctor nodded. "I think so. Probably in early adolescence. It happens more commonly than you might think." The specialist was a W.D., a Warlock Doctor, a.k.a. Warloctor. Very professional, she betrayed impatience only by adjusting her turban. Aimee could not decide whether the big, craggy woman was black or Lebanese or perhaps Hindu, but it didn't matter. Nothing seemed to matter. Not even dieting. It was this apathy that had landed Aimee here, in this office with pink cabbage roses growing down from the ceiling.

"Let's have a look," the Warloctor suggested gently. "If you'll stand up, please, and face the mirror."

Aimee stood, automatically checking her appearance in the full-length mirror: flawless, as usual. Hair in the latest style, makeup worthy of a fashion model, silk blouse, Ralph Lauren suit accessorized to perfection, and, most important of all, the sparkling diamond on her finger. Colin had bought her the biggest one she could possibly wear in good taste. He had promised her a trip to the Polynesian Islands on their honeymoon. Aimee knew herself to be a privileged young woman, in full possession of a highly desirable fiancé, a diploma from Vassar, a BMW convertible, a Fortune 500 career, designer clothing, a personal trainer to help her stay fashionably thin, and on top of all that, a symmetrical, perfectly corrected face.

Why, then, did she awaken every morning to a sense of profound, aching emptiness?

"Blessed be that the days of invasive procedures are over," the specialist was saying. "No need to undress." Murmuring, with her dark, liquid eyes out of focus, the older woman made a few passes with her unadorned hands.

Despite having been briefed on Warloctor procedure when her internist had referred her, Aimee gasped. Just like that, she saw her mirror image change. On her reflected self, all her expensive, expertly applied makeup was gone. Hair color, gone. Breast enhancement, gone. Cantilevered lingerie, carefully assembled clothing, and accessories, every artifice by which Aimee maintained an attractive feminine image was stripped away. Only nakedness remained—

No. Staring, her eyes widening but her symmetrical face disciplined into a beautiful mask, Aimee saw that what remained in the mirror was not a naked, unadorned body. Rather, it was a pale silhouette of a body, without substance, depth, or core. The edges seemed solid enough, but toward what should have been the center, it looked translucent, spectral.

It appeared to have no heart.

No guts.

And no face.

"Yes, you've lost your soul," said the W.D. comfortably. "Please, sit down." She twitched a tree-of-life Indian-print curtain over to cover the mirror.

Aimee sat in a white wicker chair, staring at her own hands layered on her knee. They seemed to be all there, complete with diamond ring and French manicure. But she felt hot bewilderment stinging at the backs of her eyes.

"It happens most commonly to fully socialized young women such as you." The Warloctor sat behind her desk, upon which stood a statuette of a Minoan goddess, bare-bosomed, lifting a serpent in each hand. "Aimee, when did you stop dreaming at night?"

"I, um . . . " Aimee glanced up, wondering.

"The soul is responsible for dreams," the Warloctor explained. "As you sleep, it flies wild and free, but tethered to your heart with a thread of silver so that it will come back to you. Something must have happened to compromise the thread. Were you abused as a child?"

"No. Not at all."

"Some other traumatic event in your childhood?"

"No. . . ."

"To return to my original question, how long has it been since you have dreamed?"

Aimee had never given the matter of her dreams much thought. "Um, I think . . . about ten years."

The W.D. nodded. "You were thirteen or thereabouts, then? At puberty, were you subjected to peer pressure?"

Aimee blinked at her. "Isn't everyone?"

"To some extent, yes. But did it change you? Did you forget about things you enjoyed? Did you focus exclusively on being attractive, restraining your intelligence to an acceptable level, and pleasing boys?"

"Of course."

The Warloctor nodded, and under the turban, her dark face betrayed some sadness.

Aimee bristled. "Are you saying it's my fault?"

"Goddess, no, dear. You were a child. Someone should have been guiding you and looking out for you."

"Wait." A new thought erased Aimee's irritation. "Are you sure it happened then? Why didn't I notice sooner?"

"It doesn't usually manifest until adulthood. Many teenage girls lose their souls, and no one notices until years later." The Warloctor sighed for some reason, then asked patiently enough, "What was your soul like, do you know?"

Somewhat recovered now, Aimee gave her the bright, edgy smile of a stressed young executive woman. "How would I know?"

"Well, as a child, perhaps sometime when you were half awake, did you ever happen to see it? Perhaps as a butterfly, or a moth, or a tiny white dove, or a honeybee?"

Aimee shook her head, feeling her mouth beginning to thin, to lose its full-lipped charm. She wanted out of this weird office. She wanted time to absorb the diagnosis. And above all she wanted a treatment. She demanded, "What do I do now?"

"Well, there are prosthetic souls available. A specialist could fabricate one for you out of your choice of poetry, music, art and so on. And the implant procedure is non-invasive." The Warloctor recited all of this without hesitation or enthusiasm. "But it's impossible to match the quality of a real, original soul." The W.P. sighed again. "Do you still have access to the place, by which I mean the physical location, where you lived when you were pubescent?"

"Yes," said Aimee. "Yes, I do."

"Then I would go back there, if I were you, and have a look for your soul."

Aimee hadn't been back in years. She hated going back. The house, like her mother, was too ice-cream-and-ruffled-curtains dowdy, and the town was too small, and it hadn't developed at all. Backyards still ended in country. There was nowhere to shop, not even a dinky strip mall. There were no nightclubs. There was nobody worth trying to impress. In short, there was nothing to do. Aimee hadn't been home since her father's funeral.

Her mother was delighted to see her, of course, and seemed to think that the unexpected visit was about wedding plans. "I know Colin is a very handsome young man," Mom said the morning after Aimee's arrival, over a breakfast of scrambled eggs, toast, and homemade strawberry jam, "and he's very well-to-do and so forth, but is he—will he—" Mother faltered, evidently attempting a kind of delicacy for which her lack of sophistication gave her no experience. "Is he good to you?" she blurted.

"He has a penthouse, Mom."

"I know, but—"

"And he's great in bed."

Aimee said this to shock, and succeeded. Her mother

gasped and blushed. "Heavens, sweetie, that's not what I meant at all."

"What do you mean, then?"

"Well, is he—will he—does he love you?"

The question seemed meaningless. Aimee brushed it aside and got down to business. "Mom, I seem to have misplaced my soul. Before I order one, I was wondering, do you happen to know where it got to?"

Her mother sat straight up and gazed at her with transparent, moist-eyed pride. "Amy, I always knew you were precocious."

Aimee scowled. It had been years since she'd changed her name. Why couldn't Mom ever seem to remember?

But Mom just babbled on. "Look at you, wanting your soul back already. I didn't start missing mine till I hit menopause." Mom turned and hollered, "Mama! Mother! Have you seen Amy's soul?"

The creaky old woman, Aimee's grandmother, shuffled into the kitchen. Mom was dowdy, but Grandma was a disaster. Mom wore polyester; Grandma wore thrift shop housedresses held together by safety pins. Mom wore Wal-Mart sneakers; Grandma wore Dollar Saver plastic slippers. Mom skipped makeup; Grandma skipped moisturizing and shaving. Above nylons rolled around her ankles, her bare hairy legs rose sturdily, their skin the texture of potato chips. Contemplating her family, Aimee suppressed a shudder. If she maintained enough steady pressure, she could probably render Mom and Grandma presentable for the wedding, but no way could she ever bring her fiancé into this house.

Grandma barked like an angry robin, "What? Have I seen what?"

"Amy's soul! She's lost her soul. Have you seen it anywhere around here?"

"No . . . no, I haven't." Grandma's voice softened to a sparrow peep. "But I ain't rightly looked yet."

"Mom found mine," Aimee's mother explained to her, "years ago."

"Laying right in plain sight on the carpet, it was." Grandma shuffled over and sat down at the kitchen table. "Like it had dropped out of her while she was heading for the door. It looked kind of like a damselfly or a lacewing. Real pretty. I picked it up gentle in the palm of my hand and tried to think how I could keep it safe for her. I knew it was no use to give it back to her then. She'd just lose it again."

"I was just starting to date," Mom explained.

"Sweet sixteen, never been kissed, and not a thought in her pretty head except how to get herself a two-piece swimsuit and permission to paint her face."

Aimee sat silent, trying very hard to follow.

"It just so happened I was canning preserves that day," Grandma chirped on, "so I put it in a jelly jar with juneberry syrup, and I put a nice thick layer of paraffin on top, and wrote your mother's name on a tape on the lid, and stuck it up in the cellar rafters. And there it stayed."

"I found it," Mom explained, "when I was helping her clean out the house after Grandpa died."

"It was like childbirth," Grandma said. "I did it and then I forgot about it as quick as I could."

Mom nodded. "Some of the most routine things in life are like that," she agreed, serene. "Like funerals. You just got to forget about them afterward so you can go on."

Aimee listened with increasing annoyance.

"Like your daughter out there running around without a soul," Grandma grumbled. "They didn't do that in my day."

"Some don't still," Mom said. "You can tell. Missy Hartzel's daughter, I don't believe she lost her soul until she went into law enforcement."

By this time Aimee felt an urge to curse, which she suppressed. She demanded, "Mom, did you find mine and stick it somewhere and forget about it?"

"Now, how would I know, sweetie, unless I happen to remember? We'd better have a look around."

By noon of the next day, the hunt had turned up nothing. The button box had been emptied and its contents gone through; ditto the sewing basket and the junk drawers of the old claw-foot dining room buffet. The jars on the spice rack had been examined, and the preserves in the pantry. Even the springhouse and root cellar had been investigated. And the attic . . . Aimee could not face the attic. She needed to get away somewhere by herself before she took a blunt object and whacked both Mother and Grandmother. But there was nowhere to go. No foreign films, no club, no mall.

Fleeing the house, Aimee found herself wandering down to the little stream winding at the bottom of the yard, to the pool by the big rock under the willow tree, where she had spent countless hours of spare time as a child. Wasted time, she was thinking—

"Amy! Welcome back!"

Standing on the flat stone amid willow fronds, Aimee gasped, and not just because a sunfish had stuck its head out of the water and spoken to her. She looked at the commonplace little fishes wafting like spirits through the sunlit and shadowy depths. As if forgetting a dream, she had forgotten all about this limpid pool bright with sunnies. For uncounted days of her childhood she had watched them, waded among them, fed them bread and Cheez Whiz and hot dog ends, tried to touch them like trying to touch angels.

And then . . . what had happened? Seemingly overnight, something had changed, not just her changing body but everything about her life, and she had left this font behind her.

Another iridescent head broke the sun-dappled surface. "Bet you forgot all about us."

"Yes, I did!"

Bubbles frothed up from the shadow-shining depths like laughter.

"I forgot a lot," Aimee murmured, remembering how she had tried to learn what kinds they were—pumpkinseed, long-ear, red-ear, bluegill, green—but their coloring and variety had bewildered her. Recognizing individuals, she had given them childish names: Blue Streak, who had cerulean markings; Robin, a ruddy-breasted bluegill; Lightning, a sleek green; Bunny, a long-ear; Sunrise, a particularly vivid pumpkinseed, colored like orange clouds over a pure yellow belly and fins. And many others, including a large perch-striped bluegill remarkable because his belly was neither ruddy, nor sunny orange, nor even buttercup yellow, but a delicate peachy pink. No name had seemed sufficient to express his uniqueness.

Finally she had called him Mariposa, which she had learned in sixth grade was Spanish for "butterfly."

Gazing down now at the lucent pool, Aimee saw her own cosmetically corrected, reflected face gazing up from the surface—yet at the same time she saw the dreams, the life, the intimations swimming in the depths behind her eyes. This place was her mirror and her mystery. She caught a glimpse of the face of a dead child in the water.

Or might the child yet live? "Hi, Sunrise," Aimee whispered to a pumpkinseed flitting through water in the vicinity of her heart. It could not be Sunrise really, not after all this time, but maybe . . . maybe another Sunrise. "Hi, Robin Redbreast."

"Hi, yourself!" They stuck their heads out at her, smiling toothlessly like babies.

"Hi, Greenie. Hi, Blue Streak. Hi—where's Mariposa?"

A chorus fountained up:

"You should know!"

"Mariposa is our hero!"

"We tell the story of Mariposa to our small fry."

"He ate the great fly—"

"Mariposa flew!"

"Someday Mariposa shall return."

"He flew to the Otherworld."

Aimee felt an almost audible echo in her mind: *flew, flew, déjà vu.* She felt her jaw sag in a way she knew to be uncouth. For a moment her breath stopped. She stood with her mouth open, remembering as if cozening back a dream.

There had been an autumn day with sun-colored leaves

floating on the water, sunfish drifting sluggish below, and a chill in the air like fate. And a knowledge in thirteen-year-old Amy that she could not much longer fight her terrible need to conform, to abandon her childhood in favor of being just like the others. A new school year had begun. Soon she would give her whole being to belonging.

But before that could happen, she had given her soul to solitude and this pool.

She had done it herself. Lying on this rock, she had day-dreamed her glimmerwisp soul out of herself and watched it dangle on its silver thread finer than spiderline. She had watched it alight like a mayfly on the pool's silver surface amid the golden leaves. She had watched the shining fish gather. And she had seen the largest one take it.

Mariposa.

Mariposa had gulped the gleaming bait and snapped the line. But then in an arc like a rainbow he had leapt clear out of the water. He had leapt so greatly that he had landed on the rock at the feet of the girl who now called herself Aimee. Bluegill Mariposa with his green fins, iridescent cerulean face, and sky pink soft underbelly, all the butterfly colors of him had lain there without even flopping. And his indigo eyes had gazed up at her with wisdom in them as deep as wells.

And then . . .

Remembering, Aimee gasped for breath as if she were drowning, then whirled and ran, bursting out of willow fronds as if rending a veil. She darted back to the house.

"Mom!" she yelled up the steep stairs. "Mother! Do you still have my fish?"

"What?" Mom's voice floated down from the attic.

"My fish!" Aimee bellowed not at all like a polished professional woman. "My sunny!"

Steps creaked down from the attic. Mom ambled to the head of the stairs and peered down at her. "Your what?"

Just like the child she used to be, Aimee wailed, "My bluegill! The only one I ever caught. Do you still have it?"

"Heavens, honey, I don't . . . "

"I told you to keep it!" Aimee screamed.

"Check the freezer. No, wait. Check the other freezer. In the garage. In the top of the old Maytag."

The white matriarch of appliances, plump and rounded yet imposing in her bulk, still hummed in a corner as if waiting for choir rehearsal to start. Aimee felt her hands shaking as she opened the heavy door to reveal a shadowy, empty womb. Her heart dropped like a stone before she saw the other, smaller door to an inner sanctum. She snatched it open, trembling.

At first she saw nothing in that tiny, heavily frosted hollow. She thrust both hands in, clawing, searching, and felt something amid all the whiteness.

From the very back she pulled a packet so hoarily crusted that she could not at first tell for sure whether it was her own. Shaking, she hugged it between her hands until her living heat had melted the years away. Then she looked at thickly wrapped white freezer paper heavily taped and labeled in a childish scrawl.

"Yes. Yes!" Aimee wanted to yell for joy, yet she started to cry.

❖ ❖ ❖

"Oh, how beautiful!" the Warloctor exclaimed, gazing into the lunch cooler Aimee had placed on her desk. Today she wore a turban of dusky pink silk like the cabbage roses growing down from the ceiling, almost the color Mariposa's belly had once been.

Aimee murmured, "He was still alive when I put him in the freezer. His gills were still gasping. I hope it didn't hurt him much."

"He's long dead now," said the Warloctor.

"Can you get my soul out of him?"

"Already did."

"What!" Aimee jumped up from her chair. "Is it—is it going to be all right?"

"It's more than just all right. As I said, it's quite beautiful, one of the loveliest I've ever seen. Come see."

Standing beside the craggy, dark woman, Aimee gawked. "It's glowing," she whispered. "Like a firefly."

"Uh-huh. I believe your mother was right, Aimee. You are a bit precocious."

Gazing at her own fragile, gauzy immortality, Aimee felt herself begin to cry again, quiet tears like warm rain wetting her face. Probably her makeup was running, but she didn't care.

The W.D. asked, "Are you ready to have it back?"

"Yes."

The Warloctor unlocked a desk drawer, drew it open, and pulled out a white silk bag. From it she fished a length of silver filament as fine as spiderwebbing. She warned, "Even though the procedure is non-invasive, there may be some degree of psycho-emotional trauma afterward. Having a soul is not always easy."

"I'll risk it," Aimee said.

"Good. Stand facing me, then. Spread your arms like wings. You'd better close your eyes."

Amy felt the return of her soul like a soundless explosion of inner light. All her dead certainties blew up and away as if in a sweet wind, and a fountain of lively contingencies flowed in to quicken her breathing and her heartbeat. She whispered, "Oh!" and her eyes snapped open.

"Oh!" Amy cried aloud. "Oh, I love your turban. What the devil am I doing in this monkey suit?" Her pantyhose itched, her waistband cut her breathing, her high-heeled shoes pinched. She had always hated to be dressed up like a Barbie doll; what had she been thinking? "Oh!" The glitter of a sizable diamond caught Amy's eye.

She stood staring at her own ring finger, remembering as if cozening back a dream:

Colin. Her fiancé. Manhattan penthouse. Porsche. Lear jet to fly to the vacation homes in Malibu, the Virgin Island, Nice.

Handsome, charming Colin with his rich-boy toys, of which she was about to become one.

Colin, who probably kissed himself in the mirror every day before the maid brought his breakfast in. Colin, who had no more soul than a steel-belted radial tire.

"Lord in heaven! What was I thinking?" Amy cried. She yanked the ring off her finger and threw it into the lunch cooler with the dead fish.

NANCY SPRINGER is the author of a number of fantasy novels for teenagers and adults, including *I Am Mordred*, *I Am Morgan le Fay*, and *The Hex Witch of Seldom* (all available from Firebird). She is a two-time Edgar Award winner.

Nancy Springer lives in East Berlin, Pennsylvania.

AUTHOR'S NOTE

We all at times come apart during our lives and have to "remember" ourselves together in order to be whole. In my own life, one thing that I'd forgotten since I was a child, and remembered forty years later, is how important it is to spend summer afternoons in company with the common sunfish. If I were a poet, maybe I could explain what it is about a cool brook pool with intimations of sunnies in the shadows like visible yet intangible dreams . . . oh, well. Someday I might remember how to be a poet, but meanwhile, I'm more of a clown. So I wrote this story.

Lloyd Alexander

max Mondrosch

"I can construct covered wagons . . . fieldpieces of beautiful and useful shape . . . designs for buildings . . . I can do whatever may be done, as well as any other whosoever he may be."
                                                    —Leonardo da Vinci

On a damp shirt of a February evening, a person named Max M. Mondrosch sat in a hotel room and drafted the following letter:

"Gentlemen," he wrote, in a hand that conveyed an insistent although respectful bid for attention.

"Gentlemen:

"Please accept this as an application for employment with your company in the capacity of—

(Here, Mondrosch left a blank space and continued.)

"I am thirty years of age, in excellent health, eager to progress with your organization. My family background, character, and education are of the highest caliber and, should you so request, I am prepared to furnish authentic references from the most unimpeachable sources.

"My experience has been varied, and has given me considerable knowledge of the type of work referred to in your advertisement.

"Hoping that you will grant me the favor of an interview and the opportunity to offer my services, I beg to remain, with best regards,

Yours very truly,

Max M. Mondrosch."

Mondrosch's hotel was one of those lodging houses found at the end of almost any mean street, where the bellboys are eighty-some years old and the accommodations no more than an iron bed, a sooty basin, a table, and a cane chair. However, even at the peeling table, Mondrosch looked like a man beginning his day at the office. His shoes were shined, his suit fairly well cut, his collar glistened as much as his cheeks. He folded the newspaper to the "Help Wanted" columns, cleared his throat, pulled back his cuffs, tucked in his chin, and made a few flourishes in the air with his pen.

He wrote out a form for most of the advertisements, fitting himself to nearly every role. Given a white apron and a crepe-paper overseas cap, he became a cheerful "Counterman." Given a sample case, he was an "Outside Salesman." A pair of spectacles could turn him into any type of "Professional Man." In a dark suit, pacing up and down with a handful of papers, he could be an "Executive" or "Manager."

Satisfied with his work, Mondrosch sealed and stamped his letters. From his briefcase he took a pair of pajamas. Overhead, the steam pipes cracked like breaking limbs, but once in the sagging bed Mondrosch plummeted into a dark well and drowned there peacefully until morning.

Mondrosch had noted down two employment agencies and by quarter to nine he was shaved, powdered, deodorized, dressed, and in the street. As he walked, he organized the points he would develop during his interviews, going carefully over his qualifications, the sequence of their presentation, and the most effective phrasing.

At the first agency, he opened the door and saw a row of chairs. Against the wall stood a high wooden table The agent sat alone at a desk, cleaning his fingernails. Mondrosch approached, hat in hand.

The agent barely looked up. "Have you filled out a form?"

"Not as yet," Mondrosch began.

"Get one filled out first." The man went back to his nails.

Mondrosch went to the table and found a clotted ballpoint pen. He completed the application and waited some while before the agent summoned him. Mondrosch sat alert while the agent glumly scanned the form. The telephone rang.

"Yes, that's right," the man said. "What? Yes. Salary?" His face brightened. "Yes, just the fellow you want. As a matter of fact, he's sitting here now."

Mondrosch looked modestly at the floor as the agent went on:

"Oh, he's one of our best. Tops. Very high type, very. I'm sending him down to you. He's leaving already. On his way now."

The employment agent jumped up, spun around the desk,

seized a hat and coat, and was out the door before Mondrosch could say a word.

In the offices of Butter & Dick, telephones and buzzers rang incessantly. Messengers arrived with handfuls of envelopes marked "Urgent," and every few minutes half a dozen applicants pushed out through the door. As Mondrosch wondered whether he should wait, a stout man reached over the wooden railing.

"I'm Butter," he shouted. "Come in, come in."

Mondrosch admitted he had not filled out an application.

The stout man waved a hand. "Don't have time. I can see you're executive material. I want you to go down to this address." He scribbled on a piece of notepaper. "You can manage an office, can't you?"

"An office?"

"A whole department. Now, let's get that fee paid and we'll all be squared away. Ten percent off for cash."

"Cash?" The word alarmed Mondrosch.

"Don't you have cash with you?"

Mondrosch made swimming motions. "Well, the cash, you see—new in town, change of banks—"

"Never mind," Butter said. "Give me a deposit. I'll take your check for the rest."

"Yes—but are you sure I'll get the job?"

The stout man slapped the desk. "Sure? I'll confirm it for you now." He picked up a telephone and, with a finger thrust in one ear, shouted at the top of his lungs.

"Department manager's spot? Yes, I filled it for you. What?"

He turned. "What's your name?" Then, at the telephone again: "Fellow by the name of Mondrosch. Will you give him an advance? That's his stipulation: advance absolutely necessary." He put down the telephone. "There you have it."

Mondrosch, embarrassed, advised him that he could only spare ten dollars. Butter shook his head. Usually, they insisted on a deposit of fifteen percent of the fee. Perhaps he had better try elsewhere. Mondrosch offered twenty dollars.

Butter's face grew bland again. "Twenty will do. I'll make an exception."

In his wallet, Mondrosch had folded away six five-dollar bills. He took out four.

Butter simultaneously took the bills and shook Mondrosch's hand. "Go right in to the personnel director. It's all arranged."

Mondrosch promised to mail a check for the remainder as soon as he got his advance. Butter helped him through the crowd and waved him out of the office.

Mondrosch did not take time to eat lunch. After two hours on a number of street cars and buses, he hurried on foot across the various lots surrounding the factory. In the personnel office, he had the impression that all the other applicants from Butter & Dick had simply transferred there. Young men in shirtsleeves collected forms. Mondrosch took hold of a clerk's elbow and asked for directions to the manager's office.

"No more interviewing today," the clerk said.

"Mr. Butter arranged an appointment for me," replied Mondrosch. "I have been selected for the position of department manager."

"Which department?"

Mondrosch hesitated. "Why—the department *manager*," he said. "I'm to take charge of—of—"

The clerk shook his head. "That vacancy is filled."

"Exactly!" exclaimed Mondrosch. "I'm the manager. You know, Mondrosch—the new department manager."

The clerk went off and brought back a file card. "I told you. The job's been taken. By a Mr. Mongoose."

"That's me!" cried Mondrosch. "I'm Mr. Mongoose. That is, my name is Max M. Mondrosch, but when Mr. Butter telephoned—"

The clerk gave Mondrosch a suspicious look. "I don't care what your name is or whether you're lying or not. But you aren't Mongoose, or Mondrosch, or whatever you call yourself, because this man reported for work two hours ago."

Dusk had fallen by the time Mondrosch reached the city again. He went directly to the offices of Butter & Dick. A sign was tacked on the door: "Out to Lunch."

He went back to the hotel.

Next morning, Mondrosch received a letter advising that if he wished to be interviewed he should report no later than noon and ask for a Mr. Munch. He left immediately and arrived at the address by nine-thirty.

At the head of a long flight of steps, Mondrosch approached a wooden box whose grilled window had been mostly covered over with cardboard. A woman sat behind the grill, a telephone receiver wired around her head and a scratch pad in front of her. Mondrosch tried to attract her attention but she did not look up. As he was about to pass, she tapped the grill. The cage was so well sealed he could hear nothing.

"To see Mr. Munch!" he shouted, holding up the letter.

She motioned him down a whitewashed corridor. Mondrosch found himself in the office area among desks, accountants, and secretaries. The employees glanced at him without much interest, then went back to adding up figures or answering telephones. Mondrosch could hear snatches of conversation:

"Hello? This is Baffle, Invincible Automatic Parts Company." Or, "Yes, Hedge speaking, Invincible Automatic." Or, "Rundle? Gildish here. Invincible."

To himself, Mondrosch repeated enthusiastically, "Hello, this is Mondrosch, Invincible Automatic."

A short man with a moustache and butcher sleeves beckoned to him. Mondrosch was a little dismayed at the prospect of being interviewed in such a public place. He preferred closed offices where, if necessary, an applicant could plead, weep, or drop to his knees without too much embarrassment.

Munch offered a cigar. Mondrosch politely declined, adding that he had cigarettes. To prove he was not lying, he took one from his pocket.

"Don't smoke cigars? Well, then." Munch tucked up his sleeves, looked sharply at Mondrosch, and began:

"This position calls for a knowledge of accounting, correspondence, administration, order handling, expediting. Are you familiar with that type of employment?"

"Very familiar," Mondrosch said. "I have performed those duties for several years."

"Ah." Munch frowned. "Computers? Calculators? Slide rules? Percentage discount tables? You know how to use them?"

"I do, sir."

"Ah." He turned Mondrosch's letter over and over in his hands. "In other words, you might say that you feel qualified to handle such a position?"

"Thoroughly."

Munch cleared his throat and again took up the letter. "You claim your name is Max N. Mondrosch."

"M. Mondrosch."

"I see. Married, of course."

"A bachelor," Mondrosch said with a certain wistfulness. "Someday, naturally, I hope there will be—"

"A Mrs. Mondrosch, yes. But not at present. Brothers and sisters?"

"A sister."

"Only one sister? No brothers at all?"

Mondrosch shook his head. He folded his hands. Munch smoked and stared at the letter. At last, he put down his cigar.

"Mondrosch," he said, "I'm afraid that we're looking for someone with a little different qualifications."

Mondrosch was obliged to vacate his lodgings, but he persuaded the hotel clerk to let him continue receiving mail there. For meals, he wandered into some cafeteria or other, briefcase under his arm, smiling, waving as if greeting a friend. When he passed a table with leftovers on it, he deftly picked up a crust here, a chop bone there, and sometimes a remnant of pie. He popped these items into a paper napkin and carried them off to the bus station where he sat in the waiting room and ate at leisure. He spent his nights, too, in the waiting room. Not wishing to call attention to himself by stretching out on the bench, he dozed upright. Mornings, he shaved in the men's room.

His weight dropped considerably over the next few weeks. His clothes fit him badly and so, during interviews, Mondrosch kept on his overcoat. It hid the bagginess of his jacket and trousers. He continued to write his applications but the positions were either filled by the time he had arrived; or the personnel manager had suddenly left town for an indefinite period; or his experience had not been in the identical work for which he presented himself.

He did receive one letter thanking him for his interest. This company was pleased to employ the latest scientific screening methods and regretted to inform him that it had already been determined that he would not be happy there.

About this time, Mondrosch developed a theory that employers tended to hire persons who in some way resembled them. At his next interview, he carefully noted the features of the personnel manager. He saw the man was heavy, with a handful of hair bunched up over his forehead. The manager's chin receded, the corners of his mouth sank down, and he had a habit of throwing out his arms when he talked, as well as a tic that made him wink constantly. Mondrosch observed that the clerks and secretaries also had their hair bunched up and their chins pulled in. As they worked, they threw their arms about and winked and blinked all they could.

MAX MONDROSCH

"I know one thing," Mondrosch told himself, "if a fellow wants to work here, he'd better look the same way. And if he can manage a bit of blinking, so much the better."

When his turn came, Mondrosch stood up, puffed out his coat to give himself more bulk, ruffled his hair, stuck in his chin, and pulled down his mouth. As he walked, he flung his arms around and winked and twitched as well as the manager himself.

Seeing Mondrosch approach, the manager turned to one of his assistants and said in a loud voice:

"Send that man away. I won't see him. He looks like some kind of imbecile."

A blizzard covered the city and for several days Mondrosch stayed in the waiting room. He feared that if he went into the streets he would be blown into a snowdrift. He was unable to visit the cafeterias. His skin grew tighter, more transparent, and his clothing weighed unbearably.

One morning he read an advertisement in a discarded newspaper:

"Blood Donors Wanted. Top price for urgently needed plasma."

Mondrosch ventured out of the station and made his way to the hospital.

At first, he feared he would be rejected because of his condition. But there were so many applicants and they were hustled through so quickly that no one paid attention.

"I'm sure it doesn't matter," Mondrosch said to himself as a nurse helped him up from the cot. "It all goes into the same pot, I daresay. Boiled up, put in bottles, away you go and who's to know, what's the difference?"

Putting on his coat in the dressing room, an old vagrant whose clothing was so covered with refuse that he looked more like a wastebasket, gave Mondrosch a wink.

"See you tomorrow, eh?"

"What?" asked Mondrosch. "Do you come here every day?"

"Why not?"

"How do you stand it?" asked Mondrosch, whose ears had started to ring.

"I'll tell you the secret," the vagrant whispered. "Vitamin pills and lots of water. And keep changing your name. They'll never recognize you. But the main thing: vitamin pills. Plenty of vitamin pills."

Mondrosch thanked him and from then on followed his advice. His head ached and spun constantly, he was troubled with fever and sudden spells of bewilderment; but the vitamins and water kept him on his feet. With the money he received, he was able to move back into his hotel. He visited the hospital several times a week and wondered if he might not go more often.

"No," he decided. "No sense being greedy."

Winter lasted through April, in long rags of sleet that wound themselves around Mondrosch's hat. Luckily, he had not completely dried up, though his legs had grown so thin and unsteady he could barely walk to the blood bank. The wind penetrated his chest and he became so inflamed with cold air that he breathed only with difficulty.

After a long spell of silence, Mondrosch found a letter in his box. He rubbed his eyes. The words kept jumping out of place and made no sense to him. He finally deciphered the address, pulled his coat around him, straightened his hat, and left the hotel.

The building was the largest he had ever seen. A dozen corridors starred from the immense lobby. Mondrosch gave his name to the receptionist. She pressed a button and in a moment a young man appeared, introducing himself as Mr. Clegg from the personnel department.

"Step this way, sir." He took Mondrosch by the arm. "The director will be glad to interview you."

Mondrosch followed his guide across an expanse of mosaic floor whose design spun like a tile pinwheel. Clegg led him down a corridor brilliant with lights. To avoid stumbling, Mondrosch kept one hand against the wall, leading Mr. Clegg to suppose he was admiring the construction.

"Special soundproofing," said Clegg. "Eliminates noise and disturbance. The company feels it makes for better working conditions."

As they went up, Clegg described the corporate pension plan, insurance, vacation policy, stock options, and bonuses. But Mondrosch felt encased in a block of ice and could hardly speak. He nodded his head and smiled as much as possible. Clegg, however, seemed disappointed at an apparent lack of enthusiasm. He lost interest in explaining further and when they reached a door he simply said, "Step in there, please," and walked away.

Mondrosch found himself in a waiting room which, to his

astonishment, was like a parlor in a home; a parlor familiar to him not because it reminded him of his own but, rather, what he had always dreamed a parlor should be. He sat down in an armchair and put his feet on an ottoman. He closed his eyes, but puffballs of orange and red exploded behind his lids. He had the disagreeable sensation that he was evaporating. He struggled against it. Fainting, he was sure, would not make a favorable impression.

The door opened. Mondrosch forced himself to stand. Before him stood the director. She was the most beautiful woman he had ever seen. Her face was that of the future Mrs. Mondrosch about whom he had speculated with Munch; it was also the face of his mother, his sister, and even of his brothers who had never existed.

"Mr. Max Mondrosch? I'm very glad to meet you, Max."

Mondrosch went to her. He loved her instantaneously, he adored her, which made it somewhat difficult for him to concentrate on what she was saying.

"Sit down, Max. I suppose you've seen a little of our operations. I hope you were favorably impressed. The corporation feels it's important for co-workers to be satisfied. We, on the other hand, require a particular kind of employee. I'd like you to answer the questions on this sheet." She handed him a form. "It will only take a few minutes."

Many of the questions, Mondrosch saw, were highly personal. Had he ever wet the bed as a child—or as an adult? Had he ever indulged in premarital heterosexual intercourse or homosexuality? Did he object to unpleasant odors? To touching people with diseases? Did he ever cry at a movie? Did he behave kindly toward animals?

Under the section marked Business Attitudes, he read: Have you ever felt unfairly treated? Have you ever gone out of your way to avoid offending someone? Would you be satisfied to stay long in one position?

He answered "Yes" to these and returned the sheet to her.

"Now, Max," she said, "before I score your test, I'd like you to tell me why you applied?"

"I applied—well, for work. That is, to have a job—"

She frowned. "The corporation feels that employees' motives are extremely important. Do they really have the corporate interest at heart; or simply looking for a job to make a living? They should derive some personal satisfaction in their work. Making a living is the least important concern, wouldn't you say? And—Are you feeling well?"

Mondrosch, whose joints felt as if they were coming unlatched and who was clutching his chest to control a spasm, nodded his head. "Quite well. Yes, quite. Thank you."

"I haven't really studied your questionnaire," the director went on, "but I note you've indicated you'd be content to stay in one position indefinitely. In your general personality constellation, I don't know how significant that response may be. But we do feel that employees should constantly wish to better themselves. They should be just a little dissatisfied. You understand that, of course?"

She folded the paper. "I shall score the test now. The results will be available by the time you reach the lobby."

The receptionist was waiting for Mondrosch with an envelope. He thanked her and tore open the flap to reveal a neatly printed form:

"We regret that we are unable at this time to offer you

employment. We trust that you will obtain a position elsewhere to which your capabilities are better suited."

At the waterfront, a cargo had come in ahead of schedule and the warehouse superintendent needed a gang of stevedores at short notice. He saw a group of vagrants standing in the lee of the sheds, and the idea came to him that he could use them and save himself a trip to the hiring hall. He put on his mackinaw, knocked out his pipe, and walked over to the sheds.

"Anybody want to offload some crates? For cash. Off the books."

Several of the vagrants stepped forward.

"Anybody else?"

As he marched his crew down the dockside, he thought he heard someone else cry, "I do!"

He turned but saw no one, only what looked like a bundle of rags flapping along the cobbles.

"Anyone else?" he called again. He heard a fading, floating sigh:

"*Max Mon—*"

The superintendent listened a moment, shrugged and walked on. A breeze blew along the docks, driving dust, papers, and the loose rags into the river.

The gulls dived for scraps.

LLOYD ALEXANDER is the author of the five-volume
Chronicles of Prydain, widely considered a classic fantasy cycle.
The Black Cauldron, the second in the series, is a Newbery
Honor Book, and the final volume, *The High King*, was award
ed the Newbery Medal. His many other books include the
three volumes of the Westmark Trilogy: *Westmark* (Winner of
the American Book Award), *The Kestrel* (A National Book
Award Finalist), and *The Beggar Queen*, all available in
Firebird editions.

Lloyd Alexander lives with his wife, Janine, and their cats
in Drexel Hill, Pennsylvania, not far from where he grew up.

AUTHOR'S NOTE
This tale of Max Mondrosch is different from anything I have
written before or since, and the darkest. Comic nightmare?
Nightmare comedy? In any case, a fantasy. Max hardly seems
the typical fantasy hero. Yet, here he is: eternally eager, res-
olute, doing his utmost. Heroism of the everyday.

Artists, as well as writers, have always had an impact on my
emotional ecology, and none more than Goya in his etchings.
I recognize shadows of those disturbing images in the present
work. But, one good thing about nightmares: We wake up
from them, hopefully stronger than when we went to sleep.

Meredith Ann Pierce

the fall of ys

The Celtic queen of Britain once had two sons, and when the time came for her to choose her successor, she set a riddle before them:

Now calm and consenting,   now cold, unrelenting—
My rhythm changes   with the moon.
When her bark rides high,   I rise and swell.
When her sphere sinks low,   I fall as well.
I buoy men up   or drag them down:
Upon me rest,   or in me drown.
I'll seize all a man owns,   never to repay—
Yet victual his table   every day.
I smile; I storm;   I do men harm—
Or else reward,   according to my whim.
Who dares to flout   my purposes,
I'll be the ruin   of him.
So wild and deep,   no fool can tame me:
Both faithless and constant.   Riddler, name me.

THE FALL OF YS

⊠ ⊠ ⊠

Gralon, the queen's younger son, answered, "A woman's heart."

His mother frowned. "You've an odd notion of women, my son," she said. "Your brother shall reign after me. His answer was, 'the Sea.'"

Hearing this, Gralon flew into a rage and stormed from the hall, cursing the queen and all women. Loading his followers onto barks, he removed himself across the channel to Brittany, there to call himself a king. Gralon had no wife, but he had a young daughter, Myramond, upon whom he doted. At times during the crossing, the channel grew so rough he feared to lose not only her, but all his barks and followers besides. But at last, the Sea spat them out, and they made safe landfall.

"You've a woman's treacherous heart, gray Sea," shouted King Gralon, standing soaked and battered on the shore. "But storm all you will, I'll not be ruled by you or any she. I'll raise a city in your very bosom. Then shall we see who reigns in Brittany."

So Gralon built his capital upon a rocky spit of land that at low tide connected to shore, but at other times stood surrounded by waves. He named this tidal island Ys, and declared it should hold the most beautiful city ever made, full of towers and bells. He ordered a great wall raised all around to hold back the Sea's fierce, churning waves and her rushing tide. Within a year, all came to pass as the king had decreed—save for the seawall. Time and again, storms rose and breakers crumbled the wall, flooding the lower reaches of Ys. Then one morning at rising tide, a moon-prowed bark appeared, bearing a tall woman robed all in white.

"I am the highest of an order of priestesses," she said, "who dwell far on yonder misty isle just at horizon's edge, forswearing the company of men and dedicating our lives to our mistress, the Sea. We have heard of the answer you gave to your mother's riddle. Our mistress is not at all pleased that you should mistake mere mortal frailty for all her plumbless depths. But she is willing to forgive, even allow you your seawall, if you will dedicate your daughter to our service."

"Give you Myramond?" King Gralon cried. "Never! My daughter is far too young."

"In a dozen years, then," the white-clad priestess said. "When she comes of age."

The king shook his head. "When my daughter comes of age, she must choose her own path. I'll not speak for her in this."

Then the priestess smiled, as though she had been testing him. "Very well," she said. "Our lady will be satisfied with this: swear that when Myramond comes of age, you will *allow* her to come to us, *if* such be her wish."

"Only that?" laughed the king. "If I swear to this, my seawall will stand? Done, then!" And the white-robed priestess took her leave. Gazing after her as she sailed away, Gralon laughed again, privily, for he meant to cheat both the priestess and the Sea.

Events proceeded just as the white lady had promised. The royal workmen completed their wall, which thereafter stood fast against even the roughest tide. King Gralon's seawalled city of Ys prospered and grew. Years passed, and Myramond, despite her father's doting, grew into a maiden as modest as she was generous of heart, laughing and kind, simple in her tastes, steady in mien, and certain of mind.

She took little interest in worldly affairs, for hers was an otherworldly bent. She saw images in seafoam and heard whispers on the wind of mysterious realms beyond our own. Her favorite pastime was to walk the seawall, gazing across the flat, gray Sea toward the horizon's edge, where the white-robed priestess's island floated, barely visible. Though her father sternly forbade her to even think of such a thing, Myramond resolved to make her home there as soon as she came of age.

She never spoke of her resolve, but her father sensed it, watching in brooding silence from the highest tower of Ys as his daughter walked the seawall below. Despite his promise to the priestess and the Sea, he was determined that Myramond should never leave him. When ten years had passed and Myramond had reached her fourteenth year, King Gralon began to tempt his daughter, seeking to turn her heart to worldly things. Sumptuous feasts he laid before her, heaping her table with delicacies. But of even the most savory dishes, the king's daughter ate only moderately, preferring simpler fare.

Undaunted, her father ordered gorgeous robes made, embroidered mantles and brooches of gold. But Myramond refused all finery, donning only the plain garb she had always worn. Concealing his frustration, the king arranged lavish entertainments of tumblers and jugglers, but his daughter only looked on politely and excused herself as early as she might, for such diversions stirred her not at all. Her heart was set on the Misty Isle.

After a year without success, King Gralon grew desperate. He knew his daughter would depart with the Sea's white priestess when she came unless he could devise some stronger snare. So, one by one, secretly, he called all the finest young men of the city to him, promising rich rewards to any who might win his daughter's heart. One by one, he sent them to her, but all in vain. The king's otherworldly daughter could not be swayed. In the end, nothing could contain the king's rage as, one by one, the young men returned to him, confessing failure.

At last, the evening before Myramond's sixteenth birthday arrived. Darkness fell. The full moon, poised overhead in the clear, dark, cloudless sky, cast a silver brilliance on the incoming tide. Myramond walked the seawall, gazing toward the far, misty isle. Tomorrow, she knew, the priestess's moon-prowed bark would come, and she would speak her decision to leave her father and Ys. Not a breath of breeze stirred. The city's watch bells were tolling the hour. Below her, strange eddies foamed about the seawall. A wild, soft moaning reached her ears.

"Myramond! Myramond . . . ," the eerie voices called.

Gazing down to where the seawall's outer steps disappeared into the waves, the king's daughter beheld the broken bodies of young men swirling through the foam. They raised their pale faces and looked at her.

"You are the dead!" gasped Myramond.

The corpses nodded. "We are the suitors whom you spurned. Your father had his servants murder us and cast our bodies to the waves."

Horrified, Myramond drew back. "Why would my father do such a thing?"

"For failing to capture your heart," they groaned. "He hoped a lover would keep you here. You spurned us to our deaths, Myramond."

"Have mercy," the king's daughter cried. "I had no notion of my father's wicked intention!"

"Fear not," the haggard spirits answered. "We come but to give warning, not to harm. Your father means to keep you in Ys by whatever means he may. You must flee the city at once, tonight."

"But on the morrow," began Myramond, "the white-robed priestess comes. . . ."

"Tomorrow will be too late!" The gray bodies slewed and washed against the seawall, muttering. "When the priestess comes, your father means to slay her as he did us. He does not mean to let you go."

"But I shall be of age," protested Myramond, "free to choose my own path. My father promised. . . ."

"Your father counts himself a king," the dead upon the waves replied, "unbound by any promises. Choose now. You are already come of age, for the midnight hour has struck. It *is* the morrow, Myramond. Flee Ys while you may!"

The king's daughter gazed hopelessly at the seething waters. "But the tide is high. Ys is an island now and shall not stand free of the waves till dawn. I have no boat; neither can I swim."

"Descend," her ghostly suitors replied. "We will make your path."

Then the spirits began rolling back the tide, bunching and

shoving it in great gray folds, like some vast, castoff mantle chased with silver where the moonlight gleamed. Back they pressed the Sea, and farther back, exposing the dank, mucky bottom beneath, strewn with flipping fish and ruffled weed. All the way to horizon's edge the Sea withdrew, so that the priestess's distant, misty isle stood suddenly high and dry as Ys itself now stood.

"Make haste!" the ragged deadmen called.

Gathering her skirts, Myramond darted down the seawall steps. The Misty Isle lay seven miles away. Just beyond it, the dark Sea rose glistening. The king's daughter's feet flew across the damp and salt-rank sand. High above, in the tallest tower of Ys, prowling sleepless, King Gralon stared in astonishment as the Sea pulled back to horizon's edge and crouched there like a huge, gray cat waiting to spring. A lone figure caught his eye, cloak flying, hair streaming, silvered by the moon. Even so far, the king knew his own daughter, already halfway to the Misty Isle.

"Myramond!" he cried. Then, "My horse! My horse!"

Bolting from the tower, Gralon pounded to the stable, snatching his charger from puzzled, sleepy grooms. He spurred through the slumbering streets of Ys. Unguarded now at the midnight hour, the seagate rose before him. In half a moment, the king had thrown the bolts, shoved wide the port, and was galloping across the watery plain.

"Faithless girl," he shouted, leaning to grasp Myramond by the arm and snatch her aloft in the saddle before him.

"I am a woman now," his daughter cried, struggling furiously, "and must choose my own path!"

"Aye, you've a woman's heart: all treachery," her father roared, wheeling and galloping back the way he had come, carrying Myramond away from the Misty Isle.

With a moan, the dead that had held back the sea released their hold. The great hill of water reared and teetered, then rushed after the king from horizon's edge. Before it surged a foaming wash, hoof-deep at first, then knee-deep, belly-deep. . . . Burdened with its double load, the king's terrified mount heaved and floundered. Myramond saw terror in her father's eye as he stared behind at the towering curve of brine hurtling nearer and nearer. His gaze flicked to the shore ahead, then down at his struggling steed and the rising Sea. Lastly he stared at his own daughter as she writhed and pulled against his grip.

"Let me go," she cried. "Father, let me go!"

"The Sea take you, then, if such will save me," he shouted suddenly and flung her savagely from him, into the churning tide.

The Sea caught at Myramond's heavy garments, dragging her down. She saw her father's charger, its burden abruptly lightened, spring on toward shore with renewed vigor just as the cold Sea closed over her. Cold forms embraced her, buoyed her, holding her fast, pulling her free of the terrible undertow. Cold, silent faces gazed at her. Innumerable cold arms raised her, lifting her upward, up toward the rippling surface above, the star-strewn night, the moonlit air—where moments later she felt strong, living hands catch hold of her and haul her choking from the foam. A dry wooden deck, firm and solid, rocked gently beneath her, only barely disturbed by the floodwaters surging all around. Soaked, gasping, shuddering, Myramond looked up into the calm gray eyes of the white-robed priestess standing above her.

"Rest easy, child," the other bade. "You are safe."

Pulling herself upright, Myramond clung to the rail of the moon-prowed bark, which stood fixed as though at anchor amid the swirling flood. Wisps of mist surrounded the craft. They began to thicken even as she regained her breath. Before her, very far away, she beheld her father's exhausted mount gaining the distant shore.

"Fool!" the tall priestess called after him, in a voice that carried even above the thunder of waters. "Did you think to rob the Sea? You did not keep your end of our agreement, and so your kingdom is forfeit. Look you to Ys!"

Myramond saw her father turn, and she, too, gazed in horror at the great wave still building, rolling toward the city, far taller now than any seawall, taller even than the highest tower of Ys.

"No!" the king's daughter cried, catching hold of the priestess's arm. "Let *me* pay the price. My father's people had no part in his broken oath. They are innocent!"

"As are you," the priestess answered. "Peace, child, and hark."

Then Myramond heard the many bells of Ys tolling, tolling riotously, and above them the ghostly voices of her suitors calling, "Awake! Rouse and arise! Your king has fled. The Sea returns. Now you, too, must flee for your lives. . . ."

Through thickening mist, as if in a dream, the king's daughter saw the populace streaming from the wide-flung city gates, abandoning Ys. Women, children, and men, courtiers and commoners alike dashed for the mainland, scrambling wildly up steep, rocky banks, clambering for higher ground. Behind them, the monstrous wave broke; the bells stilled, and the ghostly voices ceased to call as the Sea swept beautiful seawalled Ys into rubble that disappeared beneath the tide. On shore, Gralon's people stood with little more than the clothes on their backs. Their king's spent mount sank dying to the sand, while its rider knelt alongside, weeping into his hands.

"Take warning, queen's son," the tall priestess cried. "Your kingdom is no more. Our lady spared you this night for your daughter's sake, but should you ever again transgress our mistress's realm, you will pay for your trespass with your life. Myramond passes now into our lady's service of her own free will. Would that you had had honor enough to let her go. It was no woman's heart you named in answering your mother's riddle, but your own: cold, faithless, and arrogant. Farewell, Gralon, king once but nevermore of Ys."

The priestess's bark turned toward the Misty Isle, bearing its white-robed pilot and the king's daughter with it. In time, the people of Ys built a new kingdom upon the shore. But they raised no seawalls in defiance of the Sea, and Gralon himself never again set sail upon the waves. The ghosts of Myramond's murdered suitors guard the seacoast of Brittany still, sounding the phantom bells of Ys whenever storm or danger threaten. But the Misty Isle on horizon's edge disappeared from view and mortal reckoning for all time at the very hour of the fall of Ys.

MEREDITH ANN PIERCE is the author of a number of fantasy novels, all of them award-winners: the Darkangel Trilogy, the Firebringer Trilogy (Firebird), and *The Woman Who Loved Reindeer*. Her most recent novel is *Treasure at the Heart of the Tanglewood* (Viking and Firebird); a story collection, *Waters Luminous and Deep: Shorter Fictions* (Viking) is forthcoming.

She received both a B.A. and an M.A. from the University of Florida and an M.L.S. from Florida State University, and spends her days as a librarian. By night, she writes.

Her hobbies include composing music and playing the harp. She lives in the woods south of Micanopy, Florida, in a house powered by solar energy.

Visit her Web site at **www.moonandunicorn.com**

AUTHOR'S NOTE

For me, the seminal moment in the ghostly Celtic myth of the fall of Ys is when King Gralon, fleeing the destruction of the city, casts his daughter into the sea to drown. In doing so, he saves himself, for his beleaguered steed, its load thereby lightened, is then able to escape the boiling waters that have overwhelmed the kingdom and brought all to ruin.

Of the several versions that I have read of this memorable Breton legend—Margaret Hodges recounts a particularly good one in *The Other World: Myths of the Celts*—Gralon is always championed as a hero, a tragic figure, cursed by fate, who makes a noble sacrifice.

We are always asked to believe that his motive for the killing is that, just at the instant his double-mounted charger is about to be overtaken, he miraculously intuits that his beloved daughter is in actuality an inhuman monster, a supernatural being responsible for the flood and the prior deaths of many of the townspeople. The fall of Ys is all her fault.

I could never buy it. A man murders his child and afterwards claims that she deserved it. Was a demon, no less. All evidence of her supposed crimes has, of course, been obliterated in the destruction of the city. It was mere coincidence that her death just happened to result in her father's survival. A bit too convenient for my taste.

So I began to turn the story around in my head, asking myself: what if Gralon's version hadn't been the way it was, if his self-serving alibi had failed to convince? What if supernatural forces had in fact been at work, but on the side of justice, innocence, and truth? What if it had all happened another way. . . ?

Yes, I think the souls of Ys still haunt the shores of Brittany, and the phantom bells still toll, but they tell a tale far different from the one we have heretofore been asked to believe about what took place countless years ago and conspired to bring about the fall of Ys.

Michael Cadnum

MEDUSA

Sharp-eyed Athena passed among us in those days.

From shore to hilltop, little was lost on her. She was quick to spot someone attempting an unwise deed, a youth walking along the rim of a well—showing off to a maiden—or a young woman flirting with a grinning brigand just arrived on a wine ship from Samos.

The goddess of wisdom, Athena was the winged shadow who brushed the ankle just enough to tumble the lad into the well, where his cries echoed until cold water drowned them. She was the owl-shape keening lustful encouragements to the shepherd's daughter, leaving her, as time passed, pregnant and bitterly wise.

Athena was a pretty little nightbird when she took to the wing, just avoiding the snapping jaws of the vixen or the hound, too sure of herself to be afraid of a hunter's tooth. In her womanly guise, the goddess was beautiful, with a laugh like warm wind in olive trees, her step gentle music among the small, white stones.

MEDUSA

Every mortal woman learned to leap quickly from her path as the Daughter of Zeus came flirting with some demi-god or human, running her hands through her sky-bright hair, her laughter causing red poppies to flower in the field.

I was a shipwright's daughter, my hair gilded by the sun. I spent my girlhood holding a plumb line and handing my father a wood plane, helping my brothers peg planks to a ship's frame, loving my father and my brothers as the keel loves sea.

I learned the names of the winds as I grew up, my stature increasing with the summers. My shadow on the sand transformed from a girl's shape into a woman's. The wind ran through my tresses, breeze stroking my linen mantle so the outline of my still-maturing body was clear. I ran along the edge of the surf, chasing my brothers, laughing with them in the tart salt spray.

Handsome plowmen greeted me, cowherds offered me foaming cups of milk, and the wealthy vineyard keeper sang for me.

I was loved.

One day as I washed the sandy grit from my white feet, the tide began to rise. Sea rounded my ankles, lapping upward to my knees, the simmering brine chuckling, "Medusa, pretty Medusa, most lovely and playful of all the mortal maidens, listen to me."

My breath caught, and I stepped back. But I could not escape far, followed by the bubbling laughter of the foam, sporting with me, each step. It tickled pleasingly, this splashing froth. Who was I to flee?

And how could I deny the salt-silvered figure of Neptune in my bedchamber that night?

Strong-muscled, ancient and ever-youthful Neptune, the sea god himself murmured into my ear his vows of faithfulness. He said that he believed himself in love, and I think he was. My room grew bright with sea-joy.

I heard her wings when they were still far off.

I recognized the flutter of her search, circling as she spied his wet steps among the grasses of the dunes, her feathers cutting through the night.

My chamber curtain wafted and parted, flung aside by a pair of owl wings.

I knew her at once—the silken plumage, those gray raptor eyes, seeing what was happening just as Neptune took me in his arms, the ocean-god breathing my name like the surf.

An owl's cry split the hush, her shriek a curse.

My hair intertwined, locks seeking each other, coursing curls thickening, writhing. I could not make a sound, stunned. Arrayed across my pillow, my hair was a crown of serpents, each reptile hungry, rooted in my skull.

In his horror, Neptune fled me, his sea-perfume fading through the dark. Athena's voice, cold as any betrayed mortal woman's, whispered, "From this night, Medusa, every man who sees you will turn to stone."

Every lover, I thought she meant, never dreaming the weight of a goddess's curse.

At dawn, terrified of my own twisting shadow, serpents lunging, battling one another, I cried out for my father. He called my name in return, interrupted as he fastened on his shipwright's apron.

He gaped in dismay.

And froze, just as he was, early morning glittering on the marble arms of his fatherly embrace.

I called out, "Not one step closer, I pray you," to my brothers.

They rushed forward, aroused by my shriek, and they, too, cast suddenly unmoving shadows, their once-quick features forever in white stone.

I hid among the sand dunes and the brambles, my serpent diadem darting, anchored in my head, lashing the air before my eyes. I went without food. I slept among the roots of trees, and drank from black-scummed brooks. When my sandals wore thin, I cast them off and tattered my soles on thorns. I cried out to warn wandering shepherds, and hissed to frighten hunters. Spring and fall, I felt no human touch.

The story is told as far as the round sea's end—how Athena, even that sky-dwelling divine, sickened at the sight of her curse's handiwork. Regret or disgust ripened in her, until one day she found a champion.

She stroked his arm, and seduced him into courage. Bold Perseus, he of the sharp sword and ready laugh, was sailing forth to cut off my head.

I heard the village-folk murmur these tidings at the well-head, ox-drivers repeating the rumor. I hid among the ancient olive trees and stole among the village paths, as far as I could wander from the frieze of stone men, my family and the occasional traveler, rooted in the soil, permanent and lost.

I needed a plan.

The lonely have months to study the nature of the gods, and the nature of false wisdom. I heard Perseus singing, coming for miles, love songs about Athena. He had a voice that charmed. He strode through the groves carrying his mirrored shield, adorned by divinely inspired confidence, and circled around by a pair of darting, moon-silver owl wings.

I had heard it foretold by shepherds' gossip, how he had polished his shield so he could eye my reflection without harm, how Athena would guide his sword-arm, murmuring into his ear, in love with the songs about her own eternal beauty.

He smiled when he saw me in his shield.

He spoke my name—he was so in love with his own voice.

"I wish you good morning," he added, mock formal, groping for the pommel of his sword.

I said nothing, saving my speech for the prayer I had crafted during my long silence.

A sure-footed man, one who had never questioned his own destiny, he winked as he kept my reflection in his shield. He slipped his sword from its sheath. The blade's shadow lifted, and he held it high as the owl breathed encouragement.

The sword whispered as it cut through the air.

When people speak of me they tell of my head cut off. They study statues and paintings of my demise, severed head held aloft, staring with wide eyes as my power to transform men ebbs away.

No one knows the secret.

How a darting pair of wings swooped, whispering praise to the swordsman as he swung the blade. The bright owl banked, gliding ever closer, the wind from her feathers arousing my serpent-crown.

A snake goes hungry like no other living creature. Starving, voiceless and unnamed, cool nights chill the reptile, and hot sun scalds her. Within the shadow of a living quarry at last, at least one pair of reptile eyes grew bright.

A famished snake snatched the owl. The hungry serpent swallowed, working the nightbird down, enclosing the struggling wings in her belly.

The shore is white, and rippled with wind-dunes.

Sea strokes the sharp stones round. Centuries come, and the sharpest flint is softened, caressed by the tongues of surf.

Let me live, was my dying prayer to Athena, trapped in the muscled darkness of a snake.

Let me live as I deserve, I prayed, the sword stroke severing vessels and bone, my fading sight held high.

And I will let you go.

The goddess struggled, her sharp talons, her crushed wings, working—helplessly. And at that moment, she was truly wise.

The wind from the north blows cold, and summer rolls blue and empty of song. Perseus is nothing, a graven hero, a breath of air.

Athena, in her desperation, made a vow.

And she keeps her word.

Now I am stone, among the rounded, enduring company of my father and my brothers. Every time you walk along the gray and dappled pebbles of the shore you hear us, laughing with the never-dying sea.

MICHAEL CADNUM is the author of more than two dozen books, including *In A Dark Wood* and *Forbidden Forest*. His novel about the Crusades, *The Book of the Lion*, was a National Book Award Finalist. Cadnum's new novel about the Vikings, *Daughter of the Wind*, and his novel about Sir Francis Drake, *Ship of Fire*, have recently been published. He is currently at work on a series of novels based on Greek and Roman myths.

AUTHOR'S NOTE
As a boy near the Santa Ana River in Southern California I often used to pass a strange rock formation—a sandstone bluff that looked like an elephant struggling to get away from the face of the cliff. I knew this wasn't a real animal, but, as the winter rains came and went over the years, the elephant shape became attenuated—altering, escaping at last. Some part of me was captured by the sight of this living being frozen in stone—turned entirely into the living shale—as it gradually vanished.

Too often we are little more than stone—creatures of granite habit, heartless and stolid. But then something wonderful—a poem or a song, a smile or a passing greeting—touches us, and we escape again to life. Why not give such a hope to Medusa herself, a living being cursed to remain loveless, throughout time? In my version of the ancient story I remind myself that Medusa could not always have been such a terrible creature, and that even a monster can win hope from a goddess as wise and life-affirming as gray-eyed Athena.

tHe
bLack
fox

Emma Bull
(*adaptation of traditional ballad*)

Charles Vess
(*illustrations*)

EMMA BULL AND CHARLES VESS

"THE BLACK FOX"
(*Traditional ballad*)

As we went out a-hunting
One morning in the spring,
Both the hounds and the horses running well
Made the hills and the valleys ring.

But to our great misfortune
No fox there could be found.
Our huntsmen cursed and swore but still
No fox moved over the ground.

Up spoke our master huntsman,
At the head of the hounds rode he,
Saying, "Lo, we have ridden for a good three hours
But no fox did we see.

"But there is strength within me
And I will have my chase,
And if only the Devil himself come by
We'd run him such a race!"

Then up there sprung like lightning
A fox from out of his hole.
His fur was the color of a starless night,
His eyes like burning coal.

THE BLACK FOX

And we chased him over the valley,
We chased him over the field,
We chased him down to the riverbank
But never would he yield.

And he jumped into the river
And he swam to the other side.
He laughed so hard that the greenwood shook
And he turned to the huntsmen and cried:

"Ride on, my gallant huntsmen!
When must I come again?
If ever you shall want a fox
To chase all over the plain.

"And when your need is greatest,
Just call upon my name,
And I will come and you shall have
The best of sport and game."

The men looked up in wonder
And the hounds ran back to hide,
For the fox had changed to the Devil himself
Where he stood on the other side.

Then the men, the hounds and horses
Went flying back to town,
And hard on their heels came a little black fox
Laughing as he ran.

EMMA BULL is the author of *War for the Oaks*, *Bone Dance*, *Finder*, and some other novels she had way too much fun writing. Her most recent work in print is "Joshua Tree," in *The Green Man: Tales from the Mythic Forest*, edited by Ellen Datlow and Terri Windling. She's also a screenwriter and a musician. She lives in southeastern Arizona with her excellent husband, Will Shetterly, and her tyrannical cat, Buddha.

Her Web site is **www.qwertyranch.com**

AUTHOR'S NOTE

I've loved folk music since I was in third grade, especially the old ballads and the stories they tell. A few years ago, Charles Vess launched a terrific project, in which he recruited his writer friends to help him turn some of those old ballads into comic book stories. Two of my favorite media—comics and ballads—together at last! Oh, boy!

I learned this ballad, "The Black Fox," from a recording by a duo called The Pratie Heads. Intentionally or not, it has all sorts of resonances with the pre-Christian religions of Europe, from back when a hunter might meet a shape-changing horned guy and see, not the Devil, but Cernunnos, the huntsman's god.

CHARLES VESS'S award-winning work has graced the pages of numerous comic books, and has been featured in several gallery and museum exhibitions across the nation, including the first major exhibition of Science Fiction and Fantasy Art (New Britain Museum of American Art, 1980). In 1991, Charles shared the prestigious World Fantasy Award for Best Short Story with Neil Gaiman for their collaboration on *Sandman* #19 (DC Comics)—the first and only time a comic book has held this honor.

In the summer of 1997, Charles won the Will Eisner Comic Industry Award for best penciler/inker for his work on *The Book of Ballads and Sagas* (which he publishes through his own Green Man Press) as well as *Sandman* #75. In 1999, he received the World Fantasy Award for Best Artist for his work on Neil Gaiman's *Stardust*.

He is currently working with Jeff Smith on *Rose*, the prequel to Smith's *Bone*; his collaborations with his friend Charles de Lint include the picture book *A Circle of Cats* (Viking) and the illustrated novels *Seven Wild Sisters* and *Medicine Road*. His other work includes the cover and decorations for Ellen Datlow and Terri Windling's anthology *The Green Man: Tales from the Mythic Forest*.

His Web site address is **www.greenmanpress.com**

ILLUSTRATOR'S NOTE
I've been listening to English, Scottish and Irish ballads for many, many years. But it wasn't until I realized that I could draw the stories within those songs and thus take part in a centuries-old tradition of disseminating these tales into popular culture that I began what has developed into a lifelong obsession. With the help of various writers (Jane Yolen, Charles de Lint, Neil Gaiman, Sharyn McCrumb, etc.) I have so far adapted well over a hundred pages of this material and will soon collect all of it into a hardcover edition.

Patricia A. McKillip

Byndley

The wizard Reck wandered into Byndley almost by accident. He had been told so many ways to get to it that he had nearly missed it entirely. Over a meadow, across a bridge, through a rowan wood, left at a crossroads, right at an old inn that had been shut tight for decades except for the rooks. And so on. By twilight he had followed every direction twice, he thought, and gotten nowhere. He was trudging over thick oak slabs built into a nicely rounded arc above a stream when the lacy willow branches across the road ahead parted to reveal the thatched roofs and chimneys of a village. *Byndley*, said the sign on the old post leaning toward the water at the end of the bridge. That was all. But the wizard saw the mysterious dark behind the village that flowed on to meet the dusk and he felt his own magic quicken in answer.

"You want to know what?" had been the most common response to the question he asked along his journey. An incredulous snort of laughter usually followed.

How to get back again, how to get elsewhere, how to get *there*. . . .

"But why?" they asked, time and again. "No one goes look-ing for it. You're lured, you're tricked there, you don't come back, and if you do, it's not to the same world."

I went there, he thought. I came back.

But he never explained, only intimated that he was doing the king's bidding. Then they straightened their spines a bit— the innkeepers, the soldiers, those who had been about the world or heard travelers' tales—and adjusted their expres-sions. Nobody said the word aloud; everyone danced around it; they all knew what he meant, though none had ever been there. That, Reck thought, was the strangest thing of all about the realm of Faerie: no one had seen, no one had been, no one said the word. But everyone knew.

Finally somebody said, "Byndley," and then he began to hear that word everywhere.

"Ask over in Byndley; they might know."

"Ask at Byndley. They're always blundering about in magic."

"Try Byndley. It's just that way, half a day at most. Take a left at the crossroads."

And there Byndley was, with its firefly windows just begin-ning to flicker against the night, and the great oak forest beyond it, the border, he suspected, between here and there, already vanishing out of day into dream.

He stopped at the first tavern he saw and asked for a bed. He wore plain clothes, wool and undyed linen, boots that had walked through better days. He wore his face like his boots, strong and serviceable but nothing that would catch the eye. He didn't want to be recognized, to be distracted by requests for wizardry. The thing he carried in his pack grew heavier by the day. He had to use power now to lift it, and the sooner he relinquished it the better.

"My name is Reck," he told the tavern keeper at the bar as he let the pack slide from his shoulder. "I need a bed for a night or two or maybe—" He stopped, aware of a stentorious commotion as his pack hit the floor. The huge young man standing beside him, half-naked and sweating like a charger, his face flushed as by his own bellows, was rubbing one sandaled foot and snorting. "Did I drop my pack on you?" Reck asked, horrified. "I beg your pardon."

"It's been stepped on by worse," the man admitted with an effort. "What are you carrying in there, stranger? A load of anvils?" He bent before Reck could answer, hauled the pack off the floor and handed it back. Reck, unprepared, sagged for an instant under the weight. The man's dark, innocent eye met his through a drift of black, shaggy hair as Reck balanced his thoughts to bear the sudden weight. The man turned his head, puffed one last time at his foot, then slapped the oak bar with his palm.

"Ale," he demanded. "One for the stranger, too."

"That's kind of you."

"You'll need it," the man said, "against the fleas." He grinned as the tavern keeper's long gray mustaches fluttered in the air like dandelion seed.

"There are no fleas," he protested, "in my establishment. Reck, you said?" He paused, chewing at his mustaches. "Reck.

You wouldn't be the wizard from the court at Chalmercy, would you?"

"Do I look like it?" Reck asked with wonder.

"No."

Reck left it at that. The tavern keeper drew ale into two mugs. They were all silent, then, watching the foam subside. Reck, listening to the silence, broke it finally.

"Then what made you ask?"

The young man gave an astonished grunt. The tavern keeper smiled slowly. His fatuous, egg-shaped face, crowned with a coronet of receding hair, achieved a sudden, endearing dignity.

"I know a little magic," he said shyly. "Living so close"—he waved a hand inarticulately toward the wood— "you learn to recognize it. My name is Frayne. On slow nights, I open an odd book or two that came my way and never left. Sometimes I can almost make things happen. This is Tye. The blacksmith, as you might have guessed."

"It wasn't hard," Reck commented. The smith, who had a broad, pleasant face beneath his wild hair, grinned delightedly as though the wizard had produced some marvel.

"My brain's made of iron," he confessed. "Magic bounces off it. Some, though, like Linnea down the road—she can foresee in water and find anything that's lost. And Bettony—" He shook his head, rendered speechless by Bettony.

"Bettony," the tavern keeper echoed reverently. Then he came down to earth as Reck swallowed ale. "There's where you should go to find your bed."

"I'm here," Reck protested.

"Well, you shouldn't be, a wizard such as you are. She's as poor as any of us now, but back a ways, before they started disappearing into the wood for decades on end, her family wore silk and washed in perfumed water and rode white horses twice a year to the king's court at Chalmercy. She'll give you a finer bed than I've got and a tale or two for the asking."

"About the wood?"

The tavern keeper nodded and shrugged at the same time. "Who knows what to believe when talk starts revolving around the wood?" He wiped a drop from the oak with his sleeve, then added tentatively, "You've got your own tale, I would guess. Why else would a great wizard come to spend a night or two or maybe more in Byndley?"

Reck hesitated; the two tried to watch him without looking at him. He had to ask his way, so they would know eventually, he decided; nothing in this tiny village would be a secret for long. "I took something," he said at last, "when I was very young, from a place I should not have entered. Now I want to return the thing I stole, but I don't know how to get back there." He looked at them helplessly. "How can you ever find your way back to that place once you have left it?"

The tavern keeper, seeing something in his eyes, drew a slow breath through his mouth. "What's it like?" he pleaded. "Is it that beautiful?"

"Most things only become that beautiful in memory."

"How did you find your way there in the first place?" Tye the blacksmith asked bewilderedly. "Can't you find the same way back?"

Reck hesitated. Frayne refilled his empty mug, pushed it in front of the wizard.

"It'll go no farther," he promised, as earnestly as he had promised a bed without fleas. But Reck, feeling himself once more on the border, with his theft weighing like a grindstone on his shoulders, had nothing left to lose.

"The first time, I was invited in." Again, his eyes filled with memories, so that the faces of the listening men seemed less real than dreams. "I was walking through an oak wood on king's business and with nothing more on my mind than that, when the late afternoon light changed. . . . You know how it does. That moment when you notice how the sunlight you've ignored all day lies on the yellow leaves like beaten gold and how threads of gold drift all around you in the air. Cobweb, you think. But you see gold. That's when I saw her."

"Her," Tye said. His voice caught.

"The Queen of Faerie. Oh, she was beautiful." The wizard raised his mug, drank. He lowered it, watched her walking toward him through the gentle rain of golden, dying leaves. "Her hair. . . ." he whispered. "Her eyes . . . She seemed to take her colors from the wood, as she came toward me, gold threads catching in her hair, her eyes the green of living leaves. . . . She spoke to me. I scarcely heard a word she said, only the lovely sound of her voice. I must have told her anything she wanted to know, and said yes to anything she asked. . . . She drew me deep into the wood, so deep that I was lost in it, though I don't remember moving from that enchanted place. . . ."

He drank again. As he lowered the mug, the wood around him faded and he saw the rough-hewn walls around him, the rafters black with smoke, the scarred tables and stools. He smelled stale ale and onions. The two faces, still, expressionless, became human once again, one balding and innocuous, one hairy and foolish, and both avid for more.

Reck drained his mug, set it down. "And that's how I found my way there," he said hollowly, "the first time."

"But what did you steal?" Tye asked breathlessly. "How did you get free? You can't just end it—"

The tavern keeper waved him silent. "Leave him be now; he's paid for his ale and more already." He took Reck's mug and assiduously polished the place on the worn oak where it had stood. "You might come back tomorrow evening. By then the whole village will know what you're looking for, and anyone with advice will drop by to give it to you."

Reck nodded. His shoulder had begun to ache under the weight of the pack despite all his magic. "Thank you," he said tiredly. "If you won't give me a bed here, then I'll take myself to Bettony's."

"You won't be sorry," Frayne said. "Keep going down the road to the end of the village and you'll see the old hall just at the edge of the wood. You can't miss it. Tell Bettony I sent you." He raised a hand as the wizard turned. "Tomorrow, then."

Reck found the hall easily, though the sun had set by then and near the wood an ancient dark spilled out from the silent trees. Silvery dusk lingered over the rest of Byndley. The hall was small, with windows set hither and yon in the walls, and none matching. Its stone walls, patched in places, looked very old. The main door, a huge slab of weathered oak, stood open. As he neared, Reck heard an ax slam cleanly through wood, and then the clatter of broken kindling. He rounded the hall toward the sound and came upon a sturdy young woman steadying another piece on her block.

She let go of the wood on the block and swung the ax to split it neatly in two. Then she straightened, wiped her brow with her apron, and turned with a start to the stranger.

He said quickly, "Frayne sent me."

She was laughing before he finished, at her sweat, her dirty hands, her long hair sliding loosely out of its clasp. "He picked his moment, didn't he?" She balanced the ax blade in the chopping block with a blow, and tossed pieces of kindling into her apron. "You are?"

"My name is Reck. Frayne told me to find a lady called Bettony and ask her for a bed."

"I'm Bettony," she said. Her eyes were as bright and curious as a bird's; in the twilight their color was indeterminate. "Reck," she repeated. "The wizard?"

"Yes."

"Passing through?"

"No."

"Ah, then," she said softly, "you came because of the wood." She turned. "If you can bear carrying anything else, bring some kindling in with you."

Reck, wondering, gathered an armload and followed her.

"I'm my own housekeeper," Bettony said as she piled the kindling on the great, blackened hearth inside the house, and Reck let his pack drop to the flagstones with a noiseless sigh. "Though I have a boy who takes care of the cows." She flicked him a glance. "That heavy, is it? Shouldn't such a skilled wizard be able to lighten his load a little?"

"That's why I came here," Reck said grimly, and she was silent. She lit a taper from a lamp, and stooped to hold it to the kindling. He watched her coax flame out of the wood. Light washed over her face. It looked more young than old, both strong and sweet, very tranquil. Under the teasing flame, he still couldn't see the color of her eyes.

She gave him bread seasoned with rosemary, a deep bowl of savory stew, and wine. While he ate, she sat across from him on a hearth bench and talked about the wood. "My family wandered in and out of it for centuries," she told him. "Their tales became family folklore. Some were written; others just passed from one generation to the next along with the family nose. Even if the tales weren't true, truth would never stand a chance against them."

"Have you ever been—"

"To fairyland and back? No. Nor would I swear, not even on a turnip, that any of my ancestors had. But I've seen the odd thing here and there; I've heard and not quite heard . . . enough that I believe it's there, in that ancient wood, if you can find your way." He nodded, his eyes on the fire, seeing and not quite seeing, and heard her voice again. "You've been there and back."

"Yes," he said softly.

"That weight in your pack. That's what brings you here."

"Yes."

"What—" Then she smiled, waving away the unspoken question. "It's none of my business. I've just been trying to imagine what it must be that you want so badly to give to them."

"Return," he amended.

"Return." She drew a quick breath, her eyes widening, and he saw their color then: a gooseberry green, somehow pale and warm at the same time. "You stole it?"

"A more tactful innkeeper would have assumed that it was given to me," he commented.

"Yes. But if you wanted half-truths I could give you family lore by the bushel. I'm perceptive. Frayne thinks it's a kind of magic. It's not, really. It simply comes of fending for myself."

"Oh, there's some magic in you. I sense it. I think that if we picked apart your family folklore we would unravel many threads of truth in the tangle. That would take time, though. As you so quickly observed, what I carry is becoming unbearably heavy. Even my powers are faltering under it."

"Take it into the wood," she suggested. "Set it down and walk away from it. Don't look back."

"That doesn't work," he sighed. "I've lost count of the number of times and all the places I've walked away from without looking back. It always finds me. I must return it to the place where it will stay." She watched him, silent again, her eyes wide and full of questions. Is it terrible? he heard in her reluctant silence. Is it beautiful? Did you take it out of love or hate? Will you miss it, once you give it back?

"I stole it," he said abruptly, for keeping secrets from her seemed pointless, "from the Queen of Faerie. It was something she loved; her husband had his sorcerer make it for her. I took it partly to hurt her, because she stole me out of my world and made me love her and she did not love me, and partly because it is very beautiful, and partly so that I could show it to others, as proof that I had been in the realm of Faerie and found my way back to this world. I took it out of anger and jealousy, wounded pride and arrogance. And out of love, most certainly out of love. I wanted to remember that once I had been in that secret, gorgeous country just beyond imagination, and to possess in this drab world a tiny part of that one."

"All that," she said wonderingly.

"I was that young," he sighed. "Such things are so complex then."

"Do you still love her?"

"That young man I was will always love her," he answered, smiling ruefully. "That, I can't return to her."

"But how did you escape their world? And how can you be certain that this time you will be able to find your way out of it again?"

"It wasn't easy," he murmured, remembering. "The king and his greatest sorcerer came after me. . . ." He shrugged away her second question. "One problem at a time. All I know is that I must return. I can't live in my world with what I stole from theirs." He set his plate aside. "If there's any way you can help me—"

"I'll tell you what tales came down to me," she promised. "And I can show you things my ancestors wrote, describing what stream they followed that turned into a path of silver or fairy moonlight, what rose bush they fell asleep under to wake up Elsewhere, what black horse or hare they chased beyond the world they knew. It all sounds like dreams to me, wishes out of a wine cup. But who am I to say? You have been there after all." She rose, lit a pair of tapers, and handed him one.

"Come with me. I keep all those old writings in a chest upstairs, along with other odds and ends. Souvenirs of Faerie they're said to be, but none so burdensome as yours."

She told him family folklore, and showed him fragile papers stained with wine, half-coherent descriptions of improbable adventures, and rambling musings about the nature of magic, all infused with a bittersweet longing and loss that Reck felt again in his own heart, as though no time had passed at all in the realm of his memories. The writers had brought tokens back with them, as Reck had. Theirs were dead roses that never crumbled and still retained the faintest smell of summer, dried leaves that in the Otherworld had been buttons and coins of gold, a tarnished ring that once had glowed with silver fire to light the path of Bettony's great-great-grandfather as he stumbled his way from a tavern into fairyland, a rusty key that unlocked a door that had appeared in the oldest oak tree in the wood. . . .

"Such things," Bettony said, half-laughing, half-sighing over her eccentric family. "Maybe, maybe not, they all seem to say. But then again, maybe."

"Yes," Reck said softly. He glanced out a window, seeing through the black of night the faint, haunting shapes of ancient trees. "I'm very grateful that Frayne sent me to you. This must be the place I have been searching for, a part of their great wood that spills into ours and becomes the path between worlds. Thank you for your help. I'll gladly repay you with any kind of magic you might need."

"There's magic in a tale," she replied simply. "I'd like to hear the whole of yours when you come back out."

He smiled again, touched. "That's kind of you. Come to

Frayne's tavern tomorrow evening and I'll tell you as much as I know so far. That's the debt I owe to Frayne."

She closed the chest and stood up, dusting centuries from her hands. "I wouldn't miss it. Nor will the rest of Byndley," she added lightly. "So be warned."

Reck spent the next day roaming through the great wood, hoping that his heart, if not his eye, would recognize the tree that was a door, the stream that was a silver path into the Otherworld. But at the end of the day the wood was just a wood, and the only place he found his way back to was Byndley. He went to Frayne's tavern, sat down wearily and asked for supper. The pack on the floor at his feet weighed so heavily in his thoughts he scarcely noticed that the comings and goings behind him as he ate his mutton and drank his ale were all comings: feet entered but did not leave. When he turned finally to ask for more ale, he found what looked like an entire village behind him, gazing at him respectfully and waiting.

Even Bettony was there, sitting in a place of honor on a chair beside the fire. She nodded cheerfully to him. So did the blacksmith Tye behind her. He picked the ale Frayne had already poured off the counter; the mug made its way from hand to hand until it reached the wizard.

"Where did we leave off?" Tye asked briskly.

There were protests all around him from villagers clustered in the shadowy corners, sitting on tables as well as benches and stools, and even on the floor. The wizard must begin again; not everyone had heard; they wanted the entire tale, beginning to end, and they would pay to keep the wizard's glass full for as long as he needed.

The innkeeper shook his head. "The tale will pay for itself," he said, and propped himself against the bar to listen.

Reck cleared his throat and began again.

By mid-tale there was not a sound in the place. No one had bothered to replenish the fire; the faces leaning towards Reck were vague, shadowy. As he began to describe what he had stolen, he scarcely heard them breathe. Deep into his tale, he saw very little beyond his own memories, and the rise and fall of ale in his cup that in the frail light seemed the hue of fairy gold.

"I stole what stood on a table beside the queen's bed. To prove that I had been in that bed, and that once I had been among those she loved. Her husband had given it to her, she told me. It was a lovely thing. It was fashioned by the king's sorcerer of a magic far more intricate than I had ever seen, which may have been why he pursued me so relentlessly when I fled with it.

"It was like a tiny living world within a glass globe. The oak wood grew within it. Gold light filled it every morning; trees began to fade to lavender and smoke toward the end of the day. At night—their night, ours, who can say? I was never certain while I was there if time passed at all within the fairy wood—the globe was filled with the tiny countless jewels of constellations in a black that was infinitely deep, yet somehow so beautiful that it seemed the only true color for the sky. In the arms of the queen I watched the night brighten into day within that tiny wood, and then deepen once again into the rich, mysterious dark. She loved to watch it, too. And in spite of her tender laughter and her sweet words, I knew that every time she looked at it, she thought of him, her husband, who had given it to her.

"So I stole it, so that she would look for it and think of me. And because I knew that though she had stolen my heart from me, this was as close as I would ever get to stealing hers."

He heard a small sound, a sigh, in the silent room, a half-coherent word. His vision cleared a little, enough to show him the still, intent faces crowding around him. Even Frayne was motionless behind his bar; no one remembered to ask for ale.

"Show it to us," someone breathed.

"No, go on," Tye pleaded. "I want to hear how he escaped."

"No, show—"

"He can show it later if he chooses. He's been carrying it around all these years; it's not going anywhere else until he ends it. Go on," he appealed to Reck. "How did you get away from them?"

"I don't think I ever did," Reck said hollowly, and again the room was soundless. "Oh, I did what any other wizard would do, pursued by the King of Faerie and his sorcerer. I fought with fire, and with thought; I vanished; I changed my shape; I hid myself in the heart of trees, and under stones. I knew that I only had to toss that little globe in their path, and they would stop chasing me. But I refused to give it up. I wanted it more than reason. Maybe more than life. Eventually the king lost sight of me, confused by all the different shapes of bird and animal and wildflower I had taken. But I could not hide the sorcerer's own magic from him. He never lost sight of the globe, no matter how carefully I disguised it. Once, in hart-shape, I wore it as my own eye; another time I changed it into the mouse dangling from the talons of the falcon I had become. He never failed to see it. . . . Finally, for no matter which way I ran I could not seem to find my way out of that wood, I performed an act of utter desperation.

"I hid myself within the wood within the globe. And then I caused everything—globe, wood, myself—to vanish."

He heard an odd, faint sound, as though in the cellar below a cork had blown out of a keg, or somewhere a globe-sized bubble of ale had popped. He ignored it, standing once again in the tiny wood inside the globe, among the peaceful trees, the end-less, ancient light, feeling again his total astonishment.

"It was as though I had been in my own world all along, and I had mistaken all the magic in it for Faerie . . ." He lifted his glass after a moment, drank, set it down again. "But I could not linger in that illusion. It's not easy to fling yourself across a world when you are both the thrower and the object that is thrown. But I managed. When I stopped the globe's flight and stepped, with great trepidation, out of it and into my own shape, I found myself in the gray, rainy streets of Chalmercy."

He paused, remembering the grayness in his own heart at the sight of the grimy, cold, familiar world. He sighed. "But I had the globe, the world I had stolen out of fairyland. For a long time it comforted me . . . until it began to weigh upon me, and I realized that I had never been forgotten. It was what I had wanted—that the queen should remember me—but she began to grow merciless in her remembering. I had to return this to her or I could never live in any kind of peace again."

He bent then and untied his pack. The tavern was so still it might have been empty When he lifted the little globe out of the pack, its stars spangled the shadows everywhere within the room, and he heard a sigh from all the throats of the villagers of Byndley at once, as though a wind had gusted through them.

He gazed into the globe with love and rue, seeing the fairy queen again within that enchanted night, and the foolish young man who had given her his heart. After a moment he blinked. He was holding the globe in his palm as lightly as though it were a hen's egg. The strange, terrible heaviness had fallen away from it; in his surprise he almost looked into the open pack to see if the sloughed weight lay at the bottom.

Then he blinked again.

It took no small effort for him to shift his eyes from the world within the globe to the silent villagers of Byndley. Their faces, shadows and stars trembling over them, seemed blurred at first, unrecognizable. Slowly, he began to see them clearly. The wild-haired maker with his powerful face and the enigmatic smile in his dark eyes . . . The tall, silver-haired figure behind the bar, gazing quizzically at Reck out of eyes the color of the tranquil twilight within the globe . . . The woman beside the fire. . . .

Reck swallowed, haunted again, for not a mention of time had troubled that face. It was as beautiful as when he had first seen it, tinted with the fiery colors of the dying wood as she walked toward him that day long before.

She smiled, her green eyes unexpectedly warm.

"Thank you for that look," she said. There was Bettony still in her face, he saw: a glint of humor, a wryness in her smile. The faces around her, timeless and alien in their beauty, held no such human expressions. She held out her hand. Reck, incapable of moving, watched the globe float from his palm to hers under the sorcerer's midnight gaze.

"I always wondered," he told Reck, when the queen's fingers had closed around her globe, "how you managed to escape me."

"And I always wondered," the queen said softly, "why you took this from me. Now I understand."

Reck looked at the king among his mugs, still watching Reck mildly; he seemed to need no explanations. He said, "You have told your tale and been judged. This time you may leave freely. There's the door."

Reck picked up his pack with shaking hands. He paused before he opened the door, said without looking back, "The first time, I only thought I had escaped. I never truly found my way out of the wood."

"I know."

Reck opened the door. He pulled it to behind him, but he did not hear it close or latch. He took a step and then another and then did not stop until he had crossed the bridge.

He stopped then. He did not bother looking back, for he guessed that the bridge and every sign of Byndley on the other side of the stream had vanished. He looked up instead and saw the lovely, mysterious, star-shot night flowing everywhere around him, and the promise, in the faint, distant flush at the edge of the world, of an enchanted dawn.

PATRICIA A. MCKILLIP's novels include *The Forgotten Beasts of Eld*, which won the first World Fantasy Award in 1975; The Riddle-Master Trilogy, of which *Harpist in the Wind* was nominated for a Hugo; *Something Rich and Strange*, which won the 1994 Mythopoeic Award, *Winter Rose*, which was nominated for a Nebula, and *The Changeling Sea* (Firebird). Her most recent novel is *In the Forests of Serre*. She has also written a number of short stories, both science fiction and fantasy. She lives in Oregon with her husband, David Lunde.

AUTHOR'S NOTE

I was trying to write a novel one day and "Byndley" came out instead. Some stories are like that. You think you're hatching a dragon and what you get is a butterfly. The idea of fairyland fascinates me because it's one of those things, like mermaids and dragons, that doesn't really exist, but that everyone knows about anyway. Fairyland lies only in the eye of the beholder, who is usually a fabricator of fantasy. So what good is it, this enchanted, fickle land which in some tales bodes little good to humans and, in others, is the land of peace and perpetual summer where everyone longs to be? Perhaps it's just a glimpse of our deepest wishes and greatest fears, the farthest boundaries of our imaginations. We go there because we can; we come back because we must. What we see there becomes our tales.

Kara Dalkey

tHE LaDy of tHE IcE ɢARDEN

Long, long ago, before and before, there once stood two
houses side by side in Heian Kyo. They were no more
than shacks, in one of the poorer quarters of the city. In
each house lived a mother and her only child. Both women
were of once noble families that had fallen into political dis-
favor, and thereby into poverty. Such was the way of those
times, after the conflict called Heiji, in the era of Jisho.

One woman had a daughter, whom we will call Girida. The
other woman had a son, whom we will call Keiken. Both children grew up together as if they were brother and sister,
though they were not.

The two houses shared between them a garden, small but
lovingly tended, in which both children played. In the spring,
there were plum blossoms and fukujuso, peach blossoms and
azalea. In the summer, the little pond in the center of the garden would hold two sacred white lotus blossoms over which
the boy and girl would recite the Lotus Sutra. In the autumn,
there would be bluebells and cattails and crickets to catch.

But the glory of the little garden was in winter, when snow mercifully covered the patched roofs of the houses and bare boughs of the trees and made every little hillock glitter as if bedecked with silver. Girida and Keiken would chase each other, throwing snowballs and building snow dragons, laughing as if such days would never end.

But end they must. In the winter of the year when Girida turned twelve and Keiken turned thirteen, it happened. It was on a day after an ice storm, and glorious icicles, bright as sword blades, hung from the eaves of the houses and branches of the trees. The boy and girl were chasing one another through the garden when Keiken tripped on a patch of ice and slid into the wall of his house. With a great crack, icicles fell from the eaves. Keiken felt a sharp pain in his left hand, and something got into his eye. "Ei!" he cried out as he stood up.

Girida ran over. "Keiken! Are you hurt?"

Keiken blinked and rubbed his eye. The pain swiftly vanished, though his eye still felt cold.

Girida peered closely at his face. "Did you get something in your eye? I see nothing there."

"It was merely a shard of ice, I think. It has melted now."

"Keiken! Your hand!"

Keiken held up his left hand and saw that a shard of icicle had lodged in the web of flesh between his thumb and forefinger. He plucked out the ice chip and a drop of blood pooled there and then fell, a dark red stain against the pure white snow.

"Keiken, we must take you inside and let Mother bandage it."

Keiken looked up at her. And he saw Girida in a way he had never seen her before. He noticed the smudge of mud on her cheek. He noticed the many-times-mended kimono she wore. He noticed the blemishes on her sun-browned face and the slight crookedness of her teeth, the bushiness of her eyebrows. He suddenly despised her. "I will see to it myself," he grumbled. "Go away!"

"But Keiken—"

"Go!"

Girida ran into her house, weeping, and Keiken did not care.

What the two did not know is that this ice storm had been created by oni demons. They had been having a winter battle in the sky, with spears and swords made from ice, polished and sharp as steel. Such oni blades might cut the flesh of demons, but they cut the hearts and souls of mortals. A mortal hurt with such a blade will reject all that he has loved and desire what is worst for him or her. Who knows how it occurred, a stray wind or a mischievous kami, but some of the oni blades had fallen to earth as icicles in the snow.

In the days that followed, Keiken no longer played in the garden with Girida. Instead, he took up a wooden sword and went out into the street where the older boys practiced fighting. At first he had to fight fiercely, no matter what blows fell upon him, in order to gain their respect. When he had proven himself, they began to teach him things he had not known, as he had had no father to raise him.

Keiken learned that the way of the warrior is to never fear

death, to believe one is already dead and be prepared to embrace death happily when it comes. He learned that an honorable death is the sweetest thing a man might achieve. He learned that rank was what mattered in society and that a man had best marry well if he had little noble status himself. The boys would laugh about how they would someday use their bodies like swords when bedding fine ladies. Keiken learned much in a short time.

Girida would watch Keiken as he practiced and play-dueled with the other boys. She admired him all the more and tried to put aside the pain of knowing that he no longer wished her company. When Keiken finished each day, she would wave to him as he walked from the street into his house, but he would not acknowledge her. She would call upon his mother in the evening, but Keiken would not come out of his room to speak with her.

Girida's mother noticed her weeping one night and tried to console her. "It is an odd change that comes over young men of that age," her mother said. "Suddenly all they can think of is fighting and boasting and getting the better of their peers. We always assumed that the two of you were surely close in some former life and that you would someday marry. But perhaps that is not to be. A woman's life is harder than a man's and she must bear terrible burdens. Be brave and await what happens."

Weeks passed and winter deepened. One evening, when the air had turned very chill, Keiken remained in the street practicing even after the other boys had gone home. He did not mind the cold at all. It meant he could not feel the blisters on his hands, the aching in his wrists and arms as he swung his sword through the patterns. It seemed a healing cold, and he wished his soul could become as cold as well, to feel no pain, no loneliness, no loss. He watched the cloud of his warm exhalation, like dragon breath, turn to ice crystals in the air.

When at last he stopped to rest, as the twilight was fading, he noticed an ox carriage stopped at the side of the street. It was a fine, covered carriage, clearly of some noble house, and the oxen tethered to it had hides of the purest white.

The curtains of the side windows had a crest of snowflakes, or were they butterflies? Keiken could not tell.

It was not unknown for young noble ladies to stop their carriages and watch the boys practice. Some of the older boys bragged they'd gotten many a night's entertainment in such a fashion. Keiken had the feeling someone from the carriage was watching him.

A slender, white arm emerged from the carriage window. The hand curled and beckoned to him.

Keiken's breath caught in his throat. *It is a lady! What if she is a Taira? If I am desired by a lady of the most powerful warrior clan in Heian Kyo, my fortune may be made!* Keiken walked to the side of the carriage, his leg muscles aching from the exertion and the cold. "You wish to speak with me?"

"What an admirable young man you are." The woman's voice within was low and melodious, like winter wind through bare tree branches. "Such a fearsome aspect for one so young. Tell me your name and your parentage."

"I am called Keiken," he replied, and then swallowed hard. He wished he could lie about his parentage, but there were severe penalties if caught in such falsehood, particularly in a society where everyone of importance knew everyone else of importance. "As for my heritage, my father is of noble birth but was sent into exile the year after I was born and I am forbidden to speak his name. My mother's as well, though she once served at Court."

"Ah, a boy of well-born, if unfortunate family. Excellent." The back door of the carriage swung open by an unseen hand. "Please, come in and speak with me."

Keiken's heart raced. He was being offered the sort of opportunity the older boys only dreamed of. With no thought of Girida, he went to the back of the carriage and went in.

The woman who sat on the cushioned side-bench within the carriage was astonishing to look upon. She wore layers of white brocade silk kimonos, the color of purity, the color of death, as if she were a Shinto priestess. Her long, coal black hair framed a face white as porcelain, and Keiken could tell she wore no white face powder. She needed none. Her skin was as smooth and unblemished as new-fallen snow. Her eyes were black as obsidian chips, yet they held glinting light, stars in a night sky.

She beckoned him toward her. "I so admired your strength as I watched you." She untied the sash at her waist and let her kimonos fall open, revealing pale, small breasts and a smooth abdomen beneath.

Keiken stumbled into her embrace. Her skin was cold, yet he felt a warming within.

"Show me what you know of swordsmanship," she whispered.

And he did.

THE LADY OF THE ICE GARDEN

Girida worried as Keiken did not return that night. Or the next. Seven days went by. And then another seven. No one seemed to know where he had gone, not even his mother. Girida finally found an old woman who owned an herb and medicine shop on the street where the boys practiced. The old woman shook her head and said only, "He has gone with the Lady of the Ice Garden."

Girida told this to both her mother and Keiken's mother. Neither woman seemed to know any one called by such a name. "But people change names so often," said Girida's mother. "Women, particularly, whenever they change residence. This lady might even be someone we once knew at the Imperial Court."

"Well," sighed Keiken's mother. "If Keiken has made a good match for himself, then I can hardly complain." She glanced at Girida guiltily. "But it is not right that he has not sent word to us."

"Perhaps the little coward does not dare," grumbled Girida's mother. To Girida she said, "We have a distant relative whom, I heard, married recently. She is a daughter of a concubine of a former emperor and so she is sometimes called the Wisteria Princess. Perhaps it is she who took Keiken away, or she might know who did. Do you want to go ask her?"

Girida nodded.

Girida's mother brought out a set of fine, if out of fashion, winter kimonos that she had been saving. "Wear these and at least no one will laugh at you."

Girida obediently put them on, and several pairs of tabi

socks to wear under her clogs, and then set out through the snowy streets, to the address her mother gave her. The snow fell thicker and thicker and there were very few people out on the streets. Sometimes Girida had to find her way by feeling along the stone walls surrounding the great mansions in the Palace District. At last she came to the intersection of streets where the mansion she sought was supposed to be. She went to the first large gate she saw and pounded on it with her little fist.

The head of a guard appeared over the gate, his helmet comically piled with snow. "Who is there?"

"If you please, sir," said Girida, bowing respectfully, "is this the residence of a lady called the Wisteria Princess?"

"It is. Who wants to know?"

"I am Girida, no one of importance. But I believe my friend Keiken is the man she just married. I bring him a message from his mother."

"Give it to me, then."

"If you please, I should like to speak with him myself."

The samurai laughed. "If you are no one of importance, then there is no one inside you are worthy to speak to. Go away." His head disappeared behind the gate again.

Girida sighed heavily. Her feet were very cold and she stamped them. Then she turned to begin her walk home again—and gasped as a dark figure appeared, standing beside her.

"Your pardon, sir," said Girida, bowing again. "I did not see you there."

"That is quite all right."

The Lady of the Ice Garden

Girida glanced up. It was an elderly monk in black robes with a big nose who spoke to her. "Your pardon, holy one," she said with even more respect.

"It is terrible weather for a young girl like you to be out. Is anything the matter? Can I be of assistance?"

Girida said, "I do not think so. I thought that my lifelong friend Keiken might be here at this mansion. We have not heard from him in a long time and his mother and I wish to know if he is well. But even if he is here, it is not possible for me to see him. I am not of sufficient importance to get in."

"There is always a way around trouble," said the monk, with a knowing smile. "There is another entrance—the main gate, in fact. Perhaps you can get in that way."

Girida had her doubts but it seemed foolish to return all the way home without trying once more. "If you lead me to it, holy one, I will gratefully follow."

"This way, then." The monk walked away through the snow and Girida had to hurry to keep up with him. She kept her gaze on the dark shapes of his black robes flapping in the snowy wind.

He rounded the corner of the building first, disappearing from sight. When Girida rounded the corner, she nearly bumped into a man wearing the black robes and tall hat of a nobleman of the First Rank. Girida bowed very low. "Forgive me, most noble lord. I thought you were a monk who was just here, or I would have been more polite."

"I am the monk who was just here."

"But——"

"I am a tengu, and I may take any shape I wish."

"A tengu!" Girida had heard of the demons of the mountains who often took the shape of black birds. Now that she looked at the nobleman, his robes and sleeves did seem to billow out behind him as if he had black wings. "Why are you helping me?"

"Fortune is often unkind. Now and then, I like to see that Fortune does not get its way. I hate a predictable world, don't you?"

Girida did not know if she should agree, but she nodded.

"Good." The tengu nobleman strode up to the main gate in the wall and pounded on the doors.

A small panel slid open in the middle of one door and someone peered out. "Who is there?"

"What do you mean, who is there?" cried the tengu in an imperious voice. "What do you mean leaving me out in the snow like this? Here I am a very important visitor and I am treated like a servant. The Wisteria Princess herself will hear of this! Perhaps even the Chancellor!"

"Your pardon, most noble lord!" said the guard on the other side of the gate. The panel slid shut and soon Girida heard the great wooden bolts drawn from behind the doors. The doors were drawn inward with great speed and the tengu strode arrogantly in.

Girida held her sleeves up modestly in front of her face and hurried after the tengu as if she were his servant.

The tengu led her through a side garden where stone lanterns poked out from beneath mounds of snow. It did not look particularly like an ice garden to Girida, but who could say why people gave themselves the names they did?

She followed him up a flight of wooden steps into a building that formed one wing of the Wisteria Princess's mansion. They entered a room, dimly lit with little oil lanterns. The room was filled with painted folding screens, depicting men on horses hunting wild boar with spears and arrows and noblewomen in fine carriages watching the hunters. The tengu nobleman picked up an oil lamp and carried it along with him. By its flickering light, the painted hunters seemed to follow them, their horses galloping from screen to screen.

"O most noble sir," said Girida, frightened, "the screens seem to be coming to life."

"Do not worry," said the tengu. "They are only dreams. The princess hires a court painter to capture them on paper. The dreams can run from panel to panel but they can never escape. Rather sad, when you think about it."

Girida preferred not to think about it and held up her sleeves on either side of her face so that she did not have to gaze on the desperate, rushing dreams. She followed the tengu into the next chamber, which was hung with silk tapestries the color of cherry blossoms. Each banner was embroidered with wisteria blooms, in purple, blue, and white. "It is her favorite flower," said the tengu, as if reading Girida's thoughts. "Wisteria represents the impermanence of beauty. Shows wisdom on the part of the princess, I would say."

Girida merely thought it sad and gladly hurried on to the next room. There she saw a grand dais carved in the shape of an enormous lotus blossom. In the center lay two people sleeping.

One had very long hair, whom she presumed to be the

princess. The other had hair tied up in a topknot, and Girida was certain this must be Keiken.

She rushed to his side and gently shook his shoulder. "Keiken! Keiken! It is me, Girida."

The young man rolled over and gazed at her. It was not Keiken. "Who are you?" he asked sleepily. "Are you one of the dreams?"

The princess also rolled over, and regarded her, but the princess did not seem to be disturbed or angry. "Who are you? This is an awkward place to receive visitors."

Girida blushed with deep embarrassment and bowed low. "I beg your pardon, noble ones. I am called Girida, and I am a distant relative of yours. I have come looking for my dear friend Keiken who has disappeared. He has sent no message to his mother to tell her where he has gone. I have heard only that he is with the Lady of the Ice Garden. I came hoping he was here, or that you might know what this means."

"What an ill-mannered wretch," said the prince who was not Keiken, "that he should not tell his mother where he has gone."

"I do not know of such a lady," said the princess, brushing her long hair back from her face, "but if there is such a one, she must live in the mountains to the north. Only there could an ice garden last any length of time. Perhaps the monks of Kuramadera know of her. As you are a cousin who has fallen on bad fortune, it would be heartless of me not to help you. Let me lend to you my palanquin and my guards so that you may make a pilgrimage to Kuramadera."

Girida bowed very low again. "You are most kind. I doubt

that I could ever repay you sufficiently." She turned to thank the tengu also, but he seemed to have disappeared.

The princess waved her hand dismissively. "Is it not said that sympathy in the heart brings benevolence in life? Come, let us get you ready, for I am sure you are eager to leave at once."

And so Girida was fed a fine meal of rice and fish and pickled vegetables. She was given the most fashionable winter kimonos to put on—white shading to blue at the hem, with the outermost kimono bearing a pattern of cranes taking flight. She was led to an elegant wicker palanquin—a large basket, really, hung from two poles. She glanced in and saw the palanquin was full of soft cushions. Eight burly samurai in full armor of iron plates laced with purple silk cords stood ready to take up the wooden beams of the palanquin. The princess gave Girida a box full of rice cakes and pickled plums to eat along the way.

Full of gratitude and hope, Girida again thanked the princess and got into the palanquin, closing the little wicker door behind her. She felt the men take up the carrying poles and they set out upon her journey.

Kuramadera was only a few hours' travel from Heian Kyo by foot, and so Girida expected they would reach the monastery only shortly after dark. She dozed happily on the cushions as the palanquin swung gently to and fro beneath the poles, in rhythm with the marching of the warriors.

Girida was jolted awake suddenly as the palanquin crashed to the ground. She heard the warriors draw their swords, and then heard the humming of arrows. There were screams from the samurai and shouts and the clashing of metal against metal. Girida drew her knees up to her chest, very afraid.

In a way, the noise went on too long. In a way, it was over too soon. The little wicker door in the palanquin opened, and a strange, ugly face peered in. "Well, what have we here?"

Strong arms reached in and dragged Girida out of the palanquin. She screamed and kicked and shouted, "Leave me alone! The Wisteria Princess will hear of this!" But only rough laughter greeted her complaints. Her outer kimonos were torn off her, leaving her standing, shivering, in only her innermost robe.

Men with torches stood around her, their hair unbound, their garments dirty and frayed. Robbers, clearly. These were known to haunt the forests north of Heian Kyo, sometimes even venturing into the capital itself. This was why the princess had sent warriors to carry the palanquin. But now the samurai lay dead at Girida's feet.

One of the robbers, an old woman with her gray hair done up in a warrior's topknot, walked up to Girida and looked her over sourly. "What a useless bit of fluff this is," the woman robber growled. "She brings no horses or oxen to eat. Looks like we'll have to eat her instead." She drew a knife from out of her obi and pointed it at Girida's neck.

But suddenly something like a monkey jumped on the old woman's back, grabbing her arm. "No, no! Let me keep her! I always wanted a sister, a playmate. Don't kill her!" It leaned forward and bit the old woman's ears.

The old woman cried, "Ow! Ow! Oh, very well, you wicked child. Why is it I can refuse you nothing? Go on, then. We'll find something else to eat."

The creature scrambled off the old woman's back and ran up to stand nearly nose-to-nose with Girida. It was a girl, about Girida's height and age, but her skin was sun-browned and when she smiled Girida could see she was missing teeth. "Hello! Hello!" cried the robber girl. "I am Arai, and you are mine now." Arai grabbed Girida's wrist and dragged her back into the palanquin, squeezing in with her.

Girida was so afraid that she went along with the girl without struggle. Inside the palanquin, she huddled in one corner and silently watched.

The robber girl Arai rolled about on the cushions and beat her fists on the sides of the palanquin. "Carry us! Carry us!" she commanded the robbers outside. To Girida's surprise, the palanquin was hoisted into the air and again she was on her way to . . . somewhere.

Arai caught sight of the lacquered box and exclaimed, "What is this! Some overlooked riches?" She knocked the top off and gasped. "Rice cakes! And some . . . withered things."

"They're pickled plums," said Girida, morosely. "They are much prized at Court."

"Then we will eat like emperors!" said Arai. She stuffed a rice cake into her mouth and held the box out to Girida.

Girida shook her head. She was too afraid to be hungry.

"All the more for me, then," said Arai, and she finished the entire box of rice cakes and plums herself.

Girida was astonished that the robber girl was so rude as to not share any with her mother or the other robbers. But Girida did not wish to anger her—after all, Arai had saved her life, and so she said nothing.

At last the palanquin was again set down and the girls were

ordered out. Arai went first and pulled Girida out after her by the sleeve. As Girida emerged from the wicker basket she had to rub her eyes to believe what she saw.

At first it looked like a giant bush with fires burning within it. Girida blinked and saw it was a very high wall made of sticks and leaves and thorns. During the day, it would surely look like just another part of the forest.

"Come on!" cried Arai, and she pulled Girida by the arm toward the stick wall. They followed the rest of the robbers through a low opening in the wall and emerged into a torchlit clearing surrounded by little domes made of bent tree branches covered with bark. Robbers were sitting around the clearing, haggling over the clothing and weapons they had stolen off the bodies of the samurai who had accompanied Girida.

Arai pulled Girida into a little opening in the twig wall and Girida found herself in what seemed like an animal's den. The floor was lined with fox and bear skins. Bones and tiny skulls hung from overhead on silken threads. By the far wall, to Girida's surprise, stood a small red deer tethered by a leather collar to a stake in the floor. The deer stared at them and whickered but did not move.

"This is my place," said Arai. With a wave of her hand she set the bones overhead to clacking like wind chimes. "I am the Princess of Bandits."

She went over to the little deer and put her arm around its neck. The deer tried to sidle away but was trapped between Arai and the wall. "This is Beni. I caught him in the woods and now he is mine." She drew a knife from her belt and caressed the deer's neck with the blade. The deer's eyes showed white as it stared at her in terror. "I do this every night," Arai said, grinning. "He is so frightened. Isn't it delicious?"

Girida did not find it pleasant at all. She wished she could free the deer but such an action did not seem wise at the moment.

Arai came back over to her, put an arm around her shoulders, and put the knife blade against Girida's neck. "And I found you in the woods and now you are mine. I order you to tell me everything about yourself. Why were you so foolish as to come into our forest?"

Girida swallowed hard. The knife blade was cold against the skin of her neck, like ice. Wondering if she might live or die by her answer, Girida told Arai of Keiken and her search for the Lady of the Ice Garden. Arai listened with intent eyes.

"But this is a wondrous story!" cried Arai when Girida was finished. "I have never been part of a story like this. I have only been part of stories about robbing and killing and chopping people up and eating them. You must let me help you!" Arai took the knife away from Girida's neck and grabbed her sleeve. She pulled Girida roughly out of her hut and back across the open space where the robbers sat beside their cooking fires.

Girida tried not to make eye contact with the rough men, who were staring at her hungrily. Given what Arai had said about chopping and eating people, Girida couldn't be sure they weren't sizing her up for their next meal.

Arai led her to a tiny round hut made of pine branches. Dim light flickered just beyond the cloth-covered doorway. Arai stopped and grabbed Girida's shoulders. "Now, remember. You must show my Obaa great respect, even if she is a robber's grandmother. You understand?"

"Of course," said Girida.

Arai pushed aside the cloth curtain and led Girida in. The hut had a floor of flattened earth covered with woven straw mats. On a little wood platform, on tattered silk cushions, knelt an old woman, her eyes half-shut in blindness. Her face was as browned and wrinkled as pickled plums and her hands were so bony they were almost claws. Yet a benevolence seemed to radiate from her, as if her spirit had distanced itself from her horrible offspring and the deterioration of her body.

"This is something new you bring me, Arai-chan," said the old woman. "It smells like a young garden under winter snow."

"Obaa-san," said Arai, "this is Girida, who is from Heian Kyo and is my age. She came into our forest looking for her lost love Keiken, who has gone with the Lady of the Ice Garden. It is such a wonderful story, I have decided we must help her."

"I am most honored to meet you," said Girida to the old woman, bowing even though it would not be seen.

"Bring her closer," said the old woman.

Arai pushed Girida so that she fell to her knees in front of the old woman. The old woman lightly touched Girida's face and hair. At first, Girida dreaded the touch of those hands, but they were so warm and gentle that soon she didn't mind at all.

"You are on a most dangerous journey," said the old woman. "Even if you reach your goal you may very well fail."

"I know that, Obaa-san," said Girida. "But I feel as though I have no other purpose in life."

"Then I suppose you must continue, even though what you feel is not so," said the old woman.

"How can we help her?" asked Arai, eagerly.

"You cannot," said the old woman, a little sharply. "But your pet whom you keep tied up in your hidey-hole can."

"What, Beni? What can my deer do for her?"

"He is not a real deer. If he had been, you never could have caught him. He is a kirin, who was weakened by transforming himself into a deer. Because you placed a leather collar on him, he cannot return to the heavenly realm from which he came. He has been too long now in contact with sin and impurity, living among us. Perhaps if he does a kindness for this girl, he may earn his return to the Higher Paths."

"But . . . then I must lose my Beni?" asked Arai.

"You are coming to an age," said the old woman with a wry smile, "when I am sure you will soon have many more males to torment. Go and fetch him."

Arai bowed awkwardly. "As you wish, Obaa-san. I was becoming bored with him anyway." She departed and for long, awkward moments, Girida knelt with the old woman in silence.

Finally, the old woman said, "Much as it displeases me to say so, you would do well to think more like Arai, child. To devote your thoughts so much to only one thing can only lead to sorrow."

"Nonetheless," said Girida, "it is so."

The old woman sighed. "It is ever thus. I allowed my heart to be stolen by a robber king and see what has happened to me."

Arai returned, leading Beni in by the collar. "Here he is. The ungrateful wretch tried to bite me."

"Do not punish him, child. Take his collar off."

Reluctantly, Arai slipped the collar off of the red deer's

, ,

neck. At once, the deer began to change—its head became more like a dog's or a lion's with long fangs and a wispy beard and mane. Tiny horns sprouted from its forehead. Its tail became more like a donkey's and small flames flickered around its leg joints and shoulders.

"Thank you, kind lady," said the kirin in a flutelike voice, bobbing its head to the old woman. "It takes one of remarkable insight to have discerned my true nature. Surely a place awaits you in my Master's kingdom."

"Not I," said the old woman with a brusque laugh. "My offspring have seen to that. I fear I must endure another turn on the Wheel before I may approach the Pure Land. But if you can help this poor stranger girl who has come among us, you might earn yourself a return."

"To be free of this place I would gladly attempt it. What must I do?"

"Carry her to the northernmost tip of Honshu. There is an Ainu wisewoman there whom I met when I was on a pilgrimage long ago. The wisewoman should be able to help this girl find what she needs."

"Then it is done," said the kirin. So they went outside, the kirin and Arai and Girida. Arai helped Girida get on the kirin's back. Arai was pouting as if she might cry. "Take good care of her, Beni. She's as close to a sister as I ever had."

"Mend your ways," said the kirin to Arai. "May your heart find a more pure path—"

"Don't lecture me," cried the Princess of Bandits, brandishing her knife, "or I will summon my cousins to make a meal of you."

"I am gone," said the kirin and he leaped into the air.

Girida clung tightly to his mane as the kirin cantered over the clouds. The night sky was ablaze with stars and the Bridge arched across the heavens. They flew so fast the wind pulled and tore at her hair and under-robe. She should have been cold, but the flames on the kirin's legs warmed her without burning her. Along the way, Girida talked about Keiken, shouting above the wind into the kirin's ear.

Before long, the kirin alighted on a rocky shore that was lightly dusted with snow. Where the shore met the nearby hills was a single stone hut with smoke drifting out of a hole in the center of its thatched roof.

"Here we are," said the kirin. "Kindly dismount."

Girida slid off his back and together they walked toward the hut. Girida had heard little of the barbarians of the north, the Ainu, and she did not know what to expect. She was almost more afraid of meeting this wisewoman than she had been of the Princess of Bandits.

The kirin knocked at the wooden front door with his fore-hoof and presently it was opened by a short, round woman. She wore a very short cotton kimono, and her bare arms and legs were pale and hairy.

"Oh, it is you," she said to the kirin. "I expected you long ago."

"I was held captive for a time," said the kirin. "Now I bring this girl in hopes that I may be redeemed."

The wisewoman shrugged and stepped away from the door. The kirin entered as if he had been invited, and Girida followed. A great fire filed a stone circle in the center of the hut. Whole fish were roasting on an iron spit slung across the hearth. The hut was very warm and Girida was suddenly glad she was wearing no more than her one layer of kimono.

"This girl," the kirin continued, as if he'd been asked, "needs to find the Lady of the Ice Garden, who has stolen her dear companion."

The wisewoman made a pitying noise as she picked at her teeth with a fish bone. "Poor girl. No man can be stolen by the Lady of the Ice Garden unless he is more than half willing to be taken." She looked at Girida. "If you go there, you will see things that will be saddening, shocking, and painful to you. Will you still make the journey?"

Girida hesitated only a moment. "Yes. I must. My mind has been filled only with Keiken since he left."

"Must be a small mind indeed to be so easily filled," grumbled the wisewoman. "Very well, then." She picked up a dried fish and began to carve a map into it. She held out the fish to the kirin. "The Lady of the Ice Garden has her winter palace here, in the mountains to the west. Now be off with you."

"Wait!" cried the kirin. "If this Lady is so formidable a foe, should Girida not be given more protection? I know you have many potions and amulets and spells. Can't you give her the strength of ten warriors, or a magical dagger, or *something*?"

The wisewoman stared at the kirin a moment, and then laughed and laughed and laughed, her little round belly shaking. "Oh my, oh my, you have not been long in our world, have you? The Lady of The Ice Garden fights battles of the spirit, not of weapons or strength of muscle. This girl already has all the arms and armor she will ever have, within herself.

Whether it will be enough, I cannot say. Oh, wait, there is one thing I can give her." The wisewoman bustled over to a wooden chest from which she pulled a robe made from a bear skin. She waddled over to Girida and said, "Wear this."

Girida shied away. "It . . . is an unclean thing." She glanced uncertainly at the kirin.

The wisewoman sighed. "If you wear it, you will have many more years in which to chant prayers to your blessed Amida for forgiveness. If you freeze to death, you will not."

"It is a small sin," said the kirin, gently, to Girida. "You had better do as she suggests."

So Girida put on the bear-fur robe. They all went outside and the wisewoman hefted Girida onto the kirin's back. "Good fortune to you, child," said the wisewoman. "And you," she said to the kirin, "come back to me as soon as you have dropped her off and I will help you find your way home."

"Then I am gone," said the kirin, joyfully, and he leaped into the air. Again, Girida had to hold on with all her strength as the kirin dashed through the clouds up into the peaks that formed the spine of Honshu. They flew so terrifyingly close to the rocky outcroppings that Girida shut her eyes tight so as not to be frightened by what she saw.

Sooner than she expected, the kirin alighted again on solid ground and stopped. "Here we are. Dismount, please."

Girida opened her eyes and slid off his back. It was very, very cold. Her breath seemed to turn to ice before her face. She pulled the bear-skin robe tightly around herself, glad now that she had accepted the wisewoman's gift.

They were standing at a wall of high, thorned bushes, on

which grew red berries like drops of blood. The torii gateway before them was carved from cherry wood. Battling oni demons were carved into the uprights and the crossbeam.

"I must leave you now," said the kirin. "May you come to know the Amida's blessing." He rubbed his furry cheek against hers a moment and then he sprang into the air, vanishing swiftly into the surrounding mist.

Girida felt very alone. Nonetheless, she had come too far to let fear paralyze her now. She stepped across the floorbeam of the gate and entered the Ice Garden.

It was beautiful, in a strange way. There were lanterns and bridges carved of ice, grazing deer of ice, flowers of ice crystals, pine trees whose needles were ice shards. Enchanted, Girida crossed one of the ice bridges, walking deeper into the garden.

And then she saw the men. Warriors with fierce expressions standing frozen guard. But their armor was formed of slabs of ice and their swords were sharpened icicles. They stared straight ahead, eyes glazed over, facing some unseen foe. Girida tiptoed past them, but it hardly mattered. They took no notice of her. They could not.

Girida walked up ice-carved steps into the palace itself. She entered a grand hall whose pillars were ice, whose floor was ice, whose low tables were ice. In the center of the room stood a young man whose skin was a pale blue.

"Keiken!" cried Girida and she rushed to him. This time it really was Keiken and she opened her arms to embrace him.

"Stay back!" cried Keiken through jaws frozen shut. "Do not touch me!"

Girida staggered back, hurt as if a needle had been driven

into her heart. "But Keiken, it is me, Girida. Your dear friend. Aren't you happy to see me?"

"Why did you come here?" Keiken demanded. "Did I send for you? Did I give you any reason to believe I wanted you to follow me?"

Girida felt hot tears forming in her eyes. "We . . . we were so worried for you. Your mother does not know where you are. I have thought of nothing but you since you left. Don't these things matter to you?"

"Why should they matter?" growled Keiken. "Are such things a man's concern? I contemplate the Vast Emptiness, I celebrate Death, the banishment of fear. I have put pity from my heart and I now look forward to crushing enemies beneath my sandals until only I live to laugh at them. And you dare to come to me sniveling about my mother and your thoughts of me? Hah! I left because I saw what a weak, unworthy creature you are."

The tears began to run down Girida's cheeks, but they were now more tears of anger than of sorrow. She noted that all through his speech, Keiken had not moved. He was frozen in place, becoming like the guardsmen standing out in the garden. For all his brave talk, he was helpless.

Girida rushed up to him and threw her arms around him. She ignored his cries of "What are you doing? Let go of me at once!"

She wept openly on his chest, letting her hot tears flow over his shoulder and down his arm, warming his skin. She felt him begin to move beneath her.

Suddenly, he grabbed her and flung her down to the floor. "What have you done!" he cried, looking down at himself. "I was becoming strong! I was forgetting everything. I had lost my pain. I was feeling nothing. And now you want me to be weak like you. You want me to hurt and cry and need and feel shame and loneliness. I refuse! Do you hear? Don't you see? I was better off frozen. How can you say you care for me when you have ruined me?"

Keiken ran from the room. Girida stood up and watched from the veranda as he dashed into the garden and flung himself onto a frozen pond. But ice only covered the surface, and Keiken was soaked as he fell through. He managed to stagger out again, but the coldness of the air froze him swiftly, until he became as stiff and unmoving as the other guards who stood sentinel against a foe that lay only within.

Girida did not know what to do, then. She began to murmur the Lotus Sutra for him, but was stopped when a hand fell upon her shoulder.

Girida spun around. She saw a woman pale as snow, with long hair as black as night, eyes black as obsidian, dressed in kimonos of the palest blue. "Forgive me for being a poor hostess," said the woman, "but I had been occupied elsewhere. You are Girida, are you not? Keiken spoke your name sometimes, while sleeping."

"Please," begged Girida, "release him. Save him. I will give you anything."

"That is not possible, child. He has always been free to go. It is his choice to remain. But I must thank you, for you have done me a service."

"I have?"

"I search for a companion of the greatest strength and wisdom. Yet you have shown me that Keiken was weak. He rejected knowledge of himself. He was unworthy of me. Or of you." She took a stone from her sleeve and threw it at Keiken. He collapsed into a pile of ice shards on the snow.

Girida gasped, putting her hand to her mouth. "No!"

"They are so easily shattered," sighed the Lady of the Ice Garden. "The willow may look down upon the grass that grows at its roots, yet when the mighty storms blow it is the willow that breaks, not the grass. Go home, Girida. There is nothing for you here. There never was."

"Why do you do this?" Girida demanded.

"I am what I am. Men seek me out. For some reason, in this time and this place, many wish to come to me, believing that to know my embrace is the worthiest achievement. I should be flattered but, as you see, the strongest and wisest do not seek me thus and never will. Therefore I am doomed to be eternally disappointed. But you are not. Go home."

Mist gathered around Girida until her sight was obscured. When it lifted, she was standing outside her mother's hovel. The poor, shoddy place never looked so wonderful.

Years passed and Girida married a humble sandal maker. She learned how to carve the wood and handle the accounting. They had children and she laughed and cried and felt great pain and great joy with her family. When her husband and mother died, Girida put on the robes of a Buddhist nun. She became a scholar and a pilgrim, traveling the length of Honshu and writing down the wondrous things she learned and saw. And when at last she came to the Pure Land and met the kirin once more, she was able to say to him, "I have led a full life, and that has been the greatest blessing of all."

KARA DALKEY, a recent transplant to the Pacific Northwest, began her writing career as a member of the Minneapolis writers group, The Scribblies. She has had fifteen fantasy novels and twelve short stories published to date. Among her recent works are *Genpei*, a historical fantasy novel set in Japan, and *The Water Trilogy*, a YA series, which she describes as "Atlantis and Arthurian myth in a blender." Her hobbies include her two cats, Ultima Online, and playing electric bass guitar in an oldies rock 'n' roll band.

AUTHOR'S NOTE

"The Lady of the Ice Garden" is my take on the famous story "The Snow Queen," by Hans Christian Andersen. Analysts of Andersen's story have said that "The Snow Queen" is about the end of childhood and the beginning of aloof adulthood. They say that Andersen was decrying how the wide-eyed innocence and openness of children are lost as they embrace the alluring but cold-hearted attitudes of grown-ups.

The spark for writing my own version of "The Snow Queen" occurred while I was teaching a course on writing fantasy at Western State College in Gunnison, Colorado. I was explaining to the class how one can take an old story and adapt either the same plot with new themes or same themes but in a new setting. At that time, my most recent novel was *Genpei*, a historical fantasy set at the end of Heian Japan at a period when the peaceful, artistic, aristocratic culture was giving way to the civil wars and samurai warrior culture of the Kamakura period to follow.

In my research into this period, I was struck by how boys as young as twelve or fourteen years old were expected to accompany their fathers and uncles into battle, even to participate in the killing themselves, as their passage to manhood. The way of the samurai warrior is to embrace death, to consider oneself already dead, so that death will not be feared in life, and when it comes it will be no surprise. How strange it seemed that children of that time were expected to strive for such coldness of adulthood. The resonance with the themes of "The Snow Queen" suddenly seemed far more apt than even Andersen could have known.

Others, notably Kelly Link in her story "Travels with the Snow Queen," have dealt with feminist themes they saw in Andersen's tale. After all, it is about a boy who leaves, and a girl who chases after him, asking why. Because of the Late Heian transition from a "feminine" artistic culture to a masculine warrior culture, this reference to the battle of the sexes also made its way into my version.

The best stories are those that can transcend time and culture, those that have meaning and resonances in ages beyond when they were written—even if the new meanings found are far different from those the original author intended. I hope that "The Lady of the Ice Garden" can be seen as tribute to the work of Hans Christian Andersen, one of the best storytellers of any age.

Garth Nix

Hope Chest

One dusty, slow morning in the summer of 1922, a passenger was left crying on the platform when the milk train pulled out of Denilburg after its five-minute stop. No one noticed at first, what with the whistle from the train and the billowing steam and smoke and the labouring of the steel wheels upon the rails. The milk carter was busy with the cans, the stationmaster with the mail. No one else was about, not when the full dawn was still half a cup of coffee away.

When the train had rounded the corner, taking its noise with it, the crying could be clearly heard. Milk carter and stationmaster both looked up from their work and saw the source of the noise.

A baby, tightly swaddled in a pink blanket, was precariously balanced on a large steamer trunk at the very edge of the platform. With every cry and wriggle, the baby was moving closer to the side of the trunk. If she fell, she'd fall not only from the trunk, but from the platform, down to the rails four feet below.

The carter jumped over his cans, knocking two down, his heels splashing in the spilt milk. The stationmaster dropped his sack, letters and packets cascading out to meet the milk.

They each got a hand under the baby at the very second it rolled off the trunk. Both men went over the edge of the platform, and they trod on each other's feet as they landed, hard and painful—but upright. The baby was perfectly balanced between them.

That's how Alice May Susan Hopkins came to Denilburg, and that's how she got two unrelated uncles with the very same first name, her Uncle Bill Carey the stationmaster and her Uncle Bill Hoogener, the milk carter.

The first thing the two Bills noticed when they caught the baby was a note pinned to the pink blanket. It was on fine ivory paper, the words in blue-black ink that caught the sun and glinted when you held it just so. It said:

"Alice May Susan, born on the Summer Solstice, 1921. Look after her and she'll look after you."

It didn't take long for the news of Alice May Susan's arrival to get around the town, and it wasn't more than fifteen minutes later that fifty percent of the town's grown women were all down at the station, the thirty-eight of them clustering around that poor baby enough to suffocate her. Fortunately it was only a few minutes more till Eulalie Falkirk took charge, as she always did, and established a roster for hugging and kissing and gawking and fussing and worrying and gossiping over the child.

Over the next few months that roster changed to include actually looking after little Alice May Susan. She was handed from one married woman to the next, changing her surname from month to month as she went from family to family. She was a dear little girl, everyone said, and Eulalie Falkirk was hard put to decide who should adopt the child.

Her final decision came down to one simple thing. While all the womenfolk had been busy with the baby, most of the menfolk had been taking their turn trying to open up that steamer trunk.

The trunk looked easy enough. It was about six feet long, three feet wide and two feet high. It had two leather straps around it and an old brass lock, the kind with a keyhole big enough to put your whole finger in. Only no one did after Torrance Yib put his in and it came back with the tip missing, cut off clean as you please right at the joint.

The straps wouldn't come undone either, and whatever they were, it wasn't any leather anyone in Denilburg had ever seen. It wouldn't cut and it wouldn't tear and those straps drove everyone who tried them mad with frustration.

There was some talk of devilment and foreign magic, till Bill Carey—who knew more about luggage than the rest of the town put together—pointed out the brass plate on the underside that read "Made in the U.S.A. Imp. Pat. Pend. Burglar-proof trunk." Then everyone was proud and said it was scientific progress and what a pity it was the name of the company had got scratched off, for they'd get some good business in Denilburg if only they knew where to send their orders.

The only man in the whole town who hadn't tried to open the trunk was Jake Hopkins the druggist, so when Stella

Hopkins said they'd like to take baby Alice May Susan on, Eulalie Falkirk knew it wasn't because they wanted whatever was in the trunk.

So Alice May Susan joined the Hopkins household and grew up with Jake and Stella's born daughters Janice, Jessie and Jane, who at the time were ten, eight and four. The steamer trunk was put in the attic and Alice May Susan, to all intents and purposes, became another Hopkins girl. No one out of the ordinary, just a typical Denilburg girl, the events of her life pretty much interchangeable with the sisters who had gone before her.

Until the year she turned sixteen, in 1937.

Of her three sisters, only Jane was at home that birthday, enjoying a vacation. Janice and Jessie had married up and left, both of them now living more than twenty miles away. Jane was different. She'd won a scholarship that had taken her off to college back east where she'd got all sort of ideas. One of them involved criticizing everything Alice May Susan did or said, and counting the days till she could get on the train out of town and back to what she called "civilization."

"You'd better study harder so you have a chance to get away from this place," said Jane, as they sat on the porch eating birthday cake and watching the world go by. None of it had gone by yet, unless you counted the Prowell's cat.

"I like it here," said Alice May. "Why would I want to leave?"

"Because there's nothing here!" protested Jane. "Nothing! No life, no colour, no . . . events! Nothing ever happens. Everyone just gets married, has children and it starts all over again. There's no romance in anything or anyone!"

"Not everyone gets married," replied Alice May, after a short pause to swallow a too-large bite of cake.

"Gwennifer Korben, you mean," said Jane. "She's a schoolmistress. Everyone knows they're always spinsters. You don't want to be a schoolmistress."

"Maybe I do," answered Alice May. She spun her cake fork into a silver blur and snatched it handle first out of the air.

"Do you really?" asked Jane, momentarily shocked. "A schoolmistress!"

Alice May frowned and threw the cake fork into the wall. It stuck, quivering, next to the tiny holes in the wood that showed several years of practice in the gentle art of cake fork throwing.

"I don't know," she said. "I do feel . . . I do feel that I want to be something. I just don't know what it is."

"Study," said Jane firmly. "Work hard. Go to college. Education is the only way for a woman to have her own life."

Alice May nodded, to avoid further discussion. It was her birthday and she felt hot and bothered, rather than happy. The cake was delicious and they'd had a very pleasant lunch with her family and some friends from school. But her birthday somehow felt unfinished and incomplete. There was something that she had to do, but she didn't know what it was. Something more immediate than deciding her future life.

It didn't take more than two hours in the rocking chair on the porch to work out what it was she needed to do, and wait for the right moment to do it.

The steamer trunk. It had been a long time since she'd

even looked at it. Over the years she'd tried it many times, alone and in company. There had been times when she'd gone up to the attic every day to test if by some chance it had come undone. There'd been times when she'd forgotten about it for months. But no matter what, she always found herself making an attempt to open it on her birthday.

Even when she forgot about opening it, the trunk's brooding presence stayed with her. It was a reminder that she was not exactly as the other Hopkins girls. Sometimes that was pleasant, but more often not, particularly as she had got older.

Alice May sighed, and decided to give it yet another try. It was evening by then, and somewhat cooler. She picked up her lantern, trimmed the wick down a little and went inside.

"Trunk?" asked her foster father Jake, as she went through the kitchen. He was preserving lemons, the careful practice of his drugstore carried over to the culinary arts. No one else in Denilburg preserved lemons, or would know what to do with them once they were preserved.

"Trunk?" asked Stella, who was sewing in the drawing room.

"Trunk?" asked Jane on the stairs, as Alice May passed her. "Trunk?"

"Of course, the trunk!" snapped Alice May. She pulled down the attic ladder angrily and climbed up.

It was a very clean attic, in a very clean house. There was only the trunk in it, up against the small window that was letting in the last of the hot summer sun. A red glow shone on the brass lock and the lustrous leather straps.

Alice May was still angry. She set the lantern down, grabbed a strap and pulled. When it came loose, she fell over backwards and hit her head on the floor. The sound it made echoed through the house. There was a noticeable pause, then three voices carried up in chorus.

"Are you all right?"

"Yes!" shouted Alice May, angrier still. She wrenched at the other strap and it came loose too, though this time she was ready for it. At the same time, the brass lock went "click." It wasn't the sort of click that was so soft you could think you might have imagined it. This was a slow, drawn-out click, as if mighty metal gears were slowly turning over.

The lid of the trunk eased up half an inch.

Alice May whispered, "It's open."

She reached forward and lifted the lid a little further. It moved easily, the hinges free, as if they'd just been oiled.

"It's open!" screeched Alice May. "The trunk is open!"

The sound of a mad scramble below assured her that everyone had heard her this time. Before they could get there, Alice May pushed the lid completely back. Her brow furrowed as she looked at what lay within. All her life she had been waiting to open this trunk, both dreading and hoping that she would find some clue to the mystery of her birth and arrival in Denilburg. Papers, letters, perhaps a family Bible.

Nothing of that kind was obvious. Instead, clipped into the back wall of the trunk there was a lever-action rifle, an old one, with a deeply-polished stock of dark wood and an octagonal barrel of dark blue steel chased with silver flowers.

Underneath it were two holstered revolvers. Big weapons, their barrels were also engraved in silver with the flower motif, which was repeated on the holsters, though not in silver, but black thread, somber on the leather. A belt with bullet loops was folded up and pinned between the holsters. More dark leather, more flowers in black thread.

On the left side of the trunk, there was a teak box with the word "Ammunition" burnt into the lid in slim pokerwork.

On the right side, there was a jewelry case of deep purple velvet plush.

Underneath the ammunition box and the jewelry case, along the bottom of the trunk, there was a white dress laid out flat. Alice May stared at the strange combination of cowgirl outfit and bridal gown, cut from the finest, whitest shot silk, with the arms and waistcoat—it had a waistcoat—sewn with lines of tiny pearls. It looked a little big for Alice May, particularly in the region of the bust. It was also indecently short, for either wedding dress or cowgirl outfit. It probably wouldn't go much below her knees.

"A Winchester '73," said Jake behind her, pointing at the rifle. He didn't make any attempt to reach forward and touch them. "And two Colt .44s. Peacemakers, I think. Like the one my grandfather had, above the mantelpiece in the old house."

"Weird," said Jane, pushing her father so he moved to allow herself and Stella up.

"What's in the jewelry box?" asked Stella. She spoke in a hushed tone, as if she were in the temple. Alice May looked around and saw that Jake, Stella and Jane were all clustered around the top of the ladder, as if they didn't want to come any closer.

Alice May reached in to the trunk and picked up the jewelry case. As she touched the velvet, she felt a strange, electric thrill pass through her. It wasn't unpleasant, and she felt it again as she opened the case. A frisson of excitement that ran through her whole body, from top to toe.

The case held a metal star. A sheriff's badge, or something in the shape of one, anyway, though there was nothing engraved upon it. The star was shinier than any lawman's badge Alice May had ever seen, a bright silver that picked up the red sunlight and intensified and purified it, till it seemed that she held an acetylene light in her hand, a blinding light that forced her to look away and flip it over.

The light faded, leaving black spots dancing in front of her eyes. Alice May saw there was a pin on the back of the star, but again there was nothing engraved where she had hoped to see a name.

Alice May put the star back in the case and closed it, letting out the breath she didn't know she'd held. A loud exhalation from behind told her that the rest of her family had been holding their breaths as well.

Next she slid the rifle from the straps that held it in place. It felt strangely right in her hands, and without conscious thought she worked the action, checked the chamber was empty and dry-fired it. A second later she realised she didn't know what she'd done, and at the same time, that she could do it again, and more. She could load and fire the weapon, and strip and clean it too. It was all in her head, even though she'd only ever fired one firearm in her life before, and that was just her Uncle Bill's single-shot squirrel gun.

She put the rifle back and took down the twin revolvers.

They were heavy, but again she instinctively knew their weight and heft, loaded or unloaded. She put the revolvers, still holstered, across her lap. The flower pattern on the barrels seemed to move and flow as she stared at them, and the herringbone cut on the grip swung from one angle to another. The grips were some sort of bone, Alice May realised, stained dark. Or perhaps they were ebony, and had never been stained.

She drew one of the revolvers, and once again her hands moved without conscious thought. She swung the cylinder out, spun it, checked it was empty, slapped it back again, cocked and released the hammer under control and had it back in the holster almost before her foster family could blink.

Alice May put the revolvers back. She didn't even look at the box with the pokerwork "Ammunition" on it. She closed the trunk firmly. The lock clicked again, and she rapidly did up the straps. Then she turned to her family.

"Best if we don't mention this around . . ." she started to say. Then she saw the way they were looking at her. A look that was part confusion, part awe, and part fear.

"That star . . ." said Jake.

"So bright," said Stella.

"Your hands . . . a blur . . ." said Jane.

"I don't want it!" burst out Alice May. "I'm not . . . it's not me! I'm Alice May Susan *Hopkins*!"

She pushed past Jane and almost fell down the ladder in her haste to get away. The others followed more slowly. Alice May had already run to her room, and they all could hear her sobbing.

Jake went back to the kitchen and his preserved lemons.

Stella went back to her sewing. Jane went to Alice May's door, but turned aside at the last second, and went downstairs to write a letter to a friend about how nothing ever, ever happened in Denilburg.

When Alice May came down to breakfast the next morning, after a night of no sleep, the others were bright and cheerful. When Alice May tentatively tried to talk about what had happened, it became clear that the others had either no memory of what they had seen or were actively denying it.

Alice May did not forget. She saw the silver star shining in her dreams, and often woke with the feel of the rifle's stock against her cheek, or the harsh weight of the holstered revolvers on her thighs.

With the dreams came a deep sense of dread. Alice May knew that the weapons and the star were some sort of birthright, and with them came the knowledge that someday they were to be used. She feared that day, and could not imagine who . . . or what . . . she was supposed to shoot. Sometimes the notion that she might have to kill a fellow human being scared her more than anything. At other times she was more terrified by a strange notion that whatever she would ultimately face would not be human.

A year passed, and summer came again, hotter and drier than ever before. The spring planting died in the fields, and with the small seedlings went the hopes of both the farmers of Denilburg and the townsfolk who depended on the farmers making money.

At the same time, a large number of apparently solid banks went under. It came as a surprise, particularly since they'd weathered the credit famine of '30 and the bursting of the tantalum bubble two years previously. The bank crash was accompanied by a crisis of confidence in the currency, as the country shifted from gold and silver to aluminum and copper-nickel coins that had no intrinsic value.

One of the banks that failed was the Third National Faith, the bank which held most of the meager savings of Denilburg's residents. Alice May found out about it when she came home from school, to discover Stella weeping and Jake white-faced in the kitchen, mechanically chopping what might have once been a pumpkin.

For a while it looked like they'd lose the drugstore, but Janice's husband had kept a highly-illegal store of double eagles, the ones with the Dowager Empress's head on them. Selling them to a "licensed coin collector" brought in just enough to pay the Hopkins's debts and keep the store a going concern.

Jane had to leave college though. Her scholarship was adversely affected by inflation, and Jake and Stella couldn't afford to give her anything. Everyone expected her to come home, but she didn't. Instead she wrote to say that she had a job, a good job with a great future.

It took a few more months and a few letters before it turned out that Jane's job was with a political organization called the Servants of the State. She sent a tonatype of herself in the black uniform with the firebrand badges and armband. Jake and Stella didn't put it up on the mantelpiece with the shots from her sisters' lives.

The arrival of Jane's tonatype coincided with Alice May—

and everyone else—spending a lot more time thinking about the Servants. They'd seemed a harmless enough group for many years. Just another right-wing, bigoted, reactionary pseudo-military political organization with a few seats in Congress and a couple of very minor advisory positions at the Palace.

But by the time Jane joined the party, things had changed. The Servants had found a new leader somewhere, a man they called the Master. He looked ordinary enough in the newspapers, a short man with a peculiar beard, a long forelock and staring eyes. He had some resemblance to the kineto comedian Harry Hopalong, who favored the same sort of over-trimmed goatee—but the Master wasn't funny.

The Master clearly had some charisma that could not be captured by the tonatype process or reproduced in print. He toured the country constantly and wherever he appeared, he swayed local politicians, the important businesspeople and most of the ordinary population. Mayors left their political parties and joined the Servants. Oil and tantalum barons gave large donations. Professors wrote essays supporting the economic theories of the Master. Crowds thronged to cheer and worship at the Master's progress.

Everywhere the Servants grew in popularity, there were murders and arson. Opponents of the Servants died. Minorities of every kind were persecuted, particularly the First People and followers of the major heresies. Even orthodox temples whose Haruspices did not agree that fortune favored the Servants were burned to the ground.

Neither harassment, beatings, murder, arson or rape were

properly investigated when they were done by, or in the name of, the Servants. Or if they were, matters never successfully came to trial, in either State or Imperial Courts. Local police left the Servants to their own devices.

The Emperor, now a very old man roosting in the palace at Washington, did nothing. People wistfully spoke of his glory days, leading hilltop charges and shooting bears. But that was long ago and he was senile, or close to it, and the Crown Prince was almost terminally lazy, a genial buffoon who could not be stirred into any sort of action.

Off in Denilburg, Alice May was largely insulated from what was going on elsewhere. But even in that small, sleepy town, she saw the rise of the Servants. The two shops belonging to what the Servants called Others—pretty much anyone who wasn't white and a regular worshipper—had red firebrands painted across their windows and lost most of their customers. In other towns their owners would have been beaten, or tarred and feathered, but it hadn't yet come to that in Denilburg.

People Alice May had known all her life talked about the International Other Conspiracy and how they were to blame for the bank failures, the crop failures and all other failures—particularly their own failures in the everyday business of life.

The fact that something really serious was happening came home to Alice May the day that her Uncle Bill Carey walked past dressed not in his stationmaster's green and blue, but the Servants' black and red. Alice May went out in to the street to ask him what on earth he thought he was doing. But when she stopped in front of him, she saw a strange vacancy in his eyes.

It was not the Bill Carey she had known all her life. Instinctively she knew that something had happened to him, that the adopted uncle she knew and loved had been changed, his natural humanity driven deep inside him and overlaid by something horrible and poisonous.

"Praise the Master," snapped Bill as Alice May looked at him. His hand crawled up to his shoulder and then snapped across his chest in the Servants' knife-chop salute.

He didn't say anything else. His strange eyes stared into the distance until Alice May stepped aside. He strode off as she rushed inside to be sick.

Later she learned that he had been to Jarawak City, the state capital, the day before. He had seen the Master speak, out of curiosity, as had a number of other people from Denilburg. All of them had come back as committed Servants.

Alice May tried to talk to Jake and Stella about Bill, but they wouldn't listen. They were afraid to discuss the Servants, and they would not accept that anything had been done to Bill. As far as they were concerned he'd simply decided to ride with the tide.

"When times are tough, people'll believe anything that puts the blame somewhere," said Jake. "Bill Carey's a good man, but his paycheck hasn't kept up with inflation. I guess he's only just been holding on for some time, and that Master gave him hope, somehow."

"Hope laced with hatred," snapped Alice May. She still felt sick to the very bottom of her stomach at seeing Bill in his Servant's uniform. It was even worse than the tonatype of Jane. More real, more immediate. It was wrong, wrong, wrong.

A knock at the door stopped the conversation. Jake and Stella exchanged frightened looks. Alice May frowned, angry that her foster parents could be made afraid by such a simple thing as a knock at the door. They would never have flinched before. She went to open it like a whirlwind, rushing down the hall so fast she knocked the portrait of Stella's grandsire onto the floor. Glass shattered and the frame broke in two.

There was no one outside, but a notice had been pushed half under the door. Alice May picked it up, saw the black and red and the flaming torch and stormed back inside, slamming the door behind her.

"The Master's coming here! This afternoon!" she exclaimed, waving the paper in front of her. "On a special train. He's going to speak from it."

She put her finger against the bottom line.

"It says, 'Everyone must attend,'" she said grimly. "As if we don't have a choice who we listen to."

"We'd better go," muttered Stella. Jake nodded.

"What!" screamed Alice May. "He's only a politician! Stay at home."

Jake shook his head. "No. No. I've heard about what happens if you don't go. There's the store to think about."

"And my grandsire was a Cheveril—an accommodater," Stella said quietly. She looked down at the splintered glass and the smashed painting. "We mustn't give them a reason to look into the family. We must be there."

"I'm not going," announced Alice May.

"You are while you live in this house," snapped Jake, in a rare display of temper. "I'll not have all our lives and livelihood risked for some silly girl's fancies."

"I am not going," repeated Alice May. She felt strangely calm, obviously much calmer than Jake, whose face was flushed with sudden heat, or Stella, who had gone deathly pale.

"Then you'd better get out altogether," said Jake fiercely. "Go and find your real parents."

Stella cried out as he spoke, and clutched at his arm, but she didn't speak.

Alice May looked at the only parents she had ever known. She felt as if she was in a kinetoplay, with all of them trapped by the script. There was an inevitability in Jake's words, but he seemed as surprised to say them as she was to hear them. She saw a terror deep in his eyes, and shame. He was already afraid at what he was becoming, afraid of the place his fears were driving him toward.

"I'll go and pack," she said, her voice dull to her own ears. It was not the real Jake who had spoken, she knew. He was a timid man. He did not know how to be brave, and anger was his only escape from acknowledging his cowardice.

Alice May didn't pack. She stopped by her room to pick up a pair of riding boots and then went up to the attic. She opened the trunk, breathing a sigh of relief as the straps and lock gave no resistance. She took out the box marked "Ammunition" and set it on the floor, and placed the holstered revolvers and the belt next to the box.

Then she stripped down to her underclothes and put on the white dress. It fitted her perfectly, as she knew it would. She had grown in the year since her first sight of the dress, enough that two undone shirt buttons could derail the trains

of thought and conversation of most of the boys she knew—
and some of the men.

This dress was not low cut, but it hugged her breasts and
waist before flaring out, and it was daringly short at an inch
below her knees. The waistcoat that went over it was also tai-
lored to show off her figure. Strangely, it appeared to be lined
with woven strands of hair. Blonde hair, that was an identical
shade to her own.

The dress, even with the waistcoat, was cold to the touch,
as if it had come out of an ice chest. The temperature outside
had forced the mercury out the top of the old thermometer by
the kitchen door, and it was stifling in the attic. Alice May
wasn't even warm.

She strapped on the revolvers next. The gun belt rested on
her hips, with the holsters lower, against her thighs. She found
that the silk was double-lined there, to guard against wear,
and there were small ties to fix the snout of each holster to her
dress.

The ammunition box opened easily. It held a dozen smaller boxes of blue tin. Alice May was somehow not surprised by
the descriptions, which were handwritten on pasted labels. Six
of the boxes were labeled "Colt .45 Fourway Silver Cross" and
six "Winchester 44-40 Silvercutter."

She opened a tin of the .45 Fourway Silver Cross. The
squat brass cartridges were topped with lead bullets, but each
had four fat lines of silver crossed across the top. Alice May
knew it was real silver. The 44-40 cartridges looked similar,
but the bullets were either solid silver or silver over a core of
lead.

Alice May quickly loaded both revolvers and then the rifle, and filled the loops on her belt with a mixture of both cartridges. Instinctively she knew which ammunition to use in each weapon, and she put the .45 Silver Cross cartridges only on the left of the eagle buckle, and the .44-40 only on the right.

Even with the rifle temporarily laid on the floor, the revolvers and the laden bullet belt came to quite a load, heavy on her hips and thighs.

There was still one thing left in the trunk. Alice May picked up the jewelry case and opened it. The star was dull till she touched it, but it began to shine as she pinned it on. It was heavy too, heavier than it should have been, and her knees buckled a little as the pin snapped in.

Alice May stood absolutely still for a moment, breathing slowly, taking the weight that was as much imagined as real. The light of her star slowly faded with each breath, till it was no more than a bright piece of metal reflecting the sun. Everything felt lighter then. Revolvers, belt, star—and her own spirits.

She closed the trunk, sat on it, and pulled on her boots. Then she picked up the rifle and climbed down the ladder.

No one was downstairs. The broken glass and picture frame were still on the floor, in total contradiction of Stella's nature and habit. The painting itself was gone.

Alice May let herself out the back way and quickly crossed the street to her Uncle Bill's house. The other Uncle Bill, Bill Hoogener. The milk carter. She wanted to talk to him before she did . . . whatever she was going to do.

HOPE CHEST

It was unusually quiet on the street. A hot breeze blew, throwing up dust devils that whirled on the fringes of the graveled road. No one was outside. There were no children playing. No one was out walking, driving or riding. There was only the hot wind and Alice May's boots crunching gravel as she walked the hundred yards diagonally down the street to the Hoogener house.

She stopped at the picket fence. There was a red firebrand splashed across the partly-open door, the paint still wet and dripping. Alice May's hands worked the lever of her rifle without conscious thought and she pushed the door open with the toe of her boot.

The coolness of her dress was spreading across her skin, only it was colder now, a definite chill. Bill, as his surname gave away, was a descendent of Oncers, even if he wasn't practicing himself. The Servants reserved a special hatred for the monotheistic Oncers.

Everything in the hall had been broken. All of Bill's paintings of the town and its people, a lifetime of work, were smashed upon the floor. The wire umbrella stand had been wrenched apart, and the sticks and umbrellas it contained used as clubs to pummel the plasterboard. It was full of gaping holes, the wallpaper flapping around them like torn skin.

There was blood on the floor. Lots of blood, a great dark ocean of it close by the door, and then smaller pools leading back in to the house. A bloody handprint by the kitchen door showed where someone—no, not someone, Alice May thought, but Bill, her Uncle Bill—had leaned for support.

She stepped through the wreckage, colder still, colder than

she had ever been. Her eyes moved slowly from side to side, the rifle barrel with its silver flowers following her gaze. Her finger was flat and straight against the trigger guard, an instant away from the trigger, a shot, a death.

Uncle Bill was in the kitchen. He was sitting with his back against the stove, his skin pale, almost translucent against the yellow enamel of the oven door. His eyes were open, and impossibly clear, the white whiter than any milk he had ever carted, but his once bright blue pupils were dulling into black, black as the undersized bow tie which hung on his chest, the elastic broken.

His mouth was open, a gaping, formless hole. It took Alice May a moment to realize that his tongue had been cut out.

From his waist down, Bill's usually immaculate whites were black, sodden, totally saturated with blood. It still dripped from him slowly, into the patch under his legs. Someone had used that same blood to paint a clumsy firebrand symbol on the floor, and two words. But the blood had spread and joined in the letters, so it was impossible to read whatever Bill's murderers had intended. The firebrand was enough, in any case, for the death to be claimed by the Servants.

Alice May stared at her dead uncle, thinking terrible thoughts. There were no strangers in town. She would know the murderers. She could see it so easily. The men dressed up in their black and red, drinking whisky to make themselves brave. They would have passed the house a dozen times before they finally knocked on Bill's door. Perhaps they'd spoken normally for a minute to him, before they pushed him back inside. Then they'd cut and cut and cut at him as he'd reeled back down his own hallway, unable to believe what was happening and unable to resist.

Bill Hoogener had died at the hands of neighbors, without having any idea of what was going on.

Alice May knew what was going on. She knew it deep inside. The Master was a messenger of evil, a corrupter of souls. The Servants were not Servants of the State, but slaves to some awful and insidious poison that changed their very natures and made them capable of committing such dreadful crimes as the murder of her Uncle Bill.

She stepped towards him, towards the pool of blood. An echo answered her, another footfall, in the yard beyond the kitchen door.

Alice May stopped where she was, silent, waiting. The footsteps continued, then the screen door swung open. A man came in, not really looking where he was going. He wore a Servant's black coat over his blue bib-and-brace overalls. There was blood splashed above his knees. There was blood on his hands. His name was Everett Kale, assistant butcher. He had once walked out with Jane Hopkins and had given a much younger Alice May a single marigold from the bunch he'd brought for Jane.

Alice May's star flashed bright, and Everett looked up. He saw Alice May, the star, the leveled rifle. His hand flashed to the bone-handled skinning knife that rattled in the broad butcher's scabbard at his side.

The shot was very loud in the confined space, but Alice May didn't flinch. She worked the lever, the action so fast the sound seemed to fall behind it, and then she put another round into the man who had fallen back through the door. He was already dead, but she wanted to be sure.

Noise greeted her as she stepped outside. Shouts and surprised cries. There were three men in the yard, looking at the dead butcher on the ground. They had got into Bill's homebrew, and they were all holding bottles of thick, dark beer. They dropped the bottles as Alice May came out shooting.

They were armed, with slim, new automatic pistols that fit snugly into clipped holsters at the nipped-in waists of their black tunics. None of them managed to get a pistol out. They were all dead on the ground within seconds, their blood mixing with black, foaming beer, their death throes acted out upon a bed of broken glass.

Alice May looked at them from a weird and forbidding place inside her own head. She knew them, but felt no remorse. Butcher, baker, ne'er do well and ore-washer. All men of the town.

Her hands had done the killing. Her hands and the rifle. Even now those same hands were reloading, taking bullets from her belt and slipping them with a satisfying click into the tubular magazine.

Alice May realised she had had no conscious control over her hands at all. Somewhere between opening the front door of Bill's house and entering the kitchen, she had become an observer within her own body. But she didn't feel terrified by this. It felt right, and she realised she was still in charge of her actions. She wasn't a zombie or anything. She would decide where to go next, but her body—and the weapons—would help her do whatever had to be done when she got there.

She walked around the still-twitching bodies and out the back gate. On to another empty street with the unforgiving, hot wind and the dust and the complete absence of people.

There should have been a crowd, come to see what the shooting was about. The town's two lawmen should be riding up on their matching grays. But there was only Alice May.

She turned down the street, towards the railway station. Her boot heels crunched on the gravel. She felt like she had never really heard that particular sound before, not so clear, so loud.

The wind changed direction and blew against her, stronger and hotter than ever. Dust blew up, heavy dust that carried chunks of grit. But none hit Alice May, none got in her eyes. Her white dress repelled it, the wind seeming to divide as it hit her, great currents of dust and grit flying around on either side.

A door opened to her left, and she was facing it, her finger on the trigger. A man half-stepped out. Old Mr. Lacker, in his best suit, a Servants of the State flag in his trembling hand. His left hand.

"Stay home!" ordered Alice May. Her voice was louder than she expected. It boomed in her ears, easily cutting though the wind.

Lacker took another step and raised his flag.

"Stay home!"

Another step. Another wave of the flag. Then he reached inside his jacket and pulled out a tiny pocket pistol, a single-shot Derringer, all ancient, tarnished brass.

Alice May pulled the trigger and walked on, as Old Man

Lacker's best suit suddenly fountained blood from the lapel, a vivid buttonhole of arterial scarlet.

She reloaded as she walked. Inside she was screaming, but nothing came out. She hadn't wanted to kill Mr. Lacker. He was old, harmless, no danger. He couldn't have hit her even if she was standing next to him.

But her hands and the rifle had disagreed.

Alice May knew where she had to go. The railway station. Where the Master was to arrive in under an hour. She had to go there and kill him.

It didn't seem sensible to walk down the main street, so Alice May cut through the field behind the schoolhouse. From the top of the cutting beyond the field, she looked both ways, towards the station and out along the line.

The special train was already at the platform. One engine, a coal-truck and a single private car, all painted in black and red. The engine had a shield placed on the front of the boiler, above the cow-catcher. A shield with the blazing torch of the Servants. The train must have backed up all the way from Jarawak City, Alice May thought, just so the balcony at the rear of the private car faced the turning circle at the end of Main Street.

There were a lot of people gathered in that turning circle. All the people who Alice May had expected to see in the streets. They'd come down early, to make sure they weren't marked out as tardies or reluctant supporters. The whole population of the town had to be there, many of them in Servants uniform, and all of them waving red and black flags.

Alice May slid down the cutting and walked between the

rails. This was the way she'd come as a baby, all those years ago. But somehow she didn't think she'd come from Jarawak City.

All the attention was at the rear of the train, though it was clear the Master hadn't yet appeared. It was too noisy for that, with the crowd cheering and the town band playing something unrecognizable. The newspapers all made a big thing about the total silence that fell in any audience as the Master spoke.

Alice May crossed the line and crept down the far side of the engine. Just as she came to the coal-truck, an engineer stepped down. He wore denim overalls, topped with a black Servants cap, complete with the badge of the flaming brand.

Alice May's hands moved. The butt of the rifle snapped out and the engineer went down to the rails. He crawled around there for a moment, trying to get up, as Alice May calmly waited for the crowd to cheer again and the band to crescendo with drums and brass. As they did, she fired a single shot into the engineer's head and stepped over him.

I'm a murderer, she thought. Many times over.

I wish they'd stay out of my way.

Alice May stepped up to the private car's forward balcony. She tried to look inside, but the window was smoked glass.

Alice May tried the door. It wasn't locked. She opened it left-handed, the rifle ready.

She had expected a small sitting room of some kind, perhaps opulently furnished. What she saw was an impossibly long corridor, stretching off into the distance, the end out of sight.

The crowd suddenly went silent at the other end of the train.

Alice May stepped into the corridor, and shut the door behind her.

It was dark with the door closed, but her star shone more brightly, lighting the way. Apart from its length, and the fact that the far end was shrouded in mist or smoke, the corridor seemed pretty much like any other train corridor Alice May had ever seen. Polished wood and metal fittings, and every few steps a compartment door. The only strange thing was that the compartment doors all had smoked glass windows, so you couldn't see in.

Alice May was tempted to open a door, but she held out against the temptation. Her business was with the Master, and he was speaking down the far end of the train. Who knew what she would get herself into by opening a door?

She continued to walk as quietly as she could down the corridor. Every few steps she would hear a sound and would freeze for a moment, her finger on the trigger. But the sounds were not of people, or weapons, or danger. They came from behind the compartment doors, and were of the sea, or wind, or falling rain.

Still the corridor continued and Alice May seemed no closer to the end. She started to walk faster, and then began to run. She had to get there before the Master finished talking, before his poison took her foster parents and everyone she knew.

Faster and faster, boot heels drumming, breath rasping, but still cold, cold as ice. She felt like she was pushing against a barrier, that at any moment it would break and she would be free of the endless corridor.

It did break. Alice May burst out into a smoking room, one full of Servants, a long room packed with black and red uniforms.

Alice May's hands and eyes started shooting before she even knew where she was. The rifle was empty in what seemed like only seconds, but each bullet had struck home. Servants slumped in their chairs, writhed on the ground, dived for cover, clutched at weapons.

Alice May flung the rifle aside and drew a revolver, a movement so fast that to the shocked Servants the rifle appeared to transform in her hands. Six more Servants died as their nemesis fanned the hammer with her left hand, the shots sounding together in one terrible instant.

Alice May holstered one revolver and drew the other, right hand and left hand in perfect, opposite motion. But there was no one left to shoot. Gunsmoke mixed with cigar and pipe smoke, swirling up into the ceiling fans. Servants coughed out their final bloody breaths, and the last screams died away.

So this is what they mean by a charnel house, thought Alice May as she surveyed the room, calmly watching from somewhere deep inside herself as some other part of her watched the final shudders and convulsions of dying men and women, amidst the blood and brains and urine that spread and soaked into the once-blue carpet.

Her hands—but not her hands, because surely hers would be shaking—reloaded her revolvers as she watched. Then they picked up the rifle and reloaded that.

The door opened at the far end of the smoking room. Alice May caught a brief glimpse of the Master's back, caught a few of his shouted words, all of them tinged with the hint of a scream.

Her rifle came up as a young woman in black and red entered the room.

It was Jane. Alice May knew it was Jane, and still her finger tightened around the trigger.

"Hello, Alice May," said Jane. She didn't look at the newly dead around her, or bother to step back from the spreading pool of blood. "The Master said you would come. I'm to stop you, he said, because you won't shoot your own sister."

She smiled, and picked up a pistol from the table. Its previous owner had slid underneath, leaving a wet trail of blood and skin and guts against the back of his chair.

Alice May's finger pulled the trigger and she shot Jane. Only a last desperate exertion of will twitched her aim away from her sister's chest to her right arm.

"The Master is always right," said Jane. Her right arm hung at her side, her black sleeve torn apart, chips of white bone strewn along it.

"No," said Alice May, as Jane stepped across the room and picked up another pistol with her left hand. "The Master's wrong, Jane. I have shot you. I will shoot you again. I . . . I can't help it. Don't—"

"The Master is always right," repeated Jane, with serene confidence. She started to raise the pistol.

This time, Alice May wasn't strong enough to resist the inexorable pull of the rifle. It swung steadily to point at Jane's chest, and it could not be turned aside.

The shot sounded louder than any of the others, and its effect was more terrible. Jane was knocked off her feet. She was dead before she even joined the piled-up bodies on the floor.

Alice May stepped over the corpses and knelt by Jane. Tears slid from her dress like rain from glass. The white cloth could not be stained. It turned the blood and broken flesh aside, just as it had the dust.

But her hands were different, thought Alice May. Her hands would never be clean.

"Nothing ever happens in Denilburg," whispered Alice May.

She stood up and opened the door to the rear balcony. To the gathered town, and the Master.

He was shouting as she came out, his arms high above his head, coming down to pound the railing so hard that it shivered under his fists.

Alice May didn't listen to what he said. She pointed her rifle at the back of his head and pulled the trigger.

A dry, pathetic click was the only result. Alice May worked the lever. A round ejected, brass tinkling and rolling off the balcony on to the rails below. She pulled the trigger again, still with no result.

The Master stopped speaking, and turned to face her.

Alice May's star burst into light. She had to shield her eyes with the rifle so she could see.

The Master didn't look like much, up close. He was shorter than Alice May, and his goatee was ridiculous. He was just a funny little man. Till you looked into his eyes.

Alice May wished she hadn't. His eyes were like the endless corridor, stretching back to some nameless place, a void where nothing human could possibly exist.

"So you killed your sister," said the Master. His voice was almost a purr, the screaming and shouting gone. There was no doubt that everyone outside the train could still hear him. He had a voice that carried when he wanted it to, without effort. "You killed Jane Elizabeth Suky Hopkins. Just like you killed Everett Kale, Jim Bushby, Rosco O'Faln, Hubert Jenks and Old Man Lacker. Not to mention my people inside. You'd kill the whole town to get to me, wouldn't you?"

Alice May didn't answer, though she heard the crowd shuffle and gasp. She dropped the rifle and drew a revolver. Or tried to. It stayed stuck fast in its holster. She tried the left-hand gun, but it was stuck too.

"Not that easy, is it?" whispered the Master, leaning across to speak to her alone. His breath smelled like the room she had left behind. Of blood and shit and terror. "There are rules, you know, between your kind and mine. You can't draw until I do. And fast as you are, you can't be as fast as me. It'll all be for nothing. All the deaths. All the blood on your hands."

Alice May stepped back to give him room. She didn't dare look at the crowd, or at the Master's eyes again. She looked at his hands instead.

"You can give in, you know," whispered the Master. "Take your sister's place, in my service. Even in my bed. She enjoyed that, you know. You would too."

The Master licked his lips. Alice May didn't look at his long, pointed, leathery tongue. She watched his hands.

He edged back a little, still whispering.

"No? This is your last chance, Alice May. Join me and everything will turn out for the best. No one will blame you for killing Jane or the others. Why, I'll give you a—"

His hand flickered. Alice May drew.

Both of them fired at the same time. Alice May didn't even know where his gun had come from. She felt something strike her chest a savage blow and she was rammed back into the balcony rail. But she kept her revolver trained dead-centre on the Master, and her left hand fanned the hammer as she pulled the trigger one . . . two . . . three . . . four . . . five times.

Then the revolver was empty. Alice May let it fall, and fell herself, clutching her chest. She couldn't breathe. Her heart hammered with the knowledge that she'd been shot, that these were her last few seconds of life.

Something fell into her hand. It was hot, scorching hot. She gazed at it stupidly as it burned into her palm. Eventually she saw it was a bullet, a misshapen projectile that was not lead, but some sort of white and pallid stone.

Alice May dropped it, though not quickly enough to avoid a burn deep enough to scar. She tried to breathe again, and could, though there was a sharp, stabbing pain in her lungs.

She looked at her chest, expecting to see blood. But her waistcoat was as clean as ever, save for a small round hole on the right-hand side, exactly parallel with the dimming silver star on the left. Gingerly, Alice May reached in. But her hands only felt the woven hair. There was no hole in her undershirt, and no blood.

Alice May sat up. The Master was lying on his back on the far side of the balcony. He looked just like a small, dead man now. The dread that Alice May had felt for him was gone.

She crawled over, but before she could touch him, his flesh began to quiver and move. It crawled and shivered, his face changing colour from a reddish pink to a dull silver. Then the Master's flesh began to liquefy, to become quicksilver in fact as well as colour. The liquid splashed out of his clothes and dribbled across the floor into a six-spoked bronze drain-hole in the corner. Soon there was nothing left of him but a small automatic pistol, a pile of clothing, and a pair of empty boots.

Alice May looked out on the crowd. It was already breaking up. People were taking off their Servants uniforms, even down to their underwear. Others were simply walking away. All had their heads downcast, and no one was talking.

Alice May stood up, her hands pressed against her ribs to ease the pain. She looked out on the crowd for her foster parents, for her surviving Uncle Bill.

She saw them, but like everybody else, they would not look towards her. Their backs were turned, and they had their eyes set firmly towards the town.

Jake and Stella held each other tightly, and walked down the Main Street. They did not look back. Uncle Bill sidled towards the platform. For a moment, Alice May thought he was going to look at her. But he didn't.

Alice May watched them walk away and felt them take whoever she had been with them.

The fourth Hopkins girl, like the third, was dead to Denilburg.

Listlessly, she picked up her rifle and revolver and reloaded them. Her bullet belt was almost empty now.

HOPE CHEST

She was surprised when the engine whistled, but only for a moment. She had entered this life on a train. It seemed only fitting to leave it the same way.

The train gave a stuttering lurch. Smoke billowed overhead, and the wheels screeched for grip. Alice May opened the balcony door and went inside. The smoking room had disappeared, taking Jane and all the other bodies with it. There was the endless corridor again, and at her feet, the steamer trunk.

Alice May picked up one end of the trunk, opened the first compartment door she came to, and dragged it in.

From the platform, Uncle Bill the Porter watched the train slowly pull away. Before it got to the cutting, it veered off to a branch line that wasn't there, and disappeared into the mouth of a tunnel that faded away as the private car passed into its darkness.

Bill wiped a tear from his eye, for a friend who had borne the same name, for a town that had lost its innocence, and for his almost-daughter, who had paid the price for saving them all.

GARTH NIX was born in Melbourne, Australia in 1963, grew up in Canberra, and has lived in Sydney since 1987. He has a B.A. in Professional Writing from the University of Canberra, and has worked as a bookseller, book sales representative, publicist, editor, marketing consultant, and most recently as a literary agent. Garth currently writes full time. His books are published around the world and are widely translated. They include the award-winning fantasy novels *Sabriel* and *Lirael* and the *New York Times* bestseller *Abhorsen*; a fantasy series for children called *The Seventh Tower*; and several other books including *Shade's Children* and *The Ragwitch*. He lives in Sydney with his wife Anna, a publisher, and their son Thomas.

Visit his Web page at **www.ozemail.com.au/~garthnix/**

AUTHOR'S NOTE
"Hope Chest" is one of those odd stories every writer has that comes out of nowhere, gets written when you should be doing something else, and then lurks about like an unwelcome beast in the background, while you try to figure out whether it worked, what it's about and whether to send it anywhere or not.

I'm still not sure of the answers to the first two questions. I think the genesis of the story comes from watching too many Westerns (my favourites include *Winchester '73*; *Red River*; *The Good, The Bad and The Ugly*; and *They Call Me Trinity*). Certainly I've always wanted to write a Western-style story, but with my own peculiar flourishes that have made this story fantasy, though I hope it has echoes of the Westerns that once were culturally so influential all around the world.

As to whether I should send the story anywhere, I didn't, until I was fortunate enough to be invited to contribute a story to this Firebird anthology. I always have several stories in my (virtual) bottom drawer, sometimes because they are unfinished, or are actually fragments of a novel, or like "Hope Chest" strange fruit that require further thought as to what to do with them. While I always tell beginning writers to simply submit stories and let an editor decide, I don't always follow this good advice, which was given to me when I was starting out. Being invited to submit a story broke the bonds that held "Hope Chest" in the bottom drawer. I sent it out. The editor decided. So here it is.

CHASING the WIND

artha Bennett sat on her trunk in the middle of Nairobi's half-completed air terminal watching the other passengers disperse. She had been sitting there for two hours, waiting for her father, and reading over and over again the terse telegram she had received the day before she left Philadelphia:

MAY NOT MEET. TAXI WILSON AIRPORT. HART ALDEN FLY KWALE.

She was not good at waiting. It made her nervous and irritable, but Martha could not quite believe her urbane Philadelphian parents would absolutely abandon her to her own devices in the middle of Africa, and she thought there must be a chance that her father would turn up at the last minute. Although it was not really so different to being abandoned in the middle of Philadelphia, which is what they had done at the beginning of this year, 1950, when her father had started his sabbatical. He and her mother had left their city church and gone to live on a pineapple plantation and teach

English at the local school, in a place where you had to lock in your dogs at night because there might be lions around. It was also a place where the native dispossessed were sharpening knives and spears as they grew determined to throw off the rule of the colonists who had built such plantations.

Martha, who was in the middle of her junior year at Girls' High, had stayed behind with her best friend's family so she could finish the school year in Philadelphia. Now it was summer, and she was joining her parents on the pineapple farm.

MAY NOT MEET. What did that mean: Might not be able to, or *can't*? What would stop her father from leaving his voluntary job for a day? But as the terminal traffic slowed to a trickle between flight arrivals, leaving Martha a conspicuously foreign, teen-aged girl alone in the middle of Nairobi, it became clear that no one was going to meet her, and that Martha would have to TAXI WILSON AIRPORT.

She had left her hat in Cairo when she last changed planes. The palms of her cotton gloves were damp and gray with travel, and the foreign coins slipped from her fingers when she tried to count them out. She was hot and tired and hungry. And what about the trouble everyone had warned her about before she left home, what about the native uprisings, the street fights, the unrest—

Martha, Martha, you are anxious and troubled about many things; one thing is needful.

Those were the words her minister father always scolded her with, Jesus's words to Martha. She muttered them over to herself. *One thing is needful;* she only had to worry about *one thing* right now, and she would rather do anything than sit and

wait one moment longer. Martha stood up and steeled herself to go find out how to hire a taxi.

Everyone she spoke to treated her as politely as if she were a grown woman. A small boy helped her pick up her dropped coins, and she paid him to watch her trunk while she found a porter. The porter helped her find a taxi, and shook hands with her before she got in. She felt better now that she had taken action, and stared out the window with interest and apprehension at the unfamiliar streets. She was sure she had never seen a city with so little automobile traffic. Horses, wagons, donkeys, goats, bicycles, yes, but only a handful of cars other than the one she rode in. Well, there was a bus. But she had been warned not to ride the buses—Martha watched it suspiciously as it trundled around a corner and disappeared down a cross street. Nairobi's wide avenues were bright with the red-orange flames of African tulip trees, dark with their thick green foliage.

"Wilson?" said the taxi driver.

The domestic airport was a sprawl of hangars and sheds, some of them newly built of concrete blocks, some little more than shelters of thatched palm.

"I'm looking for Hart Alden?" Martha asked. "A regional airline, maybe?"

"Take you to the Aero Club," the driver answered kindly, and they bumped to the end of the service road and down a long driveway edged with hibiscus. The driver stopped the car and unloaded Martha's trunk beneath a stand of fig trees. Keyed up with all the warnings she had been given, Martha had been prepared to find Kenya frightening; but she had not expected its beauty. It mixed her up.

"Please wait till I know I'm in the right place," she begged as she paid the driver, as though the taxi were a lifeboat. Then she dragged on her limp gloves, swatted at her limp hair, and once again reluctantly steeled herself for battle.

It was late morning. The lounge of the Aero Club of East Africa was nearly empty, but not very quiet, because there was an ancient gramophone tinnily cranking out Handel's "Royal Fireworks Music." In the dimmest, most shadowy corner of the room, sunk in a wicker sofa behind an electric fan and a three-day-old newspaper, languished what appeared to be the Aero Club's only member.

"I'm looking for Hart Alden?" Martha said to the newspaper.

The pages rustled aside like a curtain lifting, to reveal a glamorous head swaddled in a green silk scarf and hidden by big dark glasses.

How can she see a thing, thought Martha.

"Are you by any chance Martha Bennett?" the starlet asked, smacking her newspaper into submission.

"Yes, ma'am," Martha answered with automatic politeness.

"Thank Christ almighty. Does Harry know you're here?"

"No. I don't know. Who? I'm looking for a flight transfer, I think."

"Oh, you *doll*," the starlet exclaimed, as suddenly happy and excited as a girl at her first Homecoming. "You're *American*."

"Uh-huh, last time I checked," said Martha, smiling.

"I thought you'd be English. Everyone's English here. They're all very sweet, but—" She let the sentence hang. Martha looked around the lounge, and knew what this woman meant without her having to explain. There was an enormous wooden propeller mounted on one wall, gleaming sad and proud above a too-long roll of honor to all the club's young pilots killed for King and Country when Martha had been a little girl. Everything about the place, from the grass-thatched ceiling to the starched white shirt front of the silent butler, whispered insistently: *British Empire*.

"My husband owns the Kwale plantation. You and me, we're going to fly there together," the starlet said. "Hart Alden, Harry, is our pilot. I'm Mrs. Copley. Mary Copley."

"Mary and Martha," Martha said. "Isn't that funny? Like in the Bible. I hope that doesn't mean you get to sit listening to stories, while I rush around cooking supper for everybody?"

Mrs. Copley's dark glasses stared toward her blankly.

"I'm a P.K.," Martha said, laughing. She had meant it as a joke. "I always talk like this."

Mrs. Copley took the glasses off, as if Martha would make more sense if she could see her more clearly.

"P.K. Preacher's kid," Martha added; then to herself, Oh, SHUT UP, Martha.

Martha had always vaguely resented being named Martha. She felt deeply dissatisfied at being automatically cast in the role of attendant. Once, right after the war ended, her father's church had hosted a visiting minister from Harlem, who had come to dinner at the Bennetts' on his first night in Philadelphia. He had been a fascinating, opinionated, hugely intelligent man, and Martha had sat over dinner riveted by his stories. When her mother had asked her to help clear the table Martha had made them all burst out laughing by complaining,

"Oh, why did you have to name me Martha when I wanted to be a Mary?"

"Do you usually rush around cooking for people?" Mrs. Copley asked now, smiling at last.

"I like to have something to *do*," Martha said. "I like to help, you know, but I'm not good at listening. My mother says I'm always so busy finding something for me to do that I don't pay attention to what anyone else wants."

"We'll get along just fine, then," Mrs. Copley said. "I like to be pampered." She put her glasses back on, and sipped at her drink.

"Do you know why no one's here to meet us?" Martha asked.

"The plane's not big enough to carry a welcoming committee, and it's not safe to go by road these days. Or train."

"Really?"

"If you're white."

"Is it *really* that bad?"

"I don't know. The British papers say it's getting worse." Mary Copley slammed down the one she had been reading. "My husband's such a goddamned entrepreneur. Bought this farm cheap from a Dutch couple who decided to go home. Like a good old Yankee carpetbagger. I can't *believe* I agreed to come live here."

Martha thought resignedly, At least my family's all going home in September.

"Is the pilot here?" she asked. "Hart Alden?"

"Harry. He's American too. He picks up customers here, he runs a kind of flying taxi service. You and me and my kitties today. We've been waiting for you. Go and let Harry know you're here, and we can get going. He's in the bar."

"I can't go in the *bar*!"

"It's mid-morning. Who cares what the rules are." Mrs. Copley picked up her paper again.

So Martha went to meet her pilot.

He was sitting at the bar, drinking coffee. He was pouring the awful remains of a battered aluminum pot into one of the Aero Club's china teacups, and the barman was already decanting fresh coffee into another, more genteel, pot, which sat on a flaring gas ring. Martha's father also drank coffee in this irreverent way, often reheating last night's leftovers in a pan and letting it bubble away into sludge, then drinking it anyway. This kinship made Martha like the pilot without knowing anything else about him. She imagined him and her father making the arrangements for her trip, on a palm-thatched veranda somewhere, over cups of black coffee as unpalatable as engine oil.

"Captain Alden?" Martha said, holding out her hand. "I'm Martha Bennett. Your passenger?"

Hart Alden stood up carefully, watching his feet, and Martha saw that he was lame. There was a walking stick hanging over the bar between his coffee cup and an ashtray, but he did not touch it. He held on to the counter with his left hand, and with his right he took Martha's in a firm handshake. He said warmly, "Welcome, Martha. We're fellow Philadelphians."

"Really?"

"You're at the Wissahickon Farm School?"

"No, my best friend is. Sally Atkins. Her mother's the secretary. I lived with the Atkins family most of this year, but I'm at Girls' High."

"My sister Lucy teaches horticulture at the Farm School. Actually, she *is* horticulture. She bullied them into hiring her, and now they've got a class of twenty girls."

Martha laughed, delighted. "She's Dr. Alden! The terror of the Flower Show! Sally talks about her all the time. So does Mrs. Atkins. Talk about a small world! You're Dr. Alden's brother?"

"That's me," Unaccountably, Hart Alden did not match her amazed delight as he answered, and his gaze wandered toward his coffee. If anything, he seemed disappointed, which made no sense at all.

"I guess you've never met her, then," he added, almost casually, and stubbed out the cigarette that was burning itself down in the ashtray. He looked up again, more brightly.

"We'd better get going, or we'll end up postponing this trip till tomorrow. I want to do it in daylight. I should have met your flight from Cairo, but—"

He stopped, and gave a wry smile. He was almost naturally apologetic. He was tall and angular, but he stooped; his light brown hair, almost the same color as his face, was graying faintly. His gray eyes were mild.

"I don't know if you want to hear my excuse or not. It'll make you think twice about letting me fly you across East Africa. I managed to get a pen to leap out of my shirt pocket and into the fuel tank of my plane while I was checking the fuel level this morning, and we had to drain the tank. It took an hour to fish the danged pen out, too. You try hooking a pen out of the wing of a small plane with a safety pin and a coat hanger! Then we all worried there'd be ink in the fuel, so we had to flush the tank—"

"Oh," Martha said. "Oh, the fuel goes in the wing? I didn't know that. That's neat."

The barman chuckled. Hart Alden gazed at Martha with a mild grin.

"That's not what Mary Copley said when I told her," the pilot commented. "You're supposed to give me a lecture about responsibility, not admire aircraft design."

"But you got the pen out, didn't you? What's the problem?"

"There isn't one. But it could kill you, if there was."

That, Martha thought, exactly summed up her first impression of Africa.

It still took another age to get going. Martha's patient taxi driver had to be paid and sent away. Mrs. Copley's cats had to be fed and watered, and Martha had to arrange to have her trunk sent on the train after her. It was too heavy, not to mention about three times too big, to take in the tiny luggage well of Hart Alden's little four-seated Cessna 170. Martha abandoned her gloves without regret and hastily packed one blouse and a sweater and some underwear in a burlap coffee sack, so that for three days all her clothes and her hairbrush and her paperback smelled of coffee, and her toothbrush tasted of it, and the smell of unground coffee beans reminded her forever after of that flight across East Africa.

Martha followed her pilot around the plane like a puppy while he gave the machine its pre-flight checks, genuinely fascinated, though not daring to touch anything herself. The wings and fuselage gleamed silver. Hart Alden ran lovingly over the front surfaces of the wings.

"Is this plane yours?"

"I've had her for a year, from brand new."

"Is that how long you've been in Kenya?"

"Oh, longer than that. Nearly five years. I left the States about a year after the war."

"Did you learn to fly in the war?"

"During," Alden answered. "But not in it. I learned as a civilian. The Air Force would have taken me, or I could have flown for England, I guess. But I don't meet their physical requirements, you know? So I didn't have to fight."

"I thought everyone wanted to fight the Axis?" said Martha, who had been seven years old when Pearl Harbor had been bombed, and remembered her father shouting the news out a bedroom window to her mother, holding her hand in the street below. She also remembered how useless it had been after that trying to get anyone's attention when the radio was on.

Hart Alden did not answer, busy pushing and pulling at the movable parts of the airplane's tail. Martha thought she must have sounded a little reproachful, so she added, "My father didn't know what to do. He was a minister, and he had a little girl, me. He didn't have to go. But he felt guilty about it. He finally applied to be posted as an Army chaplain, but then the war was over before they sent him anywhere."

"Well, I never even got that far in solving my own moral dilemma. I never signed up for anything. Maybe I would have, if it had gone on longer; or if I could have done something like your father's job. I'm not a fighter. My gosh!" He whistled.

his hands

. She should have been a
ave to leave Kenya, soon, or
I hate watching other people

n not a fighter, either, not at all,"

the difference was. She was not a
fighter, bu.   nething in her that did not like to sit
still.

"I thought maybe you got hurt in the war?"

Hart Alden smiled, faintly. He dusted his hands off, and
reached into the plane to slide his cane in on the floor alongside the seat.

"No," he said slowly. "Or anyway, not that war. Come on,
we're ready. Let's get Mary and her cats, I don't want to make
her any grouchier than she already is. I told her she couldn't
bring her make-up bag if she wanted to bring that five-pound
bag of kitty kibble. And extra water! Good thing she's not
much bigger than a cat herself."

Mrs. Copley was, in fact, considerably smaller than
Martha, a thing that Martha secretly admired and envied, as
well as envying her Christian name.

"You said it was only a three-hour flight?"

"Well, it is, but you've got to be prepared. I don't cross the
plains without water."

"Have you got a first aid kit?"

"And a coffee pot." Alden smiled his slow, mild smile, and
squeezed Martha's shoulder with one long, brown hand.
"Don't worry."

He walked slowly without his walking st
feet. He moved his long body with the lanky grac
ball player, but his stride was broken and uneven, and
his hand lightly on Martha's shoulder as they crossed t
windy airfield. But then he carried Mrs. Copley's two Siamese
cats in their rattan carrier basket, with Mrs. Copley hanging
on his other arm as though she needed the support or the
wind would knock her down. Mrs. Copley carried the cat
food, and Martha carried the small amount of luggage for all
three of them, and the coffee pot.

Mary and Martha, thought Martha again. I get to take
care of her toothbrush while she flirts with the pilot.

Well, she likes being pampered, Martha added to herself
more charitably; and I guess he's pampering her.

The plane only had doors to the front seats. The cats and
Mrs. Copley were stowed in the back seat, being the lightest
passengers. The cabin was less than half as big as the inside of
the Atkins' saloon car. Martha got to sit in the front, next to
the pilot. They strapped themselves in. Hart Alden gave her a
map.

"Now, look," he said to Martha. "I have a job for you. I
used to get Lucy to do this for me. There isn't much out here,
and we don't want to get lost, so every ten or fifteen minutes,
when you see a landmark on the map that you're sure of: a
junction of the railway and a road, or a lake, or an airstrip,
some of them are marked—"

Martha looked down at the map. He had marked the
airstrips himself.

"—then you write down next to it what time it was when

ve need to fly to find
e reason, and also we'll
Jefore we get to the next
be pretty sure where we
ay most of the way, so keep

ured, because this, above all,
what mattered to her.

Th   r his seat and pulled at the ends
of Mrs. Cop   lt with his long hands. "All tight
back there? If you   anything, you tap Martha on the
shoulder and let her know what's up, and she'll tell me."

They roared down the runway and lifted as lightly and easily as a kite on a windy beach. Martha fought with the map,
and craned to see over the dashboard as the horizon disappeared beneath their climb. She glanced out the side.

The sky was like crystal. They flew over a brown and yellow
landscape with nothing in it but elephants and giraffes.
During the first part of the journey Martha could see tiny cir-
cles of clustered huts, and cattle herds sprinkled around them,
but they soon left these behind, and for at least an hour there
was nothing but the railway line. Then she began to see the
shapeless forms of dead volcanoes, green mounds with black
pits sunk through their middles.

Alden peered out the window past Martha's bent head as
she searched for the next landmark. He shouted over the
noise of the engine, "Look, there's Kilimanjaro. WHAT a beautiful day!"

The foothills of the great mountain loomed vast and dark,

at a distance. Clouds uncurled around the sloping shoulders, and above the clouds the great twin crags of the old volcano jutted, gleaming silver at the heights where the mountain's eternal crest of snow caught the sun.

Mrs. Copley tapped Martha on the shoulder. "Where's the powder room?" Mrs. Copley shouted.

Martha blinked at her.

"What?"

"The powder room," Mrs. Copley yelled. "I need a pit stop."

They had been flying for an hour and a half. Martha remembered the gin and tonics in the flying club.

Mrs. Copley pointed at Alden, raising her eyebrows above the rims of her sunglasses and nodding encouragingly. "Did he hear me? Get his attention!"

Martha put down the map.

"Mrs. Copley needs a pit stop," she yelled.

They held a loud, heated discussion about the urgency of this matter, and then, astonishingly, Hart Alden laid his finger on the map in Martha's lap. "There. Grass strip in Amboseli. Keep your eyes peeled, it's hard to spot."

"I haven't spotted any of them!"

"Nice place for a picnic, too," Alden shouted.

"You're kidding!"

"When you've got to go—"

Martha hid her face in the wide folds of the map, spluttering. They flew for another quarter of an hour, and there where it was meant to be was a rectangular patch of darker brown against the dull olive of the empty world. The plane floated to a landing, and then bumped along as if it were taxiing over a field of potatoes.

Mrs. Copley swore through her teeth, loudly, and in a most unladylike manner.

"Let 'er out," Hart Alden said, reaching over Martha to unlatch her door. Mrs. Copley climbed over her as nimbly as one of her cats might have done.

The pilot and Martha sat side by side, both of them red in the face and shaking.

"Oh—" Martha leaned back to peer into the wicker hamper, tears leaking out of the corners of her eyes in her effort not to laugh. "That sounds like one of the cats is going to throw up—"

"Not in my plane!" Alden said, and hauled the hamper out of the back seat to drop it out the door.

"Come on, Martha. Come look at Amboseli."

It was as alien and empty as the moon. There was absolutely nothing there but low acacia scrub and cactus, and a little flower that looked like wild narcissus. It was windy, and the air smelled faintly of sage. There was no sound at all but the distant rumble of thunder.

"Huh," Alden said. "I wonder where that is." They could see no clouds. He scanned the horizon, and Martha followed his gaze, staring out toward the edge of the airstrip.

Unbelievably, there were a dozen people standing there.

They carried spears. One of them wore a khaki safari shirt not very different from Alden's, and the rest wore hardly anything. Mrs. Copley let out a little low shriek, and emerged from beneath the opposite wing, hastily pulling her clothing back into place.

"Get back in the plane," Hart Alden said in a low voice.

His passengers obeyed without question. He tossed the cats in the back, crammed his lanky body into the tiny cockpit, and slammed the doors.

"Will they attack?" Mrs. Copley gasped.

Hart Alden, who was securing his safety belt, burst out laughing.

"You've been reading too many newspapers!" he said. "Those are Masai, not Kikuyu. And anyway, they're as civil as you are."

"But you're worried about something—"

"Thunder!"

"What?"

"Everyone always wants to look at the plane, out here. That will take ages, once they get started. But there's a thunderstorm brewing somewhere. We can't hang around being ambassadors to the twentieth century if it means we might run into a thunderstorm later."

Everybody warned me about the wrong things, Martha thought. I don't need to worry about *people*. They're not going to try to kill me. I should be hoping I don't get struck by lightning, and worrying about whether I've got enough water to survive a plane crash.

But, curiously, this did not scare her; and it made her decide that the people did not scare her, either.

The engine roared. The little plane began its kangaroo progress across the savanna. The handful of tribesmen waved furiously, and Martha waved back. They frantically acknowledged one another's existence in the brief seconds it took to launch the plane aloft again, their strange worlds briefly touching for a minute.

After another hour of flying a pall of haze closed up the horizon, and it began to get bumpy.

"That's the ocean," Alden told Martha. "Only you can't see it because of the haze. And do you see that pile of cloud off to the right? That's a thundercloud. It's just about right on top of the Kwale airstrip, where we're headed."

"There's another." Martha pointed.

They flew on toward the haze.

"We'll never get down there," Alden said. He was not shouting, and Martha had to lean close to hear him. "I wouldn't dare. We'll go north a bit, and try to land at Malindi for the night, on the coast. Otherwise we'll just waste fuel, circling. There are plenty of hotels in Malindi."

Martha considered trying to relay this information to Mrs. Copley, and decided against it. Behind her dark glasses, the backseat passenger was very pale in the face, and sat with her head tilted upward against the seat back as though she were studying the ceiling. Martha could see the slight movement of her white throat as she swallowed.

The great dark clouds piled and banked up along the coast and a little way inland, southward, to their right and behind them. The little plane purred its way north, away from the storms.

Then they were coming down, leapfrogging through the air almost as violently as when they had been taxiing on the ground in Amboseli. What in the world makes you bounce in the *air* like this, Martha wondered, and looked out to see palm

fronds whipping wildly on the trees below, which had suddenly gotten very near. Martha gripped the sides of her seat.
Mrs. Copley gripped Martha's shoulder, and Martha let go of
the seat to clutch at the nervous hand.

Thump. They were down. The dirt runway seemed very
smooth.

"Well, that was the best fun I've had since my sister blew
up the professor's houseboat," Hart Alden said casually, steer-
ing the plane to a standstill in the long grass at the edge of the
runway.

Mrs. Copley let go of Martha's hand. Both cats were sick.

Alden reached across Martha to fling open her door. A
rush of warm, salty air fought with Martha's map.

"Wow, it's WINDY!"

"No kidding," said the pilot.

They piled out of the plane. At the end of the runway was
a hut made of palm thatch.

"Where are we?" said Mrs. Copley, ominously.

"Manda Island."

"*Where?*"

"Just across the bay from Lamu. We can spend the night in
Lamu, or Shela."

"Lamu's over a hundred miles from Kwale! Why, we're
practically in *Somaliland!*"

"There was lightning over Kwale?" Martha ventured. "And
over Malindi. We couldn't have landed there."

"Say it with confidence, kid," Hart Alden told her.

They crossed the bay in a dhow. One of the local people,
with the prosaic English name of Raymond, had met Alden

before. They chattered to each other in Swahili and arranged this leg of the trip without once consulting either of the passengers. Mrs. Copley bristled. Martha thought Mrs. Copley was holding up quite well under the circumstances, the pleats in her khaki skirt still crisp, her green silk scarf gallant.

They were deposited on the dock in Lamu, clutching their few possessions, and followed Alden's friend on foot. Lamu, to Martha's Pennsylvania city-bred eyes, looked like a place out of *The Arabian Nights*. The white-washed houses were jumbles of balconies and minarets, with roofs and awnings of thatched palm. The passages and streets between were narrow pathways, opening to sudden squares, or small open mosques, and filled with children and chickens, dogs and donkeys. There were no automobiles at all. The wind hurried down the gaps between the buildings and tugged at their thatched roofs.

Raymond carried the cats. Alden leaned heavily, Martha thought, on his cane. They walked out of the town and along a path by the water to Shela, the next village.

They were finally led up three staircases to a little suite of rooms opening onto a terrace, roofed, but with crenellated railings instead of walls. Martha and Mrs. Copley had to share a double bed. Out the bedroom windows were huge, white sand dunes, shielding the house a little from the wind off the Indian Ocean. In the square below the terrace, the heads of palm trees tossed sideways.

"Well, we'll have to wait till the wind drops before we start off again," said Alden. "Shall we go to the beach?"

They waited for Mrs. Copley to feed and water her cats. She let them loose in the bedroom, pulling the shutters tight. In the end she could not bear to leave them.

"You and the kid have a good run on the beach. Bring me some sand to use for litter. Then we'll have a nice long, quiet evening together," she promised.

So Martha set out with the pilot, on a mission to find cat litter, through the narrow alleyways and over the pale dunes, blushed faintly gold now by the sun of late afternoon.

Boy, am I ever a fifth wheel around here, Martha thought. What a romantic trip this would be for the two of them if I weren't along.

But no, she's married: she's going to meet her husband. And she doesn't exactly flirt, either, she just makes you carry her luggage and bring her drinks.

What about Hart Alden, though? He's not really the romantic type. He's not bad looking, but he's got other things on his mind. He's busy with his airplane, and missing his sister.

It was tough going for Alden to limp his way through the soft, deep sand at the foot of the dunes. He cocked his stick jauntily over his shoulder and carefully kept his eyes on his feet, like someone trying to climb down a mountain slope of ice. Martha watched him pick his way steadily toward the firmer sand at the water's edge. She bent to scoop sand into another coffee sack to take back to the cats. It sifted through the burlap almost as quickly as she tipped it in.

"'All is vanity,'" Martha murmured, "'and a striving after wind.'" She giggled. "This is the silliest thing I've ever tried to do."

"I never heard a girl quote so much scripture. Ecclesiastes, right?"

"I'm a P.K.," Martha said sheepishly, caught at it again. "But it is like chasing the wind."

"Try down here, where it's wetter."

He limped along the shore. Martha picked up a seashell as small and smooth and pale as the nail of her own little finger. "What war did you get hurt in?" she asked.

Hart Alden smiled, very faintly. His cane sank into the sand even down here by the foaming chocolate tide line, so he slung it over his shoulder again. "My father did it, by accident, when I was about your age. He dropped a box on my foot."

"Ouch," said Martha with sympathy.

"You could blame it on my sister," Hart Alden said. "She threw it at him. They were fighting with each other, but neither of them meant to hurt me."

I'm not a fighter, he had said.

Martha nodded. "Like being in Kenya right now. Caught in the middle," she said sympathetically, standing up. "Does your sister come visit you here? You said she used to fly with you."

"I haven't heard from her for more than five years," Alden answered. He, too, bent to pick up a shell, and pitched it low and fast out to sea. It skipped eight times before Martha lost sight of it.

"Wow," Martha breathed. "You've got an arm like Lefty Grove."

"Yeah, I do. So did my dad. Isn't Lefty Grove before your time?"

"Oh, not much. The legend lives on."

"My sisters and I were all made to worship at the altar of the Philadelphia Athletics," Alden said, and sent another shell burning into the waves.

"You really miss your family," Martha observed.

"I guess I do. But that's not because I'm here. My dad died nearly fifteen years ago, and Lucy stopped talking to me during the war. I don't miss her because I'm far away; I came away because I missed her. It's easier five thousand miles away. I couldn't stand living in the same city and never seeing Lucy, ever. She hung up if I telephoned. She moved and changed her number.

"The war was important to her," he added, consideringly, as if he were so distanced from the emotional turmoil of his family that he no longer cared about it. "She gave up on me when I wouldn't enlist."

Well, this explained his disappointment when Martha had told him it was her hosts who knew his sister, not herself. Maybe he had hoped Martha could give her a message, or find out her address. Hart Alden stood gazing out to sea, his walking stick slung over his shoulder, slouching a little, as he always did.

"Dr. Lucia Alden," he said sadly. "Talk about chasing the wind! She never did let anyone in her family tell her what to do. It'll take a bolt out of the blue to make Lucy change her mind."

Alden swung back toward the village then, and Martha followed. Clouds piled golden and silver behind the dunes. Martha and the pilot plodded silently through whipping sand to the winding path back to their guest house, where an elaborate supper, and Mary Copley, waited for them on their colonnaded court. They ate as the sun set and the wind rose.

Hart Alden kept looking around and raising his head as though he were a dog trying to pick up a scent; the wind

ELIZABETH E. WEIN

lifted his graying brown hair lightly over his young face. Mrs. Copley shivered.

"Goodness, what a wind."

"Yes." Alden brushed hair out of his eyes.

Mrs. Copley reached out to still his fluttering hand with one of hers. Her nails were perfectly manicured, straight out of Elizabeth Arden.

"What's the matter?"

"I'm worried about the plane."

"What about it?"

"It's not tied down. I should have tied it, but I was worrying about finding us a place to stay and getting a dhow, and I thought the wind would drop when the sun went down. A wind like this could easily blow a Cessna over."

There was a silence around the table then, as the wind whipped and cried in the dark, and the thatch creaked and the palms rustled, and mysterious things down at the Shela jetty clinked and knocked.

"Well, there's no point worrying about it," Mrs. Copley said. "You can't do anything about it till tomorrow."

"I've got to tie it down," said Hart Alden.

He stood up and paced to the edge of the terrace, and leaned out into the rushing dark. Then he straightened.

"I'll be back in a minute," he called over his shoulder, and cantered down the stairs.

Martha and Mrs. Copley sat staring at each other in the flickering light of a kerosene hurricane lamp, abandoned.

Then Mary Copley fell into a dither of nervousness. She paced back and forth along the terrace, clenching and unclenching her fingers around the handle of a table knife, which she waved and pointed for emphasis as she talked.

"Do you think he's gone to do it *himself*? But how can he? And are we safe here alone? What if he doesn't come back, what then?"

"He said he'd be back in a minute," said Martha.

"Well, do you trust him?"

Martha did not answer immediately. It seemed pretty much a rhetorical question, since they had both meekly submitted to his unknown expertise and judgment for a three hundred mile flight across the African bush in a plane the size of a sports car. But he should have tied it down in the first place; and there was that pen in the fuel tank. . . .

As Martha hesitated, Alden came galloping unevenly up the stairs carrying a pre-war flashlight as big as a trumpet.

"Raymond's found me a motor launch," he said. "So we're going back across to Manda to tie down the plane."

"Do you have to?" Mrs. Copley asked.

"If you want to fly out of here," he answered sharply.

"Will we be safe alone?"

Hart Alden stared at her, bewildered. "Well, you were safe this afternoon, why wouldn't you be safe now? This is a village. You're safer here than you'll be on your husband's farm, where maybe one morning you'll find your cats turned into lion hors d'oeuvres."

"I mean, *safe*," Mrs. Copley said coldly. "There aren't any locks."

"Oh!" He actually laughed. "This isn't New York City."

"No one's leaving New York because they're afraid to

live there." Mrs. Copley stood up, with queenly dignity for such a small woman, and armed herself with the cutlery she had been conducting with earlier. She stalked to the closed door of the room she was to share with Martha. "We'll just stay in here till we're sure you're back safe and sound. Come on, Martha."

Martha hesitated, took a breath, and then said all in a rush: "No, I think I'll go with Captain Alden."

There was a short silence.

"I want to come," Martha said. "Maybe I could help. Hold the flashlight, or something, while you work. It's stuffy inside, anyway."

Mrs. Copley opened her door a crack, angling a foot across it in case the cats tried to make a run for it. She shifted her grip on her table knife.

"Shela's not known for its street riots," Alden commented mildly.

"I'll see you all later, then," Mrs. Copley answered, and slipped inside the room, and closed the door.

Bet she's building a barricade with her pet carrier, Martha thought, as she followed the pilot down the terrace steps and through the narrow lanes between the houses, watching the broad but dim path illuminated by the antique flashlight.

They heard the din of an engine before they reached the Shela jetty. There were about half a dozen people standing there when they arrived—Raymond, the two owners of the launch, a short man carrying iron stakes and a coil of wire, and a couple of boys about Martha's own age contributing ropes woven of palm fronds. Nobody bothered with introductions;

they just all piled into the speedboat—which was nothing more than a dhow with a great big motor stuck on the back—and set out across the bay.

It was glorious. It was, if anything, better than flying over the foothills of Kilimanjaro. There was no light at all: no moonlight, no lights on the boat, no lights on the island where they were heading—nothing but wind and speed and night, and a million stars blazing overhead in unfamiliar positions between the clouds. Martha had no idea how anyone knew where they were going. The launch crashed over the waves like a horse leaping fences. If there was another boat with no lights out there on the water in the dark somewhere, they were all sunk.

I don't care, Martha thought. It is worth it for this ride. If I die like this I will die happy.

Manda Island loomed low and black in front of them, like the silhouette edging the artificial horizon of a planetarium's dome. The top edge of the silhouette waved and tossed: that was Manda Island's low trees moving in the wind. The stars began right behind them and got thicker, but no less bright, the higher up the sky you looked. Martha could not remember ever having noticed before how *deep* the sky is: you could see stars behind stars, on and on forever.

They all climbed out of the boat. They walked in the dark to save the batteries in the flashlight. The path seemed full of roots and rocks; Martha had to trust her feet to find their own way, and she was glad she had chosen to wear sensible oxfords for this leg of the journey, and sent the pumps and sneakers with her luggage. Hart Alden, limping at her side, was more surefooted than she was, confidently feeling the way with his cane, like a blind man.

They reached the airfield and crossed the runway. There sat the little plane in the lee of the wind, beneath a hedge of shrub that surrounded it in a small and unexpected pocket of calm.

"Not so windy here," said Raymond, in English.

Hart Alden laughed and swung the light over the plane, and it was still and quiet.

"Can I choose a parking place or can I choose a parking place? Well, let's do what we came to do."

The men tied down the plane. It took about five minutes. And Martha held the light for them, and kept track of the stakes in the dark.

They were a jovial party on the way back to Shela. The men shouted to each other in Swahili over the noise of the waves and the engine. They all stood for a moment at the dock laughing and chattering while Alden handed out cigarettes, and then the party split up as the owners of the boat sped back to wherever they had come from, and the butts were stubbed out and the boys disappeared down the narrow coast path back to Lamu, laughing and punching at each other.

"Come on, Martha."

Hart Alden beckoned her with the flashlight.

"Can I carry that? Or does it help you watch your feet?"

"Martha, Martha." He was silent for a moment, and then said, "'You are anxious and troubled about many things.' I'm a grown-up. I can carry the flashlight.

"Come on, Martha," he repeated. "Mary will be waiting up for us."

Later, lying in the dark under the mosquito net canopy, as far from Mrs. Copley and her pile of cats as she could get without falling out of bed, Martha thought over Hart Alden's gentle, enigmatic reprimand to her. He had not needed Martha to come along to tie down the plane. He had six men helping him. Mrs. Copley, on the other hand, had been sitting in the dark alone and frightened. Martha had done exactly what her mother always warned her about. She had been so busy finding something to do that she had missed seeing where she was most needed.

It deflated her like a popped balloon. It took away the joy of the boat ride. Oh, why was she born a Martha, when she wanted to be a Mary?

Mrs. Copley had to wake her for breakfast.

The wind had slackened. They made the coastal flight to Kwale in short stages, stopping at Malindi to refuel. They flew just below the clouds, out one window it was raining, out the other the sun shone. The country in the rain was lush green dotted with blue of inlet and water tank and water hole, and seemed to go on forever into distant haze, miniature and luminous. The sunlit Indian Ocean was muddy brown at the river mouths, pearl and turquoise beyond. By lunchtime Martha was scrambling out of the little plane, on another grass strip, and hurling herself into her father's arms.

Mrs. Copley held court on her husband's veranda as they ate lunch. Mary Copley made the trip sound like an even bigger adventure than it was, and described her own part in it with unashamedly self-deprecating humor.

"—The nearest bush is about five miles away. So I say to myself: Mary my dear, who is going to see you? And I get down there under the wing, in the middle of the middle of nowhere, and when I look up there are TEN PEOPLE STANDING THERE WATCHING."

Mr. Copley and Martha's father roared with laughter, and Hart Alden smiled down at his coffee, making little choked, snorting noises.

"And they were carrying spears."

Another general burst of laughter, as if it were somehow funnier to be caught with your pants down by a dozen native warriors than by a dozen Philadelphians waiting for a street-car.

"The Masai do," said Martha's mother. "They do carry spears. You would, too, if you spent your life herding cattle in lion country."

Mary Copley said, "I'd carry a pistol."

Hart Alden murmured, "Or a butter knife."

"Oh!"

Mrs. Copley banged down her fork, gesticulating wildly as much as to say that her mouth was full now but she still had the floor.

"Reverend Bennett, do you have *any idea* how brave your daughter is? Last night, in the middle of the night, she went off in a speedboat with half a dozen strange Swahili-speaking men so she could help Harry tie down his airplane. Me, I could not have done that in a million years. I was terrified, I wouldn't leave my bedroom! A thousand miles from any-where, no electricity, no telephone, no one who speaks English—"

She stopped, and spoke directly to Martha, with deep admiration. "You're a real fighter, darling."

"I'm not," Martha protested. "I just like to have something to do."

Hart Alden nodded, smiling at her. "No, Martha isn't a fighter," he agreed. "She's a doer. She gets up and gets things done. Like her namesake."

Martha sat at the big kitchen table in her parents' crazy temporary house. Her mother and the Copleys' cook were making pepper pot soup using eland instead of cow's stomach, which her mother swore produced a reasonable substitute once you got past the usual revulsion over identifying the ingredients of pepper pot in the first place. Martha was not involved in this project. She was writing a letter.

"Dear Mrs. Atkins," it began; "Thank you so much for letting me share a bedroom with Sally . . . "

Martha went on in this bread-and-buttery vein for a while, and briefly described her flight to Kwale; and then she casually mentioned the pilot.

" . . . His name is Hart Alden. His sister is the head of horticulture at your school! Please tell her—"

Martha had stopped writing. She gazed out the open door, past her mother and the Luo cook joking with each other in Swahili, which neither of them spoke fluently. Martha chewed on her pen, and stared at the violet and magenta bougainvillea cascading over the veranda rails. The house had been built between the wars, like the flashlight, and felt old and calm and solid: unlike her mother's fragile, temporary, crossing-all-the-wrong-boundaries friendship with her landlord's cook.

Martha's fingers were inky. She looked down at the page again. What lousy penmanship I have, she thought, making fingerprints on the cardboard cover of her mother's airmail pad. There was a picture of a bolt of lightning on the cover, to show how fast airmail letters went.

It'll take a bolt out of the blue to make Lucy change her mind.

Okay, Dr. Lucia Alden, here it comes. This is your bolt out of the blue. I'm going to do this, Martha thought.

She wrote:

"Please give Dr. Alden the enclosed note, from me, saying how much I liked her brother. He talked about her a lot, all good (Sally only ever complains about how strict she is!). I'd like to meet her sometime; maybe you can introduce us when I get home?

"Sorry to make you be the mailman, but I forgot to ask Captain Alden for her address.

"Coming here was much scarier than being here. I guess some kind of civil war is not far off, but I feel safe. I'll see you in September.

"Your friend, Martha."

She began the second letter. This one would be more difficult. But even if it did not work, there was still Sally, and Sally's mother, and the Philadelphia Flower Show. Martha's lightning bolt would find its mark eventually. Lightning moves faster than wind.

"Dear Dr. Alden . . ."

ELIZABETH E. WEIN has a B.A. from Yale and a Ph.D from
the University of Pennsylvania. She is the author of three novels in an ongoing Arthurian cycle: *The Winter Prince* (Firebird),
A Coalition of Lions, and the forthcoming *The Sunbird* (both
Viking).

Elizabeth and her husband both ring church bells in the
English style known as "change ringing"—they met at a
ringers' dinner!—and now live in Scotland with their two
young children.

AUTHOR'S NOTE

I originally meant this story to be set in my quasi-historical
world of sixth-century Ethiopia. It was supposed to be about
the sequestered childhood of the king of Himyar, and maybe
dragons. After six pages I stopped writing. The next page in
my notebook is scrawled with the words: "No, no, no. Actually, I want to write a story about AEROPLANES."

"Chasing the Wind" is what came out. The human charac-
ters in "Chasing the Wind" are entirely fictitious, as are their
interactions and their emotional tangles. I've made adjust-
ments to real places and events for fiction's sake. But all the
incidents of Martha's journey across Kenya in a single-engine
plane are based on my own experience as a passenger and my
husband's experience as a pilot. It didn't all happen on the
same flight, but it all really happened, from the cats as extra

passengers to the wild, lightless sea journey to Manda Island to tie down the plane.

Orville and Wilbur Wright made their momentous powered flight in a heavier-than-air, fixed-wing aircraft on December 17, 1903. My story is set in 1950, but the flying in it is much closer to the kind of flight we know and experience in 2003 than to the kind of flight the Wright Brothers experienced in 1903. This is just incredible to me. In 1933 Charles and Anne Lindbergh spent lonely months exploring possible routes across the Atlantic Ocean; twenty-five years later, planes carried more transatlantic passenger travel than did steamships. How could so much have changed *so fast*? I think air travel is the most amazing innovation of the twentieth century.

This story is my small tribute to the one-hundredth anniversary of that "first flight."

Diana Wynne Jones

Little Dot

I am lucky enough to own a wizard who talks to me. Henry knows that we cats do not like being taken by surprise. This is how I know all about my early life, when I was much too young to remember.

Henry lives in an old farm in the hills above Ettmoor and he works three days a week for the Science Institute down in the valley. It is very secret work, he says, because the Government does not want it generally known that they do magical research, but they pay him quite well. Henry is an excellent wizard. But he is far too kind-hearted for his own good.

At the time Henry came into my possession, a young lady—who, even Henry admits, was taking advantage of him horribly—had just moved out of the farm, taking with her all four of her brothers, her mother and Henry's prize pigs. The only person left was Henry's Great Aunt Harriet, who lived by herself in a cottage in the yard. Henry was lonely.

He tried keeping hens for company. He still has these, but

all they give him is eggs. (Hens, if you are an innocent town-cat, have sharp claws like we do and a *very* sharp bit on the front of their heads. A cat has to be careful around hens.)

Henry tried to console himself for the sudden quiet emptiness in the farm by buying a CD player and twenty operas, but he was still lonely. He went for long walks. He tells me that the hills are excellent for walking in, and this may be true but I have never tried it. It always seems to rain when Henry goes walking.

That particular day it was raining relentlessly, the kind of rain that is mixed up with mist and gets into all your crannies. Henry says he enjoyed it! He tramped along with his beard dripping on his chest, listening to the pattering of drops in the bracken and the gurgling of all the mountain streams, until he came to the place where the path goes over a rocky shoulder and a storm drain goes under the path. Henry says he could hear the drain rushing from a long way off. He thought this was the reason he couldn't properly hear what the black lady was saying. The water was thundering along under the path when he got near. He wondered what an old West Indian woman was doing so far up in the hills, particularly as she seemed quite dry, but she loomed out of the mist so suddenly and she was beckoning him so urgently that he didn't have time to wonder much.

He thought she said, "Hurry *up*, man!" and pointed downwards to where the storm drain came off the hill, but he was not sure.

But he galloped to where she was pointing, where he was just in time to see a tiny sodden slip of fur go sluicing down the drain and vanish under the road. He rushed to the other side of the path and went crashing down the bank, expecting me to come swirling out of the drain any second. In fact, I had caught on a stone about a foot inside the drain. I was buried in yellow frothy bubbles and practically camouflaged. Henry says he would never have found me if I hadn't had four white feet and one white ear. He plunged to his knees in the water and groped up the pipe until he had hold of me. He says I was frozen. Then he stood up, raining water from knees, elbows, and beard, and shouted up at the black lady, "Here's the kitten you dropped, madam!"

There was no sign of the lady. Henry floundered back to the path—with great difficulty, because he had me cupped in both hands and didn't want to hurt me—and stared into the mist both ways along the path and then up and down the hills, but there was no West Indian woman anywhere. He couldn't understand it. But he said he couldn't let that bother him for long, because it was obviously urgent to get me somewhere warm and dry. He ran all the way back to the farm with me.

There he put me on a towel in front of the kitchen fire and knelt beside me with a saucer of milk. I was old enough to lap, he says, and I had drunk about half the saucerful, when Great Aunt Harriet came in to borrow some sugar. Great Aunt Harriet always opens Henry's kitchen door by crashing at it with her stick. Henry says this was when I first showed my chief talent. I vanished.

Henry was most upset. He crawled about, looking under chairs and the hearthrug, and couldn't think where I'd got to.

Great Aunt Harriet said, "What *are* you doing, Henry?"

"Looking for the kitten," Henry said—or rather shouted. Great Aunt Harriet is not good at human voices unless they are very loud. Henry went on to shout about how he had found me. "And I can't think," he bellowed, "how someone can drop a kitten in a drain and then just go away!"

"Because she wasn't human probably, and there's no need to shout," Great Aunt Harriet replied. "Have you looked in the coal scuttle?"

Henry looked, and there I was, crouched up and trembling and black all over from the coal. Great Aunt Harriet sank into a chair and watched while Henry wiped the black off me and on to the towel. "What a rag-bag marked little thing!" she said. "You'll call her Dot, I suppose."

I know what Great Aunt Harriet meant. I am all over dots. Somewhere on me I have a dot of every colour a cat can have. I have looked in mirrors and Henry has checked. I have silver and grey and tabby, two kinds of ginger and almost-pink, tortoiseshell, Burmese brown, and cream, as well as white and black. I have one blue eye in a black patch and one green inside ginger. I am special. But at that time, Henry said, "Dot is a trivial sort of name, Auntie. A cat should always have a special, impressive name. I shall have to think."

"Please yourself," said Great Aunt Harriet, and began to complain that the hens kept her awake roosting in the coach house on the other side of her bedroom wall.

Henry hates people complaining. He put one of his operas on to drown Great Aunt Harriet out. This part I dimly remember. There was a lot of singing that I slept through quite happily on Henry's knees, and then, suddenly, there was this huge human woman's voice screaming, "Len Iggmy son of Trey, la moor Tay Una!"

I vanished again like a shot.

It took Henry and Great Aunt Harriet half an hour to find me. I was behind the big blue and white meat dish halfway up the Welsh dresser. We still don't know how I got there.

"That settles it," Henry said. "Her name is Turandot, out of this opera." He sat me on his left leg and stroked me with one finger while he explained that the screaming-woman was a princess called Turandot, singing a song to warn her prince that he would die if he didn't answer her three riddles. "The words mean: *There are three riddles but only one death*," he said.

So my name is Turandot and I am a princess, but somehow I am nearly always called Little Dot. Some of my chief memories of growing up—apart from chasing wisps of straw and galloping over the shed roofs and tearing up Henry's work-papers and playing with the stuffed mouse Henry had bought me—are of sitting on Henry's knee while he explained how I got my name. He played that screaming-woman a lot. And I always vanished. Henry would fish me out from behind the meat dish—and later from under the Welsh dresser and then from inside its cupboard—and sit me on his left knee, and then on both knees when I grew big enough, and explain how I got my name. At night, I slept in his beard, until after about six months he complained that I was throttling him and asked me to sleep on his head instead.

A few weeks after I started sleeping on Henry's head, Henry came home with two more cats, one under each arm. They were a dark tabby and a rippled ginger and they were both bigger than me. I was horrified. I was truly hurt. I went bounding up the coach house roof, where I drove the cockerel down and sat in his place with my back to everything, staring down at the moor. Henry came and called to me, but I was too angry and offended to listen. I sat there for hours.

In the end, Henry climbed on the roof too and sat panting astride it. "Little Dot," he said, "it's not my fault. I was in town and I met the black lady again. She was in the garden of an empty house and she called me over. Someone had moved house and left the two cats behind. They were both starving. I *had* to help them, Little Dot! Do forgive me."

It soothed me just a little, that he had come up on the roof to explain, but I couldn't let him see that. I kept my back to him and twitched my tail.

"*Please*, Little Dot!" Henry said. "You'll always be my first and only cat!"

"Prove it," I said. "Send them away again."

"I can't do that," he said. "They've nowhere to live and you can count their ribs, Little Dot. Let me look after them and I'll do anything you want."

"All right," I said, and I turned round and nosed his hand. But I didn't purr.

Henry said, "Thank God!" and more or less fell off the roof. The noise brought Great Aunt Harriet out of her cottage.

"I thought you were that dratted rooster again!" she said. "What a fuss about one little spotted cat! When are you going to build a proper henhouse?"

"Soon, soon," Henry said, rolling in the weeds.

He called those cats Orlando and Cleopatra, would you

believe! But they generally answered to Orange and Claws. Claws was a tomcat anyway and Claws suited him better. I made it very clear to them right from the start that it was me who slept on Henry's head, and I made it equally clear to Henry that I was having my food up on the Welsh dresser in future, not down on the flagstones like an ordinary cat. I wanted him to put two more catflaps in the kitchen door too, so that they wouldn't sully mine, but he said that one would have to do. He was too busy planning the hen coop Great Aunt Harriet kept on about to cut holes in doors.

Orange and Claws and I got on quite well actually. They knew I was the one who really owned Henry. And they had always lived in a town up to then, so they were quite fascinated when I showed them the farm and the hills and warned them to be careful of hens and Great Aunt Harriet's stick. Great Aunt Harriet always said she had no patience with cats and was liable to prove it by swatting you. Orange went out exploring a lot, while Claws taught me how to catch mice in the sheds. I mean, I *knew* mice before Claws came, but I hadn't known you could *eat* them.

But Henry just couldn't seem to stop himself adopting cats. "I seem to have got into the habit," he said to me apologetically, the day he arrived home from the Scientific Institute with Millamant in a basket. "Don't mind her. She's a victim of a mad scientist at the Institute. I sneaked her out of a cage there, and I'm afraid she's a bit mad herself by now."

Millamant was a skinny Burmese with a squint, and *mad* was an understatement. I mean, she liked being *wet*. The first time Claws and I found Mill swimming in the water butt, we naturally assumed she was drowning and set up a scream for help. This brought Great Aunt Harriet out of her cottage, who assumed the same thing and tried to pull Millamant out. Millamant scratched her. Deeply. In reply, Great Aunt Harriet pushed Millamant right under water and stumped off, shouting to Henry that she couldn't *abide* cats and this one was *crazy*. Later, she found Mill in the bath with her and threw her out of the window, yelling to Henry that he was to stop owning cats at *once*, before everyone else went mad too. Mill didn't care. She had a wash in the water butt and then got in the shower with Henry.

Great Aunt Harriet didn't really dislike cats. She just needed the right cat to belong to. This became clear when one of her nephews arrived for a visit. He had brought his cat, Mr Williams, in a sort of glass box pitched sideways into the back of his sports car. Mr Williams was black and well-mannered and scared of almost everything. Well, so would *I* be scared of everything if I was forced to ride around sideways in a glass box. As soon as Henry saw Mr Williams, he strode to the car and opened the box.

"That's no way to treat a cat!" Henry said. "Turn your car round and drive away. Now."

"But I've come to stay with Aunt Harriet," the nephew protested, "for a week."

"Oh no you haven't!" Great Aunt Harriet screamed from inside the cottage. "Go away at once!"

Henry looked very surprised at this. Great Aunt Harriet was supposed to be very fond of this nephew. She was leaving him her things in her Will. But as soon as Henry opened the glass box, Mr Williams had done a vanishing act almost as good as mine and ended up clamped to Great Aunt Harriet's chest. Shortly, Great Aunt Harriet arrived in the doorway of her cottage with the trembling black cat in her arms. He had his claws into her everywhere he could hang on to. Every claw said, "This human is *mine!*" Great Aunt Harriet accepted this at once, the way humans do, and she told the nephew he was not to set foot in her cottage ever again. The nephew drove sulkily away and Mr Williams stayed. He was as unbalanced as Mill in his way. He *liked* it when Great Aunt Harriet called him her cutchy-wootchy-darling-diddums and tickled his tummy—but we forgave him for that, considering what he had been through.

Great Aunt Harriet made Henry drive her into town to alter her Will, so that she could leave her things to Henry instead. Henry told me that the things were all hideous china ornaments and he hoped she would change her mind. Then he drove off to visit one of the farmers on the moor, who had asked to see him urgently, and came back with the sixth cat.

The sixth cat was called Madam Dalrymple and she was white and fluffy as a dandelion clock—or she was when Henry had washed the muck off her. Nobody knew where she had come from or who had belonged to her and Madam Dalrymple was far too stupid to explain. She certainly did not belong on the farm where Henry found her. He had discovered her struggling in the farmer's pigpen, in considerable danger from the sow who lived in the pen. Henry had to bath her four times. Unlike Millamant, Madam Dalrymple hated water and actually scratched Henry—but this was practically the only touch of spirit she ever showed. She was *stupid*. She lay about in picturesque poses and sighed to anyone who would listen that what she really, *really* needed was a blue satin bow round her neck. I mostly ignored her, except for when she tried to sit on Henry's knee. I always made her sit on his feet instead. Henry's knees are *mine*—both of them.

A couple of weeks after Madam Dalrymple arrived, all the farmers on the moor came to see Henry, looking grave and anxious. We went up on the roofs and stared at their Land Rovers and Jeeps and vans. Several of them had dogs in them, so we had to stay on the roofs until they had gone. Then I went down and sat on Henry's papers so that he could explain to me what it was all about. I am the only one who is allowed to sit on Henry's desk, or climb on his computer.

Henry was looking as upset as the farmers. It seemed that there was a Great Beast loose on Ettmoor, probably from a zoo somewhere, Henry said, although nobody really knew where it had come from or even what kind of animal it was. It had only been seen for brief moments at dusk from a long way off, but it had eaten a lot of sheep and attacked a number of other animals too. Henry spread out the various photographs the farmers had brought and I sat soberly with my tail round my legs and looked at them.

I felt the hair on my spine and my tail trying to bush out. At one photo, I had to struggle not to do a strong vanishment and end up cowering in the back of the airing cupboard or somewhere. This one had caught the Beast slinking into a distant hedge. It was dark and shaped very like a cat—but not at all like a cat either. It was—*wrong*. It was—well—a monster.

LITTLE DOT

And it was obviously huge. If I had had any doubt about its size, there was the picture of a horse it had attacked. The poor creature had lost half its hide down one side, in eight long bleeding streaks. That Beast had *claws*. And then there were pictures of the poor mutilated remains of a dog and several cats the thing had played with. My back shuddered and I thought uneasily of myself and Claws playing with the mice in the sheds. This Beast played just the same way.

"Yes," Henry said, "this is a real creature—and a real menace too, Little Dot. The farmers want me to help them track it down and shoot it. They've tried to catch it several times, but it always seems to slip away when they think they've got it cornered. They want me to apply some science to the hunt." He sighed. "They say science, Little Dot, but I can see this is going to take magic. Normally I'd hate the idea. It seems so unfair. But just look at those cats. It's got to be stopped. And until we've caught it, you cats are going to stay indoors at nights. Make that clear to the others, will you?" He sighed again, "Hens inside too, I suppose."

I explained about the Beast to the others, but I am not sure they believed me. Only Madam Dalrymple was prepared to stay inside in comfort. Every evening became a frenzy of hens running and cackling, with Henry galloping around the yard driving them into the coach house, and then getting more and more exasperated as he grabbed Orange as Orange tried to slither out into the landscape and seized Millamant dripping from the water butt. Then Claws had to be tempted out of the sheds with a slice of mackerel and Mr Williams wheedled with a chunk of melon—for some reason this was

Mr Williams's favourite food—and the rest of us thrust indoors with urgent entreaties. "Get in or I'll kick you, cat! I'm out of patience! And, no, the catflap is now *locked*, understand! Even for you, Little Dot!" This last regardless of the fact that I was only *watching*. It took nearly an hour before the five of us were moodily gathered on Henry's bed—or under it, if it was Millamant—and Mr Williams finally thrust into Great Aunt Harriet's cottage. Actually Mr Williams came straight out again through the bathroom window as soon as Henry was indoors. He gets claustrophobia, you see.

During this time, when he was not at the Scientific Institute or conferring with the farmers, Henry built the Mobile Hen Coop. Mr Williams and I both found it fascinating. It was a long, long wooden triangle, with two sloping sides and flat ends and bottom. In one sloping side there were three sliding doors for the hens to go in through and boxes full of straw inside for the hens to roost in. Once the hens were inside it for the night, Henry said, the sliding doors would be shut to keep them safe.

"But here's the clever part," Henry said. "If it stays in one place it kills all the grass."

"Weeds," said Mr Williams. "They're weeds in this yard."

"Weeds then," Henry agreed, "but I don't want them killed whatever they are."

"Finest clumps of nettles in the country," Mr Williams observed. "Thistles and camomile too."

"Medicinal and magical uses for all three," Henry said. "Do stop mewing at me, Mr Williams. It puts me off. Anyway, this Coop is designed to rise in the air and move to another place by magic. Watch."

LITTLE DOT

Mr Williams had to go away when Henry demonstrated the magic. He said it made the roots of his fur sore. But I stayed and watched. I found I understood that magic—but then I told you I was special.

Unfortunately the hens shared Mr Williams's feelings about magic. None of them would go near that Coop. They ended up being chased into the coach house every night and disturbing Great Aunt Harriet just as usual.

I used the Coop as a plaything after that. If I spread myself along the pointed top, I found I could activate the magics and send the Coop floating in any direction I wanted. To my surprise, Madam Dalrymple was the only other cat who thought this was fun. As soon as she saw me on the Coop, she hopped up behind me, and, not in the least worried that the magics bushed her coat out until she looked like a fluffy snowball, she went for sedate rides round and round the farmyard. Henry stood in the kitchen door and laughed helplessly at us whenever he took a break from making magics to catch the Beast of Ellmoor.

He had designed several rings of big black magic generators, and these were placed out on the moor to surround the areas where the Beast had been active. Every day his farmer friends moved the generators a few feet in a carefully planned direction, so that eventually the Beast would be trapped inside a small tight circle. Then they would go in with their guns.

Henry had a map laid out on the dining room table with little tiny models of the generators on it. "Do they know you're using magic?" I asked, sitting on the edge of the table to look at it.

"No, I call them field-static generators," Henry said. "They wouldn't believe they were paying for something that worked, if I said it was magic. I've had to ask them to pay for the cost of materials, you see. I made the things down at the Institute."

The little model generators looked so enticing that I couldn't resist putting out a paw to the nearest. It wobbled beautifully. To my utter indignation, Henry promptly pushed me off the table. I sat at his feet and did my Outraged Stare at him.

"No," he said. "No touching, not even for you, princess. This map is part of the magic. I think the dining room door is going to be shut from now on."

"Don't you *trust* me?" I said.

"Not where little wobbly things are concerned, no," Henry said. "Run away now, there's a good cat."

I stalked out into the yard, so furious that my tail lashed at thistles and clumps of other weeds all the way to the Coop. Henry didn't trust *me*! I couldn't believe it! I jumped up on the Coop and took it round in a great angry circle until it was pointing at the gates. The gates are always open in Henry's farm. I was almost through into the road when Madam Dalrymple bounded elegantly among the weeds and jumped up behind me.

"Where are we going?" she asked, settling herself tastefully.

"Away," I said. I didn't want her. I was angry. But I had to go somewhere now I was out in the road, so I turned right, uphill, the way that led to the hill paths. The Coop didn't like the climbing. It slewed and it slogged and it crawled. In the end I wrestled it round on to the nearest level path, which happened to be the path that Henry had taken nearly a year ago when he found me. The Coop went much better there. We were fine until a light foggy rain began to fall.

Madam Dalrymple shifted and twitched. "Where are we really going?" she said. "Is it far?" She looked very odd, with every hair on end and a raindrop on each hair. She made a silvery ball rather like the ornaments Great Aunt Harriet had hung on a tree at Christmas.

"I'm going to look at the storm drain where Henry found me," I said. I thought I might as well.

"Your birthplace," Madam Dalrymple said placidly. "How correct. He's told you all about it so often, of course. Even I can begin to understand him when he talks about it now. But I wish I could understand human talk like you do. I'd ask for a blue satin ribbon. Do you think he'd get me one?"

"No," I said. I was having problems. A peculiarity of the magic on the Coop, which had not shown up when we were just jogging round the yard, was that if you went in a straight line, you went faster and faster. It seemed to double its speed continuously. Rain was hitting my eyes like needles and whipping off my whiskers. Rocks and blurred grass raced past underneath.

"This is fun," said Madam Dalrymple, vast with magic.

I didn't think so. I could see and hear the storm drain thundering under the path already. We were whizzing up to it, and after that, the path turned a sharp corner. I knew we were going to whizz straight out over the hillside. I couldn't possibly stop us in time. "Get ready to jump off!" I gasped at Madam Dalrymple.

"Why?" she asked.

"Because," I began. And then we were at the storm drain.

"Steady, steady," said a big black lady in the middle of the path. The pale palms of her hands slapped against the triangular front of the Coop and it came to the ground with a crunch. "Where you going so fast?" she said to me.

"I—er—thought I'd look at my birthplace," I explained.

"You weren't born here, honey. It was up the hill a piece," she said. "There you got swept away."

"Good heavens!" Madam Dalrymple said, leaning over to look at the rushing water. "You might have been drowned!"

"That is so, but never you mind that now," the woman said. "There are three things I'm telling you that I want you to learn and remember. Say them after me, honey, not to forget. The first one is *The higher the fewer*. You got that?"

"*The higher the fewer*," I repeated, gazing up at her. Her face was black and wet as my nose. I'd never seen a human like her before.

"And you?" the woman said to Madam Dalrymple, but Madam Dalrymple just stared. She has no memory at all. The woman shrugged and turned back to me. "Now, *Chocolate herrings are impure*. That's two," she said.

"*Chocolate herrings are impure*," I said, still gazing. She smelled the same way the magics of the Coop did, but stronger and spicier. I began to wonder if she was quite a human.

"That's good, that's great," she told me. "Now the last is *The Beast of Ettmoor*."

"*The Beast of Ettmoor*," I said obediently. The woman had a turban on her head that stuck up in two black peaks on either side of her head. They reminded me of my own ears. "If you don't mind my asking," I said, "who are you?"

"My name is Bastet, Little Dot," she said, "and my calling is cats. Have you got my three sayings in your head? You about to need them badly."

"Yes," I said.

"Good," Bastet said. "Then walk around to the other end of this thing you riding and go home. I send a friend to you any second now. Makes seven. That's a good number."

I jumped down and picked my way over the mud and stones of the path to the opposite end of the Coop. By the time I got there, Bastet had gone. I was not surprised. I think she was very magical indeed. I jumped, rather sadly, up on to the Coop, facing the way we had come, and I was just about to get it going again, when another whiff of that spiced magic smell struck my nose. I looked up the hillside and saw something mostly white struggling down through the heather. A pleading mew came from it.

"It's all right!" I called out. "I'm waiting for you."

A large cat, almost twice my size, came scrambling and sliding down the wet rocks to the path. She was so wet and draggled and humble that I never thought of being afraid of her. "Oh dear," she said, "I'm so sorry to bother you, but *could* you find me somewhere to shelter? I've nowhere."

"You can come home with us," I said. "I'll speak to Henry. Hop up."

The large cat looked up at me and at Madam Dalrymple staring vaguely down at her. Then she looked at the Coop. "Is there a way to ride inside?" she asked diffidently.

"Well, we've got three doors," I said, "but I don't know how to open them."

"Like this, I think," the large cat said, and somehow she managed to push the middle hatch aside and crawl inside the Coop. "Lots of lovely straw," she said. "Thank you."

"You're welcome," I said. There was something about this big, wet, polite cat that made me like her.

"She's got just the same markings as you have! All those dots!" Madam Dalrymple said, craning down to look through the hatch.

I craned down to look too. Inside the hatch I could see splodges of grey, tabby, ginger, and pink, blots of black and dots of sandy brown and cream. But, to my relief, because this cat was so much larger, she seemed more white than anything. I like to think I am unique. "The effect is quite different," I said haughtily.

"Not a lot," said Madam Dalrymple. "We'll have to call her Big Dot."

I made a silently offended No Comment and moved the Coop off.

It was quite as difficult going back. The further we went, the faster the Coop moved. By the time we reached the farm road, we were scorching along as fast as a car. I worked frantically to slow us down. And of course, Madam Dalrymple, in her usual maddening way, chose the moment that I was trying to aim us at the farm gate to say, "Why did that woman tell you to remember nonsense?"

"I don't know," I spat, as we hurtled into the yard. Mr Williams, who was sitting in our way, rose six feet in the air and managed to miss us. Orange and Claws squirted out of nettle clumps to either side. We raced on until we hit the water butt and stopped. Millamant came head and shoulders out of it, squinting reproachfully. "Where's Henry?" I asked her.

"In the living room, but you won't want to go there," Mill replied.

"Of course I will. It's got the best chairs," I said.

As I bounded away towards the catflap, Mill said, "I did warn you!" but I took no notice. I raced through the kitchen and past the dining room   where the door was now closed on that map—and galloped into the living room. There I stopped as if I'd run into the water butt again.

Henry was standing there holding both the hands of a human woman. He had a beaming, dazzled look and he was staring into the human's face with the same expression that he usually saves for me. I suppose she was a handsome human, in a thin, dark way, but still . . . I mewed. Loudly.

Henry jumped. "Oh, look, Fara," he said. "Here's Turandot now!" To my extreme surprise, he swooped on me and picked me up. I'd never known him to do that without my permission before. I squirmed round and gave him my best Outraged Stare, but he took no notice and held me out towards this woman. "There," he said. "Isn't she beautiful?"

The woman narrowed her eyes at me. She shuddered. "Henry, she's *hideous*! She looks as if she's got the plague with all those blotches!" She backed away. "Don't bring her near me. I'm not a cat person."

Henry said cheerfully, "Okay." And dropped me. *Dropped* me! Just like that.

I went away, back through the catflap and over to the

Coop, where Big Dot was peering nervously out of the hatch. "I'll have to introduce you to Henry later, I'm afraid," I said. "Are you hungry?"

"Terribly," she said.

"You met that Fara creature then?" Millamant said, popping up from the water butt again. "I tried to tell you. I think she's staying here."

"Not if I have anything to say about it!" I said, leading Big Dot to the kitchen.

When we got there, Great Aunt Harriet was sitting in the best chair with Mr Williams in her lap. "Oh, we've got a Big Dot now, I see," she said, watching Big Dot fit herself humbly through the catflap. "Better than the other thing that arrived here today. I must say, Henry has a *genius* for choosing terrible women! Little Dot, *try* to make him see reason. I've never disliked anyone so much in my life as I dislike that Fara."

I jumped up on the Welsh dresser and observed that half my breakfast was still there. "Big Dot, if you'd like to come up here," I began.

But Great Aunt Harriet popped Mr Williams on the floor and sprang up, saying, "Now, Turandot, don't make that poor thing struggle up *there*, for goodness sake, not in *her* condition!" and bustled about finding saucers. She gave Big Dot most of a tin of meaty chunks, a pyramid of dry food and a soup bowl of milk. Big Dot ate it all. She was starving.

"Is this Fara woman really staying?" I asked.

Great Aunt Harriet never listens to me, but Mr Williams said gloomily, "We fear the worst. He's lent her his pyjamas."

Mr Williams was right. But it was worse than we realised.

LITTLE DOT

We expected that Fara would be given one of the spare rooms, but when we followed Henry upstairs to bed, we discovered that he and Fara were sharing Henry's room. Fara turned and stared at us. "Why are *they* here?"

"Little Dot always sleeps on my head," Henry explained. "Orange and Claws and Madam Dalrymple usually dispose themselves around on the duvet. And Millamant curls up in the chamber pot, you know."

"Well, they're not doing *that* any more," Fara said. "Get rid of them."

Henry said, in that cheerful, obliging way, "Okay." And, to our extreme distress, we found ourselves pushed outside by Henry's magic, out and down the stairs, and then out again, until we were in the farmyard. It was as if he had forgotten we were in danger from the Beast there. It was a cold night too. Claws and Orange huddled together for warmth and Madam Dalrymple sat as close to Mill as Mill would let her. I crouched by myself in the middle of the yard. I have never felt so bewildered and unhappy as I did then. Because, you see, I had seen Henry look at Fara in the way he usually looks at me. And I had seen Fara look back, and her look kept saying, Henry, you are *mine*! Just like I do. I kept wondering if I was an awful cat, the way Fara was an awful human.

After a while, something big and warm and whitish came and settled in the clump of weeds next to me. "What is so wrong, Little Dot?" Big Dot asked.

"It's Henry's new human!" I said. "She won't let us into Henry's room. And she *smells* wrong, and she doesn't even like Madam Dalrymple. I mean, most ordinary visitors who don't care for cats *always* admire Madam Dalrymple! The farmers say she's beautiful. But Fara called her a fluffy monstrosity."

"I doubt if Madam Dalrymple understood though," Big Dot said.

"No, she tried to get on Fara's knee twice," I said. "But that's not the point, Big Dot! Henry's being so *obedient* to her! He didn't listen to his operas because Fara said she didn't like opera, and he turned us *out*! How do we make Fara go away, Big Dot?"

"I'm not sure," Big Dot said, and thought about it, sitting comfortably close.

While she sat there, I noticed that Big Dot's side, where it pressed against me, was sort of squirming and jumping. "Are you all right?" I asked. "Did all that food upset you?"

"No, no," she said. "I'm going to have kittens again. Quite soon, I think. Do you know, if you can think of what to do, and if all the doors are like the door from your kitchen, I *think* I could show you how to open Henry's bedroom."

"Oh, *please* do!" I said. "I miss the smell of his head!"

As we were talking, I had been hearing a lot of noise from Great Aunt Harriet's cottage. It sounded as if Mr Williams was singing, or something. Now it suddenly rose to a climax as Great Aunt Harriet threw her door open, saying, "Oh, all right, all *right*! *Go* out and do it then! Though what's wrong with your litter box I—Oh!" she said, as the light fell on the six of us in our various huddles. "Did that creature throw you out then? Of *course* she did, she's that type. It wouldn't worry her if the Beast ate the lot of you. You'd better all come in here and be safe then."

LITTLE DOT

All of us, even Millamant, got up at once and filed politely into the cottage, where Mr Williams was sitting on the table, looking suave and smug. We arranged ourselves courteously on the hearthrug.

"Hm," said Great Aunt Harriet and picked up her mug of cocoa. She stumped up to bed, muttering to herself. "Better bend our minds to getting rid of that young woman, or she'll be sending Henry down to the vet with all the cats in a hamper to have them put down. She'd better not touch my Mr Williams, though."

This made me think very urgently all night of ways to get rid of Fara.

Of course, the first thing was to get into the house. Next morning the catflap was locked and all the windows were shut, though we could hear and smell that Fara and Henry were in the kitchen having breakfast. We gathered round the door and yowled. Orange and Millamant have particularly loud voices, so between us we raised a fine noise. Normally, it would have brought Henry to the door like a shot, but that day he took no notice of us at all. It was as if Fara had put him under a spell.

After twenty minutes of continuous din, Great Aunt Harriet stumped out of her cottage and banged the kitchen door open with her stick. We streamed in after her and stood by our empty bowls. "Aren't you going to feed your cats, Henry?" Great Aunt Harriet demanded.

Fara looked up from eating toast. "Cats are little hunting machines," she said. "They can live on the mice in the barns."

"With respect, Miss Spinks," Great Aunt Harriet said, "not

only has Claws eaten every mouse for miles around, but I don't think Madam Dalrymple would know what to do with a mouse if it ran down her throat." She got out the food and fed us, while Henry smiled dreamily at Fara and said nothing at all.

After breakfast, they chased us out again and locked the house, while Henry drove Fara into town to do some shopping. It seemed that Fara had arrived without any clothes but the flimsy black dress she was wearing.

"Which strikes me as odd," Great Aunt Harriet said, when Mr Williams fetched her. She thought a bit. "I shall borrow some lentils," she said, and let herself into the house with her key. Then she went and set the living room window very slightly ajar. "There," she said, coming out with a cup of lentils. "Go in and do your worst."

Orange muscled the window wide open and we all took turns at peeing on the rugs. But the bedroom door was firmly shut. "Not to worry," said Big Dot. She gathered us round her on the landing and showed how you stood on your hind legs and trod on the door handle, and your weight pushed the door open. Before long, all of us could do it except Madam Dalrymple, although I had to jump to reach the handle. Then Claws went in and did tomcat things until the bedroom smelt really *strong*. Millamant went along to the toilet, where she got herself extremely wet, and then lay on the pillows. I thought that had probably fixed the bedroom, so I took everyone else down to the kitchen where we spilled sugar and trod in the butter and knocked down cups so they smashed on the flagstones. Then Big Dot and Orange heaved the waste-bin over, while I went and walked behind all the plates on the Welsh dresser until most of them fell over and one or two broke. Madam Dalrymple had great fun rolling in cornflakes.

Then we went outside again and hid. Henry's car came back and he and Fara went into the house with bags and bags and bags. We could hear Fara's voice in there, screaming curses, but all that happened was that Fara came grimly outside and put our bowls outside in a row, while Henry opened windows and draped carpets and pillows out of them to air.

"Round One is a draw, I think," Great Aunt Harriet said when she let us into her cottage that night. "They've moved into the biggest spare room and *she's* hung all her new clothes there. She's bought enough stuff to last a year and *rows* of shoes. I suppose Henry paid, the poor fool!"

"What can we do with those clothes?" I said.

Madam Dalrymple suddenly came alert. "I know all about clothes," she said. "I'll show you what to do."

Next day, Henry went off to work at the Science Institute. "I must go there occasionally," he said, when I tried to get in the car with him, "or they'll wonder what they're paying me for. Out you get, Little Dot." He drove away, leaving Fara in the house with all the doors and windows shut.

Great Aunt Harriet came and knocked on the kitchen door. When Fara didn't open it, she went and rapped on the living room window. "Oh, Miss Spinks, if you would be so good! I'm afraid I've run out of sugar."

After a while, Fara came and grudgingly let her into the kitchen. I was ready. I did one of my best vanishments and was past Fara and through the kitchen before she had properly got the door open. While Great Aunt Harriet was saying, "Oh, no need to get down the tin. I can hook it with my stick and reach it that way—oh, how *kind*!" I scudded along to the dining room and opened its door the way Big Dot had taught us. I stole past the table with the map magic, very careful not to disturb it—although, from the dusty smell of it, I suspected that Fara had made Henry forget all about it—and jumped to the window sill. That window bursts open if you lean on it hard enough, so I did that. Everyone came jumping quietly inside, except for Big Dot. She was feeling poorly that day and stayed resting inside the Coop.

We all crept up to the spare bedroom. And there were all the clothes, hanging in rows, with lines of shoes underneath them. Mr Williams looked at them with great interest.

"Do we tear them up?" he asked Madam Dalrymple. "I quite fancy getting my claws into some of these."

"She'll get much more annoyed if we spoil them so that she can *almost* wear them," Madam Dalrymple said. "You make the fronts messy, as if food was spilled on them . . ."

Millamant said, "I know a pond that's full of green slime!" and hurried away.

" . . . and you put hairs all over the black things," Madam Dalrymple explained, "except you, Mr Williams, you put hairs on the *white* things. Then the knitted things, you bite a thread and then pull, to make holes, and the dresses you bite just the thread in the hems and then pull the hem half down. You bite buttons, too, so that they half come off. . . ."

She had all kinds of ideas, so many that I began to suspect that Madam Dalrymple had been dumped in that pigpen by the outraged human she once owned. And whatever she suggested, we did. Millamant came back dripping with green slime and plastered herself lovingly up the fronts of things, Mr Williams pulled down a pile of white things and wriggled in them, and while the rest of us bit and pulled threads, Orange went along methodically making messes in all of the shoes. It was fun. When everything was thoroughly treated, we went away—although Millamant paused to roll the last of her slime off on the pillows—and spent the rest of the day persuading Great Aunt Harriet to give us titbits.

You should have heard Fara shrieking when Henry came home.

"Perhaps that wasn't such a good idea," Great Aunt Harriet said, after she had been to borrow some tea the following morning. "She's telling Henry to fetch the laundry hamper and take you all down to the vet. He hasn't quite agreed yet, but he will."

"Let's get on the Coop and go away!" Madam Dalrymple said, shivering.

I didn't know what to do. I was miserable. I crouched wretchedly beside the water butt all day, hoping and hoping that Henry would come out and comfort me, but he never did, until Mr Williams came rushing across the yard, mewing excitedly. There never was a cat like Mr Williams for mewing. "Come and see! Come and look!" he mewed. "Everyone come in through the dining room window and see!"

Mill surged out of the water butt, Madam Dalrymple materialised from a hay bale, Orange and Claws shot out of the coach house, and we all galloped after Mr Williams, consumed with curiosity. He led us through the dining room and upstairs to the spare room. There was a strange new smell there. It was not coming from the shoes, which had been bundled into a plastic sack in the passage, nor the clothes, which had been thrown across the sack. It was coming from the bed, inside the room. We stood on our hind legs to look.

Big Dot was lying in the middle of the duvet there, looking tired, surrounded in rather a mess that was full of small squirming bodies. Six of them, there were six . . . "Kittens?" I said. "Oh, Big Dot, why did you have to have them *here?*"

"I didn't *mean* to," Big Dot said weakly. "But it was so comfortable—and I got rather taken short."

"We'll have to guard you," I said. "If Fara finds them . . ."

"I know. I'll move them the moment I feel stronger," Big Dot said. "Not just yet, please."

She went to sleep. Having kittens is obviously quite tiring. The rest of us crouched where we were, around the bed, waiting for what we knew was going to happen. Sure enough, just before suppertime, when the kittens had begun to move about and make squeaky noises, the door opened and Fara came in.

She stopped. She stared. Then she screamed, "Oh, this is the *last straw!* On *my* bed, of all places!"

"It isn't your bed. It belongs to Henry," I said.

She didn't hear me. She plunged forward, with both her hands out to grab. "These are going in the water butt," she said. "I'll drown them myself."

We all acted at once. We poured up over the edges of the bed, and stood there growling and spitting, so that the bed was full of our lashing tails, arched backs and glaring eyes. Big Dot stood up in the centre of us all, twice her usual size, growling loudest of all.

"*Get out of my way!*" Fara screamed and grabbed for the kittens. Upon this, Mr Williams, who was nearest—nice, mild-mannered Mr Williams—put a paw-full of claws in each of her arms and dragged. He left two rows of dark, oozing blood on her. She screamed even louder and hit Mr Williams, so that he flew across the room and crashed into the chest of drawers.

"What on earth is going on?" Henry said from the doorway.

Fara turned to Henry and went on screaming. She was so angry that she seemed to forget how to speak. "Middle of the bed!" she howled. "Water butt. Drown them. Horrible little ratty things! Drown, drown drown!"

Henry walked round her and looked down at the bed. "Kittens," he said.

"*In the middle of my bed!*" Fara screamed.

"There are other beds," Henry said. "Pull yourself together, Fara. May I?" he said to Big Dot. Big Dot, very nervously, moved aside and let him sort through her kittens. "Six," Henry murmured. "One of every colour—black, grey, white, ginger, this one's tortoiseshell, and here's a tabby. Oh, well done, Big Dot!"

"Henry," Fara said to him, in a hard, yowling voice, "I'm telling you to get rid of these cats and drown these kittens. *All* of them. Now."

"Don't talk nonsense," Henry said. He put the kittens gently back beside Big Dot. "Three boys and three girls, I make it."

"I *mean* it!" Fara shouted. "Henry, if you don't get rid of every single cat *this minute,* I shall leave!"

We all stared intensely at Henry, except for Mr Williams, who was washing his bruises beside the chest of drawers. Henry looked at Mr Williams. "The black cat," he said, "belongs to Great Aunt Harriet."

"But he *scratched* me!" Fara said. "They're all horrible creatures. So which is it to be? Do you get rid of them, or do I leave?"

Henry looked from one to another of our urgently staring pairs of eyes, and then at Fara. He seemed almost bewildered, the way he is when he wakes up in the morning. "There's no question," he said to Fara. "If that's your attitude, you'd better leave."

Fara's chest heaved with emotion. She glared. "All right," she said. "You'll regret this." And she left. She swung round and stormed out of the room. I heard her feet galloping down the stairs. I heard the kitchen door crash shut behind her. But I didn't relax until I heard her feet distantly swishing through the farmyard and then pattering on the road. Then I was so relieved that I burst out purring. I couldn't help it.

Henry sighed and said sadly, "Oh well. She did complain a lot. And she hates opera."

We had a perfect, peaceful evening. Henry invited Great Aunt Harriet to supper and played her two operas. One was *Turandot* of course. But, although I sat on his knees to comfort him, I could tell he was sad.

The next morning, all the farmers arrived again, looking grim and serious. During the night, the Beast of Ettmoor had attacked the farm next to Henry's and killed six sheep, a sheep-dog and the farm cat. They were very worried because, according to the plans, the Beast should by now have been herded down the valley inside the final ring of magical generators.

Henry was equally worried. I sat on the dining room mantelpiece and watched him show the farmers the map and scratch his hair over it. "I think," he said at last, "that what *may* have happened is that a crucial—er—field-static generator must have got moved slightly, just enough to let the Beast slip back out of our trap. This one, I think." He pointed to the wobbly little marker that I had tried to play with.

My heart banged under my fur with guilt and terror.

Henry didn't even look at me. When the farmers said they were going to patrol the area with guns in future, he said, "Yes, that seems the only thing to do. And I'll strengthen the outer ring of generators to stop it escaping back into the hills. I'm truly sorry about this. I'll go and see to it now."

He drove off in his car and he was out all that day. He came home exhausted, but instead of settling down to another opera, he went out into the dining room and worked on the map all evening. I felt so guilty that I kept well out of his way. I had messed up his magics and, on top of that, I had driven his lady away. I punished myself by not sleeping on Henry's head that night. I crouched by the kitchen fire instead and was miserable.

"There's no need to take on," Millamant said from the coal scuttle. "It's horrible Fara's fault just as much. She made him forget his magics."

"That's not the point!" I said.

Orange and Claws sat up uneasily in the best chair. They had all chosen to keep me company in my sorrow. "Speaking of the Beast," Orange said, "did you know that Big Dot has moved her kittens out into the Coop? Are they safe there?"

"Oh Lord!" I said, springing up. "They are *not*! And Mr Williams *will* stay out all night!"

I was on my way to the catflap to go and reason with Big Dot when we heard Mr Williams shriek with terror, or with pain, or both, out in the farmyard. Next second, the catflap clapped open. Mr Williams shot through it, streaked across the kitchen and went to ground under the Welsh dresser, which was almost too low even for me to get under these days.

"Hide, hide, hide!" he yowled. "It's coming!"

I stared stupidly at the path of blood Mr Williams had made, from the door to the Welsh dresser.

"*What's* coming?" said Claws.

"The Beast, the Beast!" Mr Williams gibbered. "You can't smell it till it's *there*!"

Everyone was suddenly elsewhere, Madam Dalrymple with a most unladylike howl. I did a vanishment such as I had never managed in my life before and found myself at the very top of the Welsh dresser, almost up by the ceiling. And only just in time. Something was coming through the catflap.

My outstretched hair caught on the ceiling. A big dark face was forcing its way indoors, a face twice the size of Henry's and growing bigger as it came. For a moment, I thought the thing would get stuck, but that was a vain hope. I watched the wood of the catflap and then of the door spread and enlarge as if the wood were so much rubber, to let the Beast's shoulders follow its head, and I realised hopelessly that this Beast was a magical creature. It was almost inside now. Catfight song burst from my throat as I watched it come. This was not the growling I had done at Fara, but the full-voiced, throbbing, yowling, wailing song of defiance you make when you encounter an alien cat. Amidst my terror, I was quite surprised at the noise I could make.

The others joined in, Madam Dalrymple shrilly and Millamant with deep echoes booming from the coal scuttle. Claws and Orange screamed and throbbed from two sides of the room, and Mr Williams produced unearthly yodelings from under the Welsh dresser.

But the Beast kept coming. It dragged its massive hindquarters through the door and then pulled in its long tail. The room was filling with its smell, something like tomcat and something like rotten rat, and it was beginning to rise on its hind feet, when the passage door slammed open and Henry snapped on the lights. "What. . . ?" he began.

We all blinked and stared in the dazzle for a moment. I think that was the worst moment of all. There was a human sort of face on the front of the Beast's head, blinking enormous cat's eyes, and the face was surrounded in filthy, tangled hair. It had mangy little wings dangling from its huge shoulders. Its body had patches of elderly fur on it, clinging to bare, dirty, wrinkled skin. Everything about it was old, old and decaying. The claws on the ends of its great feet were stuck with rotting meat and shreds of grass, and they were splitting with age underneath.

But the worst of it was that we all recognised the face.

"Fara?" Henry said. "My God, you're the Sphinx!"

The Beast opened its mouth, full of blue-rotting fangs, and chuckled. Oh, Henry! I thought. I'm *sorry.* I got it here. I'll never bully you again if you can only just get *rid* of it!

"You're going to ask a riddle," Henry said shakily. "Don't bother. You're going to ask what goes on four legs at dawn, on two legs at midday and three legs in the evening. And I know the answer. It's a man."

The Beast chuckled again. "Wrong," it said. It had a flat, cold voice. "I *used* to ask one riddle. Now I ask three. And I'm not going to ask *you.* I'm going to ask that conniving little spotted pet of yours, up there on top of the shelves. And when she can't answer, I shall be free to tear the lot of you to pieces. I shall gut the cats in front of you and then make you swallow those kittens before I tear your head off. Are you ready to answer, Plague-spot?"

I quivered all over at this. I thought I knew now why Bastet had made me remember those three nonsense sayings. "Ask away," I said, and licked at my shoulder to make my nervous fur lie flatter.

The Beast said, "Why is a mouse when it spins?"

"Oh, I know that one!" Henry said, and he and I answered together, *"The higher the fewer."* I couldn't think how he came to know it. It made much more sense to a cat than a human. "And?" I said.

The Beast grinned, filling the air with bad-meat smell. "When is ceramic begonias?" it said.

"That makes no sense to me," Henry said. It didn't to me, either. Nor did the answer.

"*Chocolate herrings are impure,*" I said. And I guessed that the riddles—and their answers—were the result of an ancient, tired, rotting brain. In the electric light, the Beast looked older than any creature I had ever seen. Its Fara-face was all sags and wrinkles. "And your third?" I asked. This is all back to front, I thought. I am Turandot the princess and *I* should be asking the riddles. Has Henry told me the opera wrong?

"The third," said the Beast, "is, Who kills as lion and as human wins?"

"*The Beast of Ettmoor!*" I cried out. "Now I can tear *you* to pieces!" And I was so exultant that I sprang straight down from my perch near the ceiling to the top of the Beast's head, where I began scratching and tearing at its dirty mane with all four feet. Looking back, I can't think how I came to do anything so silly. I became totally entangled in long, filthy hair. I couldn't get loose. All I could think of to do then was to sink my teeth into its nearest smelly ear. The Beast screeched and swiped at me with its claws.

The outside door crashed open, shoved by Great Aunt Harriet's stick. I think she had been getting into her clothes ever since she heard Mr Williams shrieking. She stormed in now, shouting, "What have you done to my poor little Willy-diddums?" and whacked at the Beast with her stick. Bang, bang. Clout. Feathers, dust and hairs whirled.

Henry, who was in a toweling dressing gown and his bare feet, danced around uncertainly for a moment and then seized the nearest chair—revealing Madam Dalrymple, who ran for her life—and began bashing at the Beast with it from the other side. I could feel the Beast try to protect itself with magic. Henry replied with more magic, such a furious gust of it that the chair he was wielding sizzled and the long hair wrapped round me stood out like rods. That was too much for the Beast. It turned and dived for the door.

I was thrown aside as it crashed outside. I was flung across something hard. I was so winded and frightened that it took me a second to realise that I was spread-eagled across the Coop, which Big Dot must have brought near the kitchen when she moved her kittens into it. In that second, the Beast ran, bounding into the darkness on four legs, and Claws and Orange went pelting after it as hard as they could go. Maybe they were inspired by my example. On the other hand, they never could resist chasing anything that ran. And almost in that same moment, Great Aunt Harriet galloped outside and flung herself sidesaddle across the Coop.

"After it, after it! Make this thing move, Little Dot!" she shouted, bashing the wooden side with her stick.

While I was pulling myself to my feet, Mr Williams landed on the Coop too and clung to Great Aunt Harriet's lap. He explained afterward that although the magic made him feel as if his teeth were coming loose, he had to come because Great Aunt Harriet was not behaving normally. "And one has to look after one's humans," he said.

I started the Coop and we trundled towards the gate. By then, Henry was mincing after us, gasping when he trod on a nettle, shouting, "No! *Stop!* That Beast is a killer!" but we were getting up speed by then and, what with one thing and another, I was too dazed to stop.

Catsong came throbbing out of the night. When we swept

out into the road, I saw Claws and Orange crouching in the way that led uphill, while the Beast hovered, wondering whether to kill them and go past, or turn the other way. That was clever of Claws and Orange, and brave too. If the Beast had fled up into the hills, it might have been loose forever. But it saw us coming and turned downhill. It galloped away at astonishing speed. But, as I have explained, before long the Coop got up to astonishing speed too. We fair zoomed along, and began catching up steadily to the great dark shape galloping ahead.

"We're gaining!" Great Aunt Harriet shrieked, beating on the Coop. "Go faster! Faster!"

We were still a good fifty yards away when strong lights shone out from either side of the road, pinning the Beast in their glare. It faltered. There was a BOOM like the end of the world and several crack-crack-cracks, followed by echoes that bounced round the hills until I could hardly hear straight. The Beast jumped up in a great arch and flopped back on the road, where I thought it came into several pieces. I was so shocked that I stopped the Coop dead. We came down with a crunch.

"What happened?" I said.

"Oh good!" said Great Aunt Harriet. "I mean, oh dear. I think the farmers shot it."

One of the hatches in the Coop slid aside and Big Dot stepped out. "I'll go and make sure," she said, and went trotting along towards the lights and the shapes of men and guns.

"Does that mean her kittens are in this Coop?" Great Aunt

Harriet said. "How *inconsiderate* of me! I hope the poor little things are all right."

"They will be, or she wouldn't have left them," Mr Williams said soothingly.

Here Henry came limping up. But, to my huge indignation, he limped straight on past us, saying, "I'd better go and make sure they think they've just shot a lion. Take the Coop back to the yard, Little Dot."

He passed Big Dot coming back. She said, "They used such a big gun that they blew her into several bits," and climbed back in with her kittens again.

I took the Coop back to the kitchen door, where Great Aunt Harriet scrambled down, saying things about bottles and glasses and seeing to Mr Williams's wounds. "Nothing! Just a scratch! I don't need seeing to!" I heard him saying as she banged the kitchen door shut. It took her three attempts. It was half off its hinges.

I waited, sitting on the Coop listening to Big Dot purring inside. I waited while Claws and Orange returned, very pleased with themselves. Henry was so long coming back that I got anxious. Suppose the Beast had just been faking dead and went for his throat when he got near? Then it would be all my fault. I set off out of the yard and down the road to look for him.

I'd only gone twenty yards or so, when there *was* Henry, limping along with a crowd of farmers, bringing them back to the farm for a drink. Exasperating. I sat down in the road and curled my tail primly round my legs.

Henry saw me and dashed forward, quite forgetting his

sore bare feet. "Little Dot!" he cried out. And I forgot to be exasperated and leapt up his front into his arms and draped over his shoulder, purring. "There's my brave Turandot!" Henry said.

"You keep getting things the wrong way round," I said. "I am not *your* Turandot. *You* are *my* Henry. Is that clear?"

"Perfectly," he said.

DIANA WYNNE JONES was born in London, England. At the age of eight, she suddenly *knew* she was going to be a writer, although she was too dyslexic to start until she reached twelve. There were very few books in the house so Diana wrote stories for herself and her two younger sisters. She received her B.A. at St. Anne's College in Oxford before she began to write full time.

Her many remarkable novels include the award-winning *Archer's Goon*, *Howl's Moving Castle*, *Fire and Hemlock*, the Dalemark Quartet, the Chrestomanci books (*Charmed Life*, *Witch Week*, *The Lives of Christopher Chant* and *The Magicians of Caprona*), *Dark Lord of Derkholm*, and *The Year of the Griffin*. Her most recent novel is *The Merlin Conspiracy*.

Diana Wynne Jones lives with her husband, the medievalist J.A. Burrow, in Bristol, England—the setting of many of her books. They have three grown sons and five grandchildren.

Her official Web site is **www.leemac.freeserve.co.uk**

AUTHOR'S NOTE

This story started, naturally enough, with our cat Dorabella, who is a cat of many colours and strong personality. From the moment she arrived as a tiny kitten, she revolutionised our lives. She puts us to bed at night and gets us up in the morning. And, like Little Dot in the story, her great talent is disappearing. She can vanish in the middle of an empty room if she wants to.

LITTLE DOT

Then the writer Greer Gilman came to visit and told me about a friend of hers in Yorkshire who patrols all the drains in her area, collecting kittens that people have tried to drown. The friend now has a whole tribe of cats, all with hard-luck stories.

And then another friend told me of the original of Mr Williams, who was being so inconsiderately treated by his owner that an aunt of hers simply took him away.

I put these things together and the story more or less told itself.

Nancy Farmer

Remember Me

I'm supposed to tell the therapist about my big sister, but he isn't going to believe me. I already told Dad and Ella, and they think I'm a loony tune. They're polite about it, though.

Ella's my mother—*our* mother, I mean, Flo's and mine—only she doesn't like to be called mother. It makes her feel ancient. Dad, well, he's just Dad. He doesn't notice when people feel ancient.

I have to tell this story in a way the therapist will believe. I'd better get started.

You see, Ella planned this trip to raise my I.Q. even though it's summer and we live in Arizona. It's not enough to sit under the air conditioning with a book. Ella says the only way to learn is with hands-on experience. That's one of her favorite phrases: Hands-on experience. She said I was *woefully* ignorant of state history, possibly because I got a D last spring. So the only way to fix it was to travel around from historical site to historical site in a dumb car with defective air conditioning.

I ask you!

Of course we weren't traveling around to raise Flo's I.Q. That would have been a waste of time. More about that later.

Ella loaded us into the car with Flo and me in the back. Dad drove until we all had headaches from the glare. The view was about as inspiring as a toxic waste dump. Ella had a guidebook, so we had to hunt down every clump of rocks with a bronze plaque.

I ask you. What's the difference between reading about a bunch of stupid pioneers on a nice, cool sofa, and reading about them while you're hopping around on dirt hot enough to cook a foot? Most of the pioneers would have traded in their covered wagons for a glass of ice tea anyhow.

The worst problem was I had to share the back seat with Flo. There wasn't a deodorant around that could neutralize Flo. It wasn't her fault, of course. I admit that.

Flo was *different*, you see. Even Ella refused to take credit for her. "Fourteen years ago," she told friends, "the elves were cleaning house. They opened a closet and found Flo inside. She'd been in there for nine months, growing bigger and bigger until she filled up the whole space. The elves didn't know what to do with her, so they put her in a basket and left her on my doorstep." Ella would laugh and the friends would laugh, too. Flo would look down at her feet.

It sounds mean now that I think about it. It never bothered me at the time. Flo was so big and slow. She spent hours sewing weird dresses that made her look like she ate whale sandwiches for lunch. They were in really dead colors—mud, algae, pond scum. That kind of thing. Once she made a pair of hot pants in *toad*.

Everyone at school knew she was my sister. I hated that and I hated her, too. Okay, I didn't really hate her, but I wished she lived somewhere else. Like the planet Jupiter. So I understood why Ella told the story. I, too, would have died of shame if I had a daughter who could have auditioned for *Bride of Frankenstein*.

Anyhow, about sundown Ella announced that we should start looking for a campsite. "I hate camping," said Dad, who had done a lot of it courtesy of the U.S. Army.

"Wasn't it lucky I packed sleeping bags?" said Ella, as though he'd said nothing. Ella was like that. When she got an idea, everything else melted in front of it. I don't think she even heard him. "There!" she cried. "I see a road going to a farm." She pointed at a ribbon of dirt cutting through mean little cactuses to some wrinkled-looking mountains with a green smudge at the bottom.

"What would anyone farm out here? Lizards?" said Dad.

"Let's take a vote. What do you think, Jessie?" Ella turned to me. "Would you like to sleep under nice old palm trees by a stream? Or would you prefer to sleep in the car next to Flo?"

"I vote for the palm trees," I said.

"What about you?" Ella asked Dad.

"Does it make a difference what I think?" said Dad.

"I'll count that as a yes vote. We have a majority."

"Wait a minute. You haven't asked Flo," Dad said.

Ella cocked her head to one side like a sparrow. "I don't see how it matters. We have three in favor."

"Ask her anyway," said Dad. So we all turned to Flo, who looked vaguely surprised. Dad carefully explained what the vote was about. You had to do that with her. Her mind was always somewhere else.

Flo slowly considered the decision. She looked around the car, obviously working out where we could sleep. Her blouse—a horrible brown that reminded me of cough syrup was damp under the arms. I wanted to scream *Figure it out, dummy! We have as much room in here as the inside of a panty hose.* She looked at the distant smudge at the foot of the mountains. Finally, she smiled. "I vote for the palm trees."

"Good girl," said Dad

The sky turned a deep blue after the sun set. The earth seemed to cool like a piece of metal taken from a furnace. And at the end of the road was a stream bordered by palm trees with leaves that clicked like rain. It was a quiet, secret place.

We arranged the sleeping bags next to the water and Dad built a fire. "Don't lean against that tree, Flo," Ella called. "I knew a lady who put her hand on a palm tree, and when she pulled her hand away there was a vampire bat hanging onto her finger."

Flo jumped away and brushed her shoulders. Ella was always making up stuff to amuse us. I laughed. Fortunately, Dad didn't see me. He was always after me for laughing at Flo. It was so easy to do. She believed everything you said. It was like she lived in a world where anything was possible.

We sat by the campfire. Flo watched the flames with a concentration that was slightly creepy. It was the same old flames over and over, but the way Flo watched them, it was like the most exciting novel.

What would happen when she grew up, I wondered. She had no friends. She was too slow to finish anything at school. She was rotten at sports, even when some misguided teacher put her on a team. The only people who put up with her were Dad, Ella, and me.

Did I mention she was loyal? Horribly. No matter what I did or said to keep her away, she followed me around. I hated it. My friends lied to her about where I was, to give me a break.

"Why would anyone build a road here?" Dad asked suddenly.

"What do you mean?" said Ella.

"There's no farm or mine. Why build a road?"

Dad unpacked the flashlights and we followed a path along the creek. The air had cooled, and the palm trees stirred with a gentle wind that carried a damp smell of earth and some flower that was oversweet. The moon had not yet risen, but the sky glowed with starlight. I could see the hills silhouetted against it, and in a gap where the sky came down to the path was a tall, black shape.

"It's a bear!" Ella screamed. My heart jumped to my throat.

Dad grabbed a stick and pushed ahead.

"It's a bear. It's big and awful," Ella moaned, sinking to her knees. I tried to run, but Flo put her arm around me and held me tight. Even in my terror I realized that she wasn't frightened. She seemed merely interested, as though meeting bears in the dark was perfectly normal.

"It's okay," called Dad from up ahead. "It's only a rock." He shone his flashlight on a bronze plaque fastened halfway up.

"It's a historical monument," Ella cried.

We gathered around, looking at the tall finger of stone sticking up into the night. "What does it say?" I asked.

Ella squinted at the faint writing. "'Remember Me.'"

"That's all?"

"I can't see anything else. It's so scratched, I can't be sure."

"'Remember Me.' That's a funny inscription," said Dad.

"I'm sure this monument isn't in the guidebook," said Ella.

I realized Flo was still holding me. Her sweat hung like a fog in the air. It was sort of like warm compost—the kind with grass cuttings and weeds. I decided I didn't like it and struggled free. Flo stared at the rock with her mouth open.

"Who are we supposed to remember?" Ella said.

Dad flashed the light around as though looking for the vanished person.

Then I saw that the plants here were different from the campsite. The palms had disappeared. In their place were trees with smooth bark like skin. Their roots snaked over the ground, and every crevice and crack in the mountainside was crowded with them. Beneath them was a sea of white flowers with their faces turned to the sky.

It was from these the sickly-sweet perfume came.

"That's night-blooming cereus," said Dad. "They only flower in complete darkness."

Great, I thought. You could tell they weren't waiting for anything as innocent as honeybees. Something that flowered in complete darkness had to be visited by something *else* that came out in complete darkness. The more I thought about it, the less I liked it.

"Let's go back," said Ella in a shrill voice.

Dad turned to lead the way when we ran into an unexpected snag. Flo planted herself on the ground by the monument and refused to go. It was so unusual for her to show any spirit or life that Ella and Dad didn't figure it out right away.

"Are you sick?" Dad asked.

Ella fluttered around, urging Flo to leave. "You'll feel so much better," she chirped. "Those flowers are enough to turn anyone's stomach. Why, they might even be poisonous. I read in a book that the Italians used to send poisonous flowers to their enemies."

It was another of Ella's flights of fancy, like the elves or the vampire bats that live in palm trees. She threw them around like a harem dancer throws around veils.

"I like them," said Flo.

Which stumped everyone. Flo never had an opinion about anything.

"I like the trees and rocks and sky and the stream. I never liked any place so much."

"Well, that's nice," cooed Ella, "but the rest of us simply hate it. Please, darling. You'll be so much happier in camp."

"No, I won't," said Flo. "Back there I'll just be your big, ugly daughter again. I'll have to listen to your lies and watch you push everyone around."

"Why—why—I never push anyone around," gasped Ella.

"You don't beat them over the head or anything, but you always get your way. And nothing's ever good unless you're the center of it."

"That's enough, Flo," said Dad.

"That's why you don't like this place," Flo told Ella. "It won't let you be the center."

By now Ella was crying—little, whimpering, puppyish gulps that made me feel awful. Dad put his arms around her. "She doesn't mean it," he said. "Teenagers say hurtful things sometimes, but they don't mean it." Flo walked off and looked into the stream. Dad led Ella back down the path to the camp.

I didn't know what to say. It was so incredibly unreal. I never dreamed Flo could talk like that. I never dreamed she was hurt by the things people said about her. I watched her clear a patch of ground near the monument and lie down. It seemed she was going to spend the night there.

After a while Dad came back with a sleeping bag for Flo. He waved me away. I heard his low voice and Flo's sobs. He could get to you, Dad could, in a way Ella never managed.

Ella was in her sleeping bag when I got back to camp and I guess she'd taken one of her pills. Maybe more than one. She looked completely whacked. I crawled into my sleeping bag. After a while Dad came back and went to bed, too.

The breeze freshened and carried with it a whiff of rain. A coyote yipped and thunder rumbled in the distance. An owl called from the upper air as it floated along.

I woke with the feel of rain in my face. It blew away with a loud patter. The moon shone at the edge of a cloud. "Get up!" Dad shouted. "Get up!" I was out of my sleeping bag before I even knew what I was doing. Ella was still zonked.

"It's raining in the mountains! That could mean a flash flood! Get to the car! Run!" yelled Dad. He scooped up Ella, bag and all, and staggered up the slope. In the distance was the roar of a storm. It sounded like the sky had opened up.

Flo! I thought. I grabbed my flashlight and ran down the trail.

"Jessie!" I heard Dad yell.

But I was off, going as fast as I could. Any other time I would have fallen over a tree or jammed my foot down a gopher hole. Not now. I bounded along like a mountain goat through shafts of moonlight and inky darkness. I got to the monument and saw Flo's sleeping bag. It hadn't even been unrolled.

What a dummy, I thought. Then I realized *I* was the dummy. She'd heard the storm and cleared out. I was still down at the business end of the flood. In the distance I heard a roar. It rattled and boomed as it swept towards me.

I clawed my way up the slope, but there wasn't a path here. The mountain went straight up and there weren't any branches to hold onto. I dropped the flashlight. *No branches?* I thought as I broke my fingernails on the stone. *Why aren't there any branches? What happened to the trees?*

The roar grew until it blotted out all other sounds. A swell of water washed over my feet. Spray blew in my face. I hoisted myself up a few more inches, but the rocks were slippery and the water was rising. It was at my waist now, sucking and pulling, dragging me down. I looked up.

There were the trees. But I couldn't reach them. I looked ahead at the water, which was now rising in a giant wave. Boulders so heavy it would take ten men to shift them bounced and skipped ahead of the flood. Logs of wood tossed in the foam.

I felt something reach down and grab my arm. It pulled me up just before the flood hit. I thought my arm was being torn out of the socket, it hurt so much. I screamed and screamed. I saw that the top of the mountain was covered with the strange trees. And they were swaying back and forth as though there was a high wind.

At least I think that's what I saw. The moon kept going in and out of clouds. I landed on the ground hard. "Let me go," I moaned, trying to wrestle free. I clawed at my arm. I felt a hand, a *big* hand. I looked up into a mass of leaves and in the middle—the moon came out for an instant—were eyes slitted like the eyes of a cat. The pupils opened wide as though really seeing me.

Then I did scream. And in the next instant the hand was gone. I felt someone lift me and hug me. I smelled sweat.

"Flo?" I said.

"It's okay, it's okay," she crooned.

"Flo, my arm hurts like hell." I know it sounds like a stupid thing to say after all that had happened, but it really did hurt.

"Oh! Sorry," said Flo. She laid me down again.

"We've got to get out of here," I said.

"It's okay. The flood's gone by."

"No, I mean this place is scary." I didn't want to mention the eyes. I didn't want to think about them.

"I can't go back," said Flo in a soft, sad voice I'd never heard her use before.

"What are you talking about? Ella won't stay mad forever. Heck, she's so zonked out she won't even remember what you said."

"It's not that."

"Dad never stays angry."

"I don't belong," said Flo in that sad, soft voice. "I never did. I was always too different."

"Hey, we're all weird," I said. I was anxious to get out of there. I didn't want those eyes to come back. I didn't think about the weirdest thing until later. Flo was talking! Flo, who hardly said ten words a day, was carrying on like a normal human being. She seemed wide awake and full of energy.

"Sometimes, mistakes are made," she said. "Sometimes souls are slipped into the wrong bodies. They aren't meant to go to school or hold down jobs or do the things people do. They're meant to fly like birds or run like horses . . . or simply stand and watch, like trees. The really lucky ones find their way home." And then, above the roar of water down below, I heard the sound of rushing leaves. Except there wasn't any wind at all. Not one bit.

That's when I heard Dad's voice shouting our names. I saw his flashlight beam stab through the trees.

"I'm here!" I yelled. The light swung towards me. It shone on Flo for an instant and moved on. But not before I saw the leaves sprouting from her shoulders. And the strange cat-eyes gleaming in the light.

Dad found me curled up and shaking. "Oh, God, I thought I'd lost you," he wept. "Have you seen Flo?"

What could I tell him? She was right there, but even then I was getting confused about which one she really was.

That's what I told the police later and why I'm at the therapist's now. I can tell from his face he doesn't believe me either.

REMEMBER ME

Dad went back to the stream several times with the cops and tracking dogs, but they never found a trace of Flo. One odd thing, though. In spite of the flood, all the strange trees had survived in perfect condition. It was like they hadn't even got wet. They were back down by the stream, although Dad says they had never been anywhere else.

And the monument was still there with its message: Remember Me.

NANCY FARMER grew up in a hotel on the Mexican border. As an adult, she joined the Peace Corps and went to India, where she taught chemistry and ran a chicken farm. After returning to the U.S. she joined a commune of hippies in Berkeley, California. Among other jobs, she hawked newspapers, picked peaches, worked on an oceanographic vessel, and controlled insects that ate traffic islands. After several happy years she caught a freighter to Africa in search of romance and adventure. She had $500 and a list of scientists to ask for jobs. Farmer wound up running a lab on Lake Cabora Bassa in Mozambique, in one of the wildest places on the globe, and the people she met there have since provided the background for her books. Adventure was everywhere and romance showed up in the shape of Harold Farmer, an instructor at the University of Zimbabwe. Farmer spent seventeen years in Africa before moving the family back to California. She and Harold have one son, Daniel, who is in the U.S. Navy.

Nancy Farmer is the author of five novels, including *The Ear, the Eye and the Arm* (a Newbery Honor Book), *The Warm Place*, *A Girl Named Disaster* (a National Book Award Finalist and a Newbery Honor Book), and, most recently, *The House of the Scorpion* (Winner of the National Book Award, a Newbery Honor Book, and a Michael L. Printz Honor Book).

AUTHOR'S NOTE

As a child I was addicted to fairy stories. I read thousands of them about elves, witches, talking animals and changelings. Probably the saddest stories were about changelings. They suffered not for evil they had done but for what they were: ugly babies that had been exchanged by fairies for the beautiful ones that should have been there. Very early I realized that these stories were about children with disabilities. Adults had tried to explain the existence of these unusual beings by blaming someone else. But also in these stories was the belief that changelings belonged somewhere else. And so I wrote a tale about that somewhere else where changelings are welcome and we are the unnatural ones.

Nina Kiriki Hoffman

fLotsam

aturday morning the weekend after Thanksgiving I dribbled my basketball down the street to the high school. Its basketball court had a tall fence around it so you didn't have to spend all your time chasing the ball when you missed the backboard. There was a huge field next to the court. Lots of kids lived in the houses with big picture windows, across the street. I could shoot two baskets and more players would appear.

It was best when some of them were girls. If everybody who showed up was a guy and bigger than me, they took the ball away and wouldn't let me play. I had to wait around until they got tired or called home before I got it back.

Sometimes Danny Ortega showed up. Even though he was a high school freshman like me, he was bigger than a lot of the seniors. He'd get my ball back. Then he'd say, "Becky, what did I tell you? Call me when you want to play ball."

Sometimes I called him. Sometimes I didn't want to bother him.

FLOTSAM

I mean, what if I used up his friendship? I could stare at Danny all day. I loved the way he looked, tall and strong, with black eyes and silky lashes, caramel skin and soft black hair. I loved the way he talked, and how nice he was to me even though he had no idea what I thought when I looked at him. I rationed my calls. I didn't want to change how we were together. He was relaxed around me, not nervous the way some guys get when a girl was too interested.

I couldn't stand to lose Danny, too.

That Saturday morning was cool and sunny, and I was glad. It had rained all day Thanksgiving and Friday. The way Thanksgiving had gone, rain was the perfect weather. It was the worst holiday yet. Maybe Mom-mom and Grandpop would wise up and not invite Dad to Christmas Day. Since my sister Miriam died last year, Mom and Dad couldn't stand to be in the same building with each other, let alone the same room.

I opened the gate to the basketball court and bounced the ball toward the basket to the right. I loved the *thwick-echo* sound of a pumped basketball hitting something hard. It was the sound of jump.

A kid lay bunched up against the fence in the corner of the court as though he'd been blown there. His long black hair was matted and full of leaves, his face pale and dirty, and his clothes were strange—smudged, stained dark blue velvet shirt and slacks, with gold piping along the hem and a small embroidered red flower on the chest. His feet were bare, the soles black with dirt, the tops white and frozen looking.

I caught the ball on a bounce, stood by the gate, and

wondered whether I should leave. Aside from a couple local menaces you could usually see and run away from before they could catch you, the neighborhood was safe. The kid was small, and I was strong. But he looked so weird.

I wasn't sure how I knew he was a boy.

His eyes opened. Silver blue. Nobody I knew had eyes that color, like sunlight trapped in cloudy ice. He stared at me.

I bounced the ball once and thought about Mom. If there was a beach cleanup, or a tree planting, or a Thanksgiving help-out-at-the-homeless-shelter, she used to always go, and she dragged me and my twin brother Jeff along, and our older sister Miriam, before Miriam died.

Mom had been different since Miriam died. She was a social worker, and she used to work with people who had problems. Since Miriam died, Mom had changed to an administrative job. She stopped pushing us to help people. She no longer wanted us bringing home strays. She didn't even like us bringing friends over. Sometimes I thought she didn't want us to have any friends.

Jeff was okay; he could be happy instant messaging and playing multiperson games online. He had lots of friends he'd never met, which was a good thing, as he didn't have many friends at school.

Mom loved it that she could go to Jeff's door and see him anytime she wanted to. She didn't care how many aliens and demons and martial arts fighters he killed.

I had cut way back on extracurriculars since Miriam's accident, and I hadn't figured out what to do instead. I wrote Mom a note every time I left the house. She still got bent if I went too far away. It was driving me crazy.

The boy sat up. He rubbed his eyes. His skin was as pale as the inside of a mushroom, and he had shadows under his eyes.

I took a few steps toward him, bouncing my ball.

He watched me. The closer I came, the more of a whiff of him I got. He smelled like he'd been sleeping in a sewer.

"Hey." I bounced the ball, then caught it. "You okay?"

"*Mirnama?*"

I set the ball on the asphalt near him and sat on it. His accent sounded strange. I couldn't understand what he said. There was a slidy undertone that I hadn't heard in English or Spanish, or even in the French I was taking for the first time this term.

"You okay?" I asked again. He didn't look like he was injured. No visible blood. He was probably just homeless. He sure needed a bath, and he looked cold and hungry.

"*Buzhelala zenda.*" He rubbed his hands over his face. Then he formed a triangle with his index fingers and thumbs, framed his mouth inside the triangle, and said something icy. He put his hands over his ears and said another icy thing.

The sharp cold words hurt my ears. How could words go in your ears like an ice knife? What if he said something else like that?

He blinked. "Say? Please? Say?"

I took a big breath and held it a couple seconds. Maybe I should get out of here. On the other hand, these words sounded like regular conversation.

I said, "Who are you?" I really wanted to ask, "What are you?"

He said something with a couple of "la"'s in it, then

frowned, and said, "Poppy." He touched his lips as though surprised at what had come out. Then he nodded. "Poppy."

"Poppy," I repeated.

He touched the red flower on his chest. "Poppy?"

"You're named for a flower? Boy, are you in trouble."

He wiped his hands over his face and smiled. Then: "Trouble?" His smile melted.

I stood up, the ball in my arms. "I don't think you should stay here." I could walk him to the homeless shelter, or at least give him bus fare.

He pushed himself to his bare feet. He was two inches shorter than I was, and he didn't look very strong.

"You hungry?" I asked.

"Hungry," he whispered.

The gate creaked behind me. I turned. Shoog Kelly, the biggest bully in the neighborhood, wore his trademark evil grin. "Hey, Becky. Hey. We're practically alone on this fine fall morning. Could anything be better? Who's your pretty little friend?"

Shoog was someone I ran away from if I could. Last time Shoog cornered me, he didn't just beat me up. He tried to kiss me, and he grabbed my chest, not that there was anything you could hang on to there yet.

I edged in front of Poppy and looked for anyone who could distract Shoog. Way down the block I saw Taylor Harrison mowing his lawn, and by the school, Wendy Alcala was walking her little white dog. Both of them were too far away, not strong enough, and not specifically friends.

"Hey, Shoog." I reached one hand behind me, felt Poppy's

hand slide into it. His hand was warm and thin, with a stronger grip than I had expected. I walked toward Shoog, and Poppy kept pace with me, one step behind. As we came even with Shoog I threw the basketball right at his stomach. He *oofed* loudly and bent over. I ran past him, Poppy on my heels. We left the ball bouncing away across the court.

"I'll get you for that, Silver!" Shoog yelled, his voice thin and whistly.

I glanced back at him. He was still wheezing in the court when we were halfway across the field.

I didn't slow down until we'd put a block between him and us.

Poppy could run. I had forgotten about his shoelessness, though. As I slowed on the sidewalk in front of my house, Poppy gripped my hand. I stopped.

He lifted one foot. We both stared at bright red blood on the heel.

"Oh, God. You stepped on something?"

"Ouch."

"Come inside. I'll get you a Band-Aid."

He braced his hand on my shoulder and hopped up the front walk to our door.

He tracked blood on the carpet. Mom was going to kill me. Luckily she had gone off to play tennis with her friend Valerie half an hour ago, and wouldn't be back until after her lunch date with Aunt Ariadne. Maybe I could clean everything up before she got back.

I led Poppy to the downstairs bathroom and sat him on the toilet-seat cover. "Stay here." I ran upstairs for the first aid kit.

Late Saturday morning, and Jeff was just waking up. He yelled something groggy out his half-open bedroom door as I whizzed into the upstairs bathroom, grabbed the kit, and ran downstairs.

Poppy gasped when I turned on the faucet to wet a rag with warm water.

Maybe where he came from—someplace where boys wore weird clothes and were named after flowers—they didn't have running water. I'd never read about a country like that in social studies, and that was one of the classes I stayed awake for.

I washed Poppy's wound, gentled a sliver of glass out of it. His blood stained the rag. When I rinsed it out, I got Poppy's blood on my hands, and it burned.

Oh, man. I had forgotten about diseases you could get from other people's blood. Was Poppy sick? He looked shrunken and starved, but I didn't see any skin diseases or other obvious signs. Anyway, his blood couldn't hurt me unless it got in a cut, right? I washed my hands with soap, scrubbing really hard, but even after the blood was gone, my hands tingled.

I sucked on my lower lip. Whatever had happened, it was too late to stop it now. I felt faint. I sliced the worry off and let it go. At least if I got sick it might take me a little time to die, and everybody would have a chance to say good-bye, not the way it had been with Miriam, where she was laughing and joking at dinner, teasing Mom and Dad by not answering their questions about her plans for the night, and then by midnight she was dead. Because every Friday night she went out without exactly getting permission, none of us thought that night would be any different.

I set the glass sliver on the counter by the sink. Poppy glared at it. I squeezed antibiotic ointment on his wound, then slapped a big plastic bandage over it. I hoped he didn't need stitches.

Poppy touched the Band-Aid, slid his finger over it as if he'd never seen anything like it before. "*Buzhe? Kedala,*" he muttered.

"What language is that?"

"*Zhe?* Oh. Feyan. Sorry. This is what you do for wounds here? This heals?" He stroked the Band-Aid.

"It keeps the cut safe from infection." Who didn't know that? Didn't they have Band-Aids in India? Siberia? Wherever he came from?

He gingerly picked up the glass sliver, which was about half an inch long and clear. He frowned at it, then looked at me.

"Let's toss it so it doesn't cut anybody else."

"Toss it?"

I opened the cupboard under the sink and pulled out the wastebasket. "Put it in here."

He stared at the pile of used Kleenexes, dental floss, and cotton balls in the trash, then studied the piece of glass. "There's enough of this—"

I waited a while for the rest of the sentence, but it never arrived. "Put it in here," I said.

He dropped the glass into the wastebasket. I put the wastebasket away.

"So. You want some breakfast?"

He nodded.

"You better wash first. If Mom comes home—hell, you better take a shower." I'd gotten used to his smell, but just thinking about Mom's reaction to him made me notice how bad it was. I checked him out. We were almost the same size. My hips were bigger, and my chest was just starting to grow; but I had a belt, and a T-shirt doesn't care what shape you are, only what size.

"Shower?" he repeated.

"Come on." I led him up to my room, then rummaged through my dresser until I found some old jeans and a dark blue T-shirt with a faded band logo on the back. Maybe Jeff would donate a pair of his underwear. The special exit might be a good thing for Poppy to have, supposing he—

My face heated just thinking about it.

Poppy checked out things on my desk. The globe of the world, which I had bought at a yard sale—it was thirty years old and a lot of countries had changed since it was made. My rock collection from all the geology hikes Dad had taken me on. He loved to go dig up crystals and things. I liked it too. I always thought we might find treasure. I had found some nice quartz crystals up in the Cascades, but none of them were perfect. I liked tide pooling for agates better. Less work, easier collecting, and you got to wear big rubber boots and be on the beach.

I hadn't gone on a rock hunt with Dad since he moved out. He had visitation Saturday nights. He took me and Jeff to dinner and a movie every weekend. It made me mad.

Poppy touched the cover of my *Encyclopedia of Mammals*, which showed a picture of a tiger. His eyes were wide.

"You never saw a tiger before?" I asked.

He shook his head.

"Well, I haven't really, either. Only in pictures and on TV. You ready for a shower?"

"Becky?" he said.

"Yes?"

"Your name is Becky?"

"Huh? Oh, yes. I'm sorry. I asked you your name, but I never told you mine. I'm Becky Silver. How'd you know?"

"Shoog said it. Becky, what's a shower?"

A couple of ideas drifted through my head. Maybe he was retarded. Maybe he really wasn't from around here. Maybe he was kidding. Maybe I had just hallucinated him. What had really happened was that Shoog had hit me in the head so hard that right now I was lying knocked out on the asphalt. I mean. What kid in the middle of an American town, far from any form of transportation that could have carried him here from another country, didn't know what a shower was?

Er. Well, maybe spaceships made drops here in Spores Ferry, Oregon. Weird things had been known to happen.

"Um," I said. "Do you know what a bath is?"

"A tub? With water in it?"

"Right." I handed him the jeans and the T-shirt. "I'll show you the shower." Suppose he was teasing me. I could tease back by pretending I was taking him seriously. Right?

I led him into the upstairs bathroom and opened the shower stall.

He looked inside, then glanced at me.

"Uh. Okay. This is shower gel, it's like soap. You squirt it on a wet rag and scrub your skin with it. This is shampoo— you know what shampoo is?" I checked his hair. It was horribly matted and leafy. Maybe he'd never washed it before. "You get your hair wet, and rub this through it, and wash it off, repeat, and then you're clean." I touched the faucets. "This is hot water, and this is cold." I pointed to the shower head. "The water comes out of here. You stand under this and it sprays you."

He touched a faucet. "This is water?"

"This turns the water on."

He frowned.

"Watch this." I reached in and turned on the hot water faucet.

"*Zhe!*"

I turned the faucet off.

Poppy turned the faucet on, put a hand under the falling water. He turned the faucet off and looked at me.

I went to the cupboard and got out a big fluffy towel and a washrag. "Do you understand towels and rags?"

Poppy nodded.

"Becky? What are you doing?" Jeff stood in the doorway, staring at us.

"This is my friend Poppy. He's going to take a shower."

"He? That's a *boy*?"

"Yeah. You got any clean underwear, Jeff?"

Jeff scratched his head, then wandered away and came back with a pair of underwear. Luckily Mom had done laundry last night, so it wasn't even toxic.

"Do you understand our clothes?" I asked Poppy.

He fingered the T-shirt and jeans I had handed him earlier, then leaned over to see how my jeans fastened. "Looks simple," he said.

"The zipper can kill you if you're not careful," Jeff said.

"Zipper?"

I demonstrated how the zipper worked on the jeans I had handed him.

"*Cheska*," he muttered.

"Dude. That's why you wear underwear," Jeff said.

"Thank you," said Poppy.

I turned the hot water on. Pretty soon the water was steaming. I mixed enough cold with it that it wasn't scalding. "Okay? You understand getting clean, right?"

He nodded. A lot. Jeff and I went out and closed the door.

"So who's the space case?" Jeff asked.

I shook my head. "I don't know. His name's Poppy. I found him at the basketball court. Do you think he's messing with my head?"

Jeff tugged on his lower lip, then shook his head. "I get a really strange feeling off him."

"Not from around here," I said.

"Yeah. Extremely not."

"You don't think it's all an act?"

Jeff twisted a finger through his hair, then shook his head. "Could be wrong, though."

We went downstairs. I'd already had a breakfast of Froot Loops, milk, and a banana, but that was a while back. Maybe I should make pancakes. Poppy could use some fattening up.

Jeff got out the Sugar Pops and scarfed handfuls straight from the box, dropping some on the floor with every bite. I was too distracted to tell Jeff to clean up after himself.

By the time Poppy came downstairs, I had mixed up a big bowl of buttermilk pancake batter, and the frying pan was hot enough to sizzle when I flicked water in it. Jeff sat at the kitchen table with a plate in front of him. He'd set the table, gotten out the butter and the maple syrup, and poured glasses of milk for all three of us after I suggested it.

Poppy cleaned up well. His face was interesting, angular, with a pointed chin; his eyes were startling, their ice-blue irises ringed with dark gray, the lids fringed with black lashes. His dark hair hung damp down his back all the way to his butt. It was strange to see him in my clothes—strange because he looked almost normal.

"Hey," Jeff said. "I'm Jeff."

"Shoot, I forgot my manners again. Poppy, this is my brother Jeff. Jeff, this is Poppy."

Jeff held out his hand. Poppy looked at it, then held out his. Jeff shook Poppy's hand. Poppy smiled.

"You're still hungry, right? Have a seat. You can start with milk. I'll make you some pancakes." I dropped a slice of butter into the pan and it liquefied in an instant. The kitchen smelled good. I ladled out the first test pancakes.

"Milk," Poppy said. He grabbed a glass and drank it without stopping for air. "Ahhh. Thank you."

"There's more if you want it," I said. I pointed to my glass. He lifted his eyebrows, glanced down at his stomach, and took my glass. This time he sipped instead of chugging.

Bubbles popped in the pancakes. I flipped them. The first batch usually came out a little dark and tough. I filled Jeff's plate, then dipped out another set.

Jeff sighed with happiness, dropped a dab of butter on the pancakes, and drowned them in syrup. He cut a first giant bite, then stopped, the fork in front of his mouth. "But Poppy's the guest. Shouldn't you serve him first?"

"I'm fine," Poppy said.

"Those were just practice pancakes." I flipped the new ones. Golden brown, and they smelled lovely. A minute and a half, and I scooped them onto a fresh plate and set it in front of Poppy.

He gripped knife and fork, then reached for the butter and syrup, which Jeff pushed toward him. I poured another batch of pancakes and watched Poppy mimic Jeff's earlier actions. His first bite took him by surprise. As soon as he closed his mouth with food inside, his eyes widened. Then he coughed. He should never have tried to take a Jeff-sized bite.

Poppy kept his hands in front of his mouth when he coughed. He stopped choking pretty quick, and finally swallowed. He sipped milk. Then he took a smaller bite.

"You want something else?"

He shook his head. He swallowed. "I like this. It's just not what I thought it would be when I saw it."

"So, dude, what's your story?" Jeff said. His plate was empty.

I made Jeff another batch of pancakes and then made some for myself. If Jeff finished eating his before I even cooked mine, he could make his own next time.

"My story," said Poppy. He narrowed his eyes and stared at the ceiling. "I am not sure which part to tell."

"Where'd you come from?" I asked.

"A place under a place inside a place three places ago."

So what did that mean? "Does this place have a name?" I asked.

"Feyala Durezhda."

That was a big help. "They don't have showers there, huh?"

"Not like the one you have. If I wanted water to do that, I would talk to water, not to a metal thing that talks to more metal things and tells the water where to go and how to be hot and when to stop and start."

Jeff and I exchanged glances. Maybe Poppy was crazy. Maybe we should be ready to do something about him if he started acting crazy. Together, we were pretty strong.

"How do you talk to water?" I asked.

Poppy ate three more bites, then glanced around. "Do you have water? Water in this world is not quite the same as water where I come from, but I can talk to yours. It doesn't know how to listen, but it tries."

I took a glass to the sink and filled it with water, set it in front of Poppy.

Poppy stroked the air above the glass, frowned, moved his fingers a little, said something lilting, then held out his hand, palm up.

Water flowed up out of the glass and sat in a juicy bubble on his palm.

"Whoa," said Jeff. He slumped against his chair back, his mouth wide open.

Breath went out of me, and then I couldn't breathe in. I felt faint.

"It's not used to being spoken to," Poppy said, running a finger over the globe, which quivered. "It's not sure how to respond. *Tsilla.*" The water ball shivered some more. "Hold out your hand, Becky. *Tsutelli.*"

I lifted my hand. It was shaking.

The ball floated from Poppy's hand to mine. It held its shape for only a second before splashing over my hand. It was warm. It had been cold when it came out of the tap.

I gasped for breath but couldn't find enough. Something huge inside me crumbled.

My hand was wet.

Water had traveled sideways through air without being squirted out of a gun or a hose.

Finally I pulled in a big breath. I pressed my wet palm to my cheek, touched my lips with wet fingers. What? What?

"Was that real?" Jeff whispered.

"Something's burning," said Poppy.

I whirled and jerked the pan off the burner, then turned the dial to kill the flame. The pancakes were smoking. My hands still shook. My stomach soured and sloshed.

"Could you do that again, dude?" asked Jeff.

"Why do you call me dude?"

I carried the pan over to the wastebasket and dumped my second breakfast into the trash. Suddenly pancakes were too much work. I grabbed the box of Sugar Pops, sat between Jeff and Poppy at the table, and poured some cereal into my hand.

"My name is Poppy," Poppy told Jeff.

"That's such a stupid-ass name, dude. You should change it."

Poppy's eyes narrowed to ice chips.

I chewed my mouthful of dry Sugar Pops, swallowed, and said, "You know how much water there is in your body, Jeff?"

Jeff flinched, then hunched his shoulders.

"In everybody's body." I was surprised my voice sounded steady.

Poppy looked at me, and his eyes widened to normal. "Becky? Are you frightened?"

"Yes."

"By water talk?"

"Oh, yes." By so many things. Maybe he was crazy. My hand was still wet, which gave him credibility. So when he spoke of other worlds— "What else can you talk to?"

His lips tightened. "Elements and forces. Weather. Plants, animals, and the spaces between. Where I come from, in the underground, everyone can speak some of these languages. Aboveground, no one can; they do the work of moving everything by hand. Water they move in pots and buckets and sometimes in pipes and aqueducts. They can only persuade it to go the way falling goes."

He glanced away from us, then back. "Here you have touch magic. You touch something, and something somewhere else happens." He waved toward the stove. "You touch the round white thing, and the flame goes away without your having to blow it out or tell it to go. You touch that round metal thing in the shower, and water comes from somewhere else. In the room you first took me to, you touched a thing on the wall and light came from the ceiling."

"Poppy?" Jeff leaned forward. "Seriously, dude. What else can you do that we can't?"

"What can't you do?" Poppy said.

We sat quiet. If he thought turning on a light switch was magic, how was he going to know what normal was?

"How long have you been here?" I asked.

"It was night when I arrived. I saw the houses and lights. I saw people through the windows, but I was afraid to go to the doors. Nothing looks the same here. Nothing in the last place looked the same either, or the place before that." He laid his head on the table, his face turned away from us. "All I want is to go home, but every time I go through a gate, I end up farther away."

I put my hand on his shoulder. Then I wondered if that was a deadly insult where he came from. He sighed and turned his head so he could look at me. "My father would save me if he knew where I was," Poppy said. "I think I'm too far away now."

I patted his back, since he didn't seem to mind.

He sighed again, then sat up. "I found that fenced place in the dark and went inside. If there were things roaming around in the night, I figured the fence would keep them out. I went to sleep. When I woke up, there you were, Becky. The last place where I was, I didn't find any people, only animals who wanted to eat everything that moved."

"How did you get here? You—went through a gate?"

He nodded. "My lady enjoined me against the use of gates, but I figured out a way to use them in spite of the prohibition. Only they don't work right anymore. I speak my destination and end up somewhere else. Do you have gates here?"

"Not that kind. Not that I know of."

"Is it like beaming someone up in *Star Trek*?" Jeff asked.

Poppy glanced at me. I said, "It doesn't sound the same. In *Star Trek*, they end up somewhere pretty nearby. Right? It's just ship to planet or ship to ship. Poppy came from way farther away than that. We don't have instant travel here, Poppy."

"I'll never get home," he whispered in a voice so low I almost didn't hear him.

"You could stay with us." Miriam's room was right next to mine, and nobody had touched it since she died. It was just sitting there.

"Are you crazy?" Jeff asked.

I looked at him.

"We don't know what he can do, other than that water thing, but what if it's—dangerous? What's Mom going to say, anyway? She never wants strangers in the house anymore."

"He can stay here until Mom kicks him out. Maybe he could live with Dad." How likely was that? Dad wasn't a world-saver like Mom used to be. He could be such an asshole these days. Sometimes I got the feeling he didn't want to be a father anymore.

"Becky—" Jeff began.

Poppy said, "Should I go?"

"Oh, for Pete's sake! Where would you go? You don't have money, you don't have shoes—I can get you some shoes, but I'm not sure they'll fit. The socks should be okay, though. What are you going to eat? Where are you going to sleep? What if you get sick?"

Poppy smiled slowly. His smile was so sweet I felt like I was melting. "Thank you, Becky." He looked away. "You've already given me everything I need. Now that I'm warm and clean and have had food and time to think, I should be able to take care of myself—" He muttered something. "Once I've learned how the languages are different, maybe."

"The languages," said Jeff. "How come you speak ours?"

"The ice words," I said.

"Huh?"

Poppy nodded. He held up his hands, the index fingers and thumbs forming a triangle, and framed his mouth with it. "That spell worked. I cast it on myself." He dropped his hands, unpieced the triangle.

"You can do spells, too?" Jeff asked.

Poppy cocked his head. "That's the word that came out of my mouth when I tried to describe it. You have a word for it. Is it something you do?"

Jeff shook his head. "We have stories about people who cast spells, witches, wizards, but most people think they're made up."

Poppy frowned.

"Every year around Halloween I see witches on TV, though," I said. "On CNN, talking about what the holiday means."

"Those aren't *Bewitched* type witches, the ones who can wiggle their noses and do magic," said Jeff. "Those are the ones who pretend magic is their religion."

Poppy glanced back and forth between us, his eyebrows up.

"Do you have fairy tales in your world?" I asked.

"Fey-ree tales?" He glanced past me, his eyes blank. Then he smiled. Then he laughed and shook his head. "You have tales about fey-ree?"

"Fey-ree?" I tried to pronounce it the way he had.

"Feyala Durezhda?"

I swallowed. "You're from Fairyland?"

He smiled again. His teeth looked a little pointed.

Which reminded me. "Can I see your ears?"

He sobered, lifted his hair away from the ear nearest to me, cocked his head, and raised his eyebrows.

It wasn't a big point on the top of his ear, but it wasn't round, either. Not those giant foxy ears I'd seen in fairy tale books, just the tiniest wolfish point. "That's one of the tales?" he asked. "That the fey-ree have points on their ears?"

I nodded. "Is it true?" I got this seesaw feeling the minute the question was out of my mouth. Was I really sitting in my kitchen asking a stranger about Fairyland facts?

"Mm. Mostly."

Jeff said, "Your ears are practically normal."

Poppy let his hair down. "My father is human." He frowned. "You have fey-ree tales here—"

The kitchen door opened and Mom breezed in, carrying her tennis racket and whistling. She came to a stop when she saw Poppy.

I glanced at the clock. It was only eleven. She shouldn't be back yet. She still had a lunch date. "Did something happen to Aunt Ariadne?"

"No," she said slowly. "Valerie turned her ankle, so we stopped early. Who's your friend?"

"This is Poppy, Mom."

Mom held out her hand. Poppy shook it. "Hello, Poppy," said Mom. "I'm Mrs. Silver."

Poppy nodded. "Mrs. Silver."

She used to tell my friends to call her Thea.

Mom crossed to the hall, where she hung her racket in the closet. "So you're in the middle of serving breakfast to your friend?" she asked when she came back.

"Yes," I said. "You want some more, Poppy?" He had cleared his plate. I couldn't remember when.

"Don't you want any?" Poppy asked, as Jeff said, "I'm ready for more!"

"Oh, yeah. I burned mine. I didn't start a fire, though, Mom. You want some pancakes? I still have plenty of batter left."

"I'm meeting Ari for lunch in an hour. You'll clean up when you're done, right, Becky?"

"Of course." Mom must be really out of it. I'd been cleaning up my own messes for years.

Messes. Wait a sec. I had forgotten about Poppy's blood in the front hall. I guessed Mom hadn't noticed it, but I better take care of it as soon as I could. Only how could you get blood out of a carpet? Especially weird blood like Poppy's?

"Is Poppy wearing one of your shirts, Beck?" Mom asked.

So she wasn't *that* out of it. I hadn't worn that shirt in at least three months, but she still remembered it. "Oops. That reminds me, Poppy, we should wash your clothes."

"What's wrong with her clothes?"

"They're dirty," I said.

"Poppy's a boy," Jeff said.

Mom leaned to stare at Poppy's face, glanced at Jeff, then at me. Then back at Poppy, who smiled, eyebrows up.

"You're not that girl on the cheerleading squad? I could have sworn—" said Mom.

"Oh, please!" I cried. "Just because Megan Ennis has long black hair doesn't mean Poppy looks like her!" Although now that Mom mentioned it, Megan did have a slender build and pointed features like Poppy's, and light blue eyes.

Mom straightened. "Where'd he come from, then?"

"School."

"Why did he bring his dirty clothes here?"

God, she was worse than ever. Before Miriam died she never would have asked all these rude questions in front of the guest. She would have dragged me into the other room to ask me. Or maybe she would have brought Poppy home herself and told us all to be nice to him.

"He was wearing them. He needed a shower and a change of clothes and some breakfast, Mom. He feels better now."

"Maybe I should leave," Poppy said.

I thought Mom might agree with him. *"Mom,"* I said to stop her from saying it.

She sat down beside him instead, and took his hand. "What happened?" she asked gently, in her professional counselor's voice. I hadn't seen her talk like that in at least a year. She used to get my friends to open up when there was something they weren't telling me but needed to tell someone. It was another thing that drove me crazy. How come they would talk to her when they wouldn't talk to me? Except once she knew what was wrong, she knew what to do about it, and it usually worked. I couldn't do that.

Poppy stared into Mom's face. A tear streaked down his cheek. She stroked his hand and waited.

"I can't find my way home," he said.

She pulled him into her lap.

She hadn't held me in her lap in about four years. I was supposed to be sort of grown up, and if she had tried that with me I wouldn't have let her do it. Poppy was only a little smaller than me, and Mom was only a little bigger, but she made it work somehow.

He pressed his face into her shoulder and hugged her, and she held him in the circle of her arms and hummed. She didn't tell him it would be all right. She had never said things like that, even before Miriam died. She said nothing was more toxic than an impossible promise.

She just held him.

I got up and made some more pancakes, unsettled in stomach and mind. Mom had stopped taking care of strays. She had turned into a normal grownup, as distant as most other parents I knew, the kind who said "That's nice, dear," if you told her you'd just developed a taste for fried rattlesnake.

I gave Jeff some pancakes, and me some, and slipped a couple onto Poppy's plate before he came up out of Mom's embrace. Then I sat down and ate.

"Honey," Mom said, "how can we help you?"

"I don't think you can," Poppy whispered. He lifted his head. "Maybe there's something in your tales?"

"My tails?" Mom said. "I don't have tails."

"The fey-ree tales. Do any of them talk about gates to other worlds?"

Mom took him by the shoulders and pushed him back so she could stare into his face. "Are you all right?"

What if Mom thought Poppy was crazy? She knew where to send kids who had reality problems, i.e., which facilities in the county mental health system had beds open for juveniles. I wished I could tell him to shut up.

He wiped his hand over his cheek, dashing away tears. "Oh, sure. I'm fine."

"I wouldn't go that far." She smiled. Gently she guided him back into his chair. "Let's think about this. You really want to go home?"

"More than anything."

"Is there some way we can get in touch with your parents?" She rose, got a notepad and pen from the phone table, sat down again, opened to a blank page, and looked at Poppy.

"I don't know how."

"Do you remember your phone number?"

Poppy looked at me, bewildered.

I fetched the cordless phone. "This is a phone," I said, and held it out to him.

"Oh, dear," said Mom.

Poppy held the phone in both hands, ran his fingers over it so lightly that none of the number buttons pressed down. His eyebrows pulled together. "Voices?" he whispered. "Voices come out of this into the air? Voices go into this and travel?"

"Yeah."

He held it to his ear, then away.

"It only talks to other phones, though," I said. "I don't think your parents have phones."

"No."

"What's their address?" Mom asked.

Poppy looked at me again. He turned to Mom. "They don't live in the same place. My father lives in—" he said something in lala language—"but he travels a lot, and my mother lives in—" a different lala word.

"Oh, dear," said Mom. "What country did you say you were from?"

"Feyala Durezhda."

"What continent is that on?"

"It's not really on a—a continent. It's underneath and sideways."

Mom glanced at me. I looked at Jeff. How could we possibly interpret that for her? What if she thought Poppy was nuts? What if we tried to tell Mom the truth? The truth. Still kind of up for grabs.

Mom switched topics. "What are your parents' names?"

He spoke three words in the other language, then tapped his lips. "My mother's name is—is Nightshade. My father's name is Hariyeh, Prince of Silischia."

"I *thought* they must be hippies," Mom said, "to give you a name like Poppy. Will they be looking for you?"

"I'm sure my father is looking. I don't think he can find me. I'm so far from home. I left my mother's place last year to live with my father, so she probably doesn't even know I'm gone."

"No visitation?"

Poppy looked at me.

"You don't go see your mom on a regular basis?" I asked.

He shook his head. "She said to let her know if I needed anything, but she's busy. She has three smaller children, and she trusts me to take care of myself."

Mom studied him, let silence speak for her. Poppy's cheeks colored. "If I could call her, she would come. I can't seem to call."

"How would you call her if you don't even know what a phone is?"

"I would send her a message—speak into a carrier and slip it between edges of worlds, tell it where home was, and give it the itch to get there." He studied everything on the table. "A carrier," he muttered, and picked up the salt shaker. He glanced at me and put it down. "Maybe . . . " he said.

"How far away is home from here?" Mom asked.

Poppy shook his head. "Too far."

"How did you get here?"

"I kept trying to go home, and every time I tried I got more lost."

"Was it a bus ride? A hitchhike? A train? How'd you get here?"

"I came through a gate."

Mom looked at me.

I shrugged.

She said, "No phone number, no address, no last names, not even a home continent or mode of transportation. This is complicated."

"Can he stay here until we figure it out?" I asked.

Mom's eyes went opaque. When they cleared, New Mom was back. "No," she said. "I'll call in a few favors, find him a place in emergency shelter care until I can arrange an appointment with a screener on Monday."

"You're going to put Poppy into the system on a holiday weekend?"

Mom's mouth twisted. "We don't know you," she said to Poppy in her New Mom voice. "I'm so sorry, but there's no way we can trust you."

"That's all right," said Poppy. "I'll leave. I think I can take care of myself now."

Jeff grabbed Poppy's arm. "You *can't* leave."

"Why not?"

"You have to tell us what other languages you speak."

Mom straightened. Jeff interested in a subject other than computers? We didn't see that very often.

"Becky, could you bring me his clothes? Maybe there are clues in them," she said.

"Is that all right?" I asked Poppy. I hoped it was all right. If she was interested in solving a puzzle, maybe Old Mom was still here somehow.

He nodded. "I left them on the table in the shower room."

I went upstairs to get Poppy's clothes, which were folded on the bathroom counter. He had folded the wet towel and rag and left them there, too; the shower faucet was still dripping, so I turned it off harder, and dumped his used towel and rag in the hamper.

God, his clothes stank. The smell was more swampy than sweaty. They were messier than I had remembered, the velvet matted and mud-stained. Only the red flower on the shirt was clean. I touched it, and my fingertips buzzed. I jerked my hand back.

I thought about Poppy's blood on my hands, how that, too, had tingled. Fairy blood. I didn't know what to believe.

I touched a stain on the knee of Poppy's pants. Dark, smelly, half-dried blue-gray mud flaked off, and a little purple leaf shaped like a spider fell to the floor. I picked it up. I had never seen a leaf like it. I sniffed it. Ammonia-raspberry, a stinging scent.

NINA KIRIKI HOFFMAN

I stopped in my room and put the leaf in my top desk drawer.

In the kitchen, Mom held out her hands, and I gave her Poppy's clothes. Her nose wrinkled. "Good grief! Where have you been?"

"I don't know the names of the places."

"Wetlands, apparently. Oh, my." She ran her fingers over the collar. "This was fine, fine material before it got trashed." She touched the poppy, jerked her finger away too. "Static?"

"There's a protect spell in it. My mother made it." Poppy reached past Mom and touched the flower, his face sad. "Don't know how strong it was. Maybe it protected me from those animals."

"Animals?" Mom asked. "Spells?"

I kicked Poppy's foot under the table. He glanced at me.

"In this country, only children believe in fairy tales," I said.

"Someone put a spell of confusion on the adults?" he asked.

"Uh—" said Jeff.

"Are you and Jeff children?" Poppy asked.

Another good question. Mom seemed to be waiting for an answer. Luckily the doorbell rang.

We looked at each other. I stood up. "I'll be right back."

Danny Ortega was at the door. "Hey, Becky," he said.

I pretty much forgot everything that had happened that morning and just stared at him. He had the best smile.

"You lose something?" he asked.

"Huh?"

He held out a deflated basketball. It had the name SILVER written on it with black indelible pen.

"Oh!" My ball! Dead! Maybe I could blow it up again.

"Somebody's mad at you, huh?" He turned the ball over and showed me that it had been slashed with a knife.

My stomach lurched. "Shoog Kelly," I said.

"What do I always tell you? Why didn't you call me?"

"It was way early."

"He hurt you?"

"Uh, no. I hit him in the stomach with the ball and ran away."

"Couldn't hurt you, hurt the ball instead. I'm going to have a talk with that *cabrón*. He's a very bad character." He stared down at the dead basketball. "Not like you can patch this," he said.

I took it from him and hugged it. Christmas was coming. I could ask Dad for anything, probably, maybe even one of those red-white-and-blue Wilson balls. I'd already found out on my and Jeff's birthday last summer that divorce guilt motivated a lot of gift-giving. My old ball had been a good friend, though. Helped me play well with others. "Thanks for bringing it back," I said.

"No problem. Wanted to make sure you were okay, little sister." He patted my hair.

Sister. Sigh. "Would you like some pancakes?" The pan was probably cold by now, but I still had batter left. Anyway, Danny had come over for breakfast before.

"Sure!" He followed me back to the kitchen.

Jeff handed Poppy a glass of water. "Show Mom what you did before," he said. "Then she'll have to believe."

"No," I said. I dropped the basketball and rushed forward.

Poppy checked my face, set the glass on the table, glanced past me.

"Hey, all," said Danny from behind me.

I caught my breath. What was wrong with Jeff? He shouldn't ask Poppy to reveal himself. What was Mom going to do if she found out? If Jeff and I were shocked silly the first time we saw Poppy talk to water, maybe Mom would keel over and die.

At least Poppy was listening to me. "Danny, this is Poppy," I said. "Poppy, this is my friend Danny."

Poppy stood up and held out his hand.

"Hey there." Danny shook hands.

"Hi, Danny," said Mom, her voice flat.

"Hey, Thea. You okay?"

"Well, Danny," Mom said, "mostly, but right now I have a problem. Either this child is lying to me, or he's crazy, and for some reason my BS detector isn't working the way it should."

Danny cocked his head and studied Poppy.

"He's not lying, and he's not crazy," said Jeff.

"What is that?" Poppy asked, pointing.

I glanced back, went to pick up my poor dead basketball. I brought it over and handed it to Poppy.

"Oh," he said. His fingers traveled across the gash, and his peaky eyebrows rose. "Shoog killed it?"

"Yeah," I said.

"It's your weapon."

"No, it's my toy."

"It's your friend. It protected us." He stroked his fingertips across it. "It's not so dead." He murmured to the deflated ball in lala, smiling at it, his fingertips moving over the gash. The gash blurred, melted, healed. I shook my head, wondering if there was something wrong with my eyes. Blinked. There was no knife slash in the ball anymore.

I glanced at Mom. She rubbed her eyes, stared.

"How does it breathe?" Poppy asked himself. "Air goes in and stays." He turned the ball over, his fingers tracing spirals on its skin, until he found the valve. "Air go in," he said.

The ball inflated.

He bounced it. The sound of jump. He smiled and bounced the ball toward me. I held out a hand and caught it.

"Holy shit," said Danny.

Mom blinked and blinked.

"Dude," said Jeff.

Poppy glanced at him, then at Mom and Danny. "Something else you don't do." His smile faded.

"It's good," Jeff said. "It's okay. You should do some more stuff like that for Mom. Mom, you can't send Poppy away, okay? When he says he's lost, he means really, really lost, understand?"

"No," Mom whispered.

"You a magician?" Danny asked Poppy. "You do other tricks?"

Poppy thought about that, glanced at me again, his eyebrows asking questions. "I don't think. . . ."

"A magician," whispered Mom. She nodded.

"A magician is a dealer in magic?" Poppy asked. "Maybe that is right. It doesn't feel quite right."

"You're not a magician," I said. "A magician deals in fake

magic. Tricks. Illusions. That's not what you do, Poppy."

"What you did, that was another language, right?" Jeff pointed to the basketball. I hugged it.

"Language of healing, language of air," said Poppy.

Mom whispered, "Other languages."

"He can talk to water, Mom. I bet he can talk to fire and earth too," said Jeff.

"Air and water aren't the same here," I said slowly to Poppy, "but you can still talk to them."

"Yes."

"They still behave for you."

"Yes."

"You were talking before about sending a message to your father."

"Yes."

"You could do it with that?" I put my ball on the floor and reached for the salt shaker, opened it and dumped the salt on the table.

"I—"

I handed him the empty salt shaker and its silver lid. "You said your father is human. But he could come get you if you sent him a message?"

"He was given powers of passage by my lady."

"What do you need to send a message?"

"Something that can slide through gates, past worlds." He glanced down at the salt shaker. "The language to convince it where to go and how to get there. A piece of here that could only come from here, so the gate knows where to open. Paper. Something to write with. Good fortune."

I took Mom's pad and pen and handed them to him.

FLOTSAM

"A piece of here?" Jeff said. He glanced around, pinched a piece of pancake from the ones on my plate, handed it to Poppy.

He sat down. He sniffed the bite of pancake, smiled at Jeff, shoved it into the salt shaker. He touched the paper and nodded, looked at the pen and then up at me. I took the pen from him and demonstrated how it worked. He smiled, leaned forward, and wrote on the pad. Maybe it was letters that flowed from the end of the pen, but they weren't like any alphabet I had ever seen before. Mom watched Poppy, her face blank.

Danny came to stand next to me, held out his hands. I gave him my basketball. He turned it over. My name was still on it; other than that, it looked brand new. He shook his head, thumped his forehead twice with his palm, shook his head again. He returned my ball, then grabbed my hand.

He'd never done that before. His hand was warm, large, and dry. A small piece of my brain said, *Feel this. Remember this.*

Poppy finished, tore the page off the pad, ran his fingertips across the text. The letters silvered and shimmered.

Danny's hand tightened on mine, relaxed after I thought maybe my bones were crunched. I glanced up at his face. No expression.

"Poppy," Mom said.

"Mrs. Silver." He put down his message, straightened, met her gaze.

"Only children believe fairy tales."

"Ever? Always?"

She swallowed. A tear ran from her eye. "It hurts to believe."

"Why?"

Her lips tightened. "If you can exist, why can't other things? If you can send a message between worlds, why can't I talk to my daughter again?"

My heart hurt.

"You can talk to your daughter." He looked toward me.

"My other daughter, who's dead."

Silence. Finally, he said, "That's a gate I've never gone through."

"Do people go through that gate?"

"Everyone does, but I've never spoken to anyone who's come back."

A sob shook her. Her shoulders jerked, and she gulped. Poppy touched her knee. She closed her eyes and leaned her head back. Tears leaked from her eyes.

I didn't know what to do. At Miriam's funeral, I hadn't been able to think about anything except all the ways I would miss my sister, and all the things about her that had made me mad. I had drowned in my own sadness. I had wished I could die.

I hadn't had the time or energy to wonder how Mom was doing.

My sadness came back sometimes, but it wasn't quite as deep, and it didn't last as long. I had been through it before. I knew now that I wouldn't get stuck in the middle. I could let it come and let it go.

All I knew about how Mom was dealing with Miriam's death was that she had cut a lot of things out of her life that used to mean everything to her, like caring about strangers.

Mom put her hand on top of Poppy's on her knee and covered her eyes with her other hand. After a couple minutes she stopped choking on sobs and pulled herself together. "I'm sorry."

He turned his hand over and gripped hers, then let go. "I have to send this. I know my dad's worried about me. I hope this works."

"Yes."

He folded the note in some kind of origami way that made it small and intricate. He put it in the salt shaker and screwed the lid on, then held the salt shaker in cupped hands and spoke to it in liquid lala syllables. It changed. First it smoothed out into an egg, half silver, half glass, then some rainbow shininess coated it until it was hard to look at. My gaze kept sliding away from it.

Jeff reached toward Poppy's hands. The egg shivered, though, flipped this way and that, then slid away with a faint high whistle like a distant train.

"She closed the gates to me," Poppy said, "but that wasn't me. Maybe it can get through."

Thirty seconds later a man and a woman stepped out of the air into our kitchen. They were shorter, slenderer, and smaller than most of the grown-ups I knew, but I could tell they weren't kids. The man was bare-headed, with long brown hair and blue-gray eyes. He looked ordinary, except he wore chain mail and an olive green cape, and a silver disk blazed on his forehead. The woman was shorter than I was, maybe four and a half feet tall. The pointed tips of her ears poked up through her riot of long black hair, and she had icy blue eyes just like Poppy's. Her clothes looked more like some strange black vine curling around her body than fabric.

The man and the woman burst into torrents of lala speech as they raced to the table and hugged Poppy between them. Poppy had such a blissful expression on his face that I couldn't look at him for very long. Instead I squeezed Danny's hand and stared at the floor.

The woman stepped back and cradled Poppy's face between her long-fingered hands. She kissed his forehead, then scolded him. He nodded and nodded before he turned around and the man hugged him, murmuring to him all the while, but smiling too.

It was maybe five minutes before any of them looked up. The man stroked Poppy's head, then, still smiling, glanced at me and Danny.

Just his look, just his smile, and I felt as though I were wrapped in a warm blanket of approval, love, and regard. It was an intense feeling of fatherness. I didn't know why I thought that was what it was, because I'd never felt anything like it from my own father. I just knew.

Danny relaxed beside me. He nodded. The man nodded back, then smiled at Jeff and Mom. They both shifted in their chairs.

The man held Poppy's shoulders, stroked down his arms. The man said something to Poppy, and Poppy looked at us, finally, and said, "This is my dad!" His voice squeaked.

"I figured," I said. My voice shook a little too.

"And this is my mom. They were looking for me together. They *never* do anything together!"

The woman patted Poppy's cheek, brushed fingers across his mouth, then glanced at all of us. She smiled, but on her it looked more like the smile you make when someone's taking your picture and you're totally not in the mood. She spoke.

"She says thank you for taking care of me," Poppy said.

"You're welcome," said Mom. *Her* voice shook.

Poppy's dad turned toward Mom. He asked a question, and Poppy answered. The dad let go of Poppy's hand and went to Mom. He took her hands and stared down into her eyes. Mom cried, no sobs, just tears, and stared back. My heart cracked.

The man murmured something.

Poppy said, "He says they didn't know if I was alive or dead, but they found me now, and there are people taking care of me. He says maybe on the other side of the gate someone is watching over your daughter too."

The man squeezed Mom's hands. She closed her eyes, then blinked away tears and smiled up at the man. "Oh, I hope so," she whispered.

He put his hand on her cheek and held her gaze.

The woman spoke again. Poppy nodded. "Thank you. Thank you. Mother says it feels strange here and she's not sure it's safe for her, and she wants to take me home and . . . *cook* for me. She doesn't cook. I mean, she's never cooked for me before. What?"

His father let go of Mom, returned to Poppy and the woman, embraced them both, and spoke.

"The energies here are unfamiliar and the gates may get warped, so we should leave now," Poppy translated. "I can't go through the gates by myself and get them to work, but my mother and father can take me safely." He pulled out of his dad's hug and came to me. "Becky. Thanks for saving my life." He gripped my hands and kissed my cheek. Another tingling contact, both hands and lips.

"Danny." He kissed Danny's cheek. "Jeff." He kissed Jeff's cheek. "Mrs. Silver." He kissed Mom's cheek. Danny and Jeff were in shock, but Mom patted Poppy's cheek and smiled at him.

His mother had discovered his clothes, folded and reeking on the table, and she said something that sounded nasty and flicked her fingers at them. Suddenly they were clean. The room smelled like sunshine and jasmine.

"May I keep your clothes?" Poppy asked me.

"Sure." My voice was still too high.

Poppy picked up his old clothes and brought them to me, pressed them into my arms. "You want mine? We're about the same size, yes? I don't have anything else to give you."

"Sure," I said.

He hugged me and ran back to his parents. His father said something warm to all of us. His mother and father took his hands, and his father said something else. The silver on his forehead blazed, and the three of them stepped into nowhere.

I hugged Poppy's clothes to my chest. Sunshine, jasmine, an undertone of vanilla. The mud of other worlds had vanished.

The outfit looked like something I might be able to find at the mall.

I pressed the embroidered poppy to my cheek, and it buzzed against my skin.

No, I guessed not.

"Was it— Did it— Was he even here?" Mom asked. She stared at the plate Poppy had eaten off of. Only crumbs and a pool of syrup remained. "Shared hallucination?" she muttered.

Danny said, "He kissed me. He kissed me."

"He kissed me too," Jeff said. He made a face.

"He was from another planet," I said. "It probably means something else there."

"Never tell anyone," said Danny. "Ever."

"I won't." I grabbed his hand. "You can't tell anyone about him either, okay?"

His eyebrows rose. "Oh. Yeah." He glanced around the kitchen. "Oh yeah. Is it still Saturday morning? I feel like I fell into somewhere else."

We went over to the kitchen window and looked out. The sun shone over the back yard. Starlings squabbled in the leafless horse chestnut tree. Puddles of yesterday's rain lay along the edge of the raised flowerbeds. Our winter yard.

"Saturday," said Mom, her hand pressed to her cheek where Poppy's father had touched her. "I feel like years have come and gone." She went to the sink and splashed water on her face, grabbed a towel and dried off, then glanced at the kitchen clock. "Oh, God. It's almost noon. I'm supposed to meet Ari at the India Palace in five minutes."

She gripped the edge of the sink and swayed. Color came and went in her cheeks.

"Mom? Are you all right?"

"I don't know." She turned to look at me. Her face was soft, relaxed. "I can't quite believe what just happened. But I feel better."

I went to her, dragging Danny with me. "Look." I held out Poppy's shirt.

She touched the poppy. Her hand jerked. Our eyes met.

"Protection," she said. She smiled. "Would you try it on for me?"

"Yeah."

"Would you kids come with me to lunch? Humor me. I know it doesn't make much sense, but I don't want to let any of you out of my sight right now."

"I'll go home," Danny said.

"No. Come with us, Danny. Please."

He hesitated. "Okay."

I ducked into the front hall closet and changed into Poppy's shirt. The poppy felt warm from the inside. My cheek tingled. My hands tingled. Warmth washed over my skin. I hugged myself. Today had been the best kind of strange. It was still too new a treasure for me to know what I had found, too fresh a loss for it to really hurt yet.

What had happened?

Something that shook the world.

Was it over?

I pressed my palm against the poppy and knew it wasn't.

"Becky?" Mom called. "Let's go."

Let's go.

NINA KIRIKI HOFFMAN is the author of six acclaimed novels, including *A Stir of Bones* (Viking). She has also written and sold over two hundred short stories to anthologies and magazines.

Her short stories and novels have been finalists for the Nebula, the World Fantasy, and the Endeavor awards. Her book *The Thread That Binds the Bones* won the Bram Stoker Award for first novel, and her short story "A Step Into Darkness" won a Writers of the Future Award in 1984.

Nina Hoffman lives in Eugene, Oregon, with cats, friends, and many creepy toys.

AUTHOR'S NOTE

"Flotsam" is a piece of a larger work. I've been telling myself stories about Poppy and his parents in their home world for some time now. There are dragons and lost princesses and shapeshifters and sorcerous towns and acres and pockets of Fairyland in other parts of the tale, but I knew Poppy ended up on Earth at one point, and I love stories of strangers who arrive here somehow, how they look at our culture, how they decide to deal with it.

I really like Becky, and I wonder how her brush with magic is going to shift her life.

Laurel Winter

tHe fLyɪɴɢ WoMaN

The boats rested uneasily on the surface of the sea, waiting to leave. Chief Loah gripped Raff's shoulder in one hand and tilted Dannilla's face up with the other. "Swear you will not use your unnatural power to leave this island," he said. "Swear on your father's life."

His fingers squeezed Dannilla's chin. Their father sat in one of the boats, his face shiny with tears. "I swear," she said. "I swear. Please don't hurt him."

Raff held silent, and then he gasped as the leader's hand closed on his arm. "I swear."

The leader pushed him, hard, and let go of Dannilla. Her eyes blurred and she fell to her knees in the sea.

Before Raff could regain his breath and sit up again, Chief Loah and their father and the other men and the boats were small and far away. And then gone.

Raff sat rubbing his shoulder for a long time. Dannilla felt the ocean and the beach grow larger and larger with every heartbeat, and herself grow smaller. She didn't want to ask her brother the question, because what if he didn't know? Finally, when she felt as small as one of the gritty grains of sand, she couldn't help it any longer. "What will we do?" she asked, her voice high with fear.

Raff looked at her and smiled. "We'll explore," he said. "Find some food. Build a shelter. Do some magic."

"But we promised," she said.

He shook his head. "We promised not to use it to escape the island." He smiled again, and this time it looked more real. "Find me some raw magic."

"But what about our mother? That promise?"

Raff closed his eyes for a moment. "I promised to hide the magic as well as I could, so the others wouldn't find out," he said, his voice sounding curiously young. "We both tried to be careful, didn't we?"

Dannilla nodded. Raff had mainly done small magics, strengthening snares, summoning a second tree crawler so there would be enough for a stew, ripening fruit. Away from the others. But not far enough away, it had turned out.

He continued. "But now they know. That promise doesn't count any more. We can do magic, as much as we want, whenever we want to. Find me some good raw magic."

Dannilla felt a delicious shiver run through her. They didn't have to hide here; that was the good thing about being caught. "What are you going to do?" she asked.

"You'll see."

They had always worked together—Dannilla finding the raw magic; Raff using it. For some odd reason, he couldn't sense the raw magic. She could, like smelling flowers that she didn't know how to pick. She turned slowly around now, and let her mind search. Traces of it were everywhere; no one had used magic here for a long time, if ever. A little farther up the beach it seemed deeper, richer. "Here," she said.

When he'd reached the point she had directed him to, he knelt and stretched his hands out and let it collect on his splayed fingers. Ripples flowed up his hands and wrists, until his entire lower arms were encased in glowing, translucent raw magic.

Dannilla loved this part. Raff kept gathering until she nodded to him that he had enough.

Carefully, he raised his hands and stood. Dannilla couldn't keep from dancing a bit. What was he going to do? His lips moved as he spoke silently to the raw magic, and then he snapped his hands forward.

Drops of brilliance leapt out. Sparkling air! Before, when the magic had to be secret, he had only done tiny splashes, and only a few times. Colored bits showered and she joined in, dancing wildly as the air danced around her. Raff just laughed and watched her. Dannilla leaped and twirled as the sparkles faded to pale and then disappeared, leaving her panting on the sand.

"Come on," said Raff. "We need to figure out where to stay." He snatched up the small bag of food and water that had been left for them and set off.

Dannilla set off after him, wishing he'd slow down a little, or at least wait until she rested, but the shadows lengthened around them and she didn't want darkness to come before they had shelter.

The Flying Woman

Likely-looking caves pocked the cliff face, but neither of them wanted to start climbing this late in the day. "We could build a tree house," Dannilla said, pointing at the lush forest that spilled down the hillside to the east of the cliffs.

Raff stopped and looked at her, his brown eyes wide. "You are almost as smart as your brother," he said. "A tree house it is."

None of the trees had wide spreading branches, though, so they ended up building a platform between three trees—with the help of the raw magic that had seeped to the surface. The first three logs they had to lift into place and tie up with vines, a shaky structure indeed, but then Raff used magic to make new branches grow from the ends of the dead logs and curve around the supporting trees.

After that, it was a fairly simple task to lay more logs across the triangle. Darkness crept around them, but Raff spent a few minutes growing vines over and under the logs, anchoring them to each other, to the base logs, and to the support trees. "Tomorrow we'll figure out a roof," he said, his voice hoarse with exhaustion, both from all the magic and from hefting the logs, Dannilla thought. She could barely haul herself up onto the low platform and swallow a few bites of fruit from the food bag. The logs weren't terribly comfortable, but the vines helped somewhat. She didn't spend much time tossing about before the deep velvet night crept into her mind.

She woke up hungry and thirsty. Raff still slept, one arm hanging down from the platform. Dannilla rummaged through the bag. The people had not been generous: several under-ripe pulp fruits, a twist of bread wrapped in a dry leaf, one small gourd of water. No sweets, no meat. Well, we don't need it, thought Dannilla. We are the ones who never have empty snares. She threw one of the fruits at a nearby tree.

Birds exploded from it, shrieking. Raff sat up fast, his eyes scared. Dannilla apologized and handed him half of the bread twist. "Let's go make a snare," she said, flopping down from the platform. "I'm hungry for real food." The bread tasted good, but there wasn't enough of it to make a meal.

After they had gone off in different directions to relieve themselves, they set off hunting. Dannilla also kept her senses open for some wild, hot raw magic, which Raff would need to make an ever-burning fire. There was none. They'd have to make do with the ordinary stuff for the fire, then, and hope for the best.

They set the first snare in a clump of tough grass not far from the tree house. Raff made the stems even stronger and set one of the fruits from the bag in the center of the clump— except he made it seem more luscious, ripe, bursting with sweet juice. Then, when he and Dannilla had stepped back, he set the snare.

They set several more snares, one of them with a magically-balanced log large enough to crush the spine of a pig or other large beast. Then they meandered back toward the first snare, their stomachs growling.

They heard sounds of struggle from some distance away. Success. Raff's longer legs got him there first, but Dannilla came soon after.

Usually, small snares caught small animals. Somehow, the snare had managed to wrap itself securely about the head and neck of a deer that had gone for the fruit. The frantic animal had pawed and stamped and ripped the ground up with its hooves, but it was still trapped. "Now what?" asked Dannilla, still panting.

Raff didn't answer right away. "If I had a sharp knife," he said, "we could slit its throat."

"So make one," said Dannilla. "We need one to cut it up anyway."

"It's not that easy." Raff's voice sounded angry.

The deer struggled harder as they spoke, but the snare held. Dannilla started to feel scared. The animals they usually snared were small enough that a rock to the back of the skull would kill them. And always before when they'd brought their prey back, there had been fine stone knives to cut up the meat—and grown-ups who knew just how to do it. Magic couldn't manage everything, she realized. Or maybe it could, but Raff didn't know how. Their mother hadn't had time to teach him enough before she died.

The deer thrashed, its breath coming hard. "I know," shouted Dannilla. She yanked a vine from an overhanging branch and approached the snare.

Once he saw what she planned, Raff helped. Good thing, too, as it was no easy task to strangle the deer with the vine. They both ended up with bruises, but finally the struggling animal went limp.

Raff released the snare magic, and they both stared at the sleek body at their feet.

Sharp rocks did little. Sharpened sticks did nothing. Eventually, Raff lost his patience and set the animal on fire. Or tried to, anyway. The flames sputtered and went out, time after time. Finally it caught.

Dannilla moved back, away from the smell of burning hair,

the eye-stinging smoke. She wanted to drag the deer into the circle of huts and have Kamessa slit the skin with her black-bladed knife and peel it back. She even wanted to drag the entrails away on a sled made of malek leaves and bury them. She wanted to watch the animal sizzle over the big firepit, and only get a child's share—and what she could sneak from the carcass when the adults lounged full and indulgent.

She squinted to try and keep from crying. She sank into a crouch and watched the burning deer waver and shine through a layer of tears.

After a time, Raff came up to her. "Here," he said, giving a small chunk of meat he had hacked from one of the flanks with a sharp rock. His face had streaks of black, and she could see that he had burned his fingers. He said nothing about her tears, so she wiped her face and looked at the meat. It was hot, with burnt hair and skin still clinging to the charred side. Dannilla ate, picking pieces of hair from her tongue. When she had eaten all that was edible, she went to the smoking carcass and hacked off another piece.

Most of the meat was ruined, but the two of them filled their stomachs. When they were done, they dragged the blackened body further from their tree house.

They washed in the stream when they got back. Dannilla felt weary and sore. Would every day be like this? She splashed water on her face and arms. A large bruise on her left shin marked the encounter with the deer. She missed her father. She splashed more water on her face to hide the tears.

"I know," shouted Raff, bounding from the water. He ran to the food bag and held up the last fruit triumphantly. Dannilla stared at him. "Find me some raw magic," he said.

THE FLYING WOMAN

They had used up most of the nearby raw magic and not enough time had gone by to replenish it, but Dannilla found some a little way off. Raff collected it with one hand, still holding the fruit in the other. When he had enough, he placed the fruit on the ground near the tree house and dribbled magic over it.

The fruit shuddered and split and sprouted. A stem grew, quickly becoming a trunk. Leafy branches emerged, and flowers budded and bloomed and became fruit. Raff shook off the last of the raw magic and the magic stopped. He picked a pulp fruit and handed it to Dannilla.

It was a treat after half-burned deer meat. She sucked the juices from her fingers and climbed up onto the platform. The canopy of leaves made a green ceiling—a ceiling, she knew, that would let the rain splatter down upon them. And they truly needed walls as well, or the wet wind would drench them when it came blowing almost sideways. Malek leaves, sewn together or glued with tree resin, made good temporary shelter, but they dried out and cracked. Unless they could be kept growing . . . .

Living malek leaves growing from the branches of other trees—Raff didn't find it easy, but it did work. They had a house.

They fell into a pattern. Mornings were spent checking and setting snares. Evenings, they chipped at the edges of stones and shells, trying to perfect the rough blades they used to butcher their meat. And in between, they picked fruit or swam or explored the island, Dannilla finding pools and streaks and fountains of raw magic.

It still amazed her that Raff couldn't sense it, that no one else she knew could either. Her earliest memory was of learning to walk, staggering in a twisted path so she wouldn't step in the places where the intensity was greatest.

Their mother had been able to see it, and use it. She had shown Raff secret magics and discovered his talent and pointed out raw magic to him, until her life bled away at Dannilla's birth. Her magic had not saved her.

Sometimes Dannilla wondered if she missed their mother more than Raff did, even though she had never known her. But of course she didn't, because Raff had been seven when their mother died, old enough to hold strong memories in his head. If he was in the right mood, he would tell Dannilla stories from that time, from the good time, when he and his mother worked magic together in the forest, away from everyone else.

Not long after Raff grew the roof and walls for their tree house, as they lay in the green darkness, waiting to sleep, he had been in such a mood.

"I wonder if our mother came from a place like this," he said. "She wasn't like any of the others—not even like Father, although more like him than anyone else." Vines rustled and Dannilla sensed that he was trying to see her in the darkness, skinny and tough, with frizzy brown hair and skin the same color. "She was like you."

Dannilla felt a flash of pride. "Did she look like me?"

"No," said Raff, with a laugh in his voice. "You look like her." He looked like Father and the rest of the people, tall and golden brown, with straight black hair. "She showed me raw magic and taught me to use it and Father was so happy all the time. He sometimes came from hunting in the middle of the day, just so he could be with her. The other men laughed at him and teased him, but she was rare." His voice trailed off and silence filled the darkness. Dannilla was almost asleep when he spoke again. "I want to have a woman that I will go home just to laugh with in the middle of hunting."

But there aren't any other people on the island, thought Dannilla, as she drifted into a dream.

For a while, they were reasonably content, but soon the island was explored, the stone knives sharp enough. Raff took to wandering on the beaches, staring at the sea, chasing Dannilla away with harsh words if she wandered too close. He didn't tell any more stories about their mother—or anything else, for that matter. Dannilla was more and more alone.

The tree house began to feel small and temporary. "Let's move to one of the caves," she said, more than once. Raff would nod or shrug, but he never wanted to actually do it.

And then the wet wind came.

It blew stronger here than where they had come from, or perhaps they had just built in the wrong place. It shredded even living malek leaves, pelting the two of them with cold, harsh drops and bits of debris. A splintered branch whipped through the air, cutting Dannilla's face. Even Raff looked frightened as he hauled her off the platform and dragged her beneath the logs. Dannilla couldn't keep from crying. Raff gave her a warming hug and a shaky smile.

"We should move to one of the caves," he yelled above the sound of the wind.

Dannilla let a laugh tumble into the middle of her sobs,

and then they were laughing together, in spite of being wet and miserable.

When the wind lulled the next day—a temporary thing—they clambered up the wet stone into the lowest cave. "This won't do," said Raff, fingering bits of shells he picked up from the cave floor. "The sea comes this high."

The next cliff up, though, was Dannilla's favorite. "Come see," she said, going into the twist at the back where water seeped down the rock wall.

Raff didn't follow. She peeked around the corner to see him staring out. "There's something . . . ." His voice trailed off and he shaded his eyes. "There's someone in the sea."

Dannilla ran to the opening and scanned the wild sea, turbulent from the night's storm. Nothing but waves.

Raff pointed. "There."

Near the beach. A bit of flotsam. "It's just a log," she said. "Driftwood." And then she saw the arm, and what had appeared to be part of the waves but now transformed into clothing. "You're right."

Raff was already halfway down the cliff. Dannilla followed him cautiously, her heart pounding like the waves against the beach. What if it was Father? Or one of the others from their village? The person still had to be alive, or the arm would have slipped from the log. Wouldn't it? There was going to be someone else on the island. Even if it was a stranger . . . .

By the time Dannilla had negotiated the cliff and run down to the sea's shifting edge, Raff had plunged into the surf. He reached the log just as the arm slipped off and the person disappeared beneath the surface. Raff disappeared, too, then, and Dannilla opened her mouth to scream, but there wasn't enough air in her lungs. What if he didn't come up again? What if she was alone on the island, alone forever?

But he did come up, gasping, swimming with one arm, the other holding someone by the hair. Not Father, because the hair was long and light. They made it almost to the shore, and Dannilla ran into the waves and helped Raff haul the stranger up onto the sand.

Stranger. The being was a—not a human woman, but clearly a female creature. Breasts showed through the rips in a sodden garment. The face looked human, for all that it was bruised and gray with cold, but the huge, tattered wings sprouting from the shoulders did not. It was not clear if it—she—even lived. "Help me," yelled Raff, his voice quivering with cold or emotion; Dannilla couldn't tell.

"Do what?" she asked. The creature lay like a dead thing at her feet. She shuddered.

"Find me some raw magic." He knelt and rubbed the stranger's arms and face. "And some dry wood. We need a fire."

Dannilla looked around. She couldn't concentrate, couldn't focus. Here and there were dribs and drabs of raw magic, but they didn't feel right to her. And there wouldn't be a piece of dry wood on the entire island after the wet wind had blown through. "There is none," she screamed.

Raff swore, and pulled her down. "Do this," he said, grabbing her hands and scrubbing them up and down over the cold arms.

"She's dead," Dannilla wailed, trying to pull away.

Raff wouldn't let her. "She's not," he said fiercely. "Keep rubbing. We have to warm her up." He glared at her and released her hands. "We have to," he said. He stood. Dannilla kept her hands moving over the sand-gritty arms. Raff nodded and began gathering wet fragments of driftwood thrown up on the beach by the angry waves.

Dannilla watched him. Easier than watching the strange person lying so limp beneath her hands. When Raff had a small pile of wood, he thrust his hands out blindly to gather raw magic he couldn't sense. Again and again he tried to start the fire. Nothing. Nothing. Dannilla's arms felt as if they would fall off. Nothing. Then, smoke. Finally Raff had a small fire going.

They dragged the limp figure next to it. Raff took over the rubbing, and Dannilla crouched nearby, clutching her knees with aching arms. Was she dead?

Smoke swirled on the wind and shrouded the three of them. Dannilla closed stinging eyes and coughed. She heard Raff coughing, as well, and more coughing and a retching sound. She opened her eyes to see the flying woman rolled over on her side, gasping and spitting up sea water.

It was impossible to get the shivering creature up the cliff face to the cave, and yet they did it. Raff made a ladder of logs and vines. They rested for a long time in the first cave, the waves spitting furiously at them, before they made their shaky way to the second. The winged woman wasn't pretty, thought Dannilla, with her pale, bruised skin, and her almost colorless hair, but she was young. Maybe no older than Raff.

After they climbed up, Raff going first and hauling the

stranger by one hand while Dannilla did her best to help guide her feet from the bottom, Raff pulled the ladder up and began to rip it apart. "What are you doing?" Dannilla shouted.

"We have to have a fire," he said. "There's nothing else to burn."

He tried again and again to set the remains of the ladder on fire, but there was not enough of even the wrong kind of raw magic in the cave. Finally, he had to venture out again, to the smoldering remnants of their old fire and bring back a half-burning stick. Dannilla had to turn away from the opening; it was too frightening watching his exhausted, one-handed progress up the cliff.

The flying woman lay against the wall, shivering. Her golden eyes were open, watching Dannilla with no expression. It was as if she had no strength to be grateful or scared or anything at all.

Dannilla's strength was sapped as well and there seemed no threat in the pathetic figure they had rescued, but an odd shiver of fear traveled through her.

The next day, they made many feverish trips to haul up wood and food and leaves and what was left of their belongings from the tree house. Most of the time the flying woman slept near the fire, half waking to drink down a few mouthfuls of broth.

Raff was not back from a run to the snares. Dannilla was mashing some fruit so it would be easy to swallow. The flying woman struggled up to a half-sitting position and spoke some words in a strange language with many tongue clicking sounds. Dannilla groaned. Of course, it would be too much to expect that they could understand each other. Before she could say anything, the woman tried again, with words that sounded totally different, smooth and liquid and just as incomprehensible.

"I don't understand," she said. She touched her chest with one finger. "Dannilla." She pointed to the other and made what she hoped was a questioning expression.

The flying woman let out a big breath. "Dannilla. My name is Sherremy." Her voice sounded scratchy.

"You can talk to me! How?"

"My duty is to—to exchange words in one tongue for another." She dropped back down, but didn't close her eyes again. "Many of my people do this."

"Because you can fly?" asked Dannilla. "Because you know all the people?"

Sherremy's expression made her feel like the time she had carried an armful of still-green fruit back to the village as a young child. "No one can know all the people. Not even the great ones. But, yes, we know many people, many tongues."

"What is it like to fly in the air?"

Sherremy turned to the wall and didn't answer. Her wings shook with weeping.

She wept for hours, long after Raff returned with a woven bag of dead rodents slung over his shoulder. Nothing he did consoled her, and the only words she spoke were, "Go away. Leave me alone." In the end, she fell asleep still sobbing.

Raff was elated that she could understand and speak to them. "She'll be our friend," he told Dannilla.

Dannilla shrugged. "Maybe," she said. "Or maybe she'll fly

away as soon as she's well." It seemed disloyal to Raff, who clearly wanted Sherremy to stay, but she hoped to one day see her launch into the air and disappear in the distance. Maybe it was the way Raff looked at Sherremy, but Dannilla was uneasy now in a way she had not been since they were abandoned on the island.

Their guest soon regained her strength, but she was clearly unable to fly. It was difficult for her to climb to and from the cave if the wind was blowing, as it caught at her wings and threatened to pull her from the face of the cliff. Dannilla also, with her shorter reach, found the going hazardous. So she and Sherremy were frequently stuck in the cave together while Raff checked snares or picked fruit or carried wood.

Dannilla hated these times. Sherremy talked to her only when boredom drove her to it or Dannilla asked a question—and sometimes not even then. She spent long hours preening her wings, with tears dripping from her eyes.

Raff seemed determined not to notice her unhappiness. He brought her the best fruits, checked the snares twice a day, climbed high and hazardous parts of the cliff for seabird eggs, which she swallowed from the shell. He questioned her about her world, so much larger than theirs.

For a time, this worked. Raff grew bold enough to offer to comb out her long, tangled hair, his hands moving soft and slow as whispers. Dannilla got a strange feeling in her stomach as she watched them: Sherremy sitting with her head tilted back and her eyes closed; Raff kneeling behind her, his lips parted. Sometimes Dannilla rolled on her side and stared at the cave wall, but knowing they were there behind her made the silence loud and throbbing and unbearable. Why doesn't she just go? she asked herself, again and again.

But Sherremy, despite seeming miserable except when Raff combed her hair, did not go. She didn't fly at all. Dannilla wanted to ask her why, but Sherremy drew a curtain of silence around herself that seemed impenetrable. Then, one night, when Dannilla was feigning sleep, watching them through her lashes, Raff let the carved wooden comb slip from his fingers. His hands followed the curve of Sherremy's wings.

Sherremy shuddered visibly. Her wings flared, hiding Raff from view. Only his fingers were visible—sliding along the edge of her wings—and his kneeling legs.

Dannilla closed her eyes and rolled over to face the wall.

Oddly, Sherremy seemed even less happy after that. She spent plenty of time with Raff—he followed her everywhere—but she never smiled, never laughed. Hardly ever talked, even to Raff.

On windy days, she didn't leave the cave at all, just crouched near the entrance staring out. Dannilla got the idea, though, that she wasn't seeing the waves at all, but only the sky.

"Why don't you just fly away?" Dannilla asked once.

Sherremy rocked back on her heels. "Don't you think I would, if I could?" she asked. "Do you think I would stay here with you and your pitiful brother if I had a choice?" Her face was as pale as her hair. Her wings beat the air, creating a wind in the cave that rivaled the wind outside. Dannilla shrank back. "I curse the magic that took flight from me and left me here with none of my own kind, with only ground worms."

THE FLYING WOMAN

Dannilla escaped into the wind, tears drying on her face almost as quickly as they flowed. When Raff came back, with a large bird in one hand, she sat huddled in the sand at the base of the cliff.

"What's the matter?" he shouted. The wind snatched at his words.

"She doesn't want to be here," said Dannilla. "She wants to be with people of her own kind, not with us."

Raff looked down. "It isn't true," he said, his voice fierce.

"It is. She wants to fly away but some magic won't let her." Now Dannilla looked at the sand. "Maybe you can use magic to help her fly again."

"No," he cried. "I promised—we promised not to use magic to leave the island."

"For *us* to leave," she said.

But Raff had already begun to climb the cliff, the bright feathers of the dead bird blowing sideways as he climbed.

Dannilla stayed where she was. A few minutes later, the bird plummeted to the ground before her, a brilliant stain on the sand.

Sherremy stopped eating. Not entirely, but the few bites she took each day were clearly not enough to sustain her. She paid no attention to either of them, not seeming to care when Raff combed her hair, not even seeming to notice. Her face grew hollow and drawn. Only her wings didn't change.

She slept most of the time, huddled into a ball, her wings drawn tight against her back.

Raff's face began to look drawn as well. "We have to do something," said Dannilla. "Or she'll die."

"I won't make her leave." Raff closed his eyes and clenched his fists. "I need her. I love her."

"But she's going to die," said Dannilla. "Do you want her to die? Without any of her own kind around?"

Raff slowly opened his eyes. "Find me some raw magic," he said.

"What are you going to do?" asked Dannilla.

"Remember when we used to summon more animals, when one wasn't enough?"

She nodded reluctantly. "But she's not an—"

"It should work the same way. I have to try."

They climbed down the cliff together, leaving the wasted figure alone, asleep.

Raff tapped the raw magic that Dannilla led him to. He looked up at the cave entrance, a darkness on the face of the cliff. Dannilla laced and unlaced her small brown fingers as Raff raised his glowing hands, and began to work the magic.

It was a large, difficult magic that seemed to go on and on. And then a flying woman materialized on the sand before them, a powerful woman, unclothed. Her beating wings lifted her into the air. She looked down on them with Sherremy's face, Sherremy's golden eyes.

"Raff," Dannilla screamed. "What did you do?"

"I don't know," he said, his voice almost lost in the beating of the new Sherremy's wings as she flew through the air, diving and climbing and banking. He sounded dazed. "Maybe the magic always did that, made the same animal again, rather than summoning another of that kind."

The flyer dropped to the sand. "I'm leaving now," she said.

"No," said Raff. "Wait. She needs—you need to eat first."

She nodded.

"There is food in the cave," said Raff, pointing.

This other Sherremy, so like and unlike herself, launched into in the air again.

"We're coming," shouted Raff.

"What are you doing now?" asked Dannilla as they ran for the cliff.

"She'll see herself up there," said Raff. "She'll see that she must stay."

But when they scrambled up into the cave, the original Sherremy, shaking and weak, was sobbing wildly.

The new one had a handful of meat. Fruit juice stained her chin and dripped down onto her breasts. "Keep her away from me," she said. Her eyes were fierce and cold.

"She needs you," said Raff. "You must stay with her."

The naked woman turned away, toward the opening. "She doesn't need me," she said. "She needs to fly. That's the way of us." She flexed her legs and leaped outward, her wings catching the air.

Gone. She spiraled around twice, as if for the sheer joy of flight, and then she leveled off and flew, wings beating steadily. Away. Away. Away.

"No, no, no," said a high, keening voice. "Don't go without me. Help me." She staggered to her feet and would have thrown herself from the cliff if Raff and her own lack of strength had not prevented it. "Help me," she said over and over again, her wings beating feebly.

Dannilla helped Raff hold her back and carry her to her bed when she collapsed, still sobbing and shaking.

Finally, Sherremy was still, drawn into sleep by the exertion. Dannilla wiped tears from her own face. There was nothing to say. What they had done had made things immeasurably worse. They sat together, leaning against the wall, for a very long time.

Then, in a way that made him look old, Raff got to his feet. "Come," he said, his voice lifeless.

Dannilla had to follow.

"Find me some," he said, when they were both on the sands.

"But—" Dannilla began.

"Please," said Raff. He turned away from her. "Please."

Dannilla looked at him, saw pain and resolve. She nodded.

Again, a long and difficult spell. Dannilla found herself shaking. She hugged herself tightly.

This time, no winged woman appeared before them. Raff dropped his arms to his sides: the only sign that the magic was complete.

And then a shout from the cave.

Dannilla looked up. Sherremy stood in the entrance, wings spread. She leaned against the rocks for a moment. Dannilla held her breath. Sherremy let herself fall forward, wings beating. She almost hit the sand before she gained control and surged upward. Immediately, she aimed herself for the sea.

"Don't go," whispered Raff, so softly that Dannilla could barely hear. "Don't leave me."

Together, they watched the ragged flight. Dannilla didn't say what she knew had to be true—that Sherremy wasn't strong enough to make it to land. Would she land in the sea, be eaten by a great fish? Please, thought Dannilla fiercely, let her not fall until she is out of sight. Raff could not bear it.

Somehow, in spite of the lack of food, and the days spent huddled on her bed, the tiny figure remained airborne until she dwindled into nothing.

Raff was still, his jaw muscles clenched, his eyes still trying to see her.

"She's gone," said Dannilla. "Come."

She tried to lead him to the cliff, but he shook off her hand. "Leave me alone," he said.

The cave seemed suddenly too much to bear. Dannilla went toward the jungle. She would check the snares, she thought. If there were any birds caught in them, she'd let them fly away. She would pick some fruit and swim in the cove and take care of Raff until his spirit flew back to him. In time.

And after that, somehow—Father forgive her—she would get them off the island, even if it meant using magic. They would cross the sea and find their mother's people. Raff would meet a woman who would make him laugh. Dannilla would find a teacher.

She bent and dipped her fingers into a pool of raw magic. *Someday.* She touched her forehead to seal the oath.

LAUREL WINTER'S poems and short stories have been published in a wide variety of literary magazines dedicated to speculative fiction. She has won two *Asimov*'s Reader's Poll Awards and two Rhysling Awards for her poetry, and her "Sky Eyes" won a 2000 World Fantasy Award for Best Novella. Her first novel, *Growing Wings* (Firebird), was a Finalist for the Mythopoeic Award; she has recently won a McKnight Artist's Fellowship based upon her second novel, now in progress.

Visit Laurel Winter's Web site at **www.winters.ws/laurel**

AUTHOR'S NOTE
You might think, reading my fiction (*Growing Wings*, "The Flying Woman"), that I have some sort of fixation with wings and flight. I'm not denying it, although most of my "flying" dreams are more like "hovering three inches off the ground" dreams. In some ways, though, the more important part of this story to me is that of Dannilla, who knows she has abilities trapped within her and is determined to realize them. I think that frequently people are ostracized for the very traits that make them wonderful, that make them who they are. May the magic bless all of us who stubbornly develop our inner potential, even if it means breaking a few taboos, or—at the very least—being "uncool" in the current incarnation of "cool."

acknowledgments

I hate when there are pages and pages of acknowledgments at the beginning of a book and they're all cutesy or inexplicable. Let us see if I can do better.

Since Firebird (the imprint) is really a group effort, there are a lot of people who deserve credit.

Thanks to . . .

Tracy Tang, the President and Publisher of Puffin, who has backed Firebird from the very beginning; Gerard Mancini and Phil Airoldi, our managing editors, who make sure the books get from A (my brain and/or computer and/or desk) to B (the bookshelves); Pat Shuldiner and Jennifer Tait, two very patient copy editors; Deborah Kaplan, our brilliant art director, who has an equally brilliant department—Linda McCarthy, Stefanie Rosenfeld, Nick Vitiello, Jim Hoover, and Kristina Duewell (and Lori Thorn, who designed the Firebird logo); and Amy White and Jason Primm, the truly unsung heroes, the production masters.

I couldn't ask for a better advocate than Doug Whiteman,

the head of the Penguin Group (USA) Young Readers Group, nor Mariann Donato, Eileen Kreit, Jackie Engel, Robyn Fink, and Nancy Feldman in sales; all of our reps, whom I adore; and the awesome marketing department, from Gina Maolucci, Emily Romero, Katrina Weidknecht, Susan Hawk, and Lucy del Priore onward. Special mention goes to Bill May, the initial designer of the Firebird Web site.

I want to specially thank Regina Hayes, the President and Publisher of Viking, who widened the list to include my fantasy and science fiction authors, and now calls herself "a convert."

I would be drowning in paperwork without all of my interns. They've included Stacey Bakula, Andrea Halim, Azadeh Houshyar, Jacqui Shine, and Emily Shaffer. They were and are wonderful. (So is Nancy Conescu.)

My adult analogues at Penguin are Susan Allison, Ginjer Buchanan, and Anne Sowards (Ace); Laura Anne Gilman and Jennifer Heddle (Roc); Betsy Wollheim, Sheila Gilbert, Debra Euler, and Sean Fodera (DAW), and they have all been helpful in more ways than I can count. I came into this knowing nothing about sff publishing—they have generously showed me the ropes, along with other editors in the genre (like Gordon Van Gelder, Shawna McCarthy, Patrick and Teresa Nielsen Hayden, Diana Gill, Betsy Mitchell, Anne Groell, Ellen Asher, Rodger Turner, Jaime Levine, and Charles N. Brown and Jenni Hall at *Locus*).

The science fiction and fantasy genre is full of remarkable, quirky people who have buoyed and cheered me. I've met some of them online, others at cons and readings. They all have ideas—authors and artists to recommend, publishing ideas I hadn't thought of, comments that have made a particular day. You know who you are: thanks.

I am grateful to Ellen Datlow and Terri Windling, anthologists supreme, who (without knowing it) gave me the template for this book.

The world of children's and teen publishing has its own stars—librarians, English teachers, reviewers, and booksellers who all love what they do—and they've been enthusiastic supporters from the beginning. Special thanks here to Cathi Dunn MacRae, the author of *Young Adult Fantasy Fiction* and editor of *Voice of Youth Advocates*.

I'd like to thank Angus Killick for the initial idea for this anthology, Tamora Pierce for its title, and Cliff Nielsen for his stunning cover.

The many other artists whose work has been featured on our covers deserve a round of applause—they are visionaries, mind-changers.

And I need to mention the two Firebird Editorial Boards. The "adult" board contains many authors, some of whose work you've read here, as well as librarians, reviewers, and booksellers; the teen board is all teenagers, all the time. Both boards keep me on the right track, and there are certain decisions I wouldn't have even thought about making were it not for them.

I want to again thank the authors whose work is anthologized here, and their agents. I feel so lucky to know you all and to have the chance to work with you. It is a reader's dream come true.

FIREBIRDS

Finally, I am grateful to my adopted godfather, Lloyd Alexander, whose Prydain Chronicles were the first fantasy I ever read (at age nine), and the reason why I do what I do; and Andy Burton, my boyfriend and best companion, who patiently listens to me go on about all things Firebird.

about the editor

SHARYN NOVEMBER was born in New York City, and has stayed close by ever since. She received a B.A. from Sarah Lawrence College, where she studied and wrote poetry; her work has appeared in *Poetry*, *The North American Review*, and *Shenandoah*, among other magazines, and she received a scholarship to Bread Loaf. She has been editing books for children and teenagers for over fifteen years, and working with teen readers, both online and in person, for much of that time. Her writing about this has been published in *The Horn Book* and *Voice of Youth Advocates*, and she is currently working on an essay collection. She was a regular commentator for Loose Leaf Book Company (www.looseleaf.org), and has been a board member of USBBY and ALAN, as well as being actively involved in both ALA and NCTE.

In addition to this, she's played in a variety of bands (songwriter, lead singer, rhythm guitar), and maintains an extensive personal Web site at **www.sharyn.org**. When she has time, she sleeps.

The Firebird Web site is at **www.firebirdbooks.com**